S0-BOU-658

PRAISE FOR THESE BESTSELLING AUTHORS

MIRANDA LEE

"Miranda Lee brings readers sensual scenes and sexy characters."
—*Romantic Times*

"Emotional intensity, a dash of intrigue and scorching sensuality."
—*Romantic Times* on *Secrets & Sins*

MARGARET WAY

"Margaret Way uses colourful characterization and descriptive prowess to make love and the Australian Outback blossom brilliantly."
—*Romantic Times*

"Margaret Way makes the Outback come alive."
—*Romantic Times*

MIRANDA LEE

was born and raised in Australia. Happily married with three daughters, she began writing when family commitments kept her at home. It took a decade of trial and error before her first romance, *After the Affair*, was accepted and published. She likes to create stories that are believable, modern, fast-paced and sexy. Since her career began in 1990, Miranda has become one of Mills & Boon's most prolific and popular authors.

MARGARET WAY

takes great pleasure in her work and works hard at her pleasure. She enjoys tearing off to the beach with her family on weekends, loves haunting galleries and auctions, and is completely given over to French champagne "for every possible joyous occasion." She was born and educated in the river city of Brisbane, Australia, and now lives within sight and sound of beautiful Moreton Bay.

MIRANDA LEE
AND MARGARET WAY

AUSTRALIAN NIGHTS

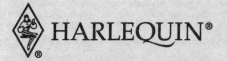

HARLEQUIN®

TORONTO • NEW YORK • LONDON
AMSTERDAM • PARIS • SYDNEY • HAMBURG
STOCKHOLM • ATHENS • TOKYO • MILAN • MADRID
PRAGUE • WARSAW • BUDAPEST • AUCKLAND

ISBN 0-373-23009-5

AUSTRALIAN NIGHTS

Copyright © 2003 by Harlequin Books S.A.

The publisher acknowledges the copyright holders of the individual works as follows:

SIMPLY IRRESISTIBLE
Copyright © 1999 by Miranda Lee

HER OUTBACK MAN
Copyright © 1998 by Margaret Way

Visit us at www.eHarlequin.com

Printed in U.S.A.

CONTENTS

SIMPLY IRRESISTIBLE
Miranda Lee

CHAPTER ONE

'WE'VE been accused of doing too many heavy stories lately,' Mervyn announced to his underlings seated around the oval table. 'From now on, one of the four segments we tape for each week's show is going to be in a lighter vein.'

Vivien looked up from where she was doodling on her note-pad, a sinking feeling in her stomach. As the last reporter to join the *Across Australia* team—not to mention the only woman—she just *knew* who would be assigned these 'lighter-veined' stories.

She hadn't long come off a *Candid Camera* style programme, and while it had been a huge success, she'd been relieved to finally have the chance to work on a television show that was more intellectually stimulating. At twenty-five going on twenty-six, she felt she was old enough to be taken seriously.

Ah, well, she sighed. One step forward and two steps backwards...

'And what constitutes lighter-veined?' demanded a male voice from across the table.

Vivien glanced over at Bob, widely known as Robert J. Overhill, their hard-hitting political reporter who wouldn't know 'lighter-veined' if it hit him in the left eye. Thirtyish, but already going bald and running to fat, he conducted every interview as a personal war out of which he *had* to emerge the victor. He had a sharp, incisive mind, but the personality of a spoilt little boy.

'I'm not sure myself yet,' Mervyn returned. 'This

directive has just come down from the great white chief himself. I've only had time to think up a try-out idea to be screened on Sunday week. Ever heard of Wallaby Creek?' he queried with a wry grin on his intelligent face.

They all shook their heads.

'It's a small town out in north-western New South Wales just this side of Bourke, but off the main highway. Once a year, in the middle of November, it's where the Outback Shearers' Association hold their Bachelors' and Spinsters' Ball.'

Everyone rolled their eyes as the penny dropped. There'd been a current affairs programme done on a similar B & S Ball a couple of years before, which had depicted the event as a drunken orgy filled with loutish yobbos and female desperadoes. The only claim to dubious fame the event seemed to have was that no girl went home a virgin.

Vivien chuckled to herself at the thought that, from what she had seen, not too many virgins had gone to that particular ball in the first place.

'I'm so glad you find the idea an amusing one, Viv,' her producer directed straight at her, 'since you'll be handling it. The ball's this Saturday night. That gives you three days to get yourself organised and out there. Now I'm not interested in any serious message in this story. Just a fun piece. Froth and bubble. Right?'

Vivien diplomatically kept her chagrin to herself. 'Right,' she said, and threw a bright smile around the table at all the smug male faces smirking at her.

It never ceased to amaze her, the pleasure men got from seeing women supposedly put in their places in the workplace, but she had always found the best line of defence was to be agreeable, rather than militant.

She defused any antagonism with feminine charm, then counter-attacked by always giving her very best, doing such a damn good job—even with froth and bubble—that her male colleagues had to give her some credit.

'I hear they drink pretty heavily at those balls,' Bob said in a mocking tone. 'We might have to send out a search party of trackers to find Viv the next day. You know what she's like after a couple of glasses. Whew…' He whistled and waved his hand in front of his face, as though he was suddenly very hot.

Vivien sighed while the others laughed. Would she *never* live down the channel's Christmas party last year? How was she to know that someone had spiked the supposedly non-alcoholic fruit punch with vodka? She was always so careful when it came to drinking, ever since she'd discovered several years before at her first university party that anything more than two glasses of the mildest concoction turned her from a quietly spoken, serious-minded girl into a flamboyant exhibitionist, not to mention a rather outrageous flirt.

Luckily for Vivien on that first occasion, her girlfriend had dragged her home before she got herself into any serious trouble. But her hangover the next morning, plus the stark memory of her silly and potentially dangerous behaviour, had made her very careful with alcohol from that moment on.

The incident at last year's Christmas party had hardly been her fault. Vivien groaned silently as she recalled how, once the alcohol took effect, she'd actually climbed up on this very table and danced a wild tango, complete with a rose in her mouth.

Earl had been furious with her, dragging her down and taking her home post-haste. He'd hardly spoken to her for a week. It had taken much longer for the people at work to stop making pointed remarks over the incident. Now, her acid-tongued colleague had brought it up again. Still, Vivien knew the worst thing she could do would be to react visibly.

'Worried you might miss out on something, Bob?' she countered with a light laugh.

'Hardly,' he scowled. 'I like my women a touch less aggressive.'

'Cut it out, Bob,' Mervyn intervened before the situation flared out of hand. 'Oh, and Viv, I can only let you have a single-man crew. You like working that way anyway, don't you?'

'I'll get Irving,' she said. Irving was a peach to work with, a whiz with camera and sound. A witty companion, too.

But the best part about Irving was that he wasn't a womaniser and never tried to chat her up. In his late twenties, he had a steady girlfriend who adored him and whom he adored back. Fidelity was his middle name. Definitely Vivien's type of man.

'It goes without saying that you'll both have to drive out. *And* in the same car,' Mervyn went on. 'You know how tight things have been since they cut our budget again. I rang the one and only hotel in Wallaby Creek to see if they had any vacancies and, luckily enough, they did. Seems the proprietor is refusing to house any revellers for the ball after a couple of his rooms were almost wrecked last year. Might I suggest you don't leave any valuable equipment in the car that night after you've retired? OK?'

'Sure thing, boss,' Vivien agreed. Maybe it wouldn't be so bad, she decided philosophically. She'd always wanted to drive out west for a look-see, having never been beyond the Blue Mountains. Not that she secretly hankered for a country lifestyle. Vivien was a Sydney girl. Born and bred. She couldn't see herself giving up the vibrant hustle and bustle of city life for wide-open spaces, dust and flies.

Not only that, but it would give her something to do this weekend, since Earl didn't want her to fly down to visit him. *Once again*, she reminded herself with a jab of dismay.

'Well, off you go, madam,' her boss announced before depression could take hold. 'Grab Irving before he's booked up elsewhere. That man's in high demand.'

'Right.' She smiled, and stood up.

'Phone call for you, Vivien,' the main receptionist called out to her as she passed through the foyer area on her way back to her office. 'I'll switch it back to your desk now. That is where you're heading, isn't it? It's STD, by the way. Your boyfriend.'

Vivien's heart skipped a beat. *Earl*? Ringing her during working hours? That wasn't like him at all...

She hurried along the corridor towards the office she shared with her three fellow *Across Australia* reporters, her heart pounding with sudden nerves.

Somehow she just knew this phone call didn't mean what she so desperately hoped it meant, that Earl wanted to say sorry for the way he'd been behaving, that he was missing her as much as she was missing him. Perhaps he'd finally given up trying to make her suffer for not dropping her career and following him to Melbourne the second he got his promotion and transfer six weeks ago.

Her heart twisted as she recalled the awful argument they'd had when he'd come home that night and made his impossible demand. She'd tried explaining that if she just quit on the spot she'd be committing professional suicide. But he hadn't been prepared to listen, his relentlessly cold logic being that if she loved him she would do what *he* wanted, what was best for *him*. If she wanted to marry him and have his children, then *her* career was irrelevant.

Although he had always shown chauvinistic tendencies, his stubborn selfishness in this matter had startled then infuriated her. She had dug in her heels and stayed in Sydney. Nevertheless, she had still been prepared to compromise, promising to look for a position in Melbourne in the New Year, which had been only three months away. To which idea Earl had sulkily agreed.

To begin with, Vivien had flown to Melbourne every weekend to be with him. These visits, however, had not been a great success, with the old argument inevitably flaring about her throwing in her job and staying with him. After three weeks of these bitter-sweet reunions, Earl had started finding reasons for her not to come, saying he was busy with one thing and another. Which perhaps he was… But underneath, Vivien believed he'd been exacting a type of revenge on her, being petty in a way he'd never been before.

She swept into the empty office and over to her corner, sending papers flying as she slid on to the corner of her desk and snatched up the receiver.

'Hello?' she said breathlessly.

'Vivien? That is you, isn't it?' Earl drawled in a voice she scarcely recognised.

Taken aback, she was lost for words for a moment. Where on earth had he got that accent from? He sounded like an upper-class snob, yet he was from a working-class background, just like herself.

'Oh—er—yes, it's me,' she finally blurted out.

His laugh had the most peculiarly dry note to it. 'You sound rattled. Have I caught you doing things you shouldn't be doing with all those men you work with?'

Now *that* was just like Earl. Jealous as sin.

She suppressed an unhappy sigh. He didn't have to be jealous. She'd never given him a moment's doubt over her loyalty from the moment she'd fallen in love with him two years before. Hadn't she even gone against her principles and agreed to live with him when he postponed their plans to marry till he was thirty?

'Don't be silly, darling,' she cajoled. 'You know you're the only man for me.'

'Do I? I'm not so sure, Vivien. And *you're* the one who's been silly. *Very* silly.'

Vivien was chilled by the tone in his voice.

'If you'd just come with me when I asked you to,' he continued peevishly, 'none of this would have happened.'

'None of w—what would have happened?' she asked, a sick feeling starting in the pit of her stomach.

'We'd probably be married by now,' he raved on, totally ignoring her tremulous question. 'The chairman of the bank down here likes his executives suitably spoused. You would have been perfect for the role of my wife, Vivien, with your personality and looks. But *no*! You had to have your own career as well, didn't you? You had to be liberated! Well, consider yourself liberated, my sweet. Set free, free of everything, including me.'

Vivien thought she made a choking, gasping sound. But perhaps she didn't.

'Besides, I've met someone else,' he pronounced with a bald cruelty that took her breath away. 'She's the daughter of a well-connected businessman down here. Not as stunning-looking as you, I admit. But then, not many women are,' he added caustically. 'But she's prepared to be a full-time wife, to devote herself entirely to *me*!'

Shock was sending Vivien's head into a spin. She wanted to drop the phone. Run. Anything. This couldn't be happening to her. Earl *couldn't* be telling her he'd found someone else, some woman he was going to *marry*?

Somehow she gathered herself with a strength that was perhaps only illusory. But she clung to it all the same.

'Earl,' she said with a quiet desperation, 'I love you. And I know you love me. Don't do this to us… not…not for the sake of ambition.'

'Ambition?' he scoffed. 'You *dare* talk to me of ambition? You, who put your career ahead of your so-called love for me? Don't make me laugh, sweetheart. Actually, I consider myself lucky to be getting out from under this…*obsession* I had for you. Any man would find it hard to give you up. But I'm cured now. I've kicked the habit. And I have my methadone at hand.' He laughed. 'Name of Amelia.'

Vivien was dimly aware that she was now in danger of cracking up on the spot. The hand that was clutching the receiver to her ear was going cold, shivers reverberating up her arm. She tried to speak, but couldn't.

'I'll be up this Saturday to get the rest of my things,' Earl continued callously. 'I'd like you to be conspicuously absent. Visit your folks or something. Oh, for pity's sake, say something, Vivien! You're beginning to bore me with this frozen silence routine. It's positively childish. You must have known the writing was on the wall once you refused to come with me.'

'I...I would have come,' she said in an emotionally devastated voice, 'if I'd known this would happen. Earl, please...I *love* you—'

'No, you bloody well don't,' he shot back nastily. 'No more than I loved you. I can see now it was only lust. I'm surprised it lasted as long as it did.'

Only lust?

Her face flamed with humiliation and hurt. She couldn't count the number of times sex hadn't been all that good for her. She'd merely pretended. For *his* sake. For his infernal male pride!

'No come-backs?' he jeered. 'Fine. I don't want to argue, either. After all, there's nothing really to argue about. You made your choice, Vivien. Now you can damned well live with it!' And he slammed down the phone.

She stared down at the dead receiver, her mind reeling as the reality of the situation hit her.

Earl was gone from her life.

Not just temporarily.

Forever.

All her plans for the future—shattered.

There would be no marriage to him. No children by him. No nothing.

Tears welled up behind her eyes and she might have buried her face in her hands and sobbed her heart out had not Robert J. Overhill appeared in the doorway of the office at that precise moment. Luckily his sharp eyes didn't go to her pale, shaken face. They zeroed in on her long, shapely legs dangling over the desk corner.

For the first time Vivien understood Bob's vicious attitude towards her. He *did* fancy her, her crime being that she didn't fancy him back.

With a desperate burst of pride she kept the tears at

bay. 'Well!' She jumped to her feet and plastered a bright smile on her face. 'I'd better stop this lounging about and get to work. You wouldn't know where Irving might be, would you?'

'Haven't a clue.' Bob shrugged, his narrowed eyes travelling slowly back up her body.

'I'll try the canteen,' she said breezily.

'You do that.'

He remained standing in the narrow doorway so that she had to turn sideways and brush past him to leave the room, her full breasts connecting with his arm.

But she said, 'Excuse me,' airily as though it didn't matter, and hurried up the corridor, hiding the shudder that ran deeply through her. All of a sudden, she hated men. The whole breed. For they were indeed hateful creatures, she decided. Hateful! Incapable of true love. Incapable of caring. All they thought about or wanted was sex.

But then she remembered her father. Her sweet, kind, loving father. And her two older brothers. Both good men with stable, secure marriages and happy wives and families. Even Irving was loyal and true, and *he* was in the television industry, hardly a hotbed of faithfulness. Was she asking for too much to want that kind of man for herself?

'Oh, Irving!' she called out, spotting the man himself leaving the canteen.

He spun round and smiled at her. 'What's up, Doc?'

'Got a job for you.'

'Thank the lord it's you and not Bob. I've had politicians up to here!' And he drew a line across his throat. 'So where are we off to this time?'

'Ever heard of Wallaby Creek?'

CHAPTER TWO

THE Wallaby Creek hotel was typical of hotels found in bush towns throughout Australia.

It was two-storeyed and quite roomy, sporting a cor-rugated-iron roof—painted green—and wooden veran-das all around, the upper one with iron lacework rail-ings—painted cream. It sat on the inevitable corner, so that any patrons who cared to wander out from their upstairs room on to the adjoining veranda would be guaranteed a splendid view of the main street below and an unimpeded panorama for miles around.

Vivien was standing on this veranda at six on the following Saturday evening, wiping the perspiration from her neck and looking out in awe at the incredible scene still taking shape before her eyes.

When she and Irving had driven into the small, dusty town the previous evening, tired and hot from the day-long trip west, they'd wondered where the ball would be held, since, at first glance, Wallaby Creek consisted of little else but this hotel, a few ancient houses, a general store and two garages.

They'd asked the hotel proprietor, a jolly soul named Bert, if there was a hall they'd missed. He'd given a good belly-laugh and told them no, no hall, then re-fused to answer their next query as to where the venue for the ball would be.

'Just you wait and see,' he'd chuckled. 'Come to-morrow afternoon, you won't recognise this place.'

He'd been right. In the short space of a few hours,

the sleepy hollow of Wallaby Creek had been transformed.

First, heavy-transport vehicles accompanied by utilities filled with men had descended on the place like a plague of locusts, and within a short while a marquee that would have done the Russian circus proud had mushroomed in a nearby paddock. Next came the dance-floor, square slabs of wooden decking that fitted together like giant parquet.

A car park was then marked out with portable fences, its size showing that they were anticipating an exceptionally large turn-out. This expectation was reinforced by the two long lines of porta-loos that stretched out on either side of the marquee, one marked 'Chicks', the other 'Blokes'.

Refreshment vans had rolled into town all day, with everything from meat pies to champagne to kegs of beer. Two enormous barbecues had been set up on either side of the front entrance to the marquee, complete with a multitude of plastic tables and chairs, not to mention plastic glasses and cutlery. Lessons had been learnt, it seemed, from accidents in previous years. Real glass was out!

Vivien had been kept busy all day, interviewing all sorts of people, from the members of the organising committee to the volunteers who helped put the venue together to the people who hoped to make a quick buck out of hot dogs or steak sandwiches or what have you.

She was amazed at the distance some of the men had travelled, though it had been patiently explained to her that Wallaby Creek was fairly central to most of the sheep properties around this section of New South Wales and country people were used to covering vast distances for their entertainment. Every unmarried jackeroo, rouseabout, stockhand and shearer in a three-hundred-kilometre radius would be in attendance to-night, she was assured, together with a sprinkling of station owners and other assorted B & S Ball fans. Apparently a few carloads of young ladies even drove out from Sydney for such occasions, in search of a man.

If Vivien hadn't been so depressed inside, she might have caught up in the general air of excited anticipation that seemed to be pervading everyone. But she couldn't even get up enough enthusiasm to start getting ready. Instead, she lingered outside, leaning on the old iron railing, staring at the horizon, which was bathed in the bold reds and golds of an outback sunset.

But she was blind to the raw, rich beauty of the land, her mind back in her flat in Sydney, where at this very moment Earl was probably taking away every single reminder she had of him. When she went back, it would almost be as though he had never existed.

Only he *had* existed, she moaned silently. And would continue to exist in her mind and heart for a long, long time.

Vivien's hands lifted to wipe moisture away from her eyes.

Damn, she thought abruptly. I can't possibly be crying again. There can't be any tears left! Angry with herself, she spun away and strode inside into the hotel room. 'No more,' she muttered, and swept up the towels off the bed for a quick visit to the bathroom. 'No more!'

And she didn't cry any more. But she still suffered, her heart heavy in her chest at having thought about Earl again, her normally sparkling eyes flat and dull as she went about transforming herself as astonishingly and speedily as Wallaby Creek had been.

By five to seven, the miracle was almost complete. Gone were the pale blue cotton trousers and simple white shirt she'd been wearing all day, replaced by a strapless ball-gown and matching bolero in a deep purple taffeta. Down was her thick black hair, dancing around her shoulders and face in soft, glossy waves. On had gone her night-time make-up, dramatic and bold, putting a high blush of colour across her smooth alabaster cheeks, turning her already striking brown eyes into even darker pools of exotic mystery, emphasising her sensually wide mouth with a coating of shimmering violet gloss.

At last Vivien stood back to give herself a cynical appraisal in the old dressing-table mirror. Now who are you trying to look so sensational for, you fool? And she shook her head at herself in mockery.

Still, the dressy dress was a must, since all patrons of the ball were required to wear formal clothes. And one did look insipid on television at night unless well made up.

There was a rapid knocking on her door. 'Viv? Are you ready?' Irving asked.

'Coming,' she said brusquely, and, slipping her bare feet into high-heeled black sandals, she swept from the room.

By ten the ball was in full swing, the heavy-metal band that had been brought up from Sydney blaring out its strident beat to a packed throng of energetic dancers. Vivien squeezed a path between the heaving, weaving bodies with her microphone and cameraman in tow, doing fleeting interviews as she went, as well as a general commentary that she probably wouldn't use except as a basis for her final voice-over.

Most of the merry-makers were co-operative and tolerant, and when she remarked to one group that some of the young people's 'formal' gear was not of the best quality she'd been laughingly told that 'experienced' B & S Ball attendees always purchased their tuxes and gowns from second-hand clothing establishments.

'Otherwise their good clothes might get ruined!' One young man winked.

'How?' she asked.

They all looked at her as though she'd just descended from Mars.

'In the creek, of course! Don't you city folks have creeks down in Sydney?'

'Er—well...' Hard to explain that one didn't go swimming in the Parramatta or St. George's River. Too much pollution. 'We do have the harbour,' she tried.

'Not as good as our creek,' someone said, and they all laughed knowingly.

They were still laughing as she moved on.

'I'm getting hot and tired, Viv,' Irving said shortly before eleven. 'I could do with a bite to eat and a cool drink.'

It was indeed becoming stuffy in the marquee and Vivien herself fancied a breath of fresh air. 'OK. Meet me back here, near the band, at midnight,' she suggested.

'Will do. Here. Give me the mike.' He rolled up the cord, slung it over his shoulder with his camera, and in seconds had disappeared, swallowed up by the throng.

Suddenly, despite being in the middle of a mêlée, Vivien felt incredibly lonely. With a weary sigh she glanced around, waffling over which of the various exits she would make for, and it was as her eyes were skating over the bobbing heads of dancers that she got the shock of her life.

For there was Earl, leaning against one of the tent poles, looking very elegant in a black evening suit, bow-tie and all.

She gasped, her view of him obscured for a moment. But when the intervening couples moved out of the way again she realised it wasn't Earl at all, but a man with a face and hair so similar to Earl's that it was scary.

She couldn't help staring at him, and as she stared his eyes slowly turned, drawn no doubt by her intense scrutiny. And then he was looking right at her.

The breath was punched from her lungs. God, but he was the spitting image of Earl! Facially, at least.

Perhaps she should have looked away, now that he was aware of her regard. But she couldn't seem to. It was as though she were hypnotised by this man's uncanny resemblance to the man who had been her lover for the past two years.

A frown formed on his handsome face as they exchanged stares, an oddly troubled frown. It struck Vivien that perhaps he thought he was getting the come-on and was embarrassed by her none too subtle stare.

But if he was, why didn't he just look away?

Suddenly, he moved—destroying his almost apparition-like quality—his spine straightening, his shoulders squaring inside his black dinner-jacket. His eyes never left her.

He was walking now, moving inexorably towards her, the gyrating crowd parting before him like the Red Sea had for Moses. Closer, he was still incredibly like Earl. The way his thick brown hair swept across his forehead from a side parting. The wide, sensuous mouth. And that damned dimple in the middle of a similarly strong square-cut jaw.

But he was taller and leaner than Earl. And his eyes weren't grey. They were a light ice-blue. They were also compellingly fixed on her as he loomed closer and closer.

Vivien's big brown eyes flicked over his elegant dinner suit. No second-hand rubbish for him, she thought, and swallowed nervously. Jackets didn't fit like that unless they were individually tailored. Of course, he was no callow youth either. He had to be at least thirty.

He stopped right in front of her, a slow and vaguely sardonic smile coming to his face. 'Care to dance?' he asked in a voice like dark chocolate.

'D-dance?' She blinked up at him, thrown by how amazingly similar that lop-sided, lazy smile was to Earl's.

His smile grew wider, thankfully destroying the likeness. 'Yes, dance. You know…two people with arms around each other, moving in unison.'

She blushed under his teasing, which rattled her even more than his looks. Good grief, she *never* blushed, having achieved a measure of fame around the channel for her sophisticated composure, her ability never to be thrown by anything or anyone. Which was perhaps why everyone had been so surprised by the wildly mad exhibition she had made of herself at that Christmas party.

'I…yes…all right,' she answered, her mind in chaos, her heart pounding away in her chest like a jackhammer.

He swept her smoothly into his arms and away on to the dance-floor, and once again there seemed to be miraculous room for him. She felt light as a feather in his arms. 'I don't disco,' he murmured, pulling her to him and pressing soft lips into her hair. 'I like my women close.'

'Oh,' was all she could manage in reply.

Good lord, she thought. What am I *doing*? I should have said no. He *had* to have got the wrong idea from my none too subtle staring, not to mention my tongue-tied schoolgirl reaction to his invitation.

Make your apologies and extricate yourself before things get awkward here, she advised herself.

Yet she stayed right where she was and said absolutely nothing, aware of little but the pounding of her heart and the feeling of excitement that was racing through her veins.

Somehow Earl's double invented a dance to the primitive beat of the music, even though it was more a rhythmic swaying than any real movement across the floor. People swirled back around them, shutting them in, making Vivien feel suddenly tight-chested and claustrophic. Someone knocked into them and her partner pulled her even closer, flattening her breasts against the hard wall of his chest.

'Put your arms up around my neck,' he murmured. 'You'll be less of a target that way.'

True, she thought breathlessly. I'll also probably cease to exist as a separate entity, because if I get any closer I'll have become part of *you*!

But she did as he suggested, amazed at herself for her easy acquiescence. The whole situation had a weird, supernatural feel to it, from the man's uncanny likeness to Earl to her out-of-character reactions to him.

Or maybe they were *in* character, she thought dazedly. Maybe her body was simply responding to the same physical chemistry she felt when she was with Earl. Her responses were not really for this man. They were merely for a face, the face of the man she loved.

A moan of dismay punched which sounded more

sensual than desolate from her throat and clearly gave her partner even more of the right—or wrong—idea.

'You feel it too, don't you?' he rasped, one of his hands sliding up under her bolero to trace erotic circles over her naked shoulder blades. 'Incredible...'

She tensed in his arms, appalled yet fascinated by her own arousal. She couldn't seem to gather the courage or common sense to pull away, to put a stop to what was happening between them. When he bent his head to kiss her neck, a betraying shiver of pleasure rippled through her. He groaned, opening his mouth to suckle softly at her flesh.

A compulsive wave of desire broke the last of her control and her fingers began to steal up into his silky, thick hair, fingertips pressing into his scalp.

'God...' he muttered against her neck.

The mindless depth of arousal in his voice plus an abrupt appreciation of where they actually were acted like a cold sponge on Vivien, snapping her back to reality.

'Dear heaven,' she cried, and, shuddering with shame, wrenched away from him.

He stared down at her, smouldering blue eyes still glazed with passion.

Her left hand fluttered up to agitatedly touch her neck where his mouth had been. The skin felt hot and wet and rough. There had to be a red mark. 'You shouldn't have done that,' she burst out. 'I...I didn't like it.'

A chill came into his eyes. 'Didn't you?'

'No, of...of course not!' she denied, her demeanour as flustered as his was now composed.

His eyes narrowed, his top lip curling with a type of sardonic contempt. 'So,' he said with a dry laugh, 'you're nothing but a tease. How ironic. How bloody ironic.'

For a moment she stared back up at him, confused by his words. But then she was angry. 'No, I'm *not*!' she retorted, chin lifting defiantly. 'And there's no need to swear!'

But when she went to whirl away his hand shot out to grab her arm, spinning her back into his body. 'Then *why*?' he flung at her in a low, husky voice. 'Why look at me the way you did? Why let me go that far before you stopped me?'

What could she say? I don't know? Maybe it wasn't *you* I was letting do that. Maybe it wasn't *you* I was wanting.

And yet…

She stared into the depths of the eyes, looking for answers, but finding only more confusion. For suddenly Earl was the furthest thing from her mind.

'You…you wouldn't understand,' she muttered.

'Wouldn't I? Try me.' And he gathered her forcefully back into his arms.

She gaped up at him. But before she could voice any bewildered protest he urged her back into their rocking, rolling rhythm, his hold firm, his eyes stubborn. 'Start explaining.'

For a second, her hands pushed at his immutable shoulders. But it was like trying to push a brick wall down with a feather.

'I deserve an explanation,' he said with maddening logic. 'So stop that nonsense and give me one.'

She glared up at him, knowing she should demand he let go of her, should tell him he had no right to use his superior male strength to enforce his will. Yet all she wanted was to close her eyes and melt back into him. It was incredible!

'I don't think I'm asking too much, do you?' he went on, disarming her with a wry but warm smile.

She groaned in defeat, her forehead tipping forwards on to his rock-hard chest. When he actually picked up her arms and put them around his neck, she glanced up at him, then wished she hadn't. He was too overwhelmingly close and too disturbingly attractive to her.

'So tell me,' he murmured. 'Why did you stare at me the way you did?'

Vivien tried to think of a plausible lie, but couldn't. How could she explain something she didn't fully understand herself? With considerable reluctance, she was forced to embrace the part she *could* grasp. 'When I first saw you I thought you were someone else. You...you look a lot like someone I know. *Used* to know,' she amended.

'An old boyfriend?'

'Sort of.'

He pulled back slightly and gave her a penetrating look. 'Would you like to be more specific?'

She sighed. 'Ex-lover, then.'

'How ex is ex? A week? A month? A year?'

'Three days. *No.*' She laughed bitterly. 'Three *weeks*. Maybe even longer. I just didn't know till three days ago.'

He stopped dancing. There was a strange stillness about his body.

'I see,' he finally exhaled, and began to move again.

'What about later?' he resumed casually enough. 'When we started to dance? What's your excuse for that?'

'I can't explain it,' she choked out.

'Neither can I,' he said, the hand on her waist lifting to hold the back of her head with surprising tenderness, forcing her face to nestle under his chin. 'I've never felt anything like it. Yet I don't even know your name.'

'Vivien,' she whispered, her lips dangerously close to his throat.

'Vivien what?'

'Roberts.'

'Mine's Ross. Ross Everton.'

'Are…are you a shearer?' she asked, trying desperately to get their conversation on to safe, neutral territory. Anything to defuse the physical tension still enveloping her.

'I *can* shear. But it's not my main job.'

She pulled her mouth away from his neck and looked up. 'Which is?'

'I manage a sheep station.'

'I would have thought you were an owner.'

He arched one of his eyebrows. 'Why's that?'

'You don't sound like a shearer or a jackeroo.' Which he didn't. He sounded very well educated.

He laughed. 'And what are they supposed to sound like? I'll have you know we had a jackeroo on our place last year who was the son of an English lord.'

'*Our* place? I thought you said you managed.'

'I do. My father's property. For the moment, that is.'

'You sound as if it's only a temporary arrangement.'

A black cloud passed over those piercing blue eyes. 'Dad had a serious stroke last month. The doctors say his chances of having another fatal one are high.'

'Oh. I…I'm sorry.'

'It's all right. You couldn't have known.'

There was a short, sharp silence between them.

'So tell me, Vivien Roberts,' he said abruptly. 'What

television programme are you representing here to-night? No, don't bother asking. I spotted you earlier doing your stuff. Is it *Country Wide*? The *Investigators*, maybe? As you can see, we country folk can watch any station we like as long as it's the ABC.'

She laughed, and felt her tension lessen. 'Sorry, but I'm from a disgusting commercial station and the show's called *Across Australia*. And if you tell me you've never heard of it I'll be mortified.'

'I've heard of it,' he admitted, 'but never seen it. Do you think I'd forget you, if I had?'

Her stomach flipped over at the intensity he managed to put into what should have been a casual compliment.

'Ross,' she began hesitantly, 'this…this attraction between us. It can't go anywhere.'

Again she felt that stilling in his body. 'Why not?'

'It…it wouldn't be fair to you.'

'In what way?'

What could she say? Because you're not just *like* the man I've loved and lost. You're almost his mirror image. I'd never know if what I felt for you was real or not. Besides, you're from a different world from me, a world I would never fit into or want to fit into.

'I'm still in love with Earl,' she said, thinking that should answer all arguments.

Ross was irritatingly silent for ages before saying, 'I presume Earl is the man I remind you of, your ex-lover?'

'Yes,' was her reluctant admission.

His laugh sounded odd. 'Even more ironic. Tell me honestly, Vivien, if dear Earl walked back into your life this minute would you take him back?'

'Never!'

'That sounded promisingly bitter. Didn't he love you?'

'I thought he did. Apparently not, however. He's moved to Melbourne and found someone else.'

'I presume you're from Sydney, then?'

'You presume right.'

'And you're going to take your broken heart and enter a convent, is that it?'

Startled, she stared up at him. There was a mocking light in his eyes.

'Very funny,' she bit out.

'Yes, it would be. Somehow I don't think the woman I held in my arms a few minutes back would make a very good nun.'

She might have wrenched herself out of his arms and stalked away at that point if they hadn't been interrupted by a third party, a good-looking young man who tapped Ross on the shoulder with one hand while he held a can of beer in the other. By the look of him, it hadn't been his first drink of the night.

'Well, well, well,' he drawled with a drunken slur. 'I thought you were supposed to be here to watch over me, big brother. But *I've* been watching *you*. What would our dear father think of his God-like first son if I told him you spent this evening so differently from the rest of us mortal men, trying to get into some woman's knickers?'

Vivien gasped, then gasped again when Ross's fist flew out, connecting with his brother's chin. For a second, the young man merely looked shocked, swaying back and forth on his heels. But then his bloodshot eyes rolled back into his head and he tipped backwards, his fall broken by the quick reflexes of the man he'd just insulted.

'Well, don't just stand there, Vivien,' Ross grated out, looking up from where he was bent over his brother, hands hooked under his armpits. 'Pick up his feet and help me get the silly idiot out into some fresh air!'

CHAPTER THREE

NO ONE seemed particularly concerned as Ross and Vivien carted the unconscious young man through the crowd towards the front exit.

'Too much to drink, eh?' was the only comment they received.

Vivien began to think one could murder someone here tonight and get away with it, by saying the corpse was 'dead' drunk as it was carried off for disposal.

'For a lightly built young man, he's darned heavy,' she complained once they made it out of the marquee and tried to prop him up in one of the plastic chairs. Vivien frowned as his head flopped forwards on to his chest. 'Do you think he'll be all right, Ross? Perhaps you hit him too hard.'

Ross made a scowling sound. 'He's lucky I didn't break his damned neck!'

'Why? He was only telling the truth.'

He flashed her a dry look. 'You do have a poor opinion of men at the moment, don't you? Look, if it was just casual sex I was after, I could have my pick of a hundred willing females here tonight. I certainly wouldn't attempt to seduce a sophisticated city broad who probably knows more counter-moves than a chess champion. Here, you pat his cheek while I get him a glass of water. But don't bat those long eyelashes at him if he comes round,' he added sarcastically over his shoulder as he strode off. 'He might get the idea you fancy him!'

She squirmed inside, a guilty blush warming her cheeks. But she busied herself doing as he'd asked, trying to awaken the slumped body in the chair. Tapping cheeks didn't work so she started rubbing hands. His head jerked back and two bloodshot blue eyes fluttered open just as Ross returned with a couple of glasses in his hands.

'Wha—what hit me?' his brother groaned, then clutched at his chin.

'What in hell do you think?' Ross snapped. 'Here, drink this water and sober up a bit.' He turned to face Vivien. 'This is for you,' he said, and pressed a fluted plastic glass of champagne into her hands. 'Your reward for helping me with lunkhead, here. I didn't think water would be your style.'

'Oh, but I...no, really, I...' She tried to give him back the glass, which brought a scoff of disbelief from his lips. 'Good God, what do you think this is, a ploy to get you drunk so that I can have my wicked way with you? Hell, honey, you have got tickets on yourself.'

Vivien stiffened with instant pique. She lifted the champagne and downed it all in one swallow, rebelliously enjoying every bubbly drop, at the same time reminding herself ruefully not to touch another single mouthful that night. She plonked the empty glass down on the littered table near by and looked Ross straight in the eye. 'Even if I were plastered,' she stated boldly, 'I wouldn't let you touch me!'

The young man sprawled in the plastic chair gave a guffaw of laughter. 'Geez, looks like the legendary Ross Everton must have lost his touch! Isn't she falling down on her knees, begging for your body, like every girl you give the eye to?'

Ross swung on his brother as though he was about to hit him again. 'Gavin, I'm *warning* you!'

'Warning me about what, big brother? What more could you possibly do to me? You've got it all now, everything I've ever wanted.' He struggled to his feet and managed to put a determined look on to his weakly handsome face. 'Let me warn *you*, brother, dear,' he blustered. 'Watch your back, because one day it's going to be *me* taking something that's *yours*! You mark my words.' And he lurched off back into the marquee, colliding with several people on the way.

'Will he be all right?' Vivien asked, worried.

'Tonight, you mean? I hope so. God knows why he has to get so damned drunk on these occasions. When he drinks to excess, he goes crazy.'

He's not the only one, Vivien thought, eyeing the empty champagne glass with a degree of concern. *I* don't even need to go to excess. My troubles start around glass number three.

She looked back at Ross, who was rubbing his temple with an agitated forefinger. She forgot about being annoyed with his earlier remarks, seeing only a human being weighed down with problems. And her heart went out to him.

But along with the sympathy she felt a certain amount of curiosity. Was his brother being sarcastic when he'd referred to him as legendary? And legendary in what way, for goodness' sake? His sexual prowess? Vivien's gaze skated over Ross's macho build. He was certainly virile-looking enough to be a womaniser.

There were other questions too teasing at her female curiosity. 'What did Gavin mean,' she asked in the end, 'when he said you've got everything he ever wanted?'

Ross shrugged. 'Who knows? The management of

the property, maybe. Or Dad's good opinion. He thinks Gavin's an irresponsible fool. Though Gavin can only blame himself if Dad thinks that. He keeps acting like one. Last year, at this ball, he drove the utility into the creek and nearly drowned. You'd think by twenty-five he'd have started to grow up.'

'Twenty-*five*? He doesn't seem that old.'

'He *looks* his age. He just doesn't act it.'

'Is that why you came along tonight? To see he didn't do it again?'

He nodded. 'I don't think Dad needs any more stress right now.'

Vivien was impressed with his warm concern for his father. 'And your mother?' she queried. 'How's she coping with your father's stroke?' One of Vivien's uncles had had a stroke a couple of years previously and her aunt had almost had a nervous breakdown coping with his agonisingly slow recuperation.

'Mum's dead,' came the brusque reply. 'There's just Dad, Gavin and me.'

'Oh...'

'Yes, I know,' he muttered, and frowned in the direction of the marquee. 'You're sorry and I'm sorry. More than you'll ever know.' His head snapped back to give her a long, thoughtful look.

She squirmed under his intense gaze, especially when his eyes dropped to inspect her considerable cleavage, which the bolero wasn't designed to hide.

'Well,' he sighed at last, eyes lifting back to her face, 'I'd better go and check up on Gavin before he picks a fight with someone else, someone who won't know to pull his punches. Goodbye, Vivien Roberts. Time for you to go back to your world and me to mine.'

He went to move away, but couldn't seem to drag

his eyes from her. 'Hell, but you're one beautiful woman. A man would have to be mad to get mixed up with you anyway. Still, I'd like to have a little more to remember than a mere dance!'

Before she realised what he had in mind, he pulled her into his arms and kissed her, his mouth grinding down on hers, his teeth hard. Only for the briefest second did his lips force hers apart, his tongue plunging forward with a single impassioned thrust before he tore his mouth away. Without looking at her again, he spun round and strode off, back into the marquee.

She stared after him, the back of her hand against her mouth. She wasn't at all aware of Irving coming to stand beside her, not till he spoke.

'Hey, Viv, what was that all about? Who *was* that guy?'

Vivien blinked and turned to focus dazedly on her colleague. 'What did you say, Irving?'

He frowned at her. 'Get with it, Viv. It's not like you to go round kissing strange blokes then looking as if you're on cloud nine. Aren't you supposed to be living with some chap back in Sydney? You're not getting swept up with the atmosphere of this Roman orgy, are you?'

She gathered herself with a bitter laugh. 'Not likely. And I'm not living with anyone any more, Irving. He tossed me over for someone else.'

Irving looked surprised. 'What is he, a flaming idiot?'

Vivien's smile was wry. 'That's sweet of you, Irving. But no, Earl's not an idiot. He's a banker.'

Since Irving didn't socialise at the channel, he had never actually met Earl. Vivien only knew as much about Irving as she did because they had worked together before and he was quite a chatterer on the job.

Irving chuckled. 'Well, a banker's not much different from an idiot, judging by the state of the economy. You're probably well rid of him. But that doesn't mean you should encourage any of the males here tonight, sweetheart. They're all tanked up and ready to fly, yet most of them don't have a flight plan. It's gung-ho and away they go! You should see them out behind the marquee.' He rolled his eyes expressively. 'No. Come to think of it, *don't* go and see. Not unless you want to research a programme on the more adventurous positions from the *Kama Sutra*!'

Vivien was astonished. 'That bad, is it? I thought everything was fairly low-key, by city standards.'

'Gracious, girl! Where have you been this last half-hour? Things are really hotting up around here.'

'*Really*?' She wasn't sure whether to believe him or not. Irving's sense of humour included exaggeration.

He nodded sagely. 'Really. The only safe place now is *inside* the marquee, but, judging by the exodus to the nether regions down by the infamous creek, that'll be empty soon except for the band. Which reminds me— you haven't interviewed them yet. Maybe you could do that during their next break.'

'Good idea.'

Vivien, re-entering the marquee, doubted that it would empty as Irving predicted, for there was still a huge crowd of fans standing around the band, clapping and singing, as well as dozens of couples dancing. She and Irving took up positions behind the bandstand to wait for the music to stop.

It didn't seem in a hurry to, one number following another. Vivien spotted Ross's tall head once, very briefly, and the sighting agitated her. She didn't want to think about him any more. She certainly didn't want to think about that disturbing kiss. It had sent sensations down to her toes that not even the longest, most sensuous kiss of Earl's could do, which was all very confusing.

Don't think about either of them, she kept telling herself. It's crazy. Futile. *Stupid*!

But to no avail. She couldn't seem to stop. She especially couldn't get her mind off Ross. He intrigued her, whether she wanted him to or not!

'Another glass of champagne?' a low male voice suddenly whispered in her ear.

She jumped and spun round, knocking an arm in the process and spilling some of the champagne Ross was holding.

'Oh, dear, I'm so sorry!' she gasped.

'So am I,' he said, and smiled with apologetic sincerity at her. 'I shouldn't have kissed you like that. Forgive me?'

She looked up into his quite beautiful blue eyes and felt a real churning in her stomach. It threw her into even more confusion.

'Oh, for Pete's sake, forgive him,' Irving drawled from beside her. 'And give me that damned mike. This band looks as if it's going to keep playing till the year 2000. I think I'll go off and take some sneaky bits down at the creek, all by myself. You go and do some flying, Viv. You deserve it if you've been banking all this time.'

'What did he mean by that?' Ross asked once he'd moved off.

'A private joke,' Vivien said, and struggled to smother a mad chuckle. Not since Earl's ghastly phone call had she felt like laughing about their breakup. And in truth, her perverse humour didn't last for long. Thinking about Earl only served to remind her that what she was feeling for Ross couldn't be real. It was an aberration. A cruel joke of nature.

'Have I said something wrong, Vivien? You look…distressed, all of a sudden.'

She gazed searchingly up into his handsome face, clinging to the various differences from Earl. But his features began to blur together and it was a few seconds before she realised tears had swum into her eyes.

'Here, drink this,' Ross urged, and pressed the plastic glass into her hands. 'It'll make you feel better.'

She hesitated, blinking madly till she had control of herself, all the while staring down into the glass, which was about three-quarters full. Perhaps it *would* make her feel better. Less uptight. Less wretched. There was no real danger. This drink wouldn't even bring her up to her two-glass limit.

'To absent bastards,' she toasted, holding the glass up briefly before quaffing the champagne down. 'Now, where's the fireplace?' she said, putting a forced smile on her face.

'*Fireplace*?'

'To smash the glass into. Oh, I can't,' she sighed, examining the glass in mock disappointment. 'It's plastic.' She looked up and flashed Ross what she thought was her most winning smile. Little did she know how brittle it looked, and how heartbreakingly vulnerable were her eyes.

'So is your Earl,' he murmured, 'if he let a girl like you get away.'

Vivien's whole throat contracted as an instant lump

claimed it. 'I...I wish you wouldn't say things like that.'

'Why? Don't you believe me?' he asked gently.

'Does anyone believe in their own worth after rejection?'

'I should hope so.'

She gave him a bitter look. 'Then you haven't ever been rejected, Ross Everton. Perhaps if you had, you'd know how I feel. And how your brother feels.'

Vivien saw she had struck a nerve with her statement, and regretted it immediately. Ross might not be a saint, but she couldn't see him deliberately hurting his younger brother. Gavin was indeed a fool, trying to blame someone else for the consequences of his own stupid and irresponsible behaviour.

Before she could formulate an apology, Ross spoke.

'Gavin's passed out in the back of his station wagon. From past experience, he'll sleep till morning. Which leaves me free to enjoy the rest of the evening. I thought that perhaps you might...' He hesitated, his eyes searching hers as though trying to gauge her reaction in advance.

'Might what?' she probed, heart fluttering.

'Go for a walk with me.'

'W—where?' she asked, feeling a jab of real alarm. Not so much at his invitation, but at the funny tingling feeling that was spreading over her skin. And now she detected a slight muzziness in her head.

She frowned down at the empty glass in her hands. Perhaps the champagne had been a particularly potent brew... Or maybe on her empty stomach the alcohol had gone to her head, almost as if it had been shot straight into her veins.

Ross shrugged. 'Not many places to go. Down towards the creek, I suppose. It's a couple of hundred yards beyond the back of the marquee.'

'Irving said I wasn't to go down there,' she said with a dry laugh, though inwardly frowning at how hot she felt all of a sudden. Her palms were clammy, too.

There was no doubt about it. The alcohol had hit her system hard. A walk in some fresh air would probably be the quickest way to sober her up, but she wasn't ignorant of the dangers such a walk presented.

She lifted firm eyes. 'Just a walk, Ross?'

He settled equally firm eyes back on her. 'I'm not about to make promises I won't keep. You're a very lovely and desirable woman, Vivien. I'm likely to try kissing you again, and I won't be in such a hurry this time.'

His eyes dropped to her mouth and she gasped, stunned by the shock of desire that charged through her.

Don't go with him, common sense warned.

Before she could open her mouth to decline he took her free hand quite forcibly and started pulling her behind the bandstand. 'There's a flap in the tent we can squeeze through back here,' he urged. 'We'll go through the car park and down to the creek, but well away from the other carousers.'

Vivien quickly found herself outside, any further argument dying on her lips when the fresh air hit her flushed face. She breathed in deeply, sighing with relief as her head started to clear. 'Oh, that *is* better.'

'I was certainly getting stuffy in there,' Ross agreed. 'It's a warm night.'

'Is it ever anything else but warm in this neck of the woods?' She laughed.

'Too right it is. Some nights it's positively freezing. Come on. It'll be very pleasant down by the creek.' He took her hand again, which brought a sharp look from Vivien.

He smiled at her warning glare and quite deliberately lifted her hand to his mouth, kissing each fingertip before turning her hand over and pressing her palm to his mouth. Her eyes widened when his lips opened and she felt his tongue start tracing erotic circles over her skin.

One small part of her brain kept telling her to yank her hand away. The rest was dazed into compliance with the sheer sensual pleasure of it all.

'You...you shouldn't be doing that,' she husked at last.

He lifted his mouth away, but kept her hand firmly in his grasp. 'Why?' Dragging her to him, he dropped her hand to cup her face, all the while staring down into her startled brown eyes. 'You're a free agent, aren't you? Why shouldn't I kiss you? Why shouldn't you kiss me?'

'Because...'

His mouth was coming closer to hers and her heart was going mad.

'Because—' she tried again.

'Because nothing,' he growled, and claimed her parted lips, his arms sweeping round her back in an embrace as confining as a strait-jacket.

When he released her a couple of minutes later, Vivien was in a state of shock. When he put his arm around her shoulder and started leading her through the car park in the direction of the creek, she was still not capable of speech.

Had Earl been able to arouse her so completely and totally with just a kiss? she was thinking dazedly. She didn't think so. When he'd made love to her, most of the time her desire had just been reaching a suitable pitch as he was finishing. Yet here…tonight…with Ross…

Perhaps she *was* tipsier than she realised. Alcohol did have a way of blasting her inhibitions to pieces.

'Are you always this silent when a man kisses you?' Ross murmured into her ear. He stopped then and turned to press her up against one of the parked cars, taking her mouth once more in another devastating kiss. She was struggling for air by the time he let her go, her heart going at fifty to the dozen. She was also blisteringly aware of Ross's arousal pressing against her. With great difficulty she ignored the excitement his desire inflamed in her, concentrating instead on the implication of what she was doing.

Truly, she could not let this continue. It wasn't fair to him. And, quite frankly, not to herself. She had never felt such desire, such excitement. In a minute or two, she wouldn't be able to stop even if she wanted to.

'Ross,' she said shakily as she tried to push him away, 'we have to stop this. We're both getting… excited, and I…I don't go in for one-night stands.'

'Neither do I,' he grated, stubbornly refusing to let her go.

'Ross, try to be sensible,' she argued, her stomach fluttering wildly. 'You're country. I'm city. After tonight we won't ever see each other again. I'm very attracted to you, but…' She shook her head, and carefully omitted to add anything about his physical resemblance to her ex-lover.

'Those problems are not insurmountable,' he said. 'Vivien, this doesn't have to stop at tonight. I often come down to Sydney to visit Dad in hospital and—'

She placed three fingers across his mouth and shook

her head again, her eyes truly regretful. 'No, Ross. It won't work. Believe me when I tell you that. And please,' she groaned when he took her hand and started kissing it again, 'don't keep trying to seduce me. I…I'm only human and you're a very sexy man. But I don't really want you.'

He stopped kissing her palm then, lifting his head to peer down at her with thoughtful eyes. 'I don't think you know what you want, Vivien,' he said tautly.

'I know I don't want to act cheaply,' she countered, cheeks flaming under his reproving gaze.

His smile was odd as he dropped her hand. 'A woman like you would never be cheap.'

'Are you being sarcastic?' she flared.

He seemed genuinely taken aback. 'Not at all.'

'Oh…I thought—'

'You think too much,' he said softly, laying such a gentle hand against her cheek that she almost burst into tears.

She swallowed the lump in her throat and lifted a proud chin. 'Better to think tonight than to wake up pregnant in the morning.'

His surprised, 'You're not on the Pill?' brought an instant flush. For of course she was. Earl had adamantly refused to take responsibility for contraception right from the start of their affair, claiming it was in *her* interests that she took charge of such matters. *She* would be the one left with an unwanted baby. Vivien could see now that it was just another example of Earl's selfishness.

'Actually, yes, I am,' she admitted. 'But there are *other* concerns besides pregnancy these days.'

'Not with me there aren't,' he bit out.

She viewed this statement with some cynicism. 'Really?' Her eyes flicked over his very male and very attractive body. 'I wouldn't have taken you for the celibate type, Ross.' His brother had implied just the opposite, Vivien remembered ruefully.

'One doesn't have to be celibate to be careful.'

'And would you have been careful tonight if I'd given you the go-ahead?' she challenged.

A slash of red burnt a guilty path across his cheeks. 'This was different,' he muttered, and lifted both hands to rake agitatedly through his hair.

Her laugh was scornful. 'I don't see how.'

His blue eyes glittered dangerously as they swung back to her. 'Then you're a fool, Vivien Roberts. A damned fool!'

For a second, she thought he was going to grab her and kiss her again. But he didn't. Instead, his mouth creased back into the strangest smile. It was both bitter and self-mocking. 'Look, let's walk, shall we? That's what you obviously came out here for. And don't worry your pretty little head. I won't lay a single finger on you unless I get a gold-edged invitation.'

He set off at a solid pace through the rows of cars, Vivien trailing disconsolately behind him. For she knew in the deepest dungeons of her mind, in the place reserved for unmentionable truths, that she didn't want Ross to lay a *single* finger on her. She wanted *all* his fingers, and *both* his hands. She wanted every wonderfully virile part of him.

CHAPTER FOUR

'CAN you slow down a bit?' she complained when the distance between them became ridiculous.

Ross had long left the car park and was almost at the tree-lined creek, while she was still halfway across the intervening paddock. If she'd tried to keep up with him she'd probably have fallen down one of the rabbit holes hidden in the grass. She'd already tripped a few times over rocks and logs and the like. Lord knew what her high heels looked like by now.

He stopped abruptly and threw a black look over his shoulder. Moonlight slanted across the angles of his face and she caught her breath as, for the first time, she saw little resemblance to Earl. His features suddenly looked leaner, harder, stronger. Yet they still did the most disturbing things to her stomach.

She slowed to a crawl as she approached, her eyes searching the ice-blue of his, trying to make sense of what she kept feeling for this man, even now, when he no longer reminded her so much of Earl. She couldn't even cling to the belief that she was tipsy, for the brisk walk had totally cleared her head.

His eyes changed as she stared up at him, at first to bewilderment, then to a wary watchfulness, and finally to one of intuitive speculation. They narrowed as they raked over her, his scrutiny becoming explicitly sexual as it lingered on specific areas of her body.

A wave of sheer sensual weakness washed through Vivien and she swayed towards him. 'Ross, I...I—'

He didn't wait for the gilt-edged invitation. He simply read her body language and scooped her hard against him, kissing her till she was totally breathless. 'God, I want you,' he rasped against her softly swollen mouth. 'I'll go mad if I don't have you. Don't say no...'

She said absolutely nothing as he lifted her up into his arms, carrying her with huge strides to the creek bank, where he lowered her on to the soft grass under a weeping willow. But her eyes were wide, her mind in chaos, her heart beating frantically in her chest.

'I won't ever hurt you, Vivien,' he whispered soothingly, and lay down beside her, bending over to kiss her, softly now, almost reverently.

Dimly she heard the sounds of distant revellers, their shouting and laughter. But even that receded as Ross's hand found her breast.

'You're so beautiful,' he muttered, and, pushing back the taffeta, he bent his mouth to the hardened peak.

Vivien closed her eyes and held his head at her breast, trying to take in the intensity of feeling that was welling up inside her. Briefly she remembered all that had happened to her over the last few days, and for a second she felt overwhelmed with guilt. She wasn't in love with Ross, couldn't possibly be. No more than he could be in love with her.

A tortured whimper broke from her lips.

'What's the matter, sweetheart?' Ross said gently, and returned to sip at her mouth. 'Tell me...'

'Oh, Ross,' she cried, her eyes fluttering open, raw pain in their depths. But as they gazed into his brilliant blue eyes, which were glittering above her with the most incredible passion in their depths, the most seductive yearning, she melted. He wanted her. He *really* wanted her. Not like Earl. Earl had never *really* wanted her.

An obsession. That's what he'd called his feelings for her. An obsession... An unhealthy, an unwanted need, one to be fought against, to be got over like something nasty and repulsive.

What she saw in Ross's eyes wasn't anything like that. It was normal and natural and quite beautiful.

She trembled as she clasped him close. 'Say that you love me,' she whispered. 'That's all I ask.'

He lifted his head to stare down at her, blue eyes startled.

'Oh, you don't have to mean it,' she cried, and clung to him. 'Just say it!'

A darkly troubled frown gathered on his brow and for a long, long moment he just looked at her. But then his hands came up to cradle her face and he gazed at her with such tenderness that she felt totally shattered. 'I love you, Vivien. I really, truly love you...'

She shuddered her despair at demanding such a pretence, but could no more deny the need to hear them than the need Ross was evoking within her woman's body.

'Show me,' she groaned. 'Make me forget everything but here...and now...'

At the first slightly vague moments of consciousness, Vivien was aware of nothing but a very fuzzy head and a throat as dry as the Simpson Desert. Her eyes blinked open to glance around her hotel room, and straight away she remembered.

With chest immediately constricted, she rolled over and stared at Ross beside her, flat on his back, sound asleep, his naked chest rising and falling in the deep and even breathing of the exhausted.

Rounded eyes went from him to the floor beside the bed, where her beautiful taffeta dress was lying in a sodden heap. Her black lace panties were still hanging from the arm-rest of the chair in the corner where Ross had carelessly tossed them. Her bolero and shoes, she recalled, were still down beside the creek.

Oh, my God, she moaned silently, the night before rushing back in Technicolor. How could I have behaved so...so outrageously? To have let Ross make love to me on the river-bank was bad enough. But what about later?

Her face flamed as guilt and shame consumed her.

She should never have allowed him to talk her into going skinny-dipping in the moonlit creek afterwards. Naked, he was even more insidiously attractive than he'd been in his dashing dinner suit, his body all brown and lean and hard.

Vivien had been fascinated by the feel of his well-honed muscles. She'd touched him innocently enough at first, holding on to his shoulders to stop herself from tiring as she trod water in the deep. But her hands hadn't stayed on his shoulders for long. They had begun to wander. Once she had started exploring his body, one thing had quickly led to another and, before she knew it, Ross was urging her into the shallows, where he'd taken her again right then and there in the water.

Afterwards, he had carried her limp body back on to the bank where he'd dressed her as best he could, then carried her back to the hotel. Vivien could still remember the look on the hotel proprietor's face when Ross had carried her past his desk and up the stairs.

By this time her conscience had begun to raise its damning head, but Ross managed to ram it back down with more drugging kisses in her room, more knowing caresses. Before she knew it, he was undressing her again and urging her to further amazing new heights of sensuality.

Vivien blushed furiously to think of her abandoned response to his lovemaking.

I have to get out of here. Fast. I couldn't possibly face him. I'd die! God, I even made him say he *loved* me!

She cringed in horror, then even more so as she recalled how after the last time here on the bed she'd actually wept. With the sheer intensity of her pleasure, not distress. Ross's lovemaking had seemed to possess not just her body but her very soul, taking her to a level of emotional and physical satisfaction she had never known before.

At least…that was how it had *seemed* at the time…

Looking back now, Vivien realised it couldn't *possibly* have been as marvellous an experience as she kept imagining. Certainly not in any emotional sense. Ross was simply a very skilled lover, knowing just what buttons to push, what words to say to make a woman melt. After all, she'd only asked him to say he loved her once, but he'd told her over and over. There were times when a more naïve woman might have believed he really *did* love her—he sounded and looked so sincere!

She darted a quick glance over at his face, at his softly parted lips. And shuddered. There wasn't a single inch of her flesh that those lips hadn't passed over at some time during the night.

Once again, she felt heat invade her face. Not to mention other parts of her body.

Thank God the bathroom is down the hall, Vivien thought shakily. I'll get my things together and slip out of this room and be gone before he opens a single one of those incredible blue eyes of his. For if I wait, I'm not sure what might happen...

A few minutes later she was knocking on Irving's door. He looked decidedly bleary as he opened it wearing nothing but striped boxer shorts.

'Viv?' He yawned. 'What are you doing up? I thought you'd be out of it for hours.' He gave her a slow, sly grin. 'Bert informed me that you were escorted back to your room at some ungodly hour by someone he called the "legendary Ross Everton". I presume he was the handsome hunk you were with earlier in the night. Did he—er—cure you of the banker?'

Vivien coloured fiercely, though her whirling mind was puzzling again over that word 'legendary'. Legendary in what way? Her colour increased when she realised it probably meant Ross's reputation with women. No doubt she had just spent the night with a very well-known local stud. Why, even his own brother had suggested Ross was a real ladies' man, with an infallible success rate.

Squashing down a mad mixture of dismay and mortification, Vivien gave Irving one of her most quelling 'shut-up-and-listen' looks. 'I need to be out of here five minutes ago, Irving. Do you think you can get a rustle on?'

'What's the emergency?'

'Shall we just say I don't want to see a certain "legendary" person when he finally wakes up?'

Irving pursed his lips and nodded slowly. 'Mornings after can be a tad sticky.'

'I would have used another word, like *humiliating*! You and I know this is not like me at all, Irving. I'm quietly appalled at myself.'

'You're only human, love. Don't be too hard on yourself. We all let our hair down occasionally.'

'Yes, well, I'd appreciate it if this particular hair-letting-down didn't get around the channel. Not all my colleagues are as good a friend as you, Irving.'

'Mum's the word.'

'Thanks. Look, I'll fix up the hotel bill and meet you at the car as soon as possible.'

'I'll be there before you are.'

Irving dropped Vivien outside her block of flats at seven that evening. She carried her overnight bag wearily up the two flights of stairs, where she inserted the key into the door numbered nine. She pushed the door open and walked in, switching on the light and kicking the door shut behind her in one movement.

Her mouth gaped open as she looked around the living-room in stunned disbelief. Because it was empty!

Well, not exactly empty. The phone was sitting on the carpet against the far wall, and three drooping pot plants huddled in a corner. Gone were the lounge and dining suites, the cocktail cabinet, the coffee-table, the television, the sound system and the oak sideboard, along with everything that had been on or in them. The walls were bare too, pale rectangles showing where various paintings had been hanging.

Vivien dropped the overnight bag at her feet and walked numbly into the kitchen. A dazed search revealed that she was still the proud owner of some odd pieces of chipped crockery and some assorted cutlery. The toaster was the only appliance still in residence, probably because it had been a second-hand one, given to them by her mother. The fridge was there too. But it had come with the flat. Vivien approached the two bedrooms with a growing sense of despair.

The main bedroom was starkly empty, except for her side of the built-in wardrobes. The guest bedroom shocked her in reverse, because it actually contained a single bed complete with linen.

'Oh, thanks a lot, Earl,' she muttered before slumping down on the side of the bed and dissolving into tears.

Five minutes later she was striding back into the living-room and angrily snatching the phone up from the floor. But then she hesitated, and finally dropped the receiver back down into its cradle.

There was no point in ringing Earl. Absolutely no point. For she hadn't paid for a single one of the items he'd taken from their flat. When she'd moved in, Earl, the financial wizard, had suggested *she* pay for the food each week while *he* paid for any other goods they needed. Over the eighteen months he'd bought quite a bit, but she'd also forked out a lot of cash on entertaining Earl's business acquaintances. He always liked the best in food and wine.

Now she wondered with increasing bitterness if he'd known all along how their affair would end and had arranged things so that he'd finish up with all the material possessions she'd assumed they co-owned.

A fair-minded person would have split everything fifty-fifty. To do what Earl had done was not only cruel. It also underlined that all he'd thrown at her over the telephone was true. He had never loved her. He'd simply used her. She'd been his housekeeper and his whore! And he'd got them both cheap!

But then she *was* cheap, wasn't she? she berated herself savagely. Only cheap women went to bed with a man within an hour or two of meeting him, without any real thought of his feelings, without caring where it led, without...

'Oh, my God!' she gasped aloud, and, with the adrenalin of a sudden shock shooting through her body, Vivien raced over to where she had dropped her bag. She reefed open the zip. But her fumbling fingers couldn't find what she was looking for. Yet they had to be here. They *had* to!

A frantic glance at her watch told her it was almost eight, thirteen hours after she usually took her pill. In the end she tipped the whole contents of the bag out on to the floor and they were were!

Snaffling them up, she pressed Sunday's pill through the foil and swallowed it. But all the while her doctor's warnings went round and round in her mind.

'This is a very low-dosage pill, Vivien, and *must* be taken within the same hourly span each day. To deviate by too long could be disastrous.'

The enormity of this particular disaster did not escape Vivien. She sank down into a sitting position on the carpet and hugged herself around the knees, rocking backwards and forwards in pained distress. 'Oh, no,' she wailed. 'Please, God...not that...I couldn't bear it...'

Vivien might have given herself up to total despair at that moment if the phone hadn't rung just then, forcing her to pull herself together.

'Yes?' she answered, emotion making her voice tight and angry. If it was Earl ringing he was going to be very, very sorry he had.

'Vivien? Is there something wrong?'

Vivien closed her eyes tight. Her mother... Her loving but very intuitive mother.

She gathered every resource she had. 'No, Mum. Everything's fine.'

'Are you sure?'

'Yes. Positive.' Smiles in her voice.

'I hope so.' Wariness in her mother's.

'What were you ringing up about, Mum?'

Vivien's mother was never one to ring for idle gossip. There was always a specific reason behind the call.

'Well, next Sunday week's your father's birthday, as you know, and I was planning a family dinner for him, and I was hoping you would come this time, now that Earl's in Melbourne. That man never seems to like you going to family gatherings,' her soft-hearted mother finished as accusingly as she could manage.

'Of course I'll be there,' she reassured, ignoring the gibe about Earl. Not that it wasn't true, come to think of it. Earl had never wanted to share her with her family.

She sighed. Perhaps in a fortnight's time she'd feel up to telling her mother about their breakup. Though, of course, in a fortnight's time she'd probably also be on the verge of a nervous breakdown, worrying if she was pregnant or not. God, what was to become of her?

'Do you want me to bring anything beside a present?' she asked. 'Some wine, maybe?'

'Only your sweet self, darling.'

The 'darling' almost did it. Tears swam into

Vivien's eyes and her chin began to quiver. 'Oh, good-ness, there's someone at the door, Mum. Must go. See you Sunday week about noon, OK?'

She just managed to hang up before she collapsed into a screaming heap on the floor, crying her eyes out.

CHAPTER FIVE

'I'M SORRY, Viv,' Mervyn said without any real apology in his voice. 'But that's the way it is. *Across Australia* has received another cut in budget and I have to trim staff. I've decided to do it on a last-on, first-to-go basis.'

'I see,' was Vivien's controlled reply. She knew there was no point in mentioning that fan mail suggested she was one of the show's most popular reporters. Mervyn was a man's man. He also never went back on a decision, once he'd made it.

'There's nothing else going at the channel?' she asked, trying to maintain a civil politeness in the face of her bitter disappointment. 'No empty slots anywhere?'

'I'm sorry, Viv,' he said once more. 'But you know how things are…'

What could she possibly say? If the quality of her work had not swayed him then no other argument would. Besides, she had too much pride to beg.

'Personnel has already made up your cheque,' he went on matter-of-factly when she remained stubbornly silent. 'You can pick it up at Reception.'

Now Vivien *was* shocked. Shocked and hurt. She propelled herself up from the chair on to shaky legs. 'But I'm supposed to get a month's notice,' she argued. 'My contract states that—'

'Your contract also states,' Mervyn overrode curtly, 'that you can receive a month's extra pay in lieu of notice. That's what we've decided to do in your case. For security reasons,' he finished brusquely.

She sucked in a startled breath. 'What on earth does that mean? What security reasons?'

'Come, now, Viv, it wouldn't be the first time that a disgruntled employee worked out their time here, all the while relaying our ideas to our opposition.'

'But…but you *know* I wouldn't do any such thing!'

His shrug was indifferent, his eyes hard and uncompromising. 'I don't make the policies around here, Viv. I only enforce them. If I hear of anything going I'll let you know.' With that, he extended a cold hand.

Vivien took it limply, turning on stunned legs before walking shakily from the room. This isn't happening to me, she told herself over and over. I'm in some sort of horrible nightmare.

In the space of a few short days, she had lost Earl, and now her job…

'Viv?' the receptionist asked after she'd been standing in front of the desk staring into space for quite some time. 'Are you all right?'

Vivien composed herself with great difficulty, covering her inner turmoil with a bland smile. 'Just woolgathering. I was told there would be a letter for me here…'

Vivien walked around the flat in a daze. She still couldn't believe what had happened back at the channel. When she'd arrived at work that morning, she'd thought Mervyn had wanted to talk to her to see how the segment at Wallaby Creek had gone over the weekend. Instead, she'd been summarily retrenched.

How ironic, she thought with rising bitterness. She

had virtually lost Earl because of that job. And now…
the job was no more.

Tears threatened. But she blinked them away. She
was fed up with crying, and totally fed up with life!
What had she ever done to deserve to be dumped like
that—first by the man she loved, then by an employer
to whom she had given nothing but her best? It was
unfair and unjust and downright unAustralian!

Well, I'll just have to get another job, she realised
with a resurgence of spirit. A *better* job!

Such as what? the voice of grim logic piped up. All
the channels are laying off people right, left and centre.
Unemployment's at a record high.

'I'll find something,' she determined out loud, and
marched into the kitchen, where she put on the kettle
to make herself some coffee.

And what if you're pregnant? another little voice inserted quietly.

Vivien's stomach tightened.

'I can't be,' she whispered despairingly. 'That would
be too much. Simply too much. Dear God, please don't
do that to me as well. *Please*…'

Vivien was just reaching for a cup and saucer when
the front doorbell rang. Frowning, she clattered the
crockery on to the kitchen counter and glanced at her
watch. 'Now who on earth could that be at four fifty-
three on a Monday afternoon?' she muttered.

The bell ran again. Quite insistently.

'All right, all right, I'm coming!'

Vivien felt a vague disquiet as she went to open the
door. Most of her acquaintances and friends would still
be at work. Who could it possibly be?

'Ross!' she gasped aloud at first sight of him, her
heart leaping with…what?

He stood there, dressed in blue jeans and a white T-shirt, a plastic carrier-bag in his left hand and a wry smile on his face.

'Vivien,' he greeted smoothly.

For a few seconds neither of them said anything further. Ross's clear blue eyes lanced her startled face before travelling down then up her figure-fitting pink and black suit. By the time his gaze returned to their point of origin Vivien was aware that her heart was thudding erratically in her chest. A fierce blush was also staining her cheeks.

Embarrassment warred with a surprisingly intense pleasure over his reappearance in her life. My God, he'd actually followed her all this way! Perhaps he didn't look at the other night as a one-night stand after all. Perhaps he really cared about her.

And perhaps not, the bitter voice of experience intervened, stilling the flutterings in her heart.

'What…what are you doing here?' she asked warily.

He shrugged. 'I had to come to Sydney to visit my father and I thought you might like the things you left behind.' He held out the plastic bag.

Her dismay was sharp. So! He hadn't followed her at all. Not really. She wasn't deceived by his excuse for dropping by. The way he'd looked at her just now was not the look of a man who'd only come to return something. Vivien knew the score. Ross was going to be in town anyway and thought he might have another sampling of what she'd given him so easily the other night.

Her disappointment quickly fuelled a very real anger. She snatched the plastic bag without looking inside, tossing it behind the door. She didn't want to see her ruined bolero and shoes, not needing any more reminders of her disgusting behaviour the other night. Ross's presence on her doorstep was reminder enough.

'How kind of you,' she retorted sarcastically. 'But how did you find out my address? It's not in the phone book.'

His eyes searched her face as though trying to make sense of her ill temper. 'Once I explained to the receptionist at the channel about your having left some of your things behind at the Wallaby Creek hotel,' he said, 'and that I had come all this way to return them, she gave me your address.'

'But you didn't come all this way just to return them, did you?' she bit out. 'Look, Ross, if you think you're going to take up where you left off then I suggest you think again. I have no intention of—'

'You're *ashamed* of what we did,' he cut in with surprise in his voice.

Her cheeks flamed. 'What did you *expect*? That I'd be *proud* of myself?'

'I don't see why not... What we shared the other night, Vivien, was something out of the ordinary. You must know how I feel about you. You must also have known I would not let you get away that easily.'

'Oh? And how *does* the legendary Ross Everton feel about little ole me?' she lashed out, annoyed that he would think her so gullible. 'Surely you're not going to declare undying love, are you?' she added scathingly. 'Not Ross Everton, the famous—or is it infamous?—country Casanova!'

His eyes had narrowed at her tirade, their light blue darkening with a black puzzlement. 'I think you've been listening to some twisted tales, Vivien. My legendary status, if one could call it such, has nothing to do with my being a Casanova.'

Now it was her turn to stare with surprise. 'Then what…what?'

He shrugged off her bumbled query, his penetrating gaze never leaving her. 'I *do* care about you, Vivien. Very much. When I woke to find you gone, I was…' His mouth curved back into a rueful smile. 'Let's just say I wasn't too pleased. I thought, damn and blast, that city bitch has just used me. But after I'd had time to think about it I knew that couldn't be so. You're too straightforward, Vivien. Too open. Too sweet…'

He took a step towards her then. Panic-stricken, she backed up into the flat. When Ross followed right on inside, then shut the door, her eyes flung wide.

'Don't be alarmed,' he soothed. 'I told you once and I'll tell you again: I won't ever hurt you. But I refuse to keep discussing our private lives in a damned hallway.' He glanced around the living-room, its emptiness clearly distracting him from what he'd been about to add. 'You're moving out?'

She shook her head. Somehow, words would not come. Her mind was whirling with a lot of mixed-up thoughts. For even if Ross was genuine with his feelings for her, what future could they have together? *Her* feelings for *him* had no foundation. They were nothing but a cruel illusion, sparked by his likeness to Earl.

'Then what happened to your furniture?' Ross asked.

She cleared her throat. 'Earl…Earl took it all.'

'*All* of it?'

Her laugh was choked and dry. 'He left me a single bed. Wasn't that nice of him?'

'Could win him the louse-of-the-year award.'

Vivien saw the pity in Ross's eyes and hated it.

Suddenly, the whole grim reality of her situation rushed in on her like a swamping wave, bringing with it a flood of self-pity. The tears she had kept at bay all day rushed in with a vengeance.

'Oh, God,' she groaned, her hands flying up to cover her crumpling face. 'God,' she repeated, then began to sob.

Despite her weeping, she was all too hotly aware of Ross gathering her into his strong arms, cradling her distraught, disintegrating self close to the hard warmth of his chest.

'Don't cry, darling,' he murmured. 'Please don't cry. He's not worth it, can't you see that? He didn't really love you…or care about you… Don't waste your tears on him… Don't…'

To Vivien's consternation, her self-pitying outburst dried up with astonishing swiftness, replaced by a feeling of sexual longing so intense that it refused to be denied. Hardly daring to examine what she was doing, she felt her arms steal around Ross's waist, her fingers splaying wide as they snaked up his back. With a soft moan of surrender, she nestled her face into his neck, pressing gently fluttering lips to the pulse-point at the base of his throat.

She felt his moment of acute stillness, *agonised* over it. Her body desperately wanted him to seduce her again. But her mind—her *conscience*—implored with her to stop before it was too late.

This is wrong, Vivien, she pleaded with herself. Wrong! You don't love him. What in God's name is the matter with you? Stop it now!

She wrenched out of his arms just as they tightened around her, the action making them both stagger backwards in opposite directions.

'I'm s—sorry,' she blurted out. 'I…I shouldn't have done that. I'm not myself today. I…I just lost my job, and coming so soon after Earl's leaving... Not that that's any excuse...' She lifted her hand to her forehead in a gesture of true bewilderment. 'I'm not even drunk this time,' she groaned, appalled at herself.

Ross stared across at her. 'What do you mean? You weren't drunk the other night. You'd only had a couple of glasses of champagne. Not even full glasses.'

Her sigh was ragged. 'That's enough for me on an empty stomach. I have this almost allergic reaction to alcohol, you see. It sends me crazy, a bit like your brother, only I don't need nearly as much. I'm a cheap drunk, Ross. A *very* cheap drunk,' she finished with deliberate irony.

'I see,' he said slowly.

'I'm sorry, Ross.'

'So am I. Believe me.' He just stood there, staring at her, his eyes troubled. Suddenly, he sighed, and pulled himself up straight and tall. 'Did I hear rightly just now? You've lost your job?'

'Yes, but not to worry. I'll find something else.' She spoke quickly, impatiently. For she just wanted him to go.

'Are you sure?' he persisted. 'Unemployment's high in the television industry, I hear.'

'I have my family. I'll be fine.'

'They live near by?'

'Parramatta. Look, it...it was nice of you to come all this way to see me again, Ross,' she said stiffly, wishing he would take the hint and leave. She had never felt so wretched, and guilty, and confused.

'Nice?' His smile was bitter. 'Oh, it wasn't nice, Vivien. It was a necessity. I simply *had* to see you again before I...' He broke off with a grimace. 'But that's none of your concern now.'

He gave Vivien an oddly ironic look. Once again, she was struck by his *dissimilarity* to Earl. His facial features might have come out of the same mould. But his expressions certainly didn't. His eyes were particularly expressive, ranging from a chilling glitter of reproach to a blaze of white-hot passion.

Vivien stared at him, remembering only too well how he had looked as he'd made love to her, the way his skin had drawn back tight across his cheekbones, his lips parting, his eyes heavy, as though he were drowning in his desire. Immediately, she felt a tightening inside, followed by a dull ache of yearning.

Did he see the desire in her eyes, the hunger?

Yes, he must have. For his expression changed once more, this time to a type of resolve that she found quite frightening. His hands shot out to grip her waist, yanking her hard against him.

'I don't care if you were drunk,' he rasped. 'I don't care if you're still in love with your stupid bloody Earl. All you have to do is keep looking at me like that and it'll be enough.'

His mouth was hard, his kiss savage. But she found herself giving in to it with a sweet surrender that was far more intoxicating than any amount of alcohol could ever be.

The doorbell ringing again made them both jump.

'Are you expecting anyone?' Ross asked thickly, his mouth in her hair, his hands restless on her back and buttocks.

Vivien shook her head.

Their chests rose and fell with ragged breathing as they waited in silence. The bell rang again. And again. Ross sighed. 'You'd better answer it.' His hands

dropped away from her, lifting to run agitatedly
through his hair as he stepped back.

Vivien ran her own trembling hands down her skirt
before turning to the door, all the while doing her best
to school her face into an expression that would not
betray her inner turmoil. One kiss, she kept thinking.
One miserable kiss and I'm his for the taking…

She was stunned to find Bob standing on the other
side of the door, a bottle of wine under his arm, a triumphant and sickeningly sleazy look on his face.

'Hello, Vivien.' He smirked. 'I dropped by to say
how sorry I was about the way Mervyn dismissed you
today. I thought we might have a drink together, and
then, if you like, we could…'

He broke off when his gaze wandered over Vivien's
shoulder, his beady eyes opening wide with true surprise when they encountered Ross standing there.

'Oh…oh, hi, there, Earl,' he called out, clearly flustered. 'I thought you were in Melbourne. Well, it's
good to know Viv has someone here in her hour of
need. I—er—only called round to offer my sympathy
and a shoulder to cry on, but I can see she doesn't need
it. I…I guess I'd better be going. Sorry to interrupt.
See you around, Viv. Bye, Earl.'

Vivien could feel Ross's frozen stillness behind her
as she slowly shut the door and turned. He looked as
if someone had just hit him in the stomach with a
sledge-hammer.

'Ross,' she began, 'I—'

'I'm not just *like* your ex-lover, am I, Vivien?' he
broke in harshly. 'I'm his damned double!'

She closed her eyes against his pained hurt. 'Almost,' she admitted huskily.

'God…'

Vivien remained silent. Perhaps it was for the best, she reasoned wretchedly. At least now he would see that there was no hope of a real relationship between them and he would leave her alone. For God only knew what would happen if he stayed.

But what if you're already pregnant by him? whispered that niggling voice.

Vivien pushed the horrendous thought aside. Surely fate couldn't be that perverse?

'I want you to open your eyes and look at me, Vivien,' Ross stated in a voice like ice.

She did, and his eyes were as flat and hard as eyes could be. She shrank from the cold fury his gaze projected.

'I want you to confirm that the main reason you responded to me the way you did the other night is because I'm the spitting image of your ex-lover. You were fantasising I was this Earl while I was making love to you, is that correct?'

No, was her instant horrified reaction. *No! It wasn't like that*!

And yet… It had to be so. For if it wasn't, then what had it been? Animal lust? The crude using of any body to assuage sexual frustration? Revenge on Earl, maybe?

None of those things felt right. She refused to accept them. Which only left what Ross had concluded. Perhaps the reason she instinctively rejected that explanation was because her memory of that night had been clouded by alcohol. She recalled thinking the next morning that her pleasure in Ross's lovemaking could not have been so extraordinary, could *not* have propelled her into another world where nothing existed but this man, and this man alone.

'I'm waiting, Vivien,' he demanded brusquely.

'Yes,' she finally choked out, though her tortured eyes slid away from his to the floor. 'Yes...'

He dragged in then exhaled a shuddering breath. 'Great,' he muttered. 'Just great. I'll remember that next time my emotions threaten to get in the way of my common sense. Pardon me if I say I hope I never see you again, Vivien Roberts. Still...you've been an experience, one I bitterly suspect I'll never repeat!'

He didn't look back as he left, slamming the door hard behind him.

It wasn't till a minute or two later that Vivien remembered something that challenged both Ross's conclusion and her own. If her responses had really been for Earl, if her memory of that night had been confused by alcohol and her pleasure not as overwhelming as she had thought, then why had she responded with such shattering intensity to Ross's kiss just now? Why?

None of it made sense.

But then, nothing made sense any more to Vivien. Her whole world had turned upside-down. Once, she had seen her future so very clearly. Now, there was only a bleak black haziness, full of doubts and fears and insecurities. She wanted quite desperately to run home to her mother, to become a child again, with no decisions to make, no responsibilities to embrace.

But she wasn't a child. She was an adult. A grown woman. She had to work things out for herself.

Vivien did the only thing a sensible, grown-up woman could do. She went to bed and cried herself to sleep.

CHAPTER SIX

'WHEN are you going to tell me what's wrong, dear?'

Vivien stiffened, tea-towel in hand, then slanted a sideways glance at her mother. Peggy Roberts had not turned away from where she stood at the kitchen sink, washing up after her husband Lionel's birthday dinner.

Vivien's stomach began to churn. There she'd been, thinking she had done a splendid job of hiding the turmoil in her heart. Why, she had fairly bubbled all through dinner, sheer force of will pushing the dark realities of the past fortnight way, way to the back of her mind.

Now, her mother's intuitive question sent them all rushing forward, stark in their grimness. She didn't know which was the worst: her growing realisation that she was unlikely to land a decent job in Sydney this side of six months, if ever; the crushing loneliness she felt every time she let herself back into her empty flat; or the terrifying prospect that her fear over being pregnant was fast becoming a definite rather than a doubtful possibility.

Her period had been due two days before and it hadn't arrived. Periods were never late when one was on the Pill. Of course, the delay might have been caused by her having forgotten one, but she didn't think so.

Just thinking about actually having a real baby—*Ross's* baby—sent her into a mental spin.

'Vivien,' her mother resumed with warmth and

71

worry in her voice, 'you do know you can tell me anything, don't you? I promise I won't be shocked, or
judgemental. But I can't let you leave here today without knowing what it is that has put you on this razor's
edge. The others probably haven't noticed, but they
don't know you as well as I do. Your gaiety, my dear,
was just a fraction brittle over dinner. Besides, you haven't mentioned Earl once today, and that isn't like
you. Not like you at all. Have you had a falling-out
with him, dear? Is that it?'

Vivien gave a small, hysterical laugh. 'I wouldn't put
it like that exactly.'

'Then how would you put it?' her mother asked
gently.

Too gently. Her loving concern sent a lump to
Vivien's throat, and tears into her eyes. Forcing them
back, she dragged in a shuddering breath then burst
forth, nerves and emotion sending the words out in a
wild tumble of awful but rather muddled confessions.

'Well, Mum, the truth is that a couple of weeks back
Earl gave me the ole heave-ho, told me he didn't love
me and that he had found someone else. I was very
upset, to put it mildly, but that weekend I had to go
out to that Bachelors' and Spinsters' Ball for work. You
know, the one they showed on TV last week. And while
I was there I met this man who, believe it or not, is
practically Earl's double, and I...well, I slept with him
on some sort of rebound, I suppose. At least, I think
that's why I did it...'

She began wringing the tea-towel. 'But I also forgot
my pill, you see, and now I think I might be pregnant.
Then on the Monday after that weekend I was retrenched at the channel and that same day Ross came
to Sydney to see me, hoping to make a go of things

between us, but he found out how much he looked like Earl and jumped to all the right conclusions, which I made worse by telling him I was sloshed at the time I slept with him anyway. Not that I was, but you know what drink does to me, and I had had a bit to drink and…and…as you can see, I'm in a bit of a mess…'

By this time tears were streaming down her face.

To give her mother credit, she didn't look too much like a stunned mullet. More like a flapping flounder, holding stunned hands out in front of her, while washing-up water dripped steadily from her frozen fingertips on to the cork-tiled floor.

But she quickly pulled herself together, wiping her soapy hands on the tea-towel she dragged out of Vivien's hands, then leading her distressed daughter quickly away from potentially prying eyes into the privacy of her old bedroom.

'Sit,' she said, firmly settling Vivien down on the white lace quilt before leaning over to extract several tissues from the box on the dressing-table and pressing them into her daughter's hands. She sat down on the bed as well, then waited a few moments while Vivien blew her nose and stopped weeping.

'Now, Vivien, I'm not going to pretend that I'm not a little shocked, no matter what I said earlier. But there's no point in crying over spilt milk, so to speak. Now, I'm not sure if I got the whole gist of your story. Ross, I presume, is the name of the man who may or may not be the father of your child?'

'Oh, he's the father all right,' Vivien blubbered. 'It's the child who's a maybe or maybe not. It's a bit too soon to tell.'

Peggy sighed her relief. 'So you don't really know yet. You might not be pregnant.'

'Yes, I am,' Vivien insisted wildly. 'I know I am.'

'Vivien! You sound as if you *want* to be pregnant by this man, this…this…stranger who looks like Earl.'

Vivien stared at her startled mother, then shook her head in utter bewilderment. 'I don't know what I want any more, Mum. I…I'm so mixed up and miserable and… Please help me. You always know just what to say to make me see things clearly. Tell me I'm not going mad. Tell me it wasn't wicked of me to do what I did. Tell me you and Dad don't mind if I have a baby, that you'll love me anyway. I've been so worried about everything.'

'Oh, my poor, dear child,' Peggy said gently, and enfolded her in her mother's arms. 'You've really been through the mill, haven't you? Of course you're not going mad. And of course you're not wicked. But as parents we *will* be worried about you having a baby all on your own, so if you are pregnant you'll have to come home and live with us so we can look after you. Come to think of it, you're coming home anyway. You must be horribly lonely in that flat all on your own.'

'You can say that again,' Vivien sniffled.

'You must be horribly lonely in that flat all on your own…'

Vivien pulled back, her eyes snapping up to her mother's. Peggy was smiling. 'Mum! This isn't funny, you know.'

'I know, but I can't help feeling glad that you're not going to marry that horrible Earl.'

'You never said you thought he was horrible before.'

'Yes, well, your father and I didn't want to make him seem any more attractive than you obviously already found him. But believe me, love, I didn't like him at all. He was the most selfish man I have ever met. Selfish and snobbish. He would have made a dreadful father, too. Simply dreadful. He had no sense of family.'

Vivien nodded slowly in agreement. 'You're right. I can see that now. I can see a lot of things about Earl that I couldn't see before. I don't know why I loved him as much as I did.'

'Well, he could be charming when he chose,' her mother admitted. 'And he was very handsome. Which makes me think that maybe you never loved him. Not really.'

Vivien blinked.

'Maybe it was only a sexual attraction,' Peggy suggested.

Vivien frowned.

'This man you slept with, the one you said looks a lot like Earl—'

'More than a lot,' Vivien muttered.

'Obviously you're one of those women who's always attracted to the same physical type. For some of us it's blond hair and blue eyes, or broad shoulders and a cute butt, or—'

'Mum!' Vivien broke in, shock in her voice.

Peggy smiled at her daughter. 'Do you think you're the only female in this family who's ever been bowled over by a sexual attraction?'

'Well, I...I—'

'Your father wasn't my first man, you know.'

'*Mum!*'

'Will you stop saying ''Mum!'' like that? It's unnerving. I don't mean I was promiscuous, but there was this other fellow first. I think if I tell you about him you might see that what happened between you and this Ross person was hardly surprising, or wicked.'

'Well, all right…if you say so…'

Peggy drew in a deep breath, then launched into her astonishing tale. At least, Vivien found it astonishing.

'I was eighteen at the time, working as a receptionist with a firm of solicitors while I went to secretarial school at night. Damian was one of the junior partners. Oh, he was a handsome devil. Tall, with black hair and flashing brown eyes, and a body to swoon over. I thought he was the best thing since sliced bread. He used to stop by my desk to compliment me every morning. By the time he asked me out four months later I was so ripe a plum he had me in bed before you could say "cheese".'

'Heavens! And was he a good lover?' Vivien asked, fascinated at the image of her softly spoken, very reserved mother going to bed with a man on a first date.

'Not really. Though I didn't know that at the time. I thought any shortcomings had to be mine. Still, I went eagerly back for more because his looks held a kind of fascination for my body which I didn't have the maturity to ignore. It wasn't till his fiancée swanned into the office one day that my eyes were well and truly opened to the sort of man he was.'

'So what did you do?'

'I found myself a better job and left a much wiser girl. Believe me, the next time a tall, dark and handsome man with flashing eyes set my heart a-flutter he had a darned hard time even getting to first base with me.'

'You gave him the cold shoulder, right?'

'Too right.'

'So what happened to him?'

'I married him.'

Vivien's brown eyes rounded. 'Goodness!'

'What I'm trying to tell you, daughter of mine, is that there's probably any number of men in this world that you might want as a lover, but not too many as your true love. When that chemistry strikes, hold back from it for a while, give yourself time to find out if the object of your desire is worth entrusting your body to, give the relationship a chance to grow on levels other than the sexual one. For it's those other levels that will stand your relationship in good stead in the tough times. You and Earl had nothing going for you but what you had in bed.'

'Which wasn't all that great,' Vivien admitted.

There was a short, sharp silence before Peggy spoke.

'I gather you can't say the same for the time you spent with this Ross person?'

Vivien coloured guiltily. There was no use in pretending any more that what she had felt with Ross that night had been anything like what she'd felt with Earl. Why, it was like comparing a scratchy old record to the very best compact disc.

Her mother said nothing for a moment. 'Have you considered an abortion?' she finally asked.

'Yes.'

'And?'

'I just can't. I know it would be an easy way out, a quick solution. Funnily enough, I've always believed it was a woman's right to make such a decision, and I still do, but somehow, on this occasion, it doesn't feel right. I'm scared, but I...I have to have this baby, Mum. Please...don't ask me to get rid of it.' She threw her mother a beseeching look, tears welling up in her eyes again.

Peggy's eyes also flooded. 'As if I would,' she said in a strangled tone. 'Come here, darling child, and give your old mother another hug. We'll work things out. Don't you worry. Everything will be all right.'

Vivien moved home the next day. Her pregnancy was confirmed two weeks later.

Once over her initial shock, her mother responded by fussing over Vivien, not allowing her to do anything around the house. Vivien responded by going into somewhat of a daze.

Most of her days were spent blankly watching television. Her nights, however, were not quite so uneventful, mostly because of her dreams. They were always of Ross and herself in a mixed-up version of that fateful night at Wallaby Creek.

Sometimes they would be on the creek bank, sometimes in the water, sometimes back in the hotel room. Ross would be kissing her, touching her, telling her he loved her. Inevitably, she would wake up before they really made love, beads of perspiration all over her body. Each morning, she would get up feeling totally wrung out. That was till she started having morning sickness as well.

Why, she would ask herself in the bathroom mirror every day, was she so hell-bent on such a potentially self-destructive path?

She could not find a sensible, logical answer.

A few days before Christmas, she made another decision about her baby, one which had never been in doubt at the back of her mind. All that had been in doubt was *when* she was going to do it.

'Dad?' she said that evening after dinner.

Her father looked up from where he was watching a movie on television and reading the evening paper at the same time. 'Yes, love?'

'Would you mind if I made a long-distance call? It doesn't cost so much at night and I promise not to talk for long.'

Now her mother looked up, a frown on her face. 'Who are you ringing, dear?'

'Ross.'

Her father stiffened in his chair. 'What in hell do you want to ring him for? He won't want anything to do with the child, you mark my words.'

'You're probably right,' Vivien returned, the image of Ross's furious departure still stark in her memory. He'd made his feelings quite clear. He never wanted to see her again.

But a few months back, she had done a segment for television on unmarried fathers, and the emotional distress of some of the men had lived with her long afterwards. One of their complaints was that some of the mothers had not even the decency to tell them about their pregnancies. Many had simply not given the fathers any say at all in their decisions to abort, adopt, or to keep their babies. Vivien had been touched by the men's undoubted pain. She knew that she would not be able to live with her conscience if she kept her baby a secret from its father.

A dark thought suddenly insinuated that she might be telling Ross about the baby simply to see him again. Maybe she wanted the opportunity to bring her erotic dreams to a very real and less frustrating fruition.

Pushing *that* thought agitatedly to the back of her mind, she addressed her frowning parents with a simplicity and apparent certainty she was no longer feeling.

'He has a right to know,' she stated firmly, and threw both her father and mother a stubborn look.

They recognised it as the same look they'd received

when they'd advised her, on leaving school, not to try
for such a demanding career as television, to do something easier, like teaching.

'You do what you think best, dear,' her mother said
with a sigh.

'It'll cause trouble,' her father muttered. 'You mark
my words!'

Vivien recklessly ignored her father's last remark,
closing the lounge door as she went out into the front
hall, where they kept the phone. Her hands were trembling as she picked it up and dialled the operator to
help her find Ross's phone number.

Three minutes later she had the number. She dialled
again with still quaking fingers, gripping the receiver
so tightly against her ear that it was aching already.

No one answered. It rang and rang at the other end,
Vivien's disappointment so acute that she could not
bring herself to hang up. Then suddenly there was a
click and a male voice was on the line.

'Mountainview. Ross Everton speaking.'

Vivien was momentarily distracted by the sounds of
merry-making in the background. Loud music and
laughter. Clearly a party was in progress.

And why not? she reasoned, swiftly dampening
down a quite unreasonable surge of resentment.
Christmas was, after all, less than a few days away.
Lots of people were having parties.

She gathered herself and started speaking. 'Ross, this
is Vivien here, Vivien Roberts. I...I...' Her voice
trailed away, her courage suddenly deserting her. It was
so impossible to blurt out her news with all that racket
going on in the background.

'I can hardly hear you, Vivien,' Ross returned.

'Look, I'll just go into the library and take this call there. Won't be a moment.'

Vivien was left hanging, quite taken aback that Ross's house would *have* a room called a library. It gave rise to a vision of an old English mansion with panelled walls and deep leather chairs, not the simple country homestead she had envisaged Ross's family living in. She was still somewhat distracted when Ross came back on the line, this time without the party noises to mar his deeply attractive voice. 'Vivien? You're still there?'

'Y…yes.'

There was a short, very electric silence.

'To what honour do I owe this call?' he went on drily. 'You haven't been drinking again, have you?' he added with a sardonic laugh.

'I wish I had,' she muttered under her breath. She hadn't realised how hard this was going to be. Yet what had she expected? That Ross would react to her unexpected call with warmth and pleasure?

'What was that?'

'Nothing.' Her tone became brisk and businesslike. 'I'm sorry to bother you during your Christmas party, but I have something to tell you which simply can't wait.'

'Oh?' Wariness in his voice. 'Something unpleasant by the sound of it.'

'*You* may think so.' Her tone was becoming sharper by the second, fuelled by a terrible feeling of coming doom. He was going to hate her news. Simply hate it!

'Vivien, you're not going to tell me you have contracted some unmentionable disease, are you?'

'Not unless you refer to pregnancy in such a way,' she snapped back.

His inward suck of breath seemed magnified as it rushed down the line to her already pained ears.

Vivien squeezed her eyes tightly shut. You blithering idiot, she berated herself. You tactless, clumsy blithering idiot! 'Ross,' she resumed tightly, 'I'm sorry I blurted it out like that. I...I—'

'What happened?' he said in a voice that showed amazing control. 'You did say, after all, that you were on the Pill. Did you forget to take it, is that it?'

She expelled a ragged sigh. 'Yes...'

Once again, there was an unnerving silence on the line before he resumed speaking. 'And you're sure I'm the father?' he asked, but without any accusation.

'Quite sure.'

'I see.'

'Ross, I...I'm not ringing because I want anything from you. Not money, or anything. I realise that I'm entirely to blame. It's just that I thought you had the right to know, then to make your own decision as to whether you want to...to share in your child's life. It's entirely up to you. I'll understand whatever decision you make.'

'You mean you're going to *have* my baby?' he rasped, shock and something else in his voice. Or maybe not. Maybe just shock.

'You don't want me to,' she said, wretchedness in her heart.

'What I want is obviously irrelevant. Does your family know you're going to have a baby?'

'Yes. I'm ringing from their place now. I moved back home a couple of weeks ago.'

'And how did they react?'

'They weren't thrilled at first, but they're resigned now, and supportive.'

'Hmm. Does Earl know?'

'Of course not!'

'Don't bite my head off, Vivien. You wouldn't be the first woman who tried to use another man's baby to get back the man she really wants. In the circumstances, I doubt you'd have had much trouble in passing the child off as his, since the father is his dead ringer.'

Vivien was shocked that Ross would even *think* of such a thing.

'Is that why you're having the baby, Vivien?' he continued mercilessly. 'Because you're hoping it will look like the man you love?'

She gasped. 'You're sick, do you know that?'

'Possibly. But I had to ask.'

'*Why?*'

'So that I can make rational decisions. I don't think you have any idea what your news has done to my life, Vivien.'

'What…what do you mean?'

'I mean that it isn't a Christmas party we're having here tonight. It's an engagement party. *Mine.*'

Vivien's mind went blank for a second. When it resumed operation and the reality of the situation sank in, any initial sympathy she might have felt for Ross was swiftly replaced by a sharp sense of betrayal.

'I see,' she bit out acidly.

'Do you?'

'Of course. You slept with me at the same time as you were courting another woman. You lied to me when you came after me, Ross. You didn't want a real relationship. All you wanted was a final fling before you settled down to your real life.'

'I wouldn't put it that way exactly,' he drawled.

'Then what way would you put it?'

'Let's just say I found you sexually irresistible. Once I had you in my arms, I simply couldn't stop.'

Vivien was appalled by the flush of heat that washed over her skin as she thought of how she had felt in *his* arms. She couldn't seem to stop either. Once she might have fancied she had fallen in love with Ross. Now she had another word for it, supplied by her mother.

Chemistry, it was called, the same chemistry that had originally propelled her so willingly into Earl's arms. Though Earl had had another word for it. *Lust*!

Vivien shuddered. God, but she hated to think her mind and heart could be totally fooled by her body. It was demeaning to her intelligence.

Men weren't fooled, though. They knew the difference between love and lust. They even seemed capable of feeling both at the same time. Ross had probably kept on loving this woman he was about to marry, all the while he was lusting after *her*.

'Let's hope you don't run into someone like me after you get married in that case,' she flung at Ross with a degree of venom.

'I won't be getting married, Vivien,' he said quite calmly. 'At least…not now, and not to Becky.'

Vivien's anger turned to a flustered outrage. Not for herself this time, but for the poor wronged woman who wore Ross's ring. 'But…but you can't break your engagement just like that. That…that's cruel!'

'It would be crueller to go through with it. Becky deserves more than a husband who's going to be the father of another woman's baby. I wouldn't do that to her. I've loved Becky all my life,' he stated stiffly. 'We're neighbours as well. I'm deeply sorry that I have to hurt her at all. But this is a case of being cruel to be kind.'

'Oh, I feel so guilty,' Vivien cried. 'I should never have rung, never have told you.'

'Perhaps. But what's done is done. And now we must think of the child. When can I come down and see you?'

'See me?' she repeated, her head whirling.

'How about Boxing Day? I really can't get away from here before Christmas. Give me your parents' address and telephone number.'

Stunned, she did as he asked. He jotted down the particulars, then repeated them back to her.

'Do me a favour, will you, Vivien?' he added brusquely. 'Don't tell your parents about the engagement. It's going to be tough enough making them accept me as the father of their grandchild without my having an advance black mark against my name. However, you'd better let them know about my remarkable resemblance to lover-boy. I don't think I could stand any more people calling me Earl by mistake.'

He dragged in then exhaled a shuddering breath. 'Ah, well…I'd better go and drop my bombshell. Something tells me this party is going to break up rather early. See you Boxing Day, Vivien. Look after yourself.'

Vivien stared down into the dead receiver for several seconds before putting it shakily back into its cradle. Normally a clear thinker, she found it hard to grasp how she really felt about what had just happened. Her emotions seemed to have scrambled her brains.

Ross, she finally accepted, was the key to her confusion. Ross…who had just destroyed the picture she had formed of him in her mind.

He was not some smitten suitor who had chased after her with an almost adolescent passion, ready to throw himself at her feet. He was the man she had first met, an intriguing mixture of sophisticate and macho male, a man who was capable of going after what he wanted with the sort of ruthlessness that could inspire a brother's hatred. He was, quite clearly, another rat!

No...she conceded slowly. Not quite.

A rat would have told her get lost. Her *and* her baby.

A rat would not have broken his engagement.

A rat would not be coming down to see her, concerned with her parents' opinion of him.

So what was he?

Vivien wasn't at all sure, except about one thing.

He was *not* in love with her.

He was in love with a woman named Becky.

Now why did that hurt so darned much?

CHAPTER SEVEN

'HE'S here,' Peggy hissed, drawing back the living-room drapes to have a better look. 'Goodness, but you should see the Range Rover he's pulled up in. Looks brand new. Can't be one of those farmers who're doing really badly, then.'

Lionel grunted from his favourite armchair. 'Don't you believe it, Mother. Graziers live on large over-drafts. Most of them are going down the tubes.'

'Well, I'd rather see my Vivien married to an over-draft*ee* than that overdraft*er* she was living with. Heavens, but I could not stand that man. Oh, my goodness, but this fellow does look like Earl. Taller, though, and fitter looking. Hmm… Yes, I can see why Vivien was bowled over. He's a bit of all right.'

'Peggy!' Lionel exclaimed, startled enough to put down his newspaper. 'What's got into you, talking like that? And don't start romanticising about our Vivien getting married just because she's having a baby. She's never been one to follow convention. Not that this Ross chap will want to marry her anyway. Young men don't marry girls these days for that reason.'

'He's not so young…'

'What's that?' Lionel levered himself out of his chair and came to his wife's side, peering with her through the lacy curtains. By this time, Ross was making his way through the front gate, his well-honed frame coolly dressed for the heat in white shorts and a pale blue polo shirt, white socks and blue and white striped Reeboks on his feet.

Lionel frowned. 'Must be thirty if he's a day.'

'Well, our Vivien *is* twenty-five,' Peggy argued.

'What on earth are you two doing?' the girl herself said with more than a touch of exasperation.

They both swung round, like guilty children found with their hands in the cookie jar.

The front doorbell rang.

Vivien folded her arms. 'If that's Ross why don't you just let him in instead of spying on him?'

'We—er—um...' came Peggy's lame mumblings till she gathered herself and changed from defence to attack.

'Vivien! Surely you're not going to let Ross see you wearing that horrible old housecoat? Go and put something decent on. And while you're at it, put some lipstick on as well. And run a brush through your hair. You look as if you've just got out of bed.'

'I *have* just got out of bed,' she returned irritably. 'And I have no intention of dolling myself up for Ross. He's not my boyfriend.'

'He *is* the father of your baby,' Lionel reminded her.

'More's the pity,' she muttered. Having been given a few days to think over the events surrounding that fateful weekend, Vivien had decided Ross was a rat after all. At least where women were concerned. He'd known she'd been upset about Earl that night, had known he himself had been on the verge of asking another woman to be his bride, one he *claimed* to have loved for years. Yet what had he done? Cold-bloodedly taken advantage of her vulnerability by seducing her, making her forget her conscience and then her pill!

'Vivien,' her mother said sternly, 'it was *your* idea

to call Ross and tell him about the baby, which was a very brave and adult decision, but now you're acting like a child. Go and make yourself presentable *immediately*!'

Vivien took one look at her mother's determined face and knew this was not the moment to get on her high horse. Besides, her mother was right. She was acting appallingly. Still, she had felt rotten all day, with a queasy stomach and a dull headache, as she had the day before. She hadn't even been able to enjoy her Christmas dinner, due to a case of morning sickness which lasted all day. If this was what being pregnant was like then it was strictly for the birds!

'Oh, all right,' she muttered, just as the front doorbell rang for the second time. 'You'd better go and let him in. Something tells me Ross Everton is not in the habit of waiting for anything.'

She flounced off, feeling ashamed of herself, but seemingly unable to do anything about the way she was acting. On top of her physical ills, the news of Ross's engagement had left her feeling betrayed and bitter and even more disillusioned about men than she already had. It was as though suddenly there were no dreams any more.

No dreams. No Prince Charming. No hope.

Life had become drearily disappointing and utterly, utterly depressing.

Vivien threw open her wardrobe and drew out the first thing her hands landed on, a strappy lime sundress which showed a good deal of bare flesh. For a second, she hesitated. But only for a second. She had always favoured bright, extrovert clothes. Her wardrobe was full of them. Maybe wearing fluorescent green would cheer her up.

Tossing aside all her clothes, she drew on fresh bikini briefs before stepping into the dress and drawing it up over her hourglass figure. With wry accession to her mother's wishes, she brushed her dishevelled hair into disciplined waves before applying a dash of coral gloss to her lips.

The mirror told her she looked far better than she felt, the vibrant green a perfect foil for her pale skin and jet-black hair. Yet when her eyes dropped to her full breasts straining against the thin cotton, Ross's words leapt back into her mind.

'I found you sexually irresistible…'

The words pained her, as Earl's words had pained her.

'It was only lust,' *he* had said.

Vivien couldn't get the dress off quickly enough, choosing instead some loose red and white spotted Bermuda shorts with a flowing white over-shirt to cover her womanly curves. The last thing she wanted today was Ross looking at her with desire in his eyes. Suddenly, she found her own sex appeal a hateful thing that stood between herself and real happiness.

Reefing a tissue out of the box, she wiped savagely at her glossed lips, though the resultant effect was not what she wanted. Sure, the lipstick was gone, but the rubbing had left her lips quite red and swollen, giving her wide mouth a full, sultry look.

'Damn,' she muttered.

'Vivien,' came her mother's voice through the bedroom door, 'when you're ready you'll find us on the back patio. Your father and Ross are having a beer together out there.'

Vivien blinked. Dad was having a beer with Ross? Already? How astonishing. He only ever offered a beer to his best mates. Perhaps he needed a beer himself, she decided. It had to be an awkward situation for him, entertaining Ross, trying to find something to talk to him about.

I should be out there, she thought guiltily.

But still she lingered, afraid to leave the sanctuary of her bedroom, afraid of what she would still see in Ross's eyes when they met hers, afraid of what she might *not* see.

Vivien violently shook her head. This was crazy! One moment she didn't want him to want her. Then the next she did. It was all too perverse for words!

Self-disgust finally achieved what filial duty and politeness could not. Vivien marched from the room, bitterly resolved to conquer these vacillating desires that kept invading her mind and body. Ross wanted to talk to her about their coming child? Well, that was all he'd ever get from her in future. Talk! She had no intention of letting him worm his way past her physical defences ever again.

She stomped down the hall, through the kitchen and out on to the back patio, letting the wire door bang as she went. The scenario of a totally relaxed Ross seated cosily between her parents around the patio table, sipping a cool beer and looking too darned handsome for words, did nothing for her growing irritation.

'Ah, here she is now,' her father said expansively. 'Ross was just telling us that he's not normally a sheep farmer. He's simply helping out at home till his father gets on his feet again. He flies helicopters for a living. Mustering cattle. Own your own business, didn't you say, Ross?'

'That's right, Mr Roberts. I've built up quite a clientele over the last few years. Mustering on horseback

is definitely on the way out, though some people like
to call us chopper cowboys.'

'Chopper cowboys... Now that's a clever way of
putting it. And do call me Lionel, my boy. No point in
being formal, in the circumstances, is there?' he added
with a small laugh.

Ross smiled that crooked smile that made him look
far too much like Earl. 'I guess not,' he drawled, and
lifted the beer to his lips.

'But isn't that rather a dangerous occupation?' Peggy
piped up with a worried frown.

'Only if you're unskilled,' Ross returned. 'Or careless. I'm usually neither.' He slanted Vivien a ruefully
sardonic look that changed her inner agitation into an
icy fury.

'Accidents do happen though, don't they?' she said
coldly.

'Now don't go getting all prickly on us, love,' Lionel
intervened. 'We all know that neither of you had any
intention of having a baby together, but you *are*, and
Ross here has at least been decent enough to come all
this way to meet us and reassure us he'll do everything
he can to support you and the child. You should be
grateful that he's prepared to do the right thing.'

Vivien counted to ten, then came forward to pick up
an empty glass and pour herself some orange juice out
of the chilled cask on the table. 'I *am* grateful,' she said
stiffly. 'I only hope no one here suggests that we get
married. I won't be marrying anyone for any reason
other than true love.'

She lifted her glass and eyes at the same time, locking visual swords with Ross over the rim. But she
wasn't the only one who could hide her innermost feelings behind a facial façade. He eyed her back without

so much as a flicker of an eyelash, his cool blue eyes quite unflappable in their steady regard.

'Believe me, Vivien,' came his smooth reply, 'neither will I.'

An electric silence descended on the group as Vivien and Ross glared at each other in mutual defiance.

'Perhaps, Mother...' Lionel said, scraping back his chair to stand up. 'Perhaps we should leave these two young people to have a private chat.'

'Good idea, dear,' Peggy agreed, and stood up also. 'Here, Vivien, use my chair. Now be careful. Don't spill your drink as you sit down.'

Vivien rolled her eyes while her mother treated her like a cross between a child and an invalid.

'Will you be staying for dinner, Ross?' Peggy asked before she left.

Ross glanced at his wristwatch which showed five to six. He looked up and smiled. 'If it's not too much trouble.'

'No trouble at all. We're only having cold meats and salad. Left-overs, I'm afraid, from yesterday's Christmas feast.'

'I love left-overs,' he assured her.

Once her parents had gone inside, Vivien heaved a heavy sigh.

'Not feeling well, Viv?' Ross ventured.

She shot him a savage look. 'Don't call me that.'

'What? "Viv"?'

'Yes.'

'Why?'

She shrugged irritably.

'Did Earl call you that?'

'No,' she lied.

He raised his eyebrows, but said nothing.

'Look, Ross, I'm just out of sorts today, OK?' Vivien burst out. 'It isn't all beer and skittles being pregnant, you know.'

'No, I don't know,' he said with a rueful note in his voice. 'But I guess I'm going to find out over the next few months. Something tells me you're a vocal type of girl.'

She darted him a dry look. 'If by that you mean I'm a shrew or a whinger then you couldn't be further from the truth. It's just that I didn't expect to be this sick all the time. I guess I'll get used to it in time. Though I'm damned if I'll get used to my mother's fussing,' she finished with a grimace of true frustration.

'You're going to live here?'

'Where else? I had no intention of staying on in Earl's flat. Besides, I'm unemployed now and I wouldn't have enough money for the rent anyway, so I have to stay here. There's no other alternative.'

'You could come home with me,' he suggested blandly.

Her mouth dropped open, then snapped shut. 'Oh, don't be ridiculous!'

'I'm not being ridiculous. Dad wants to meet you, and I'd like to have you.'

'I'll just bet you would,' she shot at him quite nastily.

Both his eyebrows shot up again. 'You have a dirty mind, Vivien, my dear.'

'Maybe it's the company I'm keeping.'

Anger glittered in his eyes. 'Perhaps you would prefer to be with a man who used you quite ruthlessly then discarded you like an old worn-out shoe!'

Vivien paled. Her bottom lip trembled.

'God,' Ross groaned immediately, placing his beer

glass down on the table with a ragged thud. 'I'm sorry, Vivien. Deeply, sincerely sorry. That was a rotten thing to say.'

'Yes,' she rasped, tears pricking at her eyes.

She stared blindly down into her orange juice, amazed at the pain Ross's words had produced. There she'd been lately, almost agreeing with her mother that she had never loved Earl. But she must have, for this reminder of his treachery to hurt so much.

Or maybe she was just in an over-emotional state, being pregnant and all. She had heard pregnancy made some women quite irrational.

With several blinks and a sigh, she glanced up, only to be shocked by the degree of bleak apology on Ross's face. He really was very sorry, it seemed.

Now she felt guilty. For she hadn't exactly been Little Miss Politeness since joining him.

'I'm sorry too, Ross,' she said sincerely, 'This can't be easy for you either. I won't pretend that I'm thrilled at finding out you only looked upon me as a "bit on the side", so to speak, but who am I to judge? My behaviour was hardly without fault. I was probably using you that night as much as you were using me, so perhaps we should try to forgive each other's shortcomings and start all over again, shall we?'

He stared at her. 'You really mean that?'

'Of course. You're the father of my baby. We should at least try to be friends. I can also see it's only sensible that I should come out to meet your family, though I really can't stay with you for my entire pregnancy. Surely *you* can see that?'

'Actually, no, I can't.'

She made an exasperated sound. 'It wouldn't be

right. I've never been a leaner. I have to make my own way.'

'That might have been all right when it was just you, Vivien,' he pointed out. 'But soon you'll have a child to support. You have no job and, I would guess, few savings. And, before you jump down my throat for being presumptuous, I'm only saying that because you're not old enough to have accrued a fortune.'

'I'm twenty-five!'

'Positively ancient. And you've been working how long? Four years at most?'

'Something like that…'

'Women never get paid as much as men in the media. Besides, in your line of work you would have had to spend a lot on clothes.'

'Yes…'

'See? It doesn't take a genius to guess at your financial position. Besides, I have a proposition to make to you.'

This brought a wary, narrow-eyed glare. 'Oh, yes?'

'Nothing like that,' he dismissed. 'My father has just come home from a stay in hospital where he's been having therapy. I have engaged a private therapist who specialises in after-stroke care to visit regularly, but there are still times when he needs someone to read to him and talk to him, or just sit with him.'

'A paid companion, you mean?'

'Yes. Something like that. Do you think you might be interested? It would kill two birds with one stone. Dad would get to know the mother of his grandchild and vice versa. And you'd feel a bit more useful than you're obviously feeling now.'

'Mmm.' Vivien gnawed away at her bottom lip. 'I've applied for social security…'

'No matter. You can either cancel it or I'll put your wages into a trust fund for the child.'

She wrinkled her nose. 'I'd rather cancel it.'

'*You would.*'

She bristled at his exasperated tone. 'Meaning?'

'You're too proud, Vivien. And too honest. You must learn that life is a jungle and sometimes the good get it in the neck.'

'Are you saying you have no pride? That you're not honest?'

A shadow passed across his eyes, turning them to a wintry grey for a second. But they were soon back to their bright icy blue. 'Let's just say that I *have* been known to go after what I want with a certain one-eyed determination.'

She gave him a long, considering look, trying not to let his physical appeal rattle her thought processes. It was hard, though. He was a devastatingly sexy man, much sexier than Earl. Oh, their looks were still remarkably similar—on the surface. But Ross had an inner energy, a raw vitality that shone through in every look he gave her, every move he made. Even sitting there casually in a deckchair with his legs stretched out, ankles crossed, he exuded an animal-like sensuality that sent tickles up and down her spine.

'Have you thought up this companion job simply to get me into a position where you can seduce me again?' she asked point-blank.

He seemed startled for a moment before recovering his cool poise. 'No,' he said firmly, and looked her straight in the eye. 'Believe me when I say there will *not* be a repeat performance of what happened that night out at Wallaby Creek.'

He sounded as if he was telling the truth, she realised

with a degree of surprise. And disappointment. The latter reaction sparked self-irritation. If *he* had managed to bring this unfortunate chemistry between them under control, then why couldn't *she*?

'Are you two ready to eat?' her mother called through the wire door. 'It's all set out.'

'Coming,' they chorused.

Thank God for the interruption, Vivien thought as she and Ross stood up.

'Vivien?' he said, taking her elbow to stop her before she could walk away.

'Yes?'

'Are you going to take me up on the offer or not?'

She tried to concentrate on all the common-sense reasons why it was a good idea, and not on the way his touch was making her pulse-rate do a tango within her veins.

'Vivien?' he probed again.

Swallowing, she lifted her dark eyes to his light blue ones, hoping like hell that he couldn't read her mind. Or her body language.

'If you trust me in this,' he said softly, 'I will not abuse that trust.'

Maybe, she thought. But could she say the same for her own strength of will? She'd shown little enough self-control once she'd found herself in his arms in the past. What if he'd been lying earlier about why he wanted her in his home? What if he was lying *now*? Men often lied to satisfy their lust. Now that she was already pregnant and his engagement was off, what was to stop Ross from using her to satisfy his sexual needs? How easy it would be with her already under his roof...

'Vivien!' her mother called again. 'What's keeping

you?' Her face appeared at the wire door. 'Come on, now, love. I've got a nice salad all ready. You must eat, you know, since you're eating for two. And I've put out the vitamins the doctor suggested you have. Ross, don't take any nonsense from her and bring her in here right away.'

'Sure thing, Mrs Roberts.'

He smiled at the pained look on Vivien's face. 'Well? What do you say? Will you give it a try for a few months?'

A few months...

Something warned her that was too long, too dangerous.

'One month,' she compromised. 'Then we'll see...'

Still looking into his eyes, Vivien would have had to be blind not to see the depth of Ross's satisfaction. Her stomach turned over and she tore her eyes away. What have I done? she worried.

As he opened the wire door and guided her into the large, airy kitchen, the almost triumphant expression on Ross's face sent an old saying into her mind.

'"Will you walk into my parlour?" said a spider to a fly...'

CHAPTER EIGHT

'WHAT did Mum say to you?' Vivien demanded to know as soon as the Range Rover moved out of sight of her waving parents.

Ross darted a sideways glance at her, his expression vague. 'When?'

'When she called you back to the front gate just now.' She eyed Ross suspiciously. 'She isn't trying to put any pressure on you to marry me, is she?'

'Don't be paranoid, Vivien. Your mother simply asked me not to speed, to remember that I had a very precious cargo aboard.'

'Oh, good grief! That woman's becoming impossible. God knows what she'll be like by the time I actually *have* this baby.'

'Speaking of the baby, are you feeling better today?'

'No,' she grumped. 'I feel positively rotten.'

'Really? You look fantastic. That green suits you.'

Vivien stiffened, recalling how she had argued with her mother over what she should wear this morning. In the end she had given in to her mother's view that she should dress the way she always dressed, not run around hiding her figure in tent dresses and voluminous tops.

But now Vivien wasn't so sure wearing such a bare dress was wise. She hadn't forgotten the way Ross had looked yesterday when she'd agreed to go home with him for a while. The last thing she wanted to do was be provocative.

'I thought you said that you wanted us to start all over again,' Ross reminded her, 'that we should try to be friends. If this is your idea of being friendly then city folk sure as hell are different from country.'

His words made Vivien feel guilty. She was being as bitchy today as she had been yesterday, and it wasn't all because she felt nauseous. When Ross had shown up this morning, looking cool and handsome all in white, she hadn't been able to take her eyes off him. Her only defence against her fluttering heart had been sharp words and a cranky countenance.

Vivien shook her head. Her vulnerability to this chemistry business was the very devil. It played havoc with one's conscience, making her want to invite things that she knew were not in her best interests. Maybe some people could quite happily satisfy their lust without any disastrous consequences. But Vivien feared that if she did so with Ross she might become emotionally involved with him.

And where would that leave her, loving a man who didn't love her back, a man whose heart had been given to another woman? It wasn't as though there was any hope of his marrying her, either. He'd made his ideas on that quite clear.

Still, none of these inner torturous thoughts were any excuse for her poor manners, and she knew it.

'I'm sorry, Ross,' she apologised. 'I'll be in a better humour shortly. This yucky feeling usually wears off by mid-morning.'

He smiled over at her. 'I'll look forward to it.'

They fell into a companionable silence after that, Vivien soon caught up by the changing scenery as they made their way up the Blue Mountains and through Katoomba. She had been the driver during this section

when she and Irving had made the trip out to Wallaby
Creek, and the driver certainly didn't see as much as
the passenger. Oddly enough, the curving road did not
exacerbate her slightly queasy stomach. In fact she was
soon distracted from her sickness with watching the
many and varied vistas.

Despite being built on at regular intervals, the moun-
tain terrain still gave one the feeling of its being totally
untouched in places. The rock-faces dropped down into
great gorges, the distant hillsides covered with a virgin
bush so wild and dense that Vivien understood only too
well why bushwalkers every year became lost in them.
She shuddered to think what would happen to the many
isolated houses if a bush-fire took hold.

'It's very dry, isn't it?' she remarked at last with
worry in her voice.

'Sure is. My father says it's the worst drought since
the early forties.'

'How old *is* your father, Ross?' Vivien asked.

'Sixty-three.'

'Still too young to die,' she murmured softly. 'And
you?'

'I'll be thirty-one next birthday. What is this, twenty
questions?'

Vivien shrugged. 'I think I should know a little about
your family before I arrive, don't you?'

'Yes. I suppose that's only reasonable. Fire away,
then.'

'Who else is there at Mountainview besides you and
your father and Gavin? I presume you three men don't
fend for yourselves.'

He laughed. 'You presume right. If we did, we'd
starve. We have Helga to look after us.'

'Helga... She sounds formidable.'

'She is. Came to us as a nurse when Mum became terminally ill. After she died, Helga stayed on, saying we couldn't possibly cope without her. I was twelve at the time. Gavin was only seven. He looks upon Helga as a second mother.'

'And you? Do you look upon her as a second mother?'

'Heaven forbid. The woman's a martinet. No, only Gavin softens that woman's heart. She'd make an excellent sergeant in the army. Still, she does the work of three women so I can't complain. Keeps the whole house spick and span, does all the washing and cooking and ironing, and still has time left over to knit us all the most atrocious jumpers. I have a drawer full of them.'

'Oh, she sounds sweet.' Vivien laughed.

'She means well, I suppose. She's devoted to Mountainview. The house, that is. Not the sheep.'

'Is it a big house? I got the impression it was on the phone.'

'Too damned big. Built when graziers were nothing more than Pitt Street farmers who used their station properties as country retreats to impress their city friends. We don't even use some sections of the house. Dad gets a team of cleaners in once a year to spring-clean. When they're finished, they cover the furniture in half the rooms with dust-cloths then lock the doors.'

'Goodness, it sounds like a mansion. How many rooms has it got?'

'Forty-two.'

Vivien blinked over at his amused face. 'You're pulling my leg.'

He glanced down at her shapely ankles. 'Unfortunately, no.'

'Forty-two,' she repeated in amazement. 'And you only have the one woman to keep house?'

'In the main. We hire extra staff if we're having a party or a lot of visitors. And there's Stan and Dave.'

'Who are they?'

'General farmhands. Or rouseabouts, if you prefer. But they don't live in the main house. They have their own quarters. Still, they do look after the gardens, so you're likely to run into them occasionally. Of course, the place is a lot busier during shearing, but that won't be till March.'

'March...' Vivien wondered if she would still be there in March. She turned her head slowly to look at Ross. In profile, he looked nothing like Earl at all, yet her stomach still executed a telling flutter.

'Do...do you think Helga will like me?' Vivien asked hesitantly.

'I don't see why not.'

Vivien frowned. Men could be so naïve at times. If Helga had been fond of Ross's Becky then she wouldn't be very welcoming to the woman who'd been responsible for breaking the girl's heart.

But *was* it broken? she wondered. Ross had confessed his long love for the woman he'd planned to marry, but Vivien knew nothing of the woman herself, or her feelings.

'Ross...'

'Mmm?'

'Tell me about Becky.'

He stiffened in his seat, his hands tightening around the wheel. 'For God's sake, Vivien...'

She bristled. 'For God's sake what? Surely I have a right to know something about the woman you were planning to marry, the woman you were sleeping with the same time you were sleeping with me?'

'I was not sleeping with Becky,' he ground out. 'I have *never* slept with Becky.'

Vivien stared over at him. 'But…but…'

'Oh, I undoubtedly would have,' he confessed testily. 'After we were properly engaged.'

Vivien could not deny that there was a certain amount of elation mixed in with her astonishment at this news. She had hated to think Ross had behaved as badly as Earl. Not that his behaviour had been impeccable. But at least he hadn't been sleeping with two women at the same time. Though, to be honest, Vivien did find his admission a touch strange.

'I'm not sure I understand,' she said with a puzzled frown. 'If you've always loved this Becky, then why haven't you made love to her? Why were you waiting till you were engaged?'

His sigh was irritable. 'It's difficult to explain.'

'*Try,*' she insisted.

He shot her an exasperated glance. 'Why do you want to know? Why do you care? You're not in love with me. What difference can it possibly make?'

'I want to know.'

'You are an incredibly stubborn woman!'

'So my mother has always told me.'

'She didn't tell *me* that,' he muttered.

'Didn't she? Well, what did she tell you, then? Were you lying to me back in Sydney whe—?'

'Oh, for pity's sake give it a rest, will you, Vivien? We've a tiresome trip ahead and you're going on like a Chinese water torture. God! Why I damned well…' He broke off, lancing her with another reproachful glare. 'You would have to be the most infuriating female I have ever met!'

Vivien's temper flared. 'Is that so? You certainly didn't find me infuriating once you got my clothes off, did you? You found me pretty fascinating then all right!'

He fixed her with an oddly chilling glance as he pulled over to the side of the road and cut the engine.

'Yes,' he grated out, then thumped the steering-wheel. 'I did. Is that what you want to hear? How I couldn't get enough of you that night? How I wouldn't have stopped at all if I hadn't flaked out with sheer exhaustion?'

He scooped in then exhaled a shuddering breath, taking a few seconds to compose himself. 'Now what else do you want to know…? Ah, yes, why I haven't slept with Becky? Well, perhaps my reasons might be clearer if I tell you she's only twenty-one years old, and a virgin to boot. Convent-educated. A total innocent where men are concerned. Somehow it didn't seem right to take that innocence away till my ring was on her finger. So I waited…

'It's just as well I did, in the circumstances,' he finished pointedly.

Vivien sat there in a bleak silence, her heart a great lump of granite in her chest. Heavy and hard and cold. My God, he had really just spelt it out for her, hadn't he? *She* could be taken within hours of their first meeting. For *she* had no innocence to speak of, no virtue to be treasured or respected. She was little better than a slut in his eyes, fit only to be lusted after, to be *screwed*!

Not so this girl he loved. She was to be treated like spun glass, put up on a pedestal, looked at but not touched, not ruthlessly seduced as he'd seduced her over and over that night.

She pressed a curled fist against her lips lest a groan of dismay escape, turning her face away to stare blindly through the passenger window. Well, at least this would give her a weapon to use against herself every time that hated chemistry raised its ugly head. She would only have to remember exactly how she stood in Ross's eyes for those unwanted desires to be frozen to nothingness. She would feel as chilled towards him as she did at this very moment.

'Haven't you any other questions you want answered?' Ross asked in a flat voice.

'No,' was all she could manage.

'In that case I'll put some music on. We've a long drive ahead of us...'

They stopped a couple of times along the way, at roadside cafés which served meals as well as petrol. Each time she climbed out of the cabin Vivien was struck by the heat and was only too glad to be underway again under the cooling fan of the vehicle's air-conditioning.

Vivien stayed quiet after their earlier upsetting encounter, even though the scenery didn't provide her bleak wretchedness with any distractions. The countryside was really quite monotonous once they were out on the Western plains. Nothing but paddock after flat paddock of brown grass, dotted with the occasional clump of trees under which slept some straggly-looking sheep. Even the towns seemed the same, just bigger versions of Wallaby Creek.

They were driving along shortly after two, the heat above the straight bitumen road forming a shimmering lake, when Vivien got the shock of her life. A huge grey kangaroo suddenly appeared right out of the mirage in front of them, leaping across the road. Ross braked, but he still hit it a glancing blow, though not enough to stop its flight to safety.

Vivien stared as the 'roo went clean over the barbed-wire fence at the side of the road and off across the paddock. Within seconds it had disappeared.

'That's the first kangaroo I've ever seen, outside a zoo!' she exclaimed, propelled out of her earlier depression by excitement at such an unexpected sight. 'I'm glad we didn't hurt it.'

'It'd take more than a bump to hurt one of those big mongrels.' Ross scowled before accelerating away again.

'Why do you call it that?' she objected. 'It's a beautiful animal.'

'Typical city opinion. I suppose you think rabbits are nice, cuddly, harmless little creatures as well?'

'Of course.'

'Then you've never met twenty thousand of the little beggars, munching their way through acres of your top grazing land. The only reason the sheep stations out here haven't got a problem with them at the moment is because there's a drought. Come the rain and they'll plague up, as they always do. The worst thing the English ever did to Australia was import the damned rabbit!'

'Well, you don't have to get all steamed up about it with me,' she pointed out huffily. 'It's not my fault!'

Suddenly he looked across and grinned at her, a wide, cheeky grin that was nothing like Earl would ever indulge in. She couldn't help it. She grinned back, and in that split second she knew she not only desired this man, but she liked him as well. Far too much.

Her grin faded, depression returning to take the place of pleasure. If only Ross genuinely returned the liking. If only she could inspire a fraction of the respect this Becky did...

'What have I done *now*?' he groaned frustratedly.

'Nothing,' she muttered. 'Nothing.'

'I don't seem to have to do anything to upset you, do I? What was it? Did I smile at you like Earl, is that it? Go on, you can tell me. I'm a big boy. I can take it!'

She shrank from his sarcastic outburst, turning her face away. What could she say to him? No, you remind me less and less of Earl with each passing moment...

'Don't you dare give me that silent treatment again, Vivien,' he snapped. 'I can't stand it.'

She sighed and turned back towards him. 'This isn't going to work out, is it, Ross?'

His mouth thinned stubbornly. 'It will, if you'll just give it a chance. Besides, what's your alternative—eight months of your mother's fussing?'

Vivien actually shuddered.

'See? At least I won't fuss over you. And neither will the rest of the people at Mountainview. They have too much to do. You'll be expected to pull your own weight out here, pregnant or not. That's what it's like in the country. You're not an invalid and you won't be treated like one.'

'Do you think that will bother me? I'm not lazy, Ross. I'm a worker too.'

'Then what *is* beginning to bother you? What have I said to make you look at me with such unhappy eyes?'

'I...I really wanted us to become friends.'

'And you think I don't?'

'Friends respect each other.'

He frowned over at her. 'I respect you.'

'No, you don't.'

'God, Vivien, what is this? Do you think I subscribe to that old double standard about sex? Do you think I think you're tainted somehow because you went to bed with me?'

'Yes,' she told him point-blank. 'If you didn't think like that, you'd have slept with Becky and to hell with her so-called innocence. Virginity is not a prize, Ross. It was only valued in the olden days because it assured the bridegroom that his bride would not have venereal disease. Making love is the most wonderful expression of love and affection that can exist between a man and a woman. Yet you backed away from it with the woman you claim you love in favour of it with a perfect stranger, in favour of a "city broad who probably knows more counter-moves than a chess champion". If that sounds as if you respect me then I'm a Dutchman's uncle!'

His face paled visibly, but he kept his eyes on the road ahead. 'That's not how it was, Vivien,' he said tautly.

'Oh?' she scoffed. 'Then how *was* it, Ross?'

'One day I might tell you,' he muttered. 'But for now I think you're forgetting a little something.'

'What?'

'The baby. *Our* baby. It's not the child's fault that he or she is going to be born. The least we can do is provide it with a couple of parents who aren't constantly at each other's throats. I realise I'm not the father you would have chosen for your child, Vivien. Neither am I yet able to fully understand your decision to actually go ahead with this pregnancy. I'm still to be convinced that it has nothing to do with my likeness to the man you're in love with.

'No, don't say a word!' he growled when she went to protest this assumption. 'You might not even recognise your own motives as yet. We all have dark and devious sides, some that remain hidden even to ourselves. But I will not have an innocent child suffer for the perversity of its parents. We're going to be mature about all this, Vivien. *You're* going to be mature. I want no more of your swinging moods or your wild, way-off accusations. You are to treat me with the same decency and respect that I will accord you. Or, by God, I'm going to lay you over my knee and whop that luscious backside of yours. Do I make myself clear?'

She eyed him fiercely, seething inside with a bitter resentment. Who did he think he was, telling her how to behave, implying that she had been acting like an immature idiot, threatening her with physical violence? As for dark and devious sides…he sure as hell had his fair share!

But aside from all that, Vivien could see that he *was* making *some* sense, despite his over-the-top threats. He even made her feel a little guilty. She hadn't really been thinking much about the baby's future welfare. She'd been consumed by her own ambivalent feelings for the man seated beside her. One moment she was desperate for him to like her, the next he was provoking her into a quite irrational anger, making her want to lash out at him. Right at this moment she would have liked to indulge in a bit of physical violence of her own!

Yes, but that's because you simply want to get your hands on him again, came a sinister voice from deep inside.

She stiffened.

'And you can cut out that outraged innocence act too!' he snapped, darting her a vicious glance. 'You're about as innocent as a vampire. *And* about as lethal! So I suggest you keep those pearly white teeth of yours safely within those blood-red lips for the remainder of this journey. For, if you open them again, I swear to you, Vivien, I'll forget that promise I made to you yesterday and give you another dose of what you've obviously been missing to have turned you into such a shrew. I'm sure you're quite capable of closing those big brown eyes of yours and pretending I'm Earl once more. And I'm just as capable of thoroughly enjoying myself in his stead!'

CHAPTER NINE

IT WAS dusk when Ross and Vivien finally turned from the highway on to a private road. Narrow and dusty, it wound a slow, steady route through flat, almost grass-less fields where Vivien only spotted one small flock of sheep, but she declined asking where the rest of the stock was. She wouldn't have lowered herself to make conversation with the man next to her. She was still too angry with him.

How dared he threaten to practically rape her? He might not literally mean it, but she couldn't abide men who used verbal abuse and physical threats to intimi-date women. It just showed you the sort of man Ross was underneath his surface charm. As for suggesting that she would actually enjoy it...

That galled most of all. Because she wasn't at all sure that she *wouldn't*!

Self-disgust kept her temper simmering away in a grimly held silence while she stared out of the passen-ger window, her lips pressed angrily together. Eventually, the flat paddocks gave way to rolling brown hills. One was quite steep, and, as they came over the crest, there, in the distance, lay some bluish-looking mountains. But closer, on the crest of the next hill, and surrounded by tall, dark green trees, stood a home of such grandeur and elegance that Vivien caught her breath in surprise.

'I did tell you it was big,' Ross remarked drily.

'So you did,' she said equally drily, then turned

flashing brown eyes his way. 'I'm allowed to talk now, am I? I won't be suitably punished for my temerity in opening my blood-red lips?'

His sigh was weary. It made Vivien suddenly feel small. What was the matter with her? She was rarely reduced to using such vicious sarcasm. She could be stubborn, but usually quietly so, with a cool, steely determination that was far more effective than more volatile methods. Yet here she was, flying off the handle at every turn. Snapping and snarling like a she-cat.

It had to be her hormones, she decided unhappily. God, but she was a mess!

She turned to look once more at the huge house, and as they drew closer an oddly apprehensive shiver trickled down her spine. Vivien knew immediately that she would not like living at Mountainview. If she stayed the full month, she would be very surprised. Yet she could not deny it was a beautiful-looking home. Very beautiful indeed.

Edwardian in style and two-storeyed, with long, graceful white columns running from the stone-flagged patio right up through the upper-floor wooden veranda to the gabled roof. An equally elegant white ironwork spanned the distance between these columns, for decoration alone downstairs, but for safety as well between the bases of the upstairs pillars.

Not that Vivien could picture too many youngsters climbing over that particular railing anyway. The house had a museum-like quality about it, enhanced possibly by the fact that only a couple of lights shone in the windows as they drove up in the rapidly fading light.

The Range Rover crunched to a halt on the gravel driveway, Ross turning to Vivien with an expectant look on his face. 'Well? What do you think of it?'

'It's—er—very big.'

'You don't like it,' he said with amazement in his voice and face.

'No, no,' she lied. 'It's quite spectacular. I'm just very tired, Ross.'

His face softened and Vivien turned hers away. She wished he didn't have the capacity to look at her like that, with such sudden warmth and compassion. It turned her bones to water, making her feel weak and vulnerable. Instinct warned her that Ross was not a man you showed such a vulnerability to.

'You must be,' he said as he opened his door. 'I'll take you inside then come back for the luggage. Once you're settled in the kitchen with one of Helga's mugs of tea you'll feel better.'

It was only after she alighted that Vivien recognised the truth of her excuse to Ross. Yet she was more than tired. She was exhausted. Her legs felt very heavy and she had to push them to lug her weary body up the wide, flagged steps. When she hesitated on the top step, swaying slightly, Ross's hand shot out to steady her.

'Are you all right, Vivien?'

She took a couple of deep breaths. 'Yes, I think so. Just a touch dizzy there for a sec.'

Before she could say another word he swept one arm around her waist, the other around her knees, and hoisted her up high into his arms. 'I'll carry you straight up to bed. Helga can bring your tea to your room. You can meet Dad in the morning.'

Suddenly, Vivien felt too drained to protest. She went quite limp in Ross's arms, her head sagging against his chest, her hands linking weakly around his neck lest they flop down by her sides like dead weights. Her eyelashes fluttered down to rest on the darkly smudged shadows beneath her eyes. She felt rather than saw Ross's careful ascent up a long flight of stairs.

'You're very strong,' she whispered once in her semi-conscious daze.

He didn't answer.

Next thing she knew she was being lowered on to a soft mattress, her head sinking into a downy pillow. She felt her sandals being pulled off, a rug or blanket being draped over her legs. She sighed a shuddering sigh as the last of her energy fled her body. Within sixty seconds she was fast asleep, totally unaware of the man standing beside the bed staring down at her with a tight, pained look on his face.

After an interminable time, he bent to lightly touch her cheek, then to draw a wisp of hair from where it lay across her softly parted lips. His hand lingered, giving in to the urge to rub gently against the pouting flesh. She stirred, made a mewing sound like a sleepy kitten that had been dragged from its mother's teat. Her tongue-tip flicked out to moisten dry lips, the action sending a spurt of desire to his loins so sharp that he groaned aloud.

Spinning on his heels, he strode angrily from the room.

Vivien woke to the sound of raised voices. For a moment she couldn't remember where she was, or whose voices they could possibly be. But gradually her eyes and brain refocused on where she was.

Once properly awake, one quick glance took in the large, darkly furnished bedroom, the double bed she was lying on, the moonlight streaming in the open french doors on to the polished wooden floors, the balcony beyond those doors. Levering herself up on to one elbow, she noticed that on the nearest bedside table rested a tray, which held a tall glass of milk and a plate on which was a sandwich, a piece of iced fruit cake and a couple of plain milk-coffee biscuits.

But neither the room nor the food was of any real interest to Vivien at that moment. Her whole attention was on the argument that was cutting through the still night air with crystal clarity.

'I don't understand why you had to bring her here,' a male voice snarled. 'How do you think Becky's going to feel when she finds out? You've broken her heart, do you know that? I was over there today and she—'

'What do you mean, you were over there today?' Ross broke in testily. 'You were supposed to be checking all the bores today.'

'Yeah, well, I didn't, did I? I'll do them tomorrow.'

'Tomorrow... You've always got some excuse, haven't you? God, Gavin, when are you going to learn some sense of responsibility? Don't you know that one day without water could be the difference between life and death in a drought like this? What on earth's the matter with you? Why don't you grow up?'

'I *am* grown-up. And I *can* be responsible. It's just that you and Dad won't give me a chance at any real responsibility. All you give me is orders!'

'Which you can't follow.'

'I can too.'

'No you bloody well can't! Just look at the bores today.'

'Oh, bugger the bores. We've hardly got any sheep left anyway. You sold them all.'

'Better sold than dead.'

'That was your opinion. You never asked me for mine. I would have kept them, hand-fed them.'

'At what cost? Be sensible, Gavin. I made the right business decision, the only decision.'

'Business! Since when has life on the land been reduced to nothing but business decisions? Since *you* came home to run things, that's when. You're a hard-hearted ruthless bastard, Ross, who'll stop at nothing to get what you want. And I know what that is. You want Mountainview. The land and the house. Not just your half, either. You want it all! That's why you were going to marry Becky. Not because you fell in love with her, but because you knew Dad was keen for one of us to marry and produce an heir before he died. That's why you dumped Becky and brought that other city bitch back here. Because she's already having your kid. You think that will sway Dad into changing his will all the sooner. Yeah, now I see it. I see it all!'

'You're crazy,' Ross snapped. 'Or crazy drunk. Is that it? Have you been drinking again?'

'So what if I have?'

'I should have known. You're only this irrational—and this articulate—when you're drunk.'

'Not like you, eh, big brother? You've got the gift of the gab all the time, haven't you? You can charm the birds right out of the trees. I'll bet that poor bitch upstairs doesn't even know what part she's playing in all this. You've got it made, haven't you? The heir you needed plus a hot little number on tap. A lay, laid on every night. I'll bet she's good in bed too. I'll bet she—'

The sounds of a scuffle replaced the voices. Vivien sat bolt upright, her heart going at fifty to the dozen, her mind whirling with all sorts of shocking thoughts. Could Gavin really be right? Was she some pawn in a game much larger and darker than she'd ever imagined? Were she and her child to be Ross's ace card in gaining the inheritance his brother seemed to think he coveted? It would explain why Ross had not made love to this Becky if he didn't really love her...

Shakily, she stood up and made her way out on to the balcony. The night air was silent now, the earlier sounds of fighting having stopped. The sky overhead was black and clear with a myriad stars, the moon a bright orb, bathing everything beneath in its pale, ghostly light.

Gingerly, Vivien looked down over the railing.

Ross was standing there on the driveway next to his Range Rover, disconsolate and alone. While she watched silently, he lifted his hands to rake back his dishevelled hair, expelling a ragged sigh. 'Crazy fool,' he muttered.

Vivien didn't think she made a move, or a sound. But suddenly Ross's head jerked up and those piercing eyes were staring straight into hers. Worried first, then assessing, he held her startled gaze for several seconds before speaking. And then it was to say only three sharp words, 'Stay right there.'

She barely had time to compose her rattled self before Ross was standing right in front of her, his big strong hands gripping her upper arms, his sharp blue eyes boring down into hers.

'How much did you hear?' he demanded to know.

'E—e-enough,' she stammered.

'Enough. Dear God in heaven. And did you believe what that fool said? *Did* you?' he repeated, shaking her.

Vivien could hardly think. 'I...I don't know what to believe any more.'

'*Don't* believe what my brother said, for Pete's sake,' Ross insisted harshly. 'He's all mixed up in the head at the moment. Believe what *I* tell you, Vivien. Your presence here has nothing to do with Mountainview. Nothing at all! You're here only because I want you here, because I...I... Goddammit, woman, why do you have to be so darned beautiful?'

And, digging his fingers into her flesh, he lifted her body and mouth to his, taking it wildly and hungrily in a savage kiss. For a few tempestuous moments, she found herself responding to his desperate desire, parting her lips and allowing his tongue full reign within her mouth. But when he groaned and swept his arms down around her, pressing the entire length of her against him, the stark evidence of a full-blooded male erection lying between them slammed her back to reality.

'No!' she gasped, wrenching her mouth from his. 'Let me go!' With a tortured cry, she struggled free of his torrid embrace, staggering back against the railing, staring up at him with wide, accusing eyes.

'You...you said this wasn't why you brought me here,' she flung at him shakily. 'You promised to keep your hands off.'

The sudden and shocking suspicion that he might have been using sex to direct her mind away from Gavin's accusations blasted into Vivien's brain, making her catch her breath. Dear heaven, he couldn't be that wicked, could he? Or that devious?

She stared at Ross, trying to find some reassurance now in his flushed face and heaving chest, as well as the memory of his explicit arousal. That, at least, was not a sham, she conceded. That was real. *Too* real.

But then his desire for her had always been real. That did not mean Gavin wasn't telling the truth. Ross could still be the ruthless opportunist his brother accused him of being, one who could quite happily satisfy his lust for her while achieving his own dark ends.

'I promised there would not be a repeat of what happened that night at Wallaby Creek,' he ground out. 'And there won't.'

'And…and what was that you were just doing if not trying to seduce me?' she blustered, still not convinced, despite his sounding amazingly sincere.

'That was my being a bloody idiot. But I was only kissing you, Vivien. Don't hang me for a simple kiss. Still, I will endeavour to keep my hands well and truly off in future. As for my reasons for bringing you here…I can only repeat it has everything to do with my child, but nothing to do with Mountainview. You have my solemn oath on that. Now go back to bed. You still look tired. I'll see you in the morning.'

Vivien stared after him as he whirled and strode off along the balcony and around the corner.

A simple kiss? There'd been nothing simple about that kiss. Nothing simple at all…

And there was nothing simple about this whole situation.

Though had there ever been?

Vivien lifted trembling hands to push the hair back off her face. God knew where all this was going to end. Perhaps it would be best if she cut her visit short here, if she declined taking the position as companion to Ross's father. There were too many undercurrents going on in this household, too many mysteries, too much ill feeling.

Vivien wanted no part in them. Life was complicated enough without getting involved in family feuds. Yes, she would tell Ross in the morning that she wanted to go back home.

Feeling marginally better, Vivien made her way back into the bedroom, intending to drink the milk then change into some nightwear before going back to bed. But she found herself lying down again, fully dressed, on top of the bed. Soon, she was sound asleep again.

CHAPTER TEN

WHEN Vivien woke a second time, it was morning. Mid-morning, by the feel of the heat already building in the closed room. Her slim silver wristwatch confirmed her guess. It was ten-fifteen.

With a groan she swung her stiffened legs over the side of the bed and sat up, thinking to herself that she could do with a shower. It was then that she remembered her decision of the night before to go straight back home.

Somehow, however, in the clear light of day, that seemed a hasty, melodramatic decision. She'd been very tired last night. Overwrought, even. Perhaps she should give Ross and his father and Mountainview a few days at least.

As for Gavin's accusations that his older brother was a ruthless bastard intent on using Vivien and her baby to gain an inheritance... Well, that too felt melodramatic, now that she could think clearly. Ross might be a typically selfish male in some ways, but she had sensed nothing from him but true affection and concern for his family. She'd also been impressed by the way he'd handled things with *her* parents. Ross was not a cruel, callous man. Not at all.

Yes. The matter was settled. She would stay a while. A week, at least. Then, if things weren't working out, she would make some excuse and go home. She could always say she couldn't stand the heat. That would hardly be a lie, Vivien thought, as beads of perspiration started trickling down between her breasts.

Feeling the call of nature, she rose and went to investigate the two panelled wooden doors that led off the bedroom. The first was an exit, leading out on to a huge rectangular gallery. The second revealed an *en suite* that, though its décor was in keeping with the house's Edwardian style, was still obviously fairly new.

Vivien was amused by the gold chain she had to pull to flush the toilet, smiling as she washed her hands with a tiny, shell-like soap.

On going back into the hot room, she started unpacking, having spied her suitcase resting on the ottoman at the foot of the bed. A shower was definitely called for, she decided, plus nothing heavier to wear than shorts and a cool top.

Since everything was very crushed she chose a simple shorts set in a peacock-blue T-shirt material, with a tropical print of yellow and orange hibiscus on it. The creases would fall out if she hung it up behind the bathroom door while she had a shower. With the outfit draped over an arm, and some fresh underwear and her bag of toiletries filling both hands, Vivien made for the shower.

The hot water felt so delicious that she wallowed in it for ages, shampooing her hair a couple of times during the process, the heat having made her thick black tresses feel limp and greasy. Once clean, however, her hair sprang around her face and shoulders in a myriad damp curls and waves. In deference to the heat, Vivien bypassed full make-up, putting on a dab of coral lipstick, a minimal amount of waterproof mascara and a liberal lashing of Loulou, her favourite perfume.

Electing to leave her hair damp rather than blow-dry

it, Vivien opened the door of the bathroom feeling refreshed but a little nervous. What was she supposed to do? Where should she go?

The unexpected sight of a large grey-haired woman in a mauve floral dress bustling to and fro across the bedroom, hanging Vivien's clothes up for her in the elegantly carved wardrobe, replaced any nerves with a stab of surprise. And a degree of dry amusement.

So this was Helga...

'And good morning to you too,' Helga threw across the room before she could say a word. 'High time you got up. Nothing worse than lying in bed too long. Bad for the digestion. I've straightened your bed and turned on the ceiling fan. Didn't you see it there? It's best to leave the windows and doors closed till the afternoon, then I'll come up and open them. We usually get an afternoon breeze. And leave your dirty washing in the linen basket in the corner.

'I'm Helga, by the way. I dare say Ross has told you about me. Not in glowing terms, I would imagine,' she added with a dry cackle. 'We never did get along, me and that lad. He's not the sort to follow orders kindly. Still, he's turned out all right, I guess. Loves his dad, which goes down a long way with me.'

She drew breath at last to give Vivien the once-over. 'Well, you certainly are one stunning-looking girl, aren't you? But then, I wouldn't expect any different from Ross. Only the best would ever do for him. Fancy schools in Sydney. Fancy flying lessons. Now a fancy woman...'

Vivien drew in a sharply offended breath, and was just about to launch into a counter-attack when Helga dismissed any defensive speech with a sharp wave of her hand.

'Now don't go getting your knickers all in a knot, lovie. No offence intended. Besides, there's no one happier than me that you put a spoke in Ross's plans to marry Becky. I presume you know who Becky is?'

Vivien found herself nodding dumbly. She'd never met anyone quite like Helga. Talk about intimidating! Ross had her undying admiration if he stood up to this bulldozer of a woman.

'Well, let me tell you a little secret about Miss Becky Macintosh,' Helga boomed on. 'She's always hankered after living at Mountainview, ever since she was knee-high to a grasshopper. She's no more in love with Ross than I am. But he's a mighty handsome man and a girl could do worse than put her slippers under his bed every night. When Oliver had his stroke and Ross came back home, Becky saw her chance and set her cap at him. Lord, butter wouldn't have melted in her mouth around him all year. But it's not the man she wants. It's Mountainview!'

Helga snapped the suitcase shut and started doing the buckles up.

'Why are you telling me all this?' Vivien asked on a puzzled note.

A sly look came over Helga's plain, almost masculine face. 'Because I don't want you worrying that you might be breaking Becky's heart if you marry Ross. That little minx will simply move on to the next brother, which will be by far the best for all concerned.'

Vivien bypassed Helga's conclusion that she wanted to marry Ross to concentrate on her next startling statement. 'You mean—'

'My Gavin loves her,' Helga broke in with a maternal passion that was unexpectedly fierce. 'He's loved her for years. But he's painfully shy around girls—

unless he's been drinking. He can't seem to bring himself to tell her how he feels. Now, after this episode with Ross, he doesn't think he'll ever stand a chance. He's always felt inferior to his big brother. But if Ross moved far away...'

'I see,' Vivien murmured. 'Yes, I see...'

'You won't want to live here, will you? A city girl like you will want the bright lights. Ross likes action too, not the slowness of station life. You'll both be happy enough well away from here.'

Looking at Helga's anxious face, Vivien was moved to pity for her. She must love Gavin very, very much. As for Gavin... Her heart really went out to him. It couldn't be easy being Ross's brother. Even harder with the two brothers loving the same girl. That was one factor Helga had blithely forgotten. What of Ross's feelings in all this? Or didn't they count?

'I'm sorry, Helga,' she explained, 'but Ross and I have no plans to marry. We're not in love, you see.'

'Not in love?' Helga looked down at Vivien's stomach with a disdainful glower. 'Then what are you doing having his child? Not in love! Well, I never! What's the world coming to, I ask you, with girls going round having babies with men they don't love? It makes one ashamed of one's own sex!'

Vivien's lovely brown eyes flashed defiance as she drew herself up straight and proud.

'I would think you should feel more ashamed of this Becky than me,' she countered vehemently. 'At least I'm honest about my feelings. She sounds like a shallow, materialistic, manipulative little witch, and I'm not sorry at all that Ross is not going to marry her. He deserves better than that. Much better. He's a...a...

And what are you laughing at?' she demanded angrily when Helga started to cackle.

Again that sly look returned. 'Just thinking what similar personalities you and Ross have. Both as stubborn as mules. Lord knows what kind of child you're going to have. He'll probably end up running the world!'

'It might be a daughter!'

'Then *she'll* run the world.'

Helga grinned a highly satisfied grin, stopping Vivien in her tracks. Against her better judgement, she found herself grinning back. She shook her head in a type of bewilderment before a sudden thought wiped the grin from her face.

'Ross doesn't know about Gavin loving Becky, does he?' she asked.

'No,' the older woman admitted. 'Gavin made me promise not to tell him.'

'I see. So you told me instead, hoping I might relay the information. That way you'd keep your promise, but get the message across.'

Helga's look was sharp. 'There's no flies on you, lovie, is there? Now how about a spot of breakfast? You'll want a good plateful, I'll warrant, since you didn't eat the supper I left you. Remember, you're eating for two.'

Vivien only just managed to suppress a groan of true dismay as she slipped on her sandals and followed Helga from the room.

The kitchen was as huge as the rest of the house. But far more homely, with copper pots hanging over the stove, dressers full of flowered crockery and knick-knacks leaning against the walls, and an enormous table in the centre.

'Do you really look after this whole place by your-self?' Vivien asked whilst Helga was piling food on to the largest plate she'd ever seen. She already had a mug of tea in front of her that would have satisfied a giant.

'Sure do, lovie. Keeps me fit, I can tell you. Here, get this into you!' And she slapped the plate down in front of her. There were three rashers of bacon, two eggs, a lamb chop and some grilled tomato, not to men-tion two slices of toast.

Vivien felt her stomach heave. Swallowing, she picked up the knife and fork and started rearranging the bacon. 'Er—do you know where Ross is this morning?' she asked by way of distraction.

'Right here,' he said, striding into the kitchen and sitting down in a chair opposite her. Vivien looked down, thinking that she would never get used to the way her heart skipped a beat every time she saw him. Of course, it didn't help that he only had a pair of jeans on. Not a thing on his top half. Sitting down, he looked naked.

'You look refreshed this morning, Vivien,' he said, virtually forcing her to look back up at him. She did, keeping her gaze well up. Unfortunately, she found her-self staring straight at his mouth and remembering how she had felt when he'd kissed her last night.

'I presume you want a mug of tea?' Helga asked Ross.

'Sure do. And a piece of that great Christmas cake you made.'

Helga threw him a dry look. 'No need to suck up to me, my lad. Your girl and I are already firm friends, aren't we, lovie?'

'Oh—er—yes,' Vivien stammered, which brought a surprised look from Ross.

'I see she appreciates your cooking as well,' he said, and gave Vivien a sneaky wink. She rolled her eyes at the food and he laughed. But laughter made the muscles ripple in his chest and she quickly looked down again, forcing a mouthful of egg in between suddenly dry lips.

'Where's Gavin?' Helga went on. 'Doesn't he want a cup too?'

'Nope. He's out checking bores. Won't be back till well after lunch.'

'Out checking bores?' Helga persisted. '*Today*? But it's going to be a scorcher. Why couldn't he go to-morrow?'

'Because he was supposed to have gone yesterday,' Ross informed her drily.

Helga looked pained and shook her head. 'That boy... Still, you have to understand he's been upset lately, Ross. He's not himself.'

'Well, he'd better get back to being himself quick smart,' Ross said firmly, 'or there won't be anything to do around here except have endless mugs of tea. Sheep don't live on love alone.'

A stark silence descended while Ross finished his tea and Vivien waded through as much of the huge break-fast as her stomach could stand. Finally, she pushed the plate aside, whereupon Helga frowned. Before her dis-approval could erupt into words Ross was on his feet and asking Vivien if he could have a few words with her in private.

It was a testimony to Helga's formidable personality that Vivien was grateful to be swept away into Ross's company when he was semi-naked.

'Don't let Helga bully you into eating too much,' was Ross's first comment as they walked along the hall-way together.

'I'll try not to. Where…where are we going?' she asked once they moved across the tiled foyer and started up the stairs.

He slanted her a look which suggested he'd caught the nervousness behind her question and was genuinely puzzled by it. 'I need to shower and change before taking you along to meet Dad,' he explained. 'I thought we could talk at the same time.'

He stopped at the top of the stairs, his blue eyes glittering with a sardonic amusement. 'Of course, I don't expect you to accompany me into my bathroom. You can sit on my bed and talk to me from there. Let me assure you the shower is not visible from the bedroom.'

Sit on his bed…

Dear heaven, that was bad enough.

Noting that he was watching her closely, Vivien lifted her nose and adopted what she hoped was an expression of utter indifference. 'I doubt it would bother me if it was,' she repudiated. 'I've seen it all before.'

His features tightened, but he said nothing, ushering her along the upstairs hall and into his bedroom, shutting the door carefully behind them. When he saw her startled look, a wry smile lifted the grimness from his face.

'You may be blasé about male nudity, Vivien, my dear, but Helga is not so sophisticated. Do sit down, however. You make me uncomfortable standing there with your hands clasped defensively in front of you. I had no dark or dastardly plan in bringing you up here, though I appreciate now that my idea of having a normal chat with you while I showered was stupid. Best I simply hurry with my ablutions and then we'll talk.'

Five minutes later he came out of the closed bath-room dressed in bright shorts and a loose white T-shirt with a colourful geometric design on the back and a surfing logo on the sleeves.

It was the longest five minutes Vivien had ever spent. Who would have believed the sound of a shower run-ning could be so disturbing?

'You look as if you're ready to shoot the waves at Bondi,' she commented, mocking herself silently for the way she was openly feasting her eyes on him this time. But she couldn't seem to help herself.

'Dad likes bright clothes. They cheer him up.'

'That's good,' she said, and bounced up on to her feet. 'Most of my clothes are bright.'

'So I noticed.'

'You don't approve?'

'Would it matter if I didn't?'

'No.'

His smile was dry. 'That's what I thought. Shall we go?'

'But you said you wanted to talk to me.'

'I've changed my mind. I'm sure you'll handle Dad OK. You seem to have a knack with men. Follow me.'

She did so in silence, her thoughts a-whirl. What was eating at Ross? Was it sexual frustration, or frustration of another kind? She seemed to be getting mixed mes-sages from him. One minute she thought he admired her, though grudgingly. The next, he was openly sar-castic.

They trundled down the stairs and along a different corridor, towards the back section of the house.

'In here,' Ross directed, and opened a door into a cool, cosily furnished bed-sitting-room. She found out later that it had once been part of the servants' quarters, when Mountainview had had lots of servants. Ross had had it renovated and air-conditioned before his father came home from hospital.

'Dad?' Ross ventured softly. 'You're not asleep, are you?'

The old man resting in the armchair beside the window had had his eyes closed, his head listing to one side. But with Ross's voice his head jerked up and around, his eyes snapping open. They looked straight at Vivien, their gaze both direct and assessing.

'Hello, Mr Everton,' she said, and came forward to hold out her hand. 'I'm Vivien.'

Pale, parched lips cracked back into a semblance of a smile. 'So...you're Vivien...' His eyes slid slowly down her body, then up over her shoulder towards his son. 'Now...I understand,' he said, the talking clearly an effort for him. Vivien noticed that one side of his face screwed up when he spoke, the aftermath, she realised, of his stroke. 'They don't...come along...like her...too often...'

Vivien was slightly put out by his remarks. Why did men have to reduce women to sex objects?

'They don't come along like Ross too often either,' she countered, quite tartly.

The old man laughed, and immediately was consumed by racking coughs. Ross raced to pick up the glass of water resting on the table beside him, holding him gently around the shoulders till the coughing subsided, then pressing the water to his lips. Vivien hovered, feeling useless and a little guilty. She should have kept her stupid, proud mouth shut! The man meant no harm.

'You should let me call in the doctor, Dad,' Ross

was saying worriedly. 'This coughing of yours is getting worse.'

'No...more...doctors,' his father managed to get out. 'No more. They'll only...put me...in hospital. I want to...to die here.'

Ross's laugh was cajoling. 'You're not going to die, Dad. Dr Harmon said that with a little more rest and therapy you'll be as good as new.'

'Perhaps,' he muttered. 'Perhaps. Now...get lost. I wish...to talk...to Vivien. *Alone*. You cramp...my style.'

'All right. But don't talk too much, mind?' And Ross lanced his father with an oddly sharp look. 'You'll find me in the library when he's finished with you, Vivien.'

'Call me...Oliver,' was the first thing Ross's father said once they were alone. 'Now, tell me...all about... yourself.'

For over an hour, Vivien chatted away, answering Oliver's never-ending questions. It worried her that he was becoming overtired, but every time she touched on the subject of his health he vetoed her impatiently.

It was clear where Ross had got his determination and stubbornness. Yet, for all his questions, Oliver never once enquired about her feelings for his son, or Ross's for her. He never asked her what she wanted for the future, either for herself or her baby. He wanted to know about her background, her growing-up years, her education, her job and her family. Finally, he sighed and leant back into the chair.

'You'll do, Vivien,' he said. 'You'll do...'

'As what, Oliver?'

His smile was as cunning as Helga's. 'Why...as the mother...of my grandchild. What else? Now run along… It's lunchtime… But tell Ross…I don't want… any.'

Vivien closed the door softly, her mind still on Ross's father.

Oliver Everton didn't fool her for one minute. He was going to try to marry her off to Ross. Not that she blamed him. Death was very definitely knocking at his door and he wanted things all tied up with pink bows before he left this world.

Gavin was accusing the wrong man when he said Ross was trying to manipulate his father. It was the father who was the manipulator, who had perhaps always been the manipulator at Mountainview. Maybe that was why Ross had chosen to follow a career away from home, and why Gavin hadn't. The stronger brother bucking the heavy hand of the father while the weaker one knuckled under.

Now, illness had brought the prodigal—and perhaps favoured—son home and the father was going to make the most of it. Vivien wouldn't put it past Oliver having been the one to insist Ross bring her out here, hoping that the sexual attraction that had once flared out of control between them would do so again, thereby making his job easier of convincing them marriage was the best course for all concerned.

And he'd been half right, the cunning old devil. That electric chemistry was still sparking as strong as ever. She could hardly look at Ross without thinking about that night, without longing to find out if the wonder of it all had been real or an illusion. How long, she worried anew, before her own body language started sending out those tell-tale waves of desire in Ross's direction? How long before his male antennae picked up on them?

He was not a man to keep promises he sensed she didn't want him to keep. He was a sexual predator, a hunter. He would zero in for the kill the moment she weakened. Of that she was certain.

So why stay? her conscience berated. Why tempt fate?

Because she had to. For some reason she just had to...

CHAPTER ELEVEN

'THERE you are!' Vivien exclaimed exasperatedly when she finally found the library. 'This house is like a maze.'

'Only downstairs,' Ross said, having glanced up from where he was sitting behind a large cedar desk in the far corner. With her arrival, he put the paperwork he was doing in a drawer and stood up. 'You must have really got along with Dad to stay so long.'

'Yes, I did,' she agreed, glancing around the room, which was exactly as she'd first imagined. Leather furniture, heavy velvet curtains and floor-to-ceiling bookshelves. 'I think he quite likes me.'

'I don't doubt it,' Ross muttered as he strode round the desk, his caustic tone drawing both her attention and her anger.

'Do you *have* to be sarcastic all the time?'

'Am I?' There was an oddly surprised note in his voice, as though he hadn't realised his bad manners.

'Yes, you are!'

'You're exaggerating, surely. I think I've been very polite, in the circumstances. Well? What did you think of Dad?'

Vivien sighed her irritation at having her complaint summarily brushed aside. What circumstances did he mean, anyway?

'He's a very sick man,' she commented at last.

'He's as strong as an ox,' came the impatient rebuttal.

'Not any longer, Ross. Maybe you've been away from home too long.'

'Meaning?'

She shrugged. 'People change. Things change.'

'I get the impression I'm supposed to read between the lines here.' Ross leant back against the corner of the desk, his arms folding. 'What's changed around Mountainview that I don't know about?'

Vivien frowned. This was not going to be easy, but it had to be done. 'Well, for one thing…did you know Gavin was in love with Becky?'

Ross straightened, his face showing true shock. 'Good God, he isn't, is he?'

She nodded slowly.

'Who told you that? It couldn't have been Dad!'

'No. Helga.'

He groaned, his shoulders sagging. 'Bloody hell. Poor Gavin…'

'Helga also says Becky doesn't really love you. She says the girl has always coveted Mountainview.'

Ross's eyes jerked up, angry this time. 'Damn and blast, what is this? You've been in this house less than twenty-four hours and already you know more about what's going on around here than I do. Why hasn't someone told me any of this? Why tell you? What do you have that I don't have?'

She looked past his anger, fully understanding his resentment. 'Objectivity, perhaps?' she tried ruefully.

'Objectivity?' His lips curled into a snarl. 'Oh, yes, you've got that all right, haven't you?'

She wasn't quite sure what he meant by that. Maybe he didn't mean anything. Maybe he just felt the need to lash out blindly. 'Ross, I…I'm really sorry.'

'For what?'

'For being the one to tell you that the woman you're in love with doesn't love you back.'

He stared at her, his blue eyes icy with bitterness. 'You don't have to be sorry about that, Vivien,' he bit out coldly. 'Because I already knew that. I've known it all along.'

'But…but—'

'You of all people should know that love is not always returned. But that doesn't stop you from loving that person, does it? Aren't you still in love with your Earl?'

'I…I'm not sure…'

'Real love doesn't cease as quickly as that, my dear,' he scorned. 'You either loved the man or you didn't. What was it?'

'I *did* love him,' she insisted, hating the feeling of being backed into a corner. But if he expected her to admit to not loving a man she'd lived with for nearly eighteen months then he was heartily mistaken. Yet even as she made the claim she knew it to be a lie. She had not loved Earl. Not really.

'Then you still do,' he insisted fiercely. 'Believe me. You still do. Now I must go and talk to my father. If what you say is all true then I have no time to waste. Things have to be done before it's too late.'

'Too late for what? What things?'

His returning look was cool. 'That is not your concern. You've done your objective duty. Now I suggest you go and have some lunch, then do what pregnant ladies do on a hot afternoon. Lie down and rest. Or, if that doesn't appeal, read one of these books. I'm sure there's enough of a selection here to satisfy the most catholic of tastes.'

'Ross!' she called out as he went to leave.

He turned slowly, his face hard.

'Please…don't be angry with me…'

The steely set to his mouth softened. He sighed. 'I'm not. Not really…'

'You…you seem to be.'

The slightest of smiles touched his mouth, but not his eyes. 'It's fate I'm angry with, Vivien. Fate…'

'Now you're being cryptic.'

'Am I? Yes, possibly I am. Let's say then that I'm angry with what I have no control over.'

'But you're not angry with me personally.'

'No.'

'Then will you show me around the house later, after you're finished with your father?'

He stared at her for a moment, his eyes searching. 'It will be my pleasure,' he said with a somewhat stiff little bow.

'I…I'll probably be here,' she said. 'I don't want any lunch. Oh, that reminds me. Your father said to tell you he didn't want any lunch either.'

A dry smile pulled at Ross's mouth. 'Helga *will* be pleased.' And, giving her one last incisive and rather disturbing glance, he turned and left the room.

Vivien stared after him, aware that her heart was pounding. Already, she was looking forward to his return, knowing full well that it wasn't the thought of a tour through this house that was exciting her. It was the prospect of being alone again with Ross.

A shiver ran through her. Oh, Oliver…you are a wicked, wicked man.

Ross returned shortly after two to find Vivien curled up in one of the large lounge chairs, trying valiantly to read a copy of *Penmarric*. The book was probably as good as everyone had told her it was, but she just hadn't been able to keep her mind on it.

Once the reason for this walked into the room she abandoned all pretence at finding the book engrossing, snapping it shut with an almost relieved sigh.

'Finished your business?' she said, and uncurled her long legs.

'For now. Come on, if you want to see the house.'

His tone was clipped, his expression harried. Clearly, his visit to his father had not been a pleasant one. Vivien wished she could ask him what it was all about, but Ross's closed face forbade any such quizzing. Instead, she put the book back and went to join him in the doorway, determined to act as naturally as possible.

But her resolve to ignore the physical effect Ross kept having on her was waylaid when he moved left just as she moved right and they collided midstream. His hands automatically grabbed her shoulders and suddenly there they were, chest to chest, thigh to thigh, looking into each other's eyes.

Vivien gave a nervous laugh. 'Sorry.'

Ross said absolutely nothing. But there was no doubting he was as agitated by her closeness as she was by his. After what felt like an interminable delay, his hands dropped from her shoulders and he stepped back. 'After you,' he said with a deep wave of his right hand and a self-mocking look on his face. See? it said. I'm a man of my word. I'm keeping my hands off.

But did Vivien want him to keep his hands off? So much had changed now. Becky didn't love him, and, while Ross might think he loved her, there was no doubting he was still very attracted to *herself*. And what of her own feelings for Ross? Had they changed too? Deepened, maybe?

She couldn't be sure, certainly not with the chemistry between them still sparking away at a million volts. Vivien would just have to wait a while longer to find out about her feelings. That was what her mother had told her to do. Wait.

'Oh, my God, *Mum*!' she gasped aloud.

Ross looked taken aback. 'What about her?'

'I forgot to ring her, let her know we arrived all right. She'll be worried to death, and so will Dad.'

'Worried?' His smile carried a wry amusement. 'About their highly independent, very sensible, grown-up girl?'

'Who happens to be on her way to being an unmarried mother,' was her droll return. 'That's really surpassing myself in common sense, isn't it? Now point me to a telephone, Ross, or you'll have my mother on your doorstep.'

'There's an extension in the foyer, underneath the stairs.'

Unfortunately, Ross sat on those stairs while she dialled the number, making her feel self-conscious about what she was going to say. The phone at the other end only rang once before it was swept up.

'Peggy Roberts here,' her mother answered in a breathless tone.

'Mum, it's Vivien.'

'Oh, Vivien, darling! I'm so glad you rang. I've been rather worried.'

'No need, Mum. I'm fine. Sorry I didn't ring sooner, but by the time we arrived last night I was so tired I went straight to bed and slept in atrociously late this morning. Then Ross wanted me to meet his father and we talked for simply ages.'

'Oh? And how is Mr Everton senior? Getting better, I hope.'

'Well, he—er—reminded me a little of Uncle Jack a few weeks after his stroke.'

'You mean just before he died?'

'Er—yes…'

'Oh, dear. Oh, how sad. Well, be nice to him, dear. And be nice to Ross. He's a sweet man, not at all what your father and I were expecting. We were very impressed with him.'

'So I noticed.'

'You don't think that you and he—er—might…' She left the words hanging. *Get married*?

Vivien knew what would happen if she even hinted marriage was vaguely possible. She'd never hear the end of it. Yet her mother's even asking the question sent an odd little leap to her heart. Who knew? If Becky didn't love Ross, there might be a chance. *If* she fell in love with him, and *if* he did with her.

That was a lot of ifs.

'Not at this stage, Mum.'

'Oh…' Disappointment in her voice.

'Give Dad my love and tell him not to worry about me. I know he worries.'

'We both do, dear. Do you know how long you'll be staying out there?' Now her voice was wistful.

'Can't say. I'll write. Tell you all about the place. Must fly. I don't like to stay on someone else's phone too long.'

'I'll write to you too.'

'Yes, please do. Bye, Mum. Keep well.'

'Bye, darling. Thanks for ringing.'

Swallowing, she replaced the receiver and walked round to the foot of the stairs. Ross was sitting a half-dozen steps up, looking rather like a lost little boy. Suddenly, Vivien thought of *his* mother. What had she been like? Did he still miss her? She knew she would die if anything happened to her mother. Much as Peggy sometimes interfered and fussed, Vivien always knew the interference and fuss was based on the deepest of loves, that of a mother for her child.

Automatically, she thought of her own baby, and a soft smile lit her face. For the first time, she felt really positive about her decision to have Ross's baby. No matter what happened, that part was right. Very right indeed.

'You look very pleased with yourself,' he remarked as he stood up. 'Anything I should know about?'

'No,' she said airily. 'Not really. Mum's fine. Dad's fine. Everything's fine.'

His eyes narrowed suspiciously. 'You look like the cat who's discovered a bowl of cream.'

Her laugh was light and carefree. 'Do I?'

'You also look incredibly beautiful...'

Her eyes widened when he started walking down the stairs towards her. Perhaps he interpreted her reaction for alarm for his expression quickly changed to one of exasperation. 'No need to panic, Vivien. I'm not about to pounce. I was merely stating a fact. You know, you look somewhat like my mother when she was young. No wonder Dad took to you.'

Vivien did her best to cool the rapid heating Ross's compliments had brought to her blood, concentrating instead on the opening he'd just given her. 'How odd,' she commented. 'I was just thinking about your mother, wondering what she was like.'

'Were you? That *is* odd. What made you think of her?'

'You wouldn't want to know,' she chuckled.

'Wouldn't I?'

'No,' she said firmly, and, linking her arm with his, turned him to face across the foyer. 'So come on, show me your house and tell me about your mother.'

Ross stared down at her for a second before moving. 'To what do I owe this new Vivien?' he asked warily.

'This isn't a new Vivien. This is the real me.'

'Which is?'

She grinned. 'Charming. Witty. Warm.'

'What happened to stubborn, infuriating and uncooperative?'

'I left them in Sydney.'

'You could have fooled me.'

'Apparently I have.'

'Vivien, I—'

'Oh, do stop being so serious for once, Ross,' she cut in impatiently. 'Life's too short for eternal pessimism.'

'It's also too short for naïve optimism,' he muttered.

His dark mood refused to lift, especially when he saw Vivien's reaction to the house. But she found it difficult to pretend real liking for the place. She favoured open, airy homes with lots of light and glass and modern furniture, not dark rooms surrounded by busy wallpaper and crammed to the rafters with heavy antiques. Still, she could see why a person of another mind might covet the place. It had to be worth heaps.

'You definitely do not like this house,' Ross announced as they traipsed upstairs.

'Well, it's not exactly my taste,' Vivien admitted at last. 'Sorry.'

'You don't have to apologise.'

'I like the upstairs better. There's more natural light in the rooms.'

The floor plan was simpler too, all the rooms coming off the central gallery and all opening out on to the upstairs veranda. There were ten bedrooms, five with matching *en suites* and five without. Any guests using the latter shared the two general bathrooms, Ross informed her. Finally, Vivien was shown the upstairs linen-room, which was larger than her mother's bedroom back home.

'My mother,' Ross explained, 'had an obsession for beautiful towels and sheets.'

Vivien could only agree as her disbelieving eyes encompassed the amount of Manchester goods on the built-in shelves. There was enough to stock a whole section in a department store.

'To tell the truth,' he went on, 'I don't think Mum liked this house any more than you do. Or maybe it was the land she didn't like. She was city, just like you.'

'Really?'

'Yes, really. Well, that's about it, Vivien,' he said as he ushered her out of the linen-room and locked the door. 'I must leave you now. I have to check on Gavin's progress with the bores. Perhaps you should have a rest this afternoon. You're looking hot. Dinner is at seven-thirty when we have visitors, and, while not formal, women usually wear a dress. I dare say I'll see you then. *Au revoir...*' And, tipping his forehead, he turned and strode away, his abrupt departure leaving her feeling empty and quite desolate.

Vivien shook her head, wishing she could come to grips with what she felt for this man. Was it still just sex? Or had it finally become more complicated than that?

There was one way to find out, came the insidious temptation. Let ~~him~~ make love to you again. See if the fires can be burn out. See if there is anything else left after the night is over...

Vivien trembled. Did she have the courage to undertake such a daring experiment. Did she?

Yes, she decided with unexpected boldness, a shudder of sheer excitement reverberating through her. Yes. She did!

But no sooner had the scandalous decision been made than the doubts and fears crowded in.

What if she made a fool of herself? What if her second time with Ross proved to be an anticlimax? What if—oh, lord, was it possible?—what if Ross *rejected* her?

No, she dismissed immediately. He wouldn't do that. Not if she offered herself to him on a silver platter. He'd admitted once he'd found her sexually irresistible. He wouldn't knock back a night of free, uncomplicated loving in her bed.

And that was what she was going to offer him.

There were to be no strings attached. No demands. No extracted promises. Just a night of sex.

Vivien shuddered with distaste. How awful that sounded. How...cheap.

Yet she was determined not to go back on her decision, however much her conscience balked at the crude reality of it. Life was full of crude realities, she decided with some bitterness. Earl had been one big crude reality. He'd made her face the fact that sex and love did not always go together. Now Vivien was determined to find out if her feelings for Ross were no more than what Earl had felt for her, or whether they had deepened to something potentially more lasting.

Maybe she wouldn't have been so desperate to find out if she weren't expecting Ross's baby. But she was, and, if there was some chance of having a real relationship with her baby's father, one that could lead to marriage, then she was going to go for it, all guns blazing. Married parents were a darned sight better for a baby's upbringing than two single ones.

Thinking about her baby's welfare gave Vivien the inner strength to push any lingering scruples aside. For the first time in weeks, she felt as if she was taking control of her life, making her own decisions for the future. And it felt good. Surprisingly good. She hadn't realised how much of her self-confidence had been undermined by what Earl had done to her. Losing her job hadn't helped either.

So it was with an iron determination that Vivien returned to her bedroom and set to pondering how one successfully seduced a man.

The practicalities of it weren't as easy as one might have imagined. She'd never had to seduce a man in her life before. Earl had made the first move. So had Ross. Neither was she a natural flirt, except when intoxicated.

Was that the solution? she wondered. Could she perhaps have a few surreptitious drinks beforehand?

It was a thought. She would certainly keep it in mind if she felt her courage failing her.

Of course, if she dressed appropriately, maybe Ross would once again make the first move. Vivien hoped that would be the case. Now what could she wear that would turn Ross on? Something sexy, but subtle. She didn't want to look as if there was a banner on her body which read: 'Here I am, handsome. Do your stuff!'

Vivien wasn't too sure what clothes she'd brought with her. Her mother had packed most of her clothes. And Helga had unpacked them. But she was pretty sure she'd spotted her favourite black dress in there somewhere when she'd rooted around for her toiletries.

Vivien walked over and threw open the wardrobe. First she would find something to wear, then she would have a bubble bath in one of the main bathrooms and then a lie-down. She didn't want to look tired. She wanted to be as beautiful as she could be. Beautiful and desirable and *simply irresistible*.

Vivien walked slowly down the huge semi-circular staircase shortly before seven-thirty, knowing she couldn't look more enticing. The polyester-crêpe dress she was wearing was one of those little black creations that looked simple and stylish, but was very seductive.

Halter-necked, it had a bare back and shoulders, a V neckline that hinted at rather than showed too much cleavage, and a line that skimmed rather than hugged the body. With her hair piled up on to her head in studied disarray, long, dangling gold earrings at her lobes and a bucket of Loulou wafting from her skin, a man would have had to have all his senses on hold not to find her ultra-feminine and desirable.

As Vivien put her sexily shod foot down on to the black and white tiled foyer a male voice called out to her from the gallery above.

'Wait on!'

Nerves tightened her stomach as she turned to watch Ross come down the stairs, looking very Magnumish in white trousers and a Hawaiian shirt in a red and

white print. It crossed Vivien's mind incongruously that
Earl would not have been seen dead in anything but a
business suit.

'Don't tell me,' she said with a tinkling laugh—one
she'd heard used to advantage by various vamps on
television. 'You've been to Waikiki recently.'

He gave her a sharp look. Had she overdone the
laugh?

'No,' he denied drily. 'This is pure Hamilton Island.'

He took the remaining few steps that separated them,
icy blue eyes raking over her. 'And what is that sweet
little number you've got on?' he drawled. 'Pure King's
Cross?'

Vivien felt colour flood her cheeks. Had she overdone *everything*? Surely she didn't really look like a
whore?

No, of course she didn't. Ross was simply being
nasty for some reason. Perhaps he'd been brooding
about Becky and Gavin. Or perhaps, she ventured to
guess, he resented her looking sexy when he was supposed to keep his hands off.

Some instinctive feminine intuition told her this last
guess was close to the mark.

Knowing any blush was well covered by her dramatic make-up, she cocked her head slightly to one side
and slanted him a saucy look. 'Been to the Cross, have
you?'

'Not lately,' he bit out, jaw obviously clenched.

'Perhaps it's time for a return visit,' she laughed.
'You seem…tense.'

Vivien was startled when Ross's right hand shot out
to grip her upper arm, yanking her close to him. 'What
in hell's got into you tonight?' he hissed.

It was an effort to remain composed when one's heart was pounding away like a jackhammer.

'Why does something have to have got into me?' she returned with superb nonchalance. 'I felt like dressing up a bit, that's all. I'm sorry you don't like the way I look, but I won't lose any sleep over it. Now unhand me, please. I don't take kindly to macho displays of male domination. They always bring out the worst in me.'

Yes, she added with silent darkness. Like they make me want to strip off all my clothes and beg you to take me on these stairs right here and now!

'Sorry,' he muttered, and released her arm. 'I...did I hurt you?'

'I dare say I'll have some bruises in the morning. I have very delicate skin.'

'So I've noticed,' he ground out, his eyes igniting to hot coals as they moved up over her bare shoulders and down the tantalising neckline.

Vivien didn't know whether to feel pleased or alarmed by the evidence of Ross's obvious though sneering admiration. There was something about him tonight that was quite frightening, as though he were balancing on a razor's edge that was only partly due to male frustration. There were other devils at work within his soul. She suspected that it wouldn't take much to tip him into violence.

'Did Gavin check all the bores?' she asked, deliberately deflecting the conversation away from her appearance and giving herself a little time to rethink the situation. Suddenly, the course of action she'd set herself upon this night seemed fraught with danger. She wanted Ross to make love to her, not assault her.

'Yes,' was his uninformative and very curt answer.

He glanced at the watch on his wrist. Gold, with a brown leather band, it looked very expensive. 'Helga gets annoyed when we're late for dinner,' he pronounced. 'I think we'd better make tracks for the dining-room.'

Vivien would never have dreamt she would feel grateful for Helga's army-like sense of punctuality.

Dinner still proved a difficult meal for all concerned. Gavin, who, unlike his brother, was dressed shoddily in faded jeans and black T-shirt, was sulkily silent. This seemed to make Helga agitated and stroppy. She kept insisting everyone have seconds whether they wanted them or not.

By the time dessert came—enormous portions of plum pudding and ice-cream—Vivien's stomach was protesting. Ross, in the end, made a tactless though accurate comment to Helga about her always giving people too much to eat. Vivien managed to soothe the well-intentioned though misguided woman by saying she would normally be able to eat everything, but that her condition seemed to have affected her appetite.

At this allusion to her pregnancy, Gavin made a contemptuous sound, stood up, and stomped out of the room, having not said a word to Vivien all evening other than a grumpy hello when she and Ross had first walked into the dining-room. Shortly, they heard his station wagon start up, the gravel screeching as he roared off.

'I...I'm sorry, lovie,' Helga apologised for Gavin. 'He's not himself at the moment.'

Vivien smiled gently. 'It's all right. I understand. He's upset.'

'He's not the only one who's upset,' Ross grated out. 'I'm damned upset that people around here chose not to tell me that my own brother was in love with the girl I was going to marry.'

He glowered at Helga, who stood up with an uncompromising look on her face. 'The boy made me promise not to tell you.'

'Then why didn't he tell me himself?'

'Don't be ridiculous!' Helga snapped. 'The boy has *some* pride.'

'Haven't we all,' he muttered darkly. 'Haven't we all…'

'Anyone for tea?' Helga asked brusquely.

'Not me,' Ross returned. 'I think I'll have some port in the library instead.'

He'd asked earlier—and with some dry cynicism, Vivien had noted—if she wanted some wine with her dinner. Vivien had politely declined, whereby Ross had still opened a bottle of claret, though he'd only drunk a couple of glasses. Gavin had polished off the rest.

'What about you, lovie?'

'Er—no, thanks, Helga.' She looked over at Ross, unsure of what to do. Swallowing, she made her decision. 'I might join Ross for some port after we've cleared up,' she said in a rush.

Ross's eyes snapped round to frown at her.

'If…if that's all right with you,' she added, battling to remain calm in the face of his penetrating stare.

He lifted a single sardonic eyebrow. 'I didn't think you liked port.'

'I do occasionally.'

Actually, she *did*, though she'd only ever indulged in small quantities before. Earl had always insisted she pretend to drink at their dinner parties, saying people hated teetotallers. She'd usually managed to tip most of her wine down the sink at intervals, but she'd often allowed herself the luxury of a few sips of Earl's vintage port at the end of the evening. It seemed to relax her after the tension of cooking and serving a meal that lived up to Earl's standards.

Vivien considered she could do with some relaxing at this point in time, while she made up her mind what she was going to do. Quite clearly, Ross wasn't going to make any move towards her. Any momentary interest on the staircase appeared to have waned. He'd barely looked at her during dinner.

'I'll see you shortly, then,' Ross said, leaving the room without a backward glance.

Vivien stood up to help Helga clear the table and then wash up. They had it all finished in ten minutes flat. Never had Vivien seen anyone wash up like Helga!

'Off you go now, lovie,' the other woman said, taking the tea-towel from Vivien's hands. 'But watch yourself. Ross is stirring for a fight tonight. I've seen him like this before. He can't stand not having what he wants, or not having things go his way. Oh, he's got a good heart but he's a mighty stubborn boy. Mighty stubborn, indeed!'

Vivien was still thinking about Helga's warning when she opened the library door. So she was startled to see Ross looking totally relaxed in the large armchair she'd been sitting in earlier in the day, his feet outstretched and crossed at the ankles, a hefty glass of port cradled in his hands.

'Close the door,' he said in a soft, almost silky voice. For some reason, it brought goosebumps up on the back of her neck.

She closed the door.

'Now lock it,' he added.

She spun round, eyes blinking wide. 'Lock it? But why?'

His gaze became cold and hard. 'Because I don't like to be interrupted when I'm having sex.'

CHAPTER TWELVE

VIVIEN froze. 'I beg your pardon?'

'You heard me, Vivien. Now just lock the door and stop pretending that your sensibilities are offended. You and I both know why you dressed like that tonight. You're feeling frustrated and you've decided once again to make use of yours truly. At least, I imagine it's me you've set your cap at. I'm the one who looks like your old boyfriend, not Gavin. Or are you going to tell me you've reverted to the tease I mistook you for that night at the ball?'

Vivien's first instinct was to flee Ross's cutting contempt. For it hurt. It hurt a lot. How could she not have realised her strategy could backfire on her so badly?

But she had faced many difficult foes during her television career. Belligerent businessmen...two-faced politicians...oily con men. She was not about to let Ross's verbal attack rout her completely, though she *was* badly shaken.

'You...you've got it all wrong, Ross,' she began with as much casual confidence as she could muster.

'In what way, Vivien?'

God, but she hated that cold, cynical light in his eyes, hated the silky derision in his voice.

'I...I did try to look extra attractive tonight, but I—'

His hard, humourless laugh cut her off. '"*Extra attractive*"? Is that how you would describe yourself tonight?' With another laugh, he uncurled his tall frame from the chair to begin moving slowly across the room

156

like a panther stalking its prey, depositing his glass of port on a side-table on the way. Nerves and a kind of hypnotic fascination kept her silent and still while he approached. What on earth was he going to do?

Finally, he stood in front of her, tension in every line of his body.

'The dress could almost have been an unconscious mistake,' he said, smiling nastily. 'Despite the lack of underwear under it. But *not* when combined with those other wicked little touches. The hair, looking as if you'd just tumbled from a lover's bed...'

When he reached out to pull a few more tendrils around her face, she just stood there, as though paralysed.

'The earrings,' he went on, 'designed to draw attention to the sheer, exquisite delicacy of your lovely neck...'

Her mouth went dry when he trickled fingers menacingly around the base of her throat.

'The scarlet lipstick on your oh, so sexy mouth...'

Vivien almost moaned when he ran a fingertip around her softly parted lips. She squeezed her eyes tightly shut, appalled that he could make her feel like this when his touch was meant to be insulting.

But at least she was finding out the bitter truth, wasn't she? This couldn't be love—or the beginnings of love. This was raw, unadulterated sex, lust in its worst form, making her want him even while he showed his contempt. His own feelings for her were apparently similar, since he quite clearly hated wanting her nearly as much.

'Close your eyes if you like,' he jeered softly. 'I don't mind. I've already accepted I'm to be just a proxy lover. But believe me, I'm going to enjoy you anyway.'

Her eyes flew open in angry defiance of his presumption.

'You keep away from me. I don't want you touching me!'

His answering laugh was so dark that she shrank back against the door, one hand searching blindly for the knob.

'Oh, no, you don't,' he ground out, turning the key in the lock and pocketing it before she had a hope of escaping. 'And don't bother to scream. This room is virtually sound-proof, not to mention a hell of a long way from the servants' quarters.'

She froze when he coolly reached out to undo the button at the nape of her neck, then peeled the dress down to the waist. When he ran the back of his hand across her bared breasts her head whirled with a dizzying wave of unbidden pleasure and excitement. She didn't have to look down to know that her nipples had peaked hard with instant arousal.

'Bitch,' he rasped, before suddenly pulling her to him, *crushing* her to him, his head dipping to trail a hot mouth over her shoulders and up her throat. Vivien began to tremble uncontrollably.

She moaned when he finally kissed her, knowing that there was no stopping him now, even if she wanted to.

And she *did* want to stop him. That was the irony of it all. But only with her brain. Her body, she had already found out once with Ross, could not combat the feelings he could evoke in her, the utterly mindless passion and need.

'No,' she managed once, when he abandoned her mouth briefly to kiss her throat again.

'Shut up,' was his harsh reply before taking possession of her lips again.

She felt his hands around her waist, then pushing the dress down over her hips. It pooled around her ankles with a silky whoosh. Now only a wisp of black satin and lace prevented her from being totally naked before him. It would have been a humiliating thought, if Vivien had been able to think. As it was she found herself winding her arms up around his neck and kissing him back with the kind of desperation no man could misunderstand. Her naked breasts were pressed flat against his chest, her hips moulded to his, her abdomen undulating against his escalating arousal with primitive force.

Ross groaned under the onslaught of her frantic desire, hoisting her up on to his hips and carrying her across the room, where he lay her back across the large cedar desk in the corner. The cool hardness of its smoothly polished surface brought a gasp of shock from Vivien, almost returning her to reality for a moment. But Ross didn't allow her mad passion any peace. His hands on her outstretched body kept her arousal at fever pitch till she was beside herself with wanting him.

His name fluttered from her lips on a ragged moan of desire and need.

'Yes, that's right,' he grated back with a satanic laugh while he removed the last items of clothing from her quivering body—her panties and her shoes. 'It's Ross. Not Earl. *Ross*!'

Vivien dimly reacted to his angry assertion, wondering fleetingly if he had been more deeply hurt over that Earl business than she'd imagined. But once he had access to her whole body, to that part of her that was melting for him, she forgot everything but losing her-

self in that erotic world of unbelievable pleasure Ross
could create with his hands and lips.

'Yes...oh, yes,' she groaned when his mouth moved
intimately over her heated flesh. She groaned even
more when he suddenly stopped, glazed eyes flying to
his.

'Say that you love me,' he demanded hoarsely as he
stripped off his trousers.

A wild confusion raced through Vivien. Dazedly, she
saw him smiling down at her, felt his flesh teasing hers.
She didn't recognise the smile for the grimace of self-
mockery it really was. All Vivien knew was that, quite
unexpectedly, a raw emotion filled her heart with his
demand, an emotion that both stunned and thrilled her.

'Go on,' he urged, his hands curving round her buttocks to pull her closer to the edge. And him. 'You
don't have to mean it. Just say it!'

'I love you,' she whispered huskily and felt the emotion swell within her chest. The words came then, ringing with passion and truth. 'I really, truly love you,
Ross.'

His groan was a groan of sheer torture. Quite
abruptly, he thrust deeply into her. Vivien felt the emotion spill over into every corner of her body, felt it
charging into every nerve-ending, sharpening them,
electrifying them. She cried out, at the same time reaching out her arms to gather Ross close, to hold him next
to her heart.

For she *did* really, truly love him. She could see it
now, see it so clearly. She'd once believed Earl the real
thing, and Ross just an illusion. But she had got it the
wrong way round. Earl had been the illusion, Ross the
real thing. He must have fallen in love with her too, to
demand such a reassurance.

So she was startled when he took her hands in an iron grip, pressing them down over the edges of the desk while he set up an oddly controlled rhythm. It was only then that she saw the ugly lines in his contorted face.

Cold, hard reality swept into her heart like a winter wind. Ross was not making love to her. He was making hate, having a kind of revenge. That was why he'd demanded she tell him she loved him. It had been nothing but a cruel parody of what she had begged of him that first night.

'Oh, God…no,' she cried out in an anguished dismay, lifting her head immediately in a valiant but futile struggle to rid herself of his flesh.

'Oh, God…yes,' he bit out and kept up his relentless surging. '*Yes!*'

She moaned in despair when she felt her body betray her, felt that excruciating tightening before her flesh shattered apart into a thousand convulsing, quivering parts. Crushingly, her climax seemed to be even more intense than anything she could remember of that night at Wallaby Creek. She almost wept with the perverse pleasure of it all, but then she felt Ross's hands tightening around hers, and he too was climaxing.

She cringed even more under his violently shuddering body. He despised her and yet he was finding the ultimate satisfaction in her body. It seemed the epitome of shame, the supreme mockery of what this act should represent.

Tears of bitter misery flooded her eyes and she began to sob.

Ross's eyes jerked up to hers as though she had struck him. When he scooped her up to hold her hard against him, his body still blended to hers, she wanted to fight him. But every muscle and bone in her body had turned to mush.

'Leave me…be,' she sobbed. 'I…I *hate* you!'

'And I hate you,' he rasped, while keeping her weeping face cradled against his shirt-front. 'Hush, now. Stop crying. You're all right. It's just a reaction to your orgasm. It was too intense. Relax, honey. Relax…'

Vivien was amazed to find herself actually calming down under the soothing way he was stroking her back. When he moved over to sit down in the huge armchair, taking her with him, she didn't even object. Her legs were easily accommodated on either side on him, the deep cushioning allowing her knees and body to sink into a blissfully comfortable position.

Vivien even felt like going to sleep, which shocked her. She should be fighting him, hitting him, telling him he was a wicked, cruel man for doing what he had just done to her. She certainly shouldn't let him go on thinking that her pleasure had been nothing but sexual, that her crying was merely an emotional reaction to a heightened physical experience.

'You're not going to sleep, are you?' he whispered, his stroking hands coming to rest rather provocatively on her buttocks.

'No. Not quite.'

God, was that her voice? When had she ever talked in such low, husky, sexy tones?

'Tell me, Vivien,' he said thickly, 'was *any* of that for me, or is it still all for Earl?'

Vivien flinched, remembering how she'd momentarily thought during Ross's torrid lovemaking that his resemblance to her ex-lover had affected him deeply. He certainly did keep harping on it. Why care, if it was just vengeful sex he was after? If that were the case it shouldn't matter to him whom she was thinking about.

Vivien's heart leapt. If Ross wanted her to want him for himself, and not for his likeness to Earl, then that could only be because his feelings for her were deeper than just lust. He might not realise that himself yet—she could understand his confusion with Becky still in his heart—but one day soon...

First, however, she had to convince him that Earl was dead and gone as far as she was concerned, then that might open the way to Ross letting his feelings for her rise to the surface.

She lifted heavy eyelids to look up into his face, that face which, though so like Earl's, feature for feature, no longer reminded her at all of the man who'd treated her so badly.

Her hand reached up to lie against his cheek. 'What a foolish man you are, Ross Everton,' she said tenderly. 'You are so different from Earl in so many ways. When I look at you now, I see no one else but you. It was you I was wanting today, you I dressed for tonight, you I wanted to make love to me. Not Earl...' And, stretching upwards, she pressed gentle lips to his mouth, kissing him with all the love in her heart.

He groaned, his hands lifting to cup her face, to hold it captive while he deepened her kiss into an expression of rapidly renewing desire and need. When Vivien became hotly aware of more stirring evidence of that renewing desire, her inside contracted instinctively, gripping his growing hardness with such intensity that Ross tore his mouth away from hers on a gasping groan.

'Did...did I hurt you?' she asked breathlessly, her own arousal having revved her pulse-rate up a few notches.

He laughed. 'I wouldn't put it quite like that. But perhaps you should do it again, just so I can make sure.' And, gripping her buttocks, he moved her in a slow up-and-down motion, encouraging her internal muscles to several repeat performances.

'No.' He grimaced wryly. 'That definitely does not hurt.' He stopped moving her to slide his hands up over her ribs till they found her breasts.

'Lean back,' he rasped. 'Grip the armrests.'

She did so, her heart pounding frantically as he began to play with her outstretched body, first her breasts, then her ribs and stomach, and finally between her thighs, touching her most sensitive part till she was squirming with pleasure. He seemed to like her writhing movements too, his breathing far more ragged than her own.

'Oh, yes, honey, yes,' he moaned when she started lifting her bottom up and down again, squeezing and releasing him in a wild rhythm of uninhibited loving. 'Keep going,' he urged. 'Don't stop...'

After it was all over, and they were spent once more, they did sleep, briefly, only to wake to the sound of thunder rocking the house.

'A storm,' Vivien whispered, and shivered.

'Just electrical, I suspect. There's no rain predicted. You don't like thunder?' he asked when she shivered again.

'I'm just cold.'

He held her closer if that was possible, wrapping his arms tightly around her. 'Want to go up to bed?'

'Uh-huh.'

'I'll carry you upstairs.'

'You can't carry me out of the room like this!' she exclaimed in a shocked tone.

'Why not? No one's likely to see us. Dad's sleeping-pill will have worked by now and Helga will be busily knitting in front of the television. As for Gavin...he's playing cards and drowning his sorrows with the boys down in the shearing shed. Won't be back till the wee small hours.'

'You're sure we won't run into anyone?'

'Positive.'

'If we do, I'll die of embarrassment.'

'Me too. I haven't got any trousers on, remember?'

They didn't run into anyone, despite Vivien giggling madly all the way up the stairs. They both collapsed into a shower together in Ross's *en suite*, which revived them enough to start making love all over again. This time, it was slow and erotic and infinitely more loving, the touching and kissing lasting for an hour before Ross moved over and into her. They looked deep into each other's eyes as the pleasure built and built, Ross bending to kiss her gasping mouth when she cried out in release, only then allowing himself to let go.

Vivien lay happily in his sleeping arms afterwards, feeling more at peace with herself than she had ever felt.

So this was what really being in love was like. She smiled softly to herself in the dark, pressing loving lips to the side of Ross's chest.

'And I think you love me too,' she whispered softly. 'You just don't know it yet...'

CHAPTER THIRTEEN

THREE days rolled by and Vivien was blissfully happy. Ross was sweet to her during the day, and madly passionate every night. With each passing day she became more and more convinced that he loved her, despite his never saying so. Her own love for him was also growing stronger as she discovered more about him.

Helga had been right when she'd said they had similar personalities. They also had similar likes and dislikes in regard to just about everything. They were both mad about travel and Tennessee Williams's plays and the Beatles and playing cards, especially Five Hundred. It was uncanny. With Earl, she had had to pretend to like what he liked, just to keep him happy. With Ross, there was no pretending. Ever. She'd never felt so at one with a person.

There was another matter that did wonders for her humour as well. She didn't have morning sickness any more. How wonderful it was to be able to wake and not have to run to the bathroom! Her appetite improved considerably once her stomach was more settled, which was just as well since Helga had decided she needed 'building up'.

Yes, Vivien couldn't have been happier. Even Oliver seemed a little better, though he still tired quickly. The couple of hours she sat with him each morning and afternoon were mostly spent with her reading aloud while he relaxed in his favourite armchair. Occasionally they watched a video which Ross brought out from town.

The only fly in the ointment was Gavin, who remained as sour and uncommunicative as ever. He'd hardly spoken a dozen words to Vivien since her arrival, but she refused to let his mood upset her new-found happiness.

He was only young, she reasoned. He would get over his love for this Becky girl, as Ross was obviously getting over his. Every now and then, Vivien found herself puzzling over exactly what sort of girl this Becky Macintosh was to command such devotion.

She found out on New Year's Eve.

Vivien had just finished her morning visit with Oliver. Ross and Gavin were out mending fences. She and Helga were sitting in the kitchen having a mug of tea together when suddenly they heard a screeching of brakes on the gravel driveway. Before they could do more than raise their eyebrows, a slender female figure in pale blue jeans and a blue checked shirt came racing into the kitchen, her long, straight blonde hair flying out behind.

'Where's Ross?' she demanded breathlessly of Helga.

'Down in the south paddocks, mending fences. What is it, Becky? What's happened?'

'There was a small grass fire on the other side of the river. Dad and I put it out, but not before the wind picked up and a few sparks jumped the river. Now the fire's growing again and heading straight for our best breeding sheep. I've rung the emergency bush-fire brigade number, but apparently all of the trucks are attending two other scrub fires. They said they'd send a few men along in a helicopter, one of those that can

water-bomb the fire. The trouble is the only pilot available is a real rookie. I thought Ross might be able to
help.'

'I'll contact him straight away,' Helga said briskly.
'They have a two-way radio with them. I won't be a
moment. The gizmo's in the study. I'll send them
straight over to your place.'

'Thanks, Helga, I'd better get back. Mum's in a
panic. Not that the fire's anywhere near the house. But
you know what she's like.'

'Can I help in any way?' Vivien offered. 'Maybe I
could stay with your mother while you do what you
have to do.'

Vivien found herself on the end of a long look from
the loveliest blue eyes. There was no doubt about it.
Becky had not been behind the door when God gave
out looks. Though not striking, she had a fragile delicacy about her that would bring out the protective instinct in any man. Too bad they never saw the tough-
ness behind those eyes.

'I presume you're Vivien,' she said drily.

Vivien stood up, her shoulders automatically squaring. 'Yes, I am.'

Those big blue eyes flicked over her face and figure
before a rueful smile tugged at her pretty mouth. 'If I'd
known the sort of competition I had, I would have
given up sooner. What odds, I ask myself, of Ross
meeting someone like you at that horrid ball? Still, I
have more important things to do today than worry over
the fickle finger of fate. Yes, you can come and hold
Mum's hand. That'll free me to help outside.'

Helga bustled back into the kitchen just in time to
be told Vivien was going with Becky. Oddly enough,
the older woman didn't seem to think this at all strange.

For all her earlier criticisms about the girl's behaviour
with Ross, she seemed to like Becky.

It came to Vivien then that there was more worth in
this girl than she'd previously believed. That was why
Helga wanted her for Gavin—to put some fire in his
belly. Becky had a positive attitude and energetic drive
Vivien could only admire.

'So when are you and Ross getting married?' Becky
enquired while she directed the jeep at a lurching speed
down the dusty road that led back to the highway.

'I don't know,' came the truthful answer. 'He—er—
hasn't asked me yet.'

Becky slanted a frowning glance her way. 'Hasn't
asked you yet? That's odd. When he confessed to me
that he'd fallen in love with someone else the night of
the ball at Wallaby Creek, and that the girl in question
was pregnant by him, I naturally thought you'd be married as quickly as possible.'

Vivien held her silence with great difficulty. Ross
had said that? Back *then*? That meant he'd virtually
fallen in love with her straight away.

Oh, my God, she groaned silently. My God...

Her heart squeezed tight at the thought of all she had
put Ross through that night, especially making him tell
her he loved her like that. It also leant an ironic and
very heart-wrenching meaning to Ross's statement a
few days ago that he had always known the girl he
loved didn't love him back, but that didn't stop him
loving her. Of course Vivien had thought he meant
Becky. But he had meant herself!

Vivien felt like crying. If only she'd known. But, of
course, why would he tell her? No man would, certainly not after that day when he'd followed her to
Sydney, only to discover that he was the dead-ringer

of her previous lover, the man she supposedly still
loved. God, it was a wonder his love for her hadn't
turned to hate then and there.

Maybe it almost had for a while, she realised, remembering the incident in the library.

But if only he had told her later that night that he
loved her, instead of letting her think his feelings were
only lust.

And what of you? a reproachful voice whispered.
Have you told him you love him? Have you reassured
the father of your child that your feelings for him are
anything more than just sexual?

She almost cried out in dismay at her own stupidity.

Oh, Ross...darling...I'll tell you as soon as I can,
she vowed silently.

'Of course I always knew he wasn't madly in love
with me, or I with him,' Becky rattled on. 'But we go
back a long way, Ross and I. Gavin too, for that matter.
We've always been great mates, the three of us. We
love each other, but I think it's been more of a friendship love than anything else To be honest, I wasn't at
all desperate to go to bed with Ross. But then...I've
never been desperate to go to bed with any man as yet.'
She sighed heavily. 'Maybe I will one day, but something tells me I'm not a romantic at heart.'

Vivien only hesitated for a second. After all, nothing
ventured, nothing gained. 'Has it ever occurred to you
that you might have been looking for passion with the
wrong brother?'

The jeep lurched to one side before Becky recovered.
She darted Vivien a disbelieving glance. 'You're not
serious!'

'Never been more serious. Helga says Gavin's crazy

about you. He was simply crushed by your intention to marry Ross.'

'*Really*?'

'Yes, really. He's been as miserable as sin lately because he thinks you're suffering from a broken heart. He blames me and Ross.'

'But…but if he loves me, the stupid man, why hasn't he said so? Why hasn't he *done* something?'

'Too shy.'

'Too *shy*? With *me*? That's ridiculous! Why, we've been skinny dipping together!'

'Not lately, I'll bet.'

'Well, no…'

'Perhaps you should suggest you do so again some time. See what happens.'

Becky looked over at Vivien, blue eyes widening. 'You city girls don't miss a trick, do you? Skinny dipping, eh? Yes, well, I—er—might suggest that some time, but I can't think about Gavin right now. I have a fire to help put out.'

They fell silent as Becky concentrated on her driving. Not a bad idea, Vivien thought, since the girl drove as she no doubt did most things—with a degree of wild recklessness. Or maybe all country people drove like that on the way to a fire. Whatever, Vivien was hanging on to the dashboard for dear life.

Ross and Gavin must have gone across land, picking up Stan and Dave on the way, for all four men arrived at the homestead simultaneously with Becky and Vivien. A plump, fluttery lady raced out to greet them all with hysteria not far away.

'Oh, thank God, thank God,' she kept saying.

'Now, now, Mrs Macintosh,' Ross returned, patting her hand. 'Calm down. The cavalry's here.'

He turned to give Vivien a questioning look, but she merely smiled, hugging to herself the wonderful knowledge of his love for her. Later today, she would tell him of her own love. Not only would she tell him, but she would show him.

'There's the helicopter!' Becky shouted, pointing to the horizon. 'It's a water-bombing helicopter,' she explained to Ross, 'but the pilot's not very experienced. Do you think you might be able to help him?'

'Sure. I haven't exactly done that kind of thing myself before, but it can't be too difficult.'

The dark grey helicopter landed in a cloud of dust, forestalling any further conversation. It was all business. A side-door slid back to reveal several men inside. Stan, Dave and Gavin piled in with them. Ross climbed in next to the pilot, shouting back to Becky to collect some cool drinks and to drive down in the jeep.

Becky didn't look at all impressed at being given such a tame job to do, but in the end she shrugged resignedly. Within minutes of the helicopter taking off, she'd successfully filled two cool boxes with ice and drinks, refusing to let Vivien help her carry them to the jeep.

'You shouldn't be carrying heavy things when you're in the family way,' she was told firmly.

'Where will they get the water from to bomb the fire with?' Vivien asked as Becky climbed in behind the wheel.

'The dam, I guess, though there isn't too much water in it. Maybe the river.'

Vivien frowned. 'But wouldn't that be dangerous? The river's not very wide and there are trees all along the bank.'

'*Dangerous*? For the legendary Ross Everton?' Becky laughed.

'I've heard him called that before, but I don't know what it means.'

'It means, duckie, that you've got yourself hooked to the craziest, most thrilling-seeking chopper cowboy that ever drew breath. Ross prides himself on being able to fly down and hover low enough to open gates by leaning out of the cockpit. He'll heli-muster anything that moves in any kind of country, no matter how rough and wild. Cattle. Brumbies. Buffalo. He's a legend all over the outback for his skill and daring.' She gave Vivien a wry look as she fired the engine. 'Having second thoughts, are we?'

'Of course not!' she returned stalwartly, and waved Becky off.

But a type of fear had gripped her heart. Ross might be very skilled, but hadn't he just admitted he hadn't done this kind of job before? What if he made a mistake? What if the helicopter crashed?

Vivien felt sicker than she ever had with morning sickness. She felt even sicker an hour later while she and Mrs Macintosh stood together on the back veranda of the homestead, from where they had a first-class view of what was going on, both in the far paddocks and in the air. The helicopter had indeed scooped up a couple of loads of water from the dam, but clearly not enough. The grass fire was still growing. Now, the helicopter was being angled around to head for the river. Vivien just knew who it was at the controls.

'Oh, God, no,' she groaned when the machine skimmed the tops of trees in its descent to the narrow strip of water below.

She watched with growing horror when the helicopter dipped dangerously to fill the canvas bag, the rotor blades almost touching the surface of the water before the craft straightened and scooped upwards. 'I can't watch any more,' she muttered under her breath.

But she did, her heart aching inside her constricted chest as she watched Ross make trip after dangerous trip to that river then back to the fire. At last, the flames died, leaving nothing but a cloud of black smoke. Mrs Macintosh turned to hug her when, even from that distance, they heard the men's shouts of triumph.

Vivien couldn't feel total triumph, however. Fear was still gripping her heart. How could she bear Ross doing this kind of thing for a living? How could she cope with the continuous worrying? She wanted the father of her baby around and active when their child grew up. Not dead, or a paraplegic.

Her fears were compounded when the men came back to the house and Ross was laughing—actually laughing!—as the rookie pilot relayed tales of near-missed fences and trees. In the end, she couldn't bear it any more. She walked right up to him and said with a shaking voice, 'You might think that risking your life is funny, but I don't. I've been worried sick all afternoon, and I...I...' Tears flooded her eyes. Her shoulders began to shake.

Ross gathered her against his dusty chest. 'Hush. I'm all right, darling. Don't cry now...' He led her away from the others before tipping her tear-stained face up to him. 'Dare I hope this means what I think it means?'

'Oh, Ross, I love you so much,' she cried. 'I can't bear to think of you risking your life every day. Don't ever go back to doing that helicopter business. Please. I couldn't bear it if you had an accident.'

'I won't have an accident.'

'You don't know that. You're not immortal. Or infallible. No one is. If you love me even a little—'

'A *little*? My God, Vivien, I *adore* you, don't you know that?'

She stared up at him, stunned, despite what Becky had told her. It sounded so much more incredibly wonderful coming from Ross's actual lips. 'You…you've never actually told me,' she choked out. 'Not in words.'

'Well, I'm telling you now. I've loved you since the first moment I set eyes on you, looking at me across that crowded ballroom. You mean the world to me. But you don't understand. I won't have an accident because—'

Mr Macintosh's tapping him on the shoulder interrupted what Ross was going to say.

'Ross…'

Ross turned. 'Yes?'

'Er—Helga just called. I'm sorry, but I have some bad news.'

'Bad news?'

'Yes…your father…'

Vivien closed her eyes as a wave of anguish washed through her, for she knew exactly what the man was going to say. Fresh tears flowed, tears for the man who'd become her friend. More tears for the man she loved. He was going to take this hard.

Mr Macintosh cleared his throat. 'He…he passed away…this afternoon. I'm so sorry, lad.'

Ross's hold tightened around Vivien. Yet when he spoke, his voice sounded calm. Only Vivien could feel him shaking inside. 'It's all right. Dad's dearest wish was that he would die at Mountainview. He…he's probably quite happy.'

*   *   *

Oliver Everton was cremated, in keeping with his
wishes, and his ashes sprinkled over the paddocks of
his beloved Mountainview. They had a large wake for
him at the house, again in keeping with his wishes, and
it was towards the end of this wake that Mr Parkinson,
Oliver's solicitor, called the main beneficiaries of his
will into the study.

Mr Parkinson sat behind the huge walnut desk while
Ross and Vivien, Helga and Gavin pulled up chairs.
Vivien was perplexed—and a little worried—over what
she was doing there. If she was to be a beneficiary, that
meant Oliver had changed his will recently. She was
suddenly alarmed at what she was about to hear.

'I won't beat about the bush,' Mr Parkinson started.
'It appears that Oliver saw fit to write a new will a
couple of days ago without consulting me. Oh, it's all
legal and above-board, witnessed by Stan and Dave.
Helga had it in her safe keeping...'

Vivien stared at Helga, who kept a dead-pan face.

'But I have to admit that the contents came as a
shock to me. I think they might come as a shock to
you too, Ross.'

Vivien finally dared to look at Ross, who didn't look
at all worried. It crossed her mind then that he knew
full well what was in that will. She went cold with
apprehension.

'Aside from Ross being left a couple of real estate
properties around Sydney and Helga being left a pen-
sion trust fund to ensure she won't want for money for
the rest of her life, it seems that Oliver has left the bulk
of his estate, including the property Mountainview and
all it contains, to his second son, Gavin.'

Gavin sat bolt upright in his chair, clearly stunned.
'But that's not fair. Mountainview is worth millions!

Ross…' He swivelled to throw a distressed look at his brother. 'You must know…I had no hand in this.'

'I know that,' Ross replied equably. 'Dad told me what he was going to do. I fully agreed with his decision.'

Vivien almost gasped at his obvious twisting of the truth. It had been Ross, she realised, who had insisted on the change of will. This was what he had gone to see his father about a few days ago, before it was too late. He knew his father had actually left control of Mountainview to *him*. He had sacrificed his inheritance for love of his brother, for he knew his brother needed it more than he did, in more ways than one.

Gavin was looking even more stunned. 'You *agreed* with my having Mountainview?'

'Yes. I've been made an excellent offer for my fleet of helicopters and the goodwill of my business. I'm going to take it. Believe me, Gavin, I won't be wanting for a bob, if that's what's worrying you. And don't forget about those Sydney properties Dad left me.'

'But they'd be nothing compared to Mountainview!'

'That depends on the point of view. One of them is that penthouse unit at Double Bay Mum inherited. It's hardly worth peanuts. The other is a substantial acreage Dad bought years ago just outside Sydney on the Nepean River. I've always had a dream to set up an Australian tourist resort, catering for people who want to experience typical Australian country life without having to actually travel out there. That piece of land on the Nepean would be the ideal site.'

'You've never mentioned this before,' Gavin said, clearly still worried.

Ross gave him a ruefully affectionate smile. 'We don't always talk about our dreams out loud, do we, little brother? I thought my duty lay here till I saw you had more heart for this place than I ever would.'

'And what will this tourist resort have in it, Ross?' Vivien joined in, intrigued by the thought of it all.

Smiling widely, he turned to her. 'Lots of things. There'll be a miniature farm with examples of all our animals, shearing exhibitions, sheep-dog trials. Individual cabins for people to stay in. Restaurants that serve typical Australian food. Barbecue and picnic facilities. Souvenir shops. All sorts of things. I think it could be a great success, especially if my wife joins in and helps me. She's a whiz with people…'

She stared back at him, having only heard the word—'wife'. He bent over and kissed her before turning back to face his brother.

'So don't worry about Dad leaving you Mountainview, Gavin. He's put it in the best of hands. And I think there might be a girl somewhere around here who might like to help you and Helga look after the place.'

'Gosh, I don't know what to say.'

Neither did Helga, it seemed. Tears were streaming down her face.

Vivien reached out to take Ross's hand. 'You are a wonderful, wonderful man,' she murmured. 'Do you know that?'

'Yes,' he said, and leant close. 'You will marry me, won't you?'

'You know I will.'

'That's what your mother told me that day. She said if I were patient you'd come around. She said you loved me, but you just didn't know it yet.'

Vivien was astonished. 'Mum said that?'

'Sure thing. She told me her daughter didn't go

round having babies with men she didn't love. I should have believed her sooner.'

A lump filled Vivien's throat. Dear heaven...her mother knew her better than she knew herself. But she'd been so right. So very right.

Mr Parkinson coughed noisily till they were all paying attention to him again. 'I have one more bequest to read out. It seems the late Mrs Everton had a sizeable amount of very valuable jewellery which has been kept in a bank vault in Sydney all these years. Mr Everton senior left it all to the mother of his first grandchild, Miss Vivien Roberts. To be worn, his will states. Not locked away. He says it could only be enhanced by Miss Roberts's beauty.'

Vivien tried not to cry, but it was a futile exercise. The tears had already been hovering. She began to sob quietly, Ross putting an arm round her shoulder to try and comfort her. Helga stood up abruptly and left the room, returning quickly with a tray full of drinks. She passed them all around.

'I wish to propose a toast to my employer and friend, Oliver Everton.'

They all stood up.

'May I?' Ross asked thickly.

Helga nodded.

'To Oliver Everton,' he said. 'He was a good father and a good friend. He was a good man. They don't come along like him too often...'

CHAPTER FOURTEEN

'IRVING! What do you think you're doing?' Vivien remonstrated. 'I asked you to film just the christening, but you've been following me around all afternoon with that darned camera. I came out here on my own back patio to catch a breath of fresh air and up you pop like a bad penny.'

Irving continued filming as he spoke. 'Now, Viv, sweetie, I don't often have such a gorgeous-looking subject to film. You're looking ravishing today in that white dress, especially with that pearl choker round your lovely neck. Have pity on me. I've been doing nothing but film sour old politicians for the channel lately. Of course, if a certain lady journalist would heed her old boss's pleas to return to work then I might get assigned some more interesting jobs…like that one out at Wallaby Creek.'

Vivien's laughter was dry. 'Mervyn can beg till he's blue in the face. I have no intention of ever returning to work for a man who's so stupid. Fancy keeping Bob on instead of me. No intelligence at all.'

'Didn't I tell you? Bob's moved to Western Australia. He's decided the politicians are more interesting over there.'

'Oh, so that's it! Now Mervyn has a hole in his staff and he thinks he can fill it with yours truly. No way, José. I'm very happy helping Ross build this place.' And she swept an arm round to indicate the mushrooming complex. Already their own house was finished on a spot overlooking the river. So was the gardener's cottage. The foundations of the restaurant and shops had been poured that week.

'That's what I told him,' Irving said. 'But he's a stubborn man.'

'Who's a stubborn man?' Ross remarked on joining them. Vivien thought he looked heart-stoppingly handsome in a new dark grey suit. And very proud, with his six-week-old baby son in his arms.

'Mervyn,' she explained. 'You know he keeps asking me to go back to work for him.'

'Why don't you?'

Vivien blinked at her husband. 'But you said—'

Ross shrugged. 'I always believe in letting people do what they want to do, regardless. If you're missing work then by all means go back. You know your mother's dying to get her hands on Luke here, and since your father agreed to quit the railways and take on the job as chief gardener you've got a built-in babysitter. Your parents will be living only a hundred yards away.'

Vivien could hardly believe her ears. That was one aspect of Ross's character that never ceased to amaze her: his totally selfless generosity. So different to Earl, who'd been greedily possessive of her time. He'd hated her working.

Thinking about the differences between Ross and Earl brought a small smile to her lips, for they were more different now than ever. Her mother had shown her a picture in a women's magazine the other day, of a couple at the Flemington races. Vivien had not recognised the man till she'd read the caption below the photograph:

Mr and Mrs Earl Fotheringham enjoying a day at the races.

She had stared at the photograph again, then had difficulty suppressing a burst of laughter. For Earl was not only grossly overweight, but he was going bald. In less than a year, he looked ten years older, and nothing like Ross at all. She'd shown the picture to Ross, who'd looked at it, then stared at her.

'And *this* is who I'm supposed to look like?' he said.

'Once upon a time,' she said, trying to keep a straight face.

When Ross had burst out laughing she had too. But from relief, rather than any form of mockery, for now Ross could put Earl's ghost to rest once and for all.

Vivien's father opened the sliding glass doors and popped his head out. 'Is this a private session, or can anyone join in?'

'By all means join us, Lionel,' Ross said warmly. 'Get Peggy out here too and we can have a family shot.'

Lionel looked sheepish. 'Well, actually I was told to bring you all back inside. Your mother says it's getting late, Vivien, and you should be opening the baby's presents.'

They all were soon gathered in the large living area of the modern, airy house, Vivien sitting down on the white leather sofa to begin opening the gifts and cards that were piled high on the coffee-table, while everyone looked on. Irving kept happily filming away. Vivien decided to ignore him as best she could, and began ripping off paper with relish.

There were all the usual christening presents from toys to teddies, clothes to engraved cups, all beautiful and much gushed over by everyone. Gavin, who had become ecstatically engaged to Becky the previous month, had already sent down their excuses at not being able to attend, since they were in the middle of shearing. He'd posted down the cutest toy lamb Vivien had ever seen. The card attached had a small note from Becky.

'What does she mean,' Ross asked, 'about how she's been practising her swimming a lot lately?'

Vivien felt her lips twitching. 'I—er—told her the only way to get good at anything was to practise it.'

Ross frowned. 'Becky practising swimming? That's silly. She's a fantastic swimmer. Why, we used to go…' His voice trailed off as suspicion dawned in his eyes. He gave Vivien a narrow-eyed stare. She busied herself with another present by way of distraction.

'Here's one from Helga,' she announced, feeling it all over before opening it. 'I wonder what it is.' It was quite bulky, but soft.

Ross groaned. 'I have an awful feeling of premonition that Helga's been knitting again.'

Vivien ripped the paper off and everyone just stared. It was, she supposed, a rug of some sort, knitted in the most ghastly combination of colours she had ever seen, not to mention different ply wools. Now she knew why Ross's jumpers had never seen the light of day. Who would think to combine mauve with orange with black with red with purple in a series of striped and checked squares that had no regular pattern? On the card was the following explanation:

I began this before I knew whether your baby would be a boy or a girl, so I decided that neutral colours would be best.

These were *neutral* colours? Vivien stared down at the rug, unable to think of a thing to say.

'What...what is it?' Vivien's mother finally asked.

'A horse blanket,' Ross stated with a superbly straight face. 'For Luke's first pony. Helga's horse blankets are quite famous. Horses love them.'

'Oh,' Peggy said.

'We'll put it in a drawer for him, sweetheart,' Ross said to Vivien. 'Perhaps we should put a special drawer aside in which to save up all of Helga's marvellous gifts.'

'Yes, dear,' she returned with an even better poker-face. 'I think that would be best.'

They were lying in bed that night after Luke had finally condescended to go to sleep, chuckling over the incident.

'I almost died when I first saw it,' Vivien giggled.

'Don't you mean ''almost died laughing''? And now, madam, would you like to tell me in the privacy of our bedroom what decadent advice you gave Becky?'

'Decadent advice? Who, me?'

'Yes, *you*, city broad.'

She laughed. 'That's for me to know and you to find out.'

'I think I already have...'

'Then why are you asking? Besides, it worked, didn't it? They're engaged and happy.'

'Not as happy as we are,' Ross insisted, pulling her close.

Vivien lifted her mouth to his in a tender kiss. 'No one's as happy as we are.'

'Too true.'

'Which is why I'm not going back to work.'

'You're not?'

'No. I'm happy doing what I'm doing, looking after Luke and helping you. Maybe some day I might want to go back to television, but not right now. I want to be right here when Luke cuts his first tooth, says his first word, takes his first step. Let Mervyn find someone else,' she went on without any regret. 'I can see I'm not going to be available for at least ten years, till our last child has gone to school.'

Startled, Ross propped himself up on his elbow and stared down at her. 'Our *last* child? How many are we going to have, for heaven's sake?'

'Oh, at least four. Kids these days need brothers and sisters to stick up for them. It's a tough world.'

He shook his head in a type of awed bewilderment. 'You never cease to amaze me, Mrs Everton. First, you bravely went ahead and had my baby when most women in your shoes wouldn't have. Now, after you've just been through a rotten long labour, you tell me you want a whole lot more! I'm beginning to wonder if you're a glutton for punishment or just plain crazy.'

'I'm crazy,' she said, and with a soft, sexy laugh pulled him down into her arms. 'Crazy about you...'

HER OUTBACK MAN

Margaret Way

CHAPTER ONE

VAST as the homestead was, everywhere Dana looked
there were people; in the drawing room, the library,
Logan's study, the entrance hall of grand dimensions,
even the broad verandas that surrounded the marvellous
old homestead on three sides were crowded with
mourners. There must have been four hundred at least.
They had been arriving since early morning in their
private planes and their charter planes set down like a
flock of birds on the station's runway, or in the small
army of vehicles that had made the long hot trek over-
land; all of them come to pay their last respects to
James Tyler Dangerfield, second son of this powerful
and influential landed family, dead at twenty-eight,
killed in a car crash after a wild all-night party. Not
many people would know that. Logan, as always, had
taken charge very swiftly, gathering them all in, issuing
a brief statement to the press, making all the arrange-
ments while the entire Dangerfield clan, pastoralists,
judges, scientists and politicians, one a Government
minister, closed ranks behind him.

Logan was the cattle baron. As direct descendant of
the Dangerfield founding father in colonial Australia,
he was head of one of the country's richest families
and Chairman of the Dangerfield pastoral empire and a
network of corporations since the death of his late father, Sir Matthew Dangerfield some two years earlier.
Jimmy had been the playboy, the second son, forever
doomed to walk in Logan's tall shadow. Logan was the

real Dangerfield, Jimmy had often said, never quite able to conceal his envy and a kind of half-bitter, half-wry resentment at his being second best. Jimmy, with his easy, happy-go-lucky charm, spoiled by the family fortune. Logan was the chip off the old block. The son with unlimited skills and matchless energies. Sir Matthew had worshipped Logan, Jimmy had told her, and Dana had seen that with her own eyes. It had always been perfectly obvious Jimmy could never hope to measure up to his big brother.

Stepbrother.

Logan's mother, Elizabeth Logan Dangerfield, had died giving him birth, something that would not have happened had she elected to have her firstborn in hospital instead of on historic Mara Station to please her husband. Matthew Dangerfield had married Jimmy and Sandra's mother, Ainslie, a few years later, a marriage as nearly a business merger as the first one had been an ecstatic romance. Both Jimmy and Sandra favoured their mother's side of the family, with their golden-brown colouring. Logan was all dark, dangerous Dangerfield, which was to say, unfairly endowed with all of Nature's attributes.

Her expression bleak, Dana turned away from the elegant white wrought-iron balcony to look over to where Logan stood, perhaps on this awful day a little stiffly, his head characteristically thrown up but in perfect control of his emotions as was expected of the head of the family.

Logan, strikingly handsome in his formal dark clothes relieved only by the immaculate white of his shirt, thick blue-black hair, a piercing regard, not that ''piercing'' fully described the beauty of his sapphire eyes, at six-three, towering over the people around him, a lean and splendid physique. One might have thought it unnecessary to endow him with other qualities, but he had a razor-sharp intelligence he never bothered to conceal and a natural air of command; a capacity for leadership he hadn't developed but had been born with. If there were scores of people who adored Logan Dangerfield, scores more *women,* Dana wasn't one of them. She and Logan looked on one another with a mixture of feelings. Liking wasn't one of them. In the six years since she had first met him they had maintained an uneasy and often electric truce.

The thing was, she would never have moved into his rarified world if it weren't for Melinda. Melinda was her cousin, orphaned child of her mother's sister. Melinda's parents had been killed in a train accident when Melinda was eight and Dana six, and Dana's mother had insisted Melinda come to them. Pretty as a picture, blond-haired and blue-eyed, strangely no one else in the family had wanted her, so Melinda arrived. More than a cousin, a sister, settling into the house as softly and quietly as a little cat. Dana knew better than anyone all about Melinda.

When they were at University, Melinda, two years ahead of eighteen-year-old Dana, had met the Golden Boy, Jimmy Dangerfield, a playboy even then. Jimmy was studying for a degree in Commerce, though he cared little for study. Jimmy was a "dabbler" with no interest in getting on with his work yet he had a perfectly good brain. Something he apparently liked to keep to himself. But Jimmy always had all the money he needed. He got to all the parties and he always had the pretty girls. Jimmy thought being serious about anything was dull and boring. When it was all said and done, all he wanted out of life was fun.

He hadn't really wanted Melinda, though his roving eye had singled out her soft, seemingly vulnerable prettiness. He had taken her out for a time without the slightest awareness of what Melinda was really like. Melinda had an overriding ambition in life. To find *security*. No doubt a consequence of her early traumas. Not the security that mattered, but *money* above all else. Golden Boy Dangerfield was the beginning and end of her search. Known for his love of freedom, Melinda had set Jimmy a trap. She deliberately got herself pregnant, feeling no guilt when Jimmy was forced into a marriage he didn't want, though to his everlasting credit he recognised his responsibilities to Melinda and his coming child. This child was a Dangerfield. He would never have been forgiven had he turned his back on her. Melinda was pretty, intelligent, and from a respectable background. Jimmy had believed she loved him passionately. It wasn't long into the marriage before Jimmy found out she didn't.

Melinda.

At this moment she was lying supposedly sedated in one of the upstairs bedrooms, unable to attend the service, which had been held in the old two-storeyed stone chapel some distance from the homestead, or see her young husband laid to rest on Eagle's Ridge, the family plot surrounded by a six-foot-high wrought-iron fence with ornate double gates. Melinda wasn't prostrate from grief. Dana knew that for a fact. Melinda needed to hide away from all the condemnatory eyes. Dana, who had had a lifetime of fronting for Melinda, was acutely aware of all the subterranean surges and the long speculative glances levelled at her. Everyone knew who she was just as they knew ''Tyler's'' marriage had not been a happy one. Inevitable some would say when it had started out so badly.

Dana couldn't bear to look back on those days. The image of Melinda, her face paper-white, blue eyes blazing, smiling at her in a sort of conspiratorial triumph.

"He doesn't really want to but I pulled it off, didn't I? He's going to marry me. I'll be a Dangerfield. I'll be rich and important. Mara is *famous*."

Dana then as now felt a sick dismay but she had little room in her heart for condemnation. Melinda's dream had turned to ashes. Jimmy had been laid to rest. Life might have been very different for both of them had Melinda been more a woman of heart and mind. Going over to visit them mostly for Alice's, her beloved little goddaughter's sake had been like going onto a battle ground. Jimmy had not finished his degree any more than Melinda had. After an initial period of trying, Jimmy had quickly settled back into having a good time while Melinda, to everyone's horror, turned into a shrew, complaining bitterly to anyone who would listen, having Alice had caused her to miss out on her youth. Small wonder Alice growing up in such a household was as troubled a child as she could be. Dana was her refuge and they both knew it. Dana could never abandon Alice. Especially *now*.

What to do with the pain? Dana thought. What to do with the pain?

She knew Logan blamed her for lots of things, but he had only said it once. The night of the wedding. The first time she had ever laid eyes on John Logan Dangerfield.

CHAPTER TWO

THIS wedding was different. He had known instinctively something was wrong when Tyler came home crowing with delight he had fallen love and wanted to get married immediately.

"She's my blond enchantress," he told them, shocking Ainslie, who had different plans for her son. "I've never met anyone like her. So cool and clever."

It didn't fit the description of the young woman who later flew in to meet them with her coy almost cloying prettiness and shy downcast eyes. The disturbing beauty and the cool intelligence belonged to her cousin. He could never understand how Tyler had looked beyond Dana until it all became clear. But on that day Tyler had his eyes firmly set on Melinda, his young wife, soon to be the mother of his child. Logan had managed to get that out of his beleaguered brother almost at once, backing Tyler's wish to have a quiet wedding on the station attended by family and a few close friends; something that upset Melinda terribly. She had wanted a big wedding with all the trimmings, but the family took no notice of that. It was, after all, a marriage that had been manipulated from the start. But in all fairness, though bitterly disappointed, Ainslie had arranged a wedding pageant and they all did their level best, about fifty in all, to make it a festive occasion. The bride wore virginal white, a soft flowing dress cut to skim the waistline, her pale face hidden by her veil; the cousin wore the same sort of fabric, silk chiffon, he later learned, but in a frosted gold, the bodice leaving her shoulders bare, the long skirt billowing from a small cinched waist. Like the bride, she carried an exquisite bouquet of roses from Mara's home gardens combining all the creams and yellows and golds...

He had been caught up on one of the outstations all morning. The manager there had been foolish enough to try to make a bit extra for himself periodically selling off a few head of prime cattle, so he had to attend to that, a rough confrontation out in the bush, flying back into Mara just over an hour before the ceremony in the family chapel was due to begin. He had never felt less like attending a wedding in his life, knowing Ty, for all his efforts to put on a good face, wasn't happy and he himself was deeply uncomfortable with the idea the bride wasn't just a kitten-faced innocent caught up in an all too common situation but a first-rate opportunist. The cousin she had lived with from childhood was probably the same. He had left before the cousin's flight was due in. She had paid for her ticket to the domestic terminal herself. Something that had surprised him. Melinda had taken to being "looked after" like a duck to water.

Feeling strung out and dishevelled, he had entered the house at the precise moment a young woman in a beautiful strapless gown set her foot on the first landing of the central staircase. She was young, very young, perhaps eighteen or nineteen, but her expression as she looked down at him was one of dignity and maturity.

Tyler's *enchantress,* he thought in one revelatory second, while something hot and hostile flared behind his rib cage.

"You must be Logan," she said sweetly, an answering heat in her flush. "I'd heard you'd been called out."

Her voice, too, was alluring and he gave himself a moment to level out. "To one of our outstations, as it happens." He didn't smile, the formality of his tone in sharp contrast to her natural warmth. "And you must be Dana?" Stupid. Of course she was Dana. The cousin. Yet he couldn't quite believe it. She was blond, like Melinda, but an ash-blond, very nearly platinum, her long, thick, straight hair caught back from her face with a sparkling diadem and allowed to fall down her back. But where one might have expected Melinda's white skin and blue eyes, this girl's skin gleamed ivory, her eyes set in a slight upward slant like the wings of her eyebrows, velvet brown. It was a stunning combination.

What was even more stunning was the fact he was staring, but her physical beauty seized his imagination. Woman magic. A quality that could bring great joy or havoc or both in equal measure.

She hesitated, perhaps baffled and a little alarmed at his attitude, while sunlight from the high arched casements lent a startling radiance to her hair and her gown. He almost felt like calling out, "Come down, I won't bite you," when she suddenly descended the stairs in cool challenge, holding up the folds of her skirt with one hand, the other outstretched towards him.

"How do you do, Logan," she said with the utmost composure. "I'm so pleased to meet you at last. Jimmy speaks of you all the time."

Jimmy. Who was *Jimmy?* To the family, he was Tyler. He knew from the glitter in her velvet eyes she was suddenly angry, as hostile in her fashion as he was. Even the brief contact of hands sent out warning signals as if to say we may never be open about it but we will never be friends.

Friends with this young woman? One might as well be friends with some creature who wrought spells. The danger was plain. He felt a powerful urge to question her, to try to get to the bottom of what had happened to his brother, only it was all too late.

"Please *don't*," she said, surprising him, her upturned face betraying a certain anguish. *Guilt?*

"I'm sorry. I don't follow," he lied, every nerve jangling.

"I think you do." She took a little breath. "We both want Jimmy to be happy."

His voice when it came was so sharp it was like he had splinters in his throat. "You speak of *Tyler* as though you know him very, very well."

Something flickered in her eyes and she flushed as if knowing he had insulted her. "Jimmy is my friend." Still she remained controlled. "I have a warm feeling towards him as befitting someone who is to marry my cousin. I don't want to see him hurt. Melinda, either."

That touched a raw spot. "Are you suggesting *I* do?"

She half turned away from him so he could see her delicate winging shoulder-blades above the low back of her gown. For a moment disconcerted and thoroughly on edge, he felt a strange piercing tenderness for her youth, her beauty, and the fact he had offended her.

"I can look behind your words," she said. "I can see into your eyes. You're upset about the whole situation. Your family, too."

"Well you would know better than anybody how it all came about." He answered too harshly but he was unable to prevent himself.

Her eyes went very dark. "*I* had little part to play in it."

"Well you know," he retorted crisply. "You fit the role of enchantress."

She managed to appear genuinely bewildered. "Why ever are you saying *that?*"

"When Tyler came home he told us he'd fallen hopelessly in love with a *blond enchantress.*"

Her delicate brows rose. "Melinda *is* very pretty."

"So she is, in a conventional way," he replied bluntly. "You on the other hand have a quite different look."

Her expression gained a dismayed intensity. "You surely can't think Jimmy and I shared a romance?"

"I'm sure you dazzled him." He smiled at her, looking very dangerous and powerful, but that simply didn't occur to him.

She appeared, for her part, appalled. Perhaps she was. At being found out. "We simply didn't move in the same circles. I barely knew Jimmy until Melinda started going out with him."

"This isn't actually how she tells it." He didn't quite know *how* Melinda was telling it, but she had certainly thrown out lots of veiled hints.

One of the girl's hands fluttered to her breast. She looked for a moment enormously vulnerable. "I can't imagine what Melinda said, but I assure you you've misinterpreted it. This is ridiculous."

"Yes it is." His tone was laced with irony. "Especially as my brother is to marry your cousin in—" he lifted an arm and glanced at his watch "—under an hour. What I really have to do is shower and change. We can talk again."

*   *   *

The chapel was luminous with white flowers, roses, lilies, carnations, stephanotis, great clouds of baby's breath literally transforming it into a fairyland. The bride and her attendant looked as lovely as anyone could wish, the reception in the homestead's ballroom was sumptuous, but hectic circles of colour burned on the bridegroom's cheeks and Logan had to tell him very quietly he was drinking too much.

"Nerves, J.L.! It's not every day a man finds himself married."

Ainslie and Sandra quietly cried into lace-edged handkerchiefs. On the air was a kind of sulphur, like after a thunderstorm. The happy couple, Melinda *did* appear radiant, were to leave on the first leg of their honeymoon journey that would take them to Europe, only at the very last minute Tyler pulled their brides-maid to him and kissed her full on the lips with a kind of mad jubilation. Something that made Dame Eleanor Dangerfield turn to Logan with consternation on her imperious old face. The girl, Dana the cousin, had made a singularly good impression on her, but what in the world was *that* all about?

Logan faced Dana with it hours later when the household had finally settled. He caught her hand, risk-ing those warning tingles, drawing her into his study and shutting the door. "I have to be gone fairly early in the morning, Dana, so I'll say my goodbyes now. Your charter flight has been arranged for 1:00 p.m. I've taken the liberty of securing you your on-going ticket. You'll find it waiting for you at the terminal."

"I didn't want you to do that," she protested, as much on edge as he was.

"Nevertheless I have. My pleasure. Everything went off very well."

"It was a beautiful ceremony and the reception was superb. I must tell you Melinda and I are very appreciative of everything you've done. She was too emotional to begin to tell you."

"Perhaps she was marvelling at that kiss Tyler gave you just as they were leaving?" he said in a tone, half silk, half steel.

Colour stained her cheeks. "Tyler scarcely knew what he was doing."

"My God, the rest of us did." Now came the hard irony.

"Please, Logan, don't you see Jimmy was full of emotion?" she appealed to him

"I actually thought he was begging you to go with him." This was disastrous, but he couldn't stop.

"So it's not a marriage made in heaven—" her voice rang with pain "—but we've got to give it every chance."

He could only marvel at her stricken look. "So what does this involve?" he taunted her. "Do you plan to move out of their lives?"

She looked at him aghast. "Melinda and I are very close. We were reared as sisters."

"But Tyler fell in love with *you* first?" Anyone would.

"Tyler never fell in love with me at all." She shook her head in a kind of desperation.

"Are you sure of that?" The disbelief was thick in his voice.

"Where and when did you learn differently?" she challenged, her eyes sparkling brilliantly, a pulse in her throat at full throttle.

He shifted his gaze unwilling to admit he, too, felt

her power. "You must know it shocked a lot of people seeing Tyler reach for you?"

"He wanted comfort." She dropped her head in seeming defeat, but on pure reflex he tilted her chin.

"My dear girl, he had just married your cousin. A very sweet girl. I think *now* Tyler was on the rebound from you. Melinda did tell us he was spellbound by your beauty. I don't know whether you realise it, but your cousin has a problem with you. Sibling rivalry it's called."

"And you'd know a great deal about that yourself." She pushed his hand away, anger lilting out of her voice. "As much as I care about Melinda, she talks a great deal of nonsense at times."

"You don't mind her going off with Tyler?" Better, far better, he shut up, but he couldn't.

"All I want for them is to be happy."

"Well, *good,*" was his sardonic answer. "I don't want to have to worry about you, to tell the truth."

"Worry about *me?*" She spun so the long flowing skirt of her dress flared out around her.

It came to him with amazement his own emotions were surging dangerously. "You must see it will be better for you to get on with your life."

Again her face flamed. "If I weren't stuck in the middle of the Never-Never I'd be out of here in a second."

"Forgive me." He could hear the ringing arrogance in his apology. "You are a guest in my home."

"And you're a very powerful and dangerous man," she said, looking out at him accusingly from her great dark eyes. "It hasn't just occurred to me. I've listened to everything Jimmy has said about you."

His downward stare was more daunting than he

knew. "Tyler loves me as I love him," he said coldly. "I know he has his hangups—who doesn't?—but he knows he can always count on my support."

"Surely that's to be expected of a brother?" Her scorn was genuine.

"And what can be expected of cousins?" he countered harshly. "Cousins as close as *sisters?*"

Her slender body fairly danced with fury mixed up with a kind of anguish that showed in her eyes. He saw the bright flash in them, like a flame set to oil, then she brought up her hand incredibly to strike him. He couldn't for the life of him think why, but it made him want to laugh. He hadn't seen such spirit for ages. He caught her hand in mid-flight, his own blood aflame, then for one extraordinary never-to-be-repeated moment swept her into his arms, covering her romantic soft mouth in a kiss so raw and ruthless it later filled him with a kind of horror and self-contempt. For all her beauty and female allure she was little more than a schoolgirl.

She didn't speak afterwards, as shocked as he was and close to tears. He knew he had to keep hold of her all the time he was apologising, his senses swimming and his veins continuing to run lava. He knew she would never forgive him and God knows he had his own intense forebodings about her. Certain women because of their female power and seductiveness could bring destruction to a family.

Ainslie's long distinguished face was distorted with grief. Dana's heart ached for her but she knew from the outset Ainslie wanted no words of sympathy from her.

"That dreadful girl," Ainslie moaned, her fine skin

mottled with red. "I knew the moment I laid eyes on her she would bring grief to this family."

What matter now? Dana had thought it herself. Still she tried to defend her cousin, so ingrained with the habit. "Ainslie, Melinda is bereft. We're full of anguish. It's so dreadfully, dreadfully tragic."

"Ah don't defend her, Dana," Ainslie admonished her. "No more. We women can't fool one another. There's something twisted about my daughter-in-law. Look how she is with poor little Alice. She never loved my son, either. Why couldn't *you* have been the one?"

Dana couldn't hide her shock. "But it wasn't that way, Ainslie. Jimmy had no romantic feelings towards me."

"Tyler *loved* you," Ainslie said, sounding utterly convinced.

Dana laboured hard to correct her. "As a friend. A *good* friend."

"No, my dear." Ainslie gave her a small, sad smile. "He told me he loved you."

"Jimmy did?" Dana's shock was total.

Ainslie sighed heavily, patting Dana's hand. "Please don't call him Jimmy in my presence, dear."

Dana flushed with dismay. "Forgive me but it's what—Tyler called himself. The very last thing I want to do is upset you, Ainslie. What Tyler *meant* was, he loved me as family. Alice's godmother."

Ainslie looked obliquely at her, drying her deeply shadowed eyes. "You're much too intelligent and intuitive a young woman to say that. Tyler admired as well as loved you. Surely you know Melinda was sick with jealousy?"

Dana set her jaw against her sudden anger. Anyone who knew Melinda knew she habitually lied. "That's not possible, Ainslie.'' Dana felt like she was drowning in deception. ''Believe me on this terrible day when I say there was nothing between Tyler and me but a deep friendship. I was his confidante when—''

''When things got bad with Melinda,'' Ainslie interrupted. ''I know. Tyler told me. In those early days I prayed and prayed the marriage would work. But I hadn't reckoned on what Melinda was really like. She planned her pregnancy to trap my son.''

''But we have Alice, don't we?'' Dana pointed out with great gentleness.

''Yes, we have Alice.'' Ainslie gave a shuddering sigh. ''We have no choice but to go on, but I don't want to be near Melinda today, Dana. I don't think anyone else does, either. It's sad, but that's life. She has always pretended to be so quiet and sweet, yet all the time she's been causing trouble. The marriage would have worked had she really been what she pretended, instead Tyler's gone and we're all punished.''

Sandra was less restrained, off balance with grief and swollen-eyed.

''This is a house of mourning, Dana,'' she cried, her hazel eyes clouded with her inner rage. ''It's a good thing Melinda has chosen to hide away upstairs. I knew last night she was in a panic about fronting up. *You* had to do that for her. I know she's your cousin, but I really think you shouldn't bother with your loyalty anymore. She depends on you, I know, but she's not your friend.''

Hold the presses, Dana thought dismally. It was no news. ''Sandra, don't compound all this grief,'' she warned, leaning forward to kiss Sandra's cheek.

''I'm sorry, Dana, I can't seem to stop. What we should have stopped was the wedding. It was never destined to work out. Look at Alice, the sheer misery of that little girl. You don't think Logan's going to let Melinda take her out of our lives? A cat's a better mother. A cat is kinder.''

Dana took Sandra's hand between her own and rubbed it. It was icy cold. ''Melinda doesn't want to do that. You're Alice's family.''

''We are,'' Sandra replied fiercely, ''so we can't desert her. Melinda has never found a place in her life for Alice. Anyone would think Alice was thrust upon her instead of...''

''Alice is very important to me, as well.'' Dana led the tormented Sandra farther away from the other mourners.

''She loves you. She adores you.'' Sandra nodded her head frantically. ''She wants to belong to you. So did Tyler.''

Dana wanted to protest the truth from the rooftops. ''Sandy, why are you saying this? It makes me sick with dismay. Tyler and I were friends. That was the extent of our relationship. Why are you speaking out like this now? Why the sudden doubts?''

''And Melinda *dreamed* up all the rest?'' Sandra gave a broken laugh.

''I don't want to have to say this, but I must.'' Dana looked back at the other woman very directly. ''Melinda has a gift for twisting the truth.''

''We learned that,'' Sandra confirmed bleakly. ''She was born to breed trouble. I don't think badly of you, Dana. I can't. You're too honourable and decent. If Tyler loved you, I do, too.''

The crushing burden of misunderstanding was too much for Dana to bear. She withdrew at the first opportunity and went upstairs to Melinda's bedroom, shutting the door behind her and moving over to the huge four-poster bed where her cousin lay her golden head pressed into a mound of pillows.

"Is it *too* ghastly?" Melinda asked in a sympathetic tone.

Dana felt a powerful tide of revulsion. "Ghastly, why *wouldn't* it be ghastly? I keep seeing Jimmy striding along the beach holding Alice on his shoulders, both of them laughing. Jimmy, my God, my God, he was only twenty-eight. The family is devastated."

"That's it. Ignore *me*."

Dana heard the tremble in Melinda's voice and tried desperately to rein herself in. "I know your suffering in your way, Melinda."

"Don't think for a moment I'm not," Melinda retorted, admonishing her. She sat up, plumping the pillows behind her. "And what about you? You look wonderful in black, darling. As though you didn't know," she added archly.

Dana shook her head slowly. "I simply don't understand you, Melinda, and the things you say."

"Oh, yes, you do." Melinda gave a brittle laugh. "I've never been able to fool you, from day one. Worst of all, in some subtle way you've become my enemy."

"Ah, cut the act," Dana snapped. "I don't want to listen to your nonsense anymore."

"It's not an act, I mean it," Melinda shouted. "I bet they all hate me downstairs."

"Well, you haven't tried very hard, have you?" Dana all but abandoned herself to her disgust.

"I never did have Jimmy completely to myself, did I?" Melinda said, her voice hard and sullen.

"I know there were other women," Dana said heavily, forced to agree.

"Other women?" Melinda sneered. "The only one who counted was *you*."

"So this is how you mean to play it." Finally Dana saw the light. "Are you never going to stop playing fast and loose with the truth?"

"I'm not going to change," Melinda confirmed. "I saw the way he looked at you. The innocent temptress in our midst."

The colour drained entirely from Dana's face. "Spread that lie and I don't see how you can live with yourself. It's a bid for sympathy, isn't it? You want the family to forgive you. Let you back in. I'm to be the scapegoat. The marriage couldn't work because *I* came between you both. It won't wash, Melinda. *You* know it. *I* know it. The only feeling I had for Jimmy was friendship."

Melinda gave a bitter laugh. "You've always been too good to be true. I really can't help what anyone else thinks. They didn't get it from me. Jimmy was the stupid one. He opened his big mouth. You know Logan hates you."

Dana pulled back from the bed like it had caught fire. "He does not. We mightn't be compatible but he doesn't hate me."

"He does, too," Melinda confirmed as though she'd just heard it straight from Logan's mouth. "I'm amazed you refuse to believe it. Logan's ten times the man Jimmy was, but *you* couldn't catch him in a million light-years." There was a glitter of pure malice in Melinda's blue eyes.

Dana's breath came so hard she nearly choked. "Catch him? Aren't you mixing me up with someone else?"

At that, Melinda's cheeks burned. "You've been dying to say that all these years, haven't you?"

"It would never have helped anyone to have said it," Dana answered bluntly. "Be warned, I'm not going to allow you to make up lies about me, Melinda. And about Jimmy. I can't help what Logan thinks. You must be some sort of a monster. I've done everything I could to support you since we were kids."

"I know. You're a bred-in-the-bone do-gooder," Melinda replied almost cheerfully with her odd capacity to confound. "Logan thinks it was good old you who first captured Jimmy's heart. Which you did. But it was *later,* and all unaware. I used to watch the two of you together and enjoy a good laugh. Jimmy knew you would never look at him. Then you got engaged to your precious Gerard. What a swathe you two cut. You so blond, he so dark. Both of you so damned clever. You never did tell me what happened there."

"I couldn't love Gerard in the way he wanted," Dana said in a voice as quiet as possible. "I realise now it wasn't love. It was deep affection. Gerard deserved the lovely girl he has since married."

"And you're all friends," Melinda crowed. "That's the really funny part. Your lovely friend Lucy is a bit of an idiot if you ask me."

"You can't hurt her, Melinda," Dana said. "You can't hurt Gerard and you can't hurt me, though you've tried often enough."

Melinda's shoulders against the pillows went rigid. "I'm scared, Dana," she suddenly confessed. "I'm so terrified I'm shaking inside. What if Jimmy changed his will?"

Dana caught the panic in her cousin's voice. "You think he did?"

"Well, he didn't love me, darling." Melinda was back to mockery.

"He might have had you given him a chance. He never mentioned anything about changing his will to me. You are his widow."

"And Alice was his dear little changeling. How she ever got to be so plain I'll never know. I've been complimented on my looks all my life. Jimmy was very good-looking. Not like Logan, of course, but then, who the hell is?"

"Alice will come into her own as she matures," Dana said sharply, her condemnation of Melinda spilling out. "Ainslie is a distinguished-looking woman. Alice takes after her grandmother."

"With a face like a horse," Melinda said waspishly.

"A *thoroughbred,* that's the thing. It's terrible what you're doing to Alice, Melinda. One day you're going to bitterly regret it. You're starving her of your love."

"I am not and I never have been. I just don't pander to her like you do. In many ways she's a big disappointment to me. You might think of that while you're ticking me off. She's difficult, she's plain, and she doesn't know how to *behave.* I've had to put up with her tantrums for years on end. I've had no life. I lost all that when I married Jimmy. I thought we were going to travel the world staying in the best hotels. But he had to stay close to you and his adored family. Well close enough. No way anyone could expect me to live out here. It's like another planet. Maybe Mars."

"Until it turns into the biggest garden on earth. I must go back, Melinda," Dana said tiredly. It was impossible to get through to her cousin.

"Do that," Melinda called after her bitterly. "Don't forget to give them all my love. I'm sure you've been

answering queries about the bereaved widow around
the clock.''

By late afternoon everyone had left except two elderly
relatives who couldn't face the return journey and had
elected to retire with a light supper to be served later
in their rooms. Ainslie was at the end of her tether and
had retired, as well, taking a sedative at the behest of
her doctor. Sandra, wishing to escape for a few hours
and openly hostile to Melinda, had flown out for the
night with her boyfriend, Jack Cordell, and his family.
The Cordells owned Jindaroo Station on Mara's north-
east border, some sixty miles away. Alice, tired out by
her accumulated tears and fears, had for once climbed
quietly into her bed and instantly fell into a deep sleep
from which she was not to wake until dawn the following morning.

Left to her own devices, Dana sat on the veranda
looking over the extraordinary sweeping vista of
Mara's home gardens. It never failed to move her how
the early settlers through their sense of nostalgia had
tried to recreate something of ''home'' in a landscape
as remote from the misty beauty of the British Isles as
the far side of the moon, yet the Dangerfields had succeeded to a remarkable degree. Every last mistress of
Mara had been a passionate gardener, but it took
Ainslie to begin the long task of replacing exotics extremely difficult to get to flourish with the wonderful
natives that abounded but had hitherto been considered
too ''strange.''

Dana would never forget her first visit to Mara.
Nothing could have prepared her for the heart-stopping
sight of a magnificent green oasis in the middle of a
red desert. The splendid homestead was sheltered by

magnificent old trees planted to mark the birth of each
child through the generations. For one family to have
established all this was inspiring. Even more incredu-
lous was the garden's dimensions. Fed by underground
bores, it included its own huge informal lake with its
colony of black swans and wealth of water plants.
There were sunken rose gardens with long beds of
massed plantings and wonderful old statuary brought
out from England, native gardens, fruit gardens and
vegetable gardens all tended by a small army of
groundsmen under a Mr. Aitkinson who had been with
the family since forever and was a horticulturist of
some note. Great sheaves of flowers from Mara's gardens had covered Jimmy's casket.

At the memory, tears rushed into Dana's eyes and
she stood up, twisting her body as though trying to
shake off a great burden of sadness. She couldn't fully
take in what the family was saying about her and
Jimmy. She would have to make a great effort to remember to call him Tyler. Certainly they had grown
close over the years, their love and concern for Alice
their common bond, but to suggest Jimmy had loved
her in any romantic sense simply wasn't true. He had
never shown a hint of it in his behaviour. Indeed he
had treated her more like a sister with a tender affection. Was it possible she had been blinded by her own
immunity? Had she failed to divine his true feelings?

It was an unhappy fact Jimmy had turned to other
women for comfort and sexual release. Melinda, so ea-
ger for his lovemaking before their marriage, had inexplicably turned off physical intimacy after the birth
of their child. Or so Jimmy had thought. Dana knew
her cousin better. Even as a child Melinda, behind the
soft smiles, had been a cold and manipulative little per-

son. "Grasping" one of Dana's friends had called her. A charge that had upset Dana at the time but one she was later forced to admit was impossible to defend. The same friend had suggested to Dana that her cousin's "love" for her contained an element of deep resentment.

In her heart Dana knew it. There had been many little betrayals through the years. It was Melinda who had planted the seed. To cause doubt in them all. To lessen Dana's standing in the eyes of the family. She was the third person in a doomed relationship. Whatever Melinda's purpose, the strategy had succeeded. Dana had won over Ainslie and Sandra, all three of them naturally compatible, but as for Logan? Logan had distrusted her from day one.

Logan, too, had a failed engagement. Dana had met Phillipa Wrightsman on several occasions although she had not attended the engagement party nor had she been invited. Phillipa, as a member of the landed gentry, was eminently suitable to succeed Ainslie as mistress of Mara. But the engagement hadn't worked. No one seemed to know why. Logan never spoke about it other than to say the decision was mutual. The family wouldn't have it any girl in her right mind would reject Logan. In fact Dana, with her excellent eye, had taken note this very day Phillipa was still in love with her ex-fiancé. Logan had driven Phillipa and her family down to the airstrip some twenty minutes before with Phillipa holding on to Logan's arm. Phillipa had tried to be friendly but Dana knew she would never be regarded as anyone else but Melinda's cousin. Melinda was deeply disliked, although the extended family had tried hard to disguise it in the name of good manners.

Melinda's blond curls and big blue eyes had rarely seduced her own sex, either.

Even as Dana stood at the balcony, her hands gripping the wrought-iron railing, a jeep swept through the open gates of the main compound. Logan returning. There was no time to retreat. He brought the jeep to a halt near the central three-tiered fountain, swung out, slammed the door and took the short flight of stone steps to the homestead in two lopes.

If Dana had been asked to sum up Logan Dangerfield with one word it would have been: *electric*. He radiated power. It crackled and flew in the very air around him. She had never in her life met anyone who could equal Logan for sheer impact and she had met many high-profile people in the course of her work as a professional photographer. Though he would be amazed and not too pleased to hear it, she had a framed photograph of him in her apartment. She had taken it herself, an action shot of him on horseback, controlling his favourite stallion, Ebony King, spooked by a visitor's flyaway hat. It was a great shot. All her girlfriends who saw it thought she had to be madly in love with him. Not really believing her when she said all that had ever been between her and Logan was a kind of cold war. Nothing but that unspeakable, unbanishable kiss. Not a kiss. A punishment.

"You look terribly on edge," Logan now said, his brilliant eyes moving over her with extraordinary intensity yet that curious reserve.

"So do you," she responded tightly, taking a chair.

"God, why not? On this horrendous day." He had removed his suit jacket sometime earlier, now he jerked at his black tie, pulling it off and throwing it over the back of one of the wicker armchairs. "Where's everyone?'' He unloosened the top button of his shirt then another, exposing the strong brown column of his throat.

"Ainslie has retired," she told him quietly.

"Poor Ainslie!" His voice was deep with sympathy. "For a mother to lose her son and in such a way. Uncle George and Aunt Patricia? What about them?"

"They're played out. They're having a light supper in their room. Alice is asleep, as well. She's worn out by her tears. It's been a terrible day for her."

"I know." Under his dark copper tan was a distinct pallor. "And Melinda? I have to tell you, Dana, I hope I'm not seeing her tonight. I just couldn't take it."

"She's staying in her room." Dana's voice firmed. "She said to tell you she'll be taking the plane out in the morning."

"After the will reading, I bet. What about you?" He shot her a quick look. A recent assignment on the Great Barrier Reef had gilded her skin. It glowed like a pale golden pearl against the sombre black of her two-piece suit.

"I'll be going, as well, of course." She looked back at him in consternation.

"I thought you might think of family for once," he replied bitingly. "Ainslie and Sandra. They could do with your company."

"I can't stay here without Melinda, Logan. Surely you see that?"

"No, I *don't*," he clipped off. "The best thing you could do, Dana, is get shot of your cousin."

"And what about Alice?" she retaliated, her own brown eyes suddenly blazing. It was always like this with Logan.

He pulled out a chair and slumped into it moodily.

"Yes, yes. Poor little Alice. My heart bleeds for that child. At least when Tyler was there…" He broke off in grief and anger.

"*I'm* here, Logan." Her eyes welled with tears and she turned away abruptly so he couldn't see.

His laugh was discordant. "And we're very grateful for that. Why don't you and Alice stay on for a few days? I'm sure Melinda won't mind. She's let you take care of Alice often enough."

Dana turned, feeling a queer stab of regret. One part of her would have loved to stay but as a fellowship-winning photographer and currently "hot" property on the art scene, she had numerous commitments. "Logan, I'd do what I could," she said, "but I have assignments and a set of pictures for a Sydney showing due in. Besides, when have you ever wanted me around the place?"

His eyes were as hot and stormy as the electric blue sky. "Don't be so bloody ridiculous," he rasped.

"I'm not being ridiculous at all," she retorted, stung by his long-held attitudes. "You've never liked me, Logan, any more than I like you."

"So what do you want from me?" he taunted, deliberately trying to stir her. "What you're used to? Men who worship the ground you walk upon?"

"If that were true, we'd have an awful lot in common," she flared. "Phillipa is still in love with you.

He looked back dispassionately. "Like most women, Phillipa doesn't want to let go. She'll meet someone soon."

"I hope so, for her sake," Dana answered, suddenly sounding very cool, though it cost her dearly. "It's been three years."

"Really?" He shifted position abruptly so he could

stare at her. Face to face. "I didn't realise you kept such tabs on me."

Before she could prevent herself she arched back in her chair, her two hands gripped together. It was a significant move, one he appreciated from the mocking look on his face. "How could I not know what was happening in your life. I saw Jimmy—"

Logan winced, dangerously close to breaking loose. "Can't you say Tyler?"

"Of course I can." She took a deep breath, trying to hold on to her own escalating emotions. "But it will take time. Tyler was Jimmy to us. I suppose he was trying for a new life." She stopped abruptly, continued in a gentler tone. "He used to love to talk about you. About Mara. When you were boys. He had such great love for you, Logan. Such respect and admiration."

His knuckles gripped until they gleamed bone white. "But I wasn't able to help him at the end?" There was a whole world of regret in it.

"He was a grown man," Dana offered in the spirit of reconciliation, though every nerve in her body was on edge. This had been such a terrible day for everybody. She could see the depth of Logan's grief.

"And he had the great misfortune to marry Melinda. Just about any other girl would have made a go of it." It was said not in anger, more a point of fact.

Dana sighed, a sad and haunted look in her eyes. "Tragically they weren't suited to each other at all." She put back a hand, lifted her long hair away from her hot nape, unaware a beam of sunlight was streaming through it turning it to a waterfall of ash gold. When she looked back at Logan, some expression in his eyes made her heart pound. It wasn't anger or even the sexual hostility that often flared between them, but something more primitive and dangerous. "Is something wrong?" she asked, a betraying tremor in her voice.

He shoved back his chair, stood up, all six foot three, flexing the muscles in his back. No one better than Logan to throw a long shadow. "Sometimes I can't take your feminine wiles," he growled.

She stared up at him in amazement. "I've never met anyone in my life who fires up like you do," she protested. "*What* feminine wiles?"

He shot her a sharp, potent glance. "Hell, every time I see you, you've got a new one. I guess you're the sort of woman a man would do anything to have." There was condemnation mixed up with the grudging admiration.

"Well, I haven't made my mark on you." Dana, in her turn, jumped up from her chair. What *was* this between her and Logan? A kind of love-hate? Nothing else came to mind.

"On the contrary, you made your mark," he said moodily. "You were dangerous as little more than a schoolgirl," he brooded. "Now you're a woman and ten times more alluring. Ah, what the hell! Let's get away from the house," he said with a kind of urgency. "Change your clothes. We'll ride. I feel like galloping to the very edge of the earth."

CHAPTER THREE

AND gallop he did, with the kind of desperate anguish
Dana shared. Though an excellent rider, well mounted,
she couldn't hope to match him, but she drove her
beautiful spirited mare until her aching head started to
clear and the awesome splendour of the sky entered her
blood.

A storm was coming. The very air sizzled with the
build up of electricity. On the western horizon huge
mushrooming clouds of purple and silver were shot
with flame as the slanting rays of the sun cut a great
swathe through them. Even the sandhills on the desert
border glowed like furnaces against the eerie, super-
charged sky. It was a barbaric scene and, despite her
grief, Dana felt a rising wave of excitement.

Birds, great flights of them, were coming from all
points of the compass, splitting the air with their cries.
They passed overhead at lightning speed, homing into
the shadowy sanctuary of swamps, billabongs and lagoons that crisscrossed the vast landscape. The air vi-
brated with the whirr of a million brilliantly coloured
wings. Often such spectacular atmospheric effects came
to nothing or little more than a fine beading of rain-
drops, but Dana could tell from the violent and acid-
green streaks in the heatwaves this was going to be big.
She believed wholeheartedly the storm was sent to
mark Tyler's passing.

Logan thought so, too. She could see it in his face,
dark, brooding, despairing.

"We'd better take shelter," he shouted to her, lifting his voice as the first clap of thunder rolled across the heavens. Even as they turned the horses towards the line of shallow caves the aboriginals called Yamacootra, a jagged spear of lightning flashed through the low canopy of clouds. The caves right in the heart of Mara were prehistoric sites, hallowed ground inhabited by Dreamtime spirits, the largest of them pitched high at the dome allowing easy access to a man as tall as Logan. It was there they headed. Incandescent light seething around them as they galloped up the slope. Once a pair of brolgas shot up from a huge clump of cane grass, causing Dana's mare to rear in sudden fright. So strong was the tension in the atmosphere she thought she would be thrown but Logan closed in on her, grabbing at the reins and subduing the mare with his superior strength.

When they arrived at the entrance Logan settled the excited, sweating horses in an overhang partially screened by high tangled vegetation and a spindly ghost gum growing out of rock. A bank of flowering lantana all but blocked the mouth of the cave but Logan ripped it aside as the driving wind turned the fallen leaves into a whirlwind of green and purple. Temporarily blinded by the whirling cloud Dana lurched over a half-hidden rock, clawing at Logan's shirt to keep her balance.

"Here, steady, I've got you." His strong arm whipped around her and he muffled a violent oath as a disturbed goanna, fully six feet in length, shot out of the cave opening like a projectile, hissing at them hoarsely.

Dana held a hand over her face for protection. Her heart was thudding behind her ribs. Logan was holding her so painfully close she had to grit her teeth against a whole range of electrifying sensations.

Logan shouted at the giant lizard, watching it race down the slope. "Go on, get. I just hope he hasn't got a mate." Shielding her body with his own, Logan entered the cave, his eyes darting swiftly around the interior. There was plenty of light now as brilliant spears of lightning forked down the sky. The ancient stone walls glowed with ochres, red, yellow, burnt orange, black and white and charcoal.

Moving very quietly, Dana moved back into the cave, further unnerved by the presence of little lizards that dashed across the sand at her feet. This wasn't the first time she had been inside the cave. Logan had permitted her access several times, but for once she felt threatened by the forces that were at work all around them. The cave was eerie, hushed, dim except for the brilliant flashes of light. There was hardly an inch of wall and roof space that wasn't covered in drawings of totemic beings and creatures. Like the great undulating coils of the Rainbow Snake executed on ochres, stark white and charcoal. As the lightning flashed, the snake seemed to move, causing Dana an irrational spasm of fear. She continued to move about, trying to cover her agitated state of mind though it must have been obvious to Logan. A great crocodile was incised and painted on the wall, its broad primeval snout peering out of what appeared to be a clump of reeds. A crocodile in the desert? Either the aboriginal artist was a nomad or the drawing dated back to the inland sea of prehistory. In a sort of desperation she stopped and focused on it, murmuring more to herself than Logan who was standing at the entrance of the cave staring out at the brilliant pyrotechnics.

"I'd love to photograph all this. It would sell like hot cakes."

"The answer is no," he threw over his shoulder.

"I understand why."

"That's why you've been allowed in."

"No need to snap my head off." Damn, his tone of voice wasn't the problem. It was being alone with him. Both of them usually took care it didn't happen. He was standing quite still but his whole aura told her he was on full alert. Would she ever find an answer to the mystery that was Logan Dangerfield? The rain was coming down harder now, falling in a solid silver sheet from the overhang. They might have been sealed in some ancient temple.

For the first time she noticed Logan's tanned skin, taut over his chiselled bones, was sheened with rain. His blue-black hair was damp, as well, curling over the collar of his denim shirt. He always wore his thick waving hair full and a little long, not wasting much time looking for hairdressers. He didn't have to. Most women would give anything to have hair like that. Once or twice she had seen him with a beard when he'd been away for weeks on end visiting the outstations. The sight of him *wild* with his blue eyes blazing had all but dried up her mouth. She realised now she had always revelled in his arrogance and splendid male beauty even as she buried it in the wary banter they indulged in.

Another bolt of thunder flashed across the heavens, then a flash of lightning so harsh it was almost withering, filled the cave.

Dana in sheer reaction fell to her knees holding both hands across her ears.

"It's okay." Logan tried to comfort her though he

spoke between his clenched teeth. He crossed to her, easing himself down on his haunches. "Dana?"

She didn't answer, her ash-blond head down between her arms. He took a thick silky fistful of hair, lifting her face to him. He had never seen her eyes so huge, so dark, pools of an answering tension. Her body might have been wired it was so electric to his touch. "No need to panic. You've seen a storm before." Even as he spoke his words were almost drowned out by the violent crack of thunder that crashed like a giant drum. There were massive thunder-heads backlit by flashes that rivalled the brilliance of the sun. If the rain kept coming, all the gullies would be overflowing, bringing precious water to the eternally thirsty land. A strong wind had blown up outside the cave, parting the silver curtain of rain so that it flew into the mouth of the cave. They were forced to pull back into the interior. Logan, with one arm, half dragged her across the sand.

Today of all days he thought he could just lose his last hold on control, do something both of them would regret all their lives. But his feeling for her ran contrary to his will. It was an urgent pulse drumming deep inside of him. Desire that had been buried deep since the first time he had taken her in his arms. "Damn you, Dana," he said explosively.

"And damn you, too," Dana answered with equal fervour, trying to break his strong grip. "I can't bear to be with you, Logan."

The knowledge tore at him. "So what are you waiting for?" He jerked her to her feet, overcome by sexual hostility that fairly crackled and spat. "This isn't the biggest storm I've ever seen. In a minute or so it will be all over. You can ride."

That sent her wild. "Why do you hate me?" she

hurled at him. "Melinda told me you did but I wouldn't believe it. But it's *true*. You're so cruel. Then I see another side of you. You're so bloody charming, so bloody *perverse!*"

His blue eyes blazed an ominous warning. "I don't hate you, Dana. Far from it. But my heart and mind are locked and barred against you."

"Why?" She cursed herself for asking but she was obsessed with knowing. "Can't you tell me *why?*"

"You've known since the day I met you," he returned harshly. "For what happened between you and Tyler. Melinda wasn't alone in this disaster. *Your* hold on Tyler was too powerful for him to break."

Any sense of balance disappeared entirely. She closed her eyes, shuttering them with her lashes. "What you're saying is terrible. It's so ugly."

"Yes, it *is,*" he agreed with terrible irony. "You may not have broken any code of honour but there were consequences, Dana. Consequences for us all. You were forbidden to Tyler, just as you're forbidden to me."

Forbidden? Was that the awful truth? "You're crazy," Dana said in dull despair.

"He told me you were the best thing in his life," Logan said just as bleakly.

"The best thing in his life was *Alice*." Her voice picked up power. "My only role was *friend*. Can't you get that through your fool head?" A dull roaring had begun in her ears. Fool? Logan Dangerfield. What was she saying?

"I don't give a damn for words, Dana."

"You're calling me a liar? I don't like that."

His blue eyes *burned*. "Then how come Tyler spoke so lovingly of you to us all? Ainslie, Sandra, me. Even

Alice. You were in all his letters. I can show them to you. Hell, Dana. He was my brother. I understood him.''

''He couldn't have said we were *lovers*. He could never have said that,'' Dana waivered, wondering if she had ever known Jimmy at all.

''*Were* you?'' Logan caught her face between his hands, forced her to look at him.

''I would swear on his grave.'' She was trembling so violently she thought she might fall.

''Do you mean that?'' He shook her as though unable to deal with his anger.

''Of course I mean it. Why are you trying to ruin my life? Why are you trying to force this role of seductress on me?''

''Because I have to *know*.''

''Why is it so terribly important to you?'' she demanded. ''You act as if you can't stand it.'' In another minute she knew she'd either cry or lunge at him.

''Maybe I *can't*.'' His voice was very bitter. ''I knew the minute you stopped my breath with your beauty you would know how to wreck lives.''

She felt ravaged, full of pain. What he was saying was monstrous.

''I want to leave.'' Dana held up her hand as if to ward off danger.

''I'm not going to stop you,'' he rasped.

''Because you're afraid. The great Logan Dangerfield, master of all he surveys, is afraid. Afraid of a woman.'' Hostility flooded her, an aching desire to punish him as he punished her. ''You know in your heart there was nothing between Jimmy and me, but you have to tear at me anyway. You know why? Because you don't want to answer to your own desires.

It must be really bad for you to want a woman you profess to despise.''

It was a moment of such tremendous tension Dana feared a dizzy spell. What was happening was more powerful than either of them. Adrenaline coursed through her overheated veins, so her body flushed. She turned on her heel, determined to rush out into the driving storm, but he came after her, locking a steely arm around her, staring down into her face framed by the blond turbulence of her hair.

''Don't be a damned fool,'' he said, feeling on this day of all days just touching her would set off a landslide.

''Better the storm than you,'' Dana cried tempestuously, feeling all the air was being sucked out of her body. Didn't he know his long fingers were cupping her breast?

''Dana, don't do this. *Don't.*'' His nerves were so jangled his hands were rough, but she continued to struggle as if she didn't care, more invited it. Her struggles and the high soft moans that went with it like a keening bird, only served to inflame him.

Finally he lost it. Lost whatever had held him in check all these years. Furiously, a driven man, he spun her into his arms, his mouth moving with insatiable hunger all over her face, her temples, her eyes, her cheeks, her breathtaking mouth, her high arched throat, bending her backwards until he could taste the sweet satin swell of her breast. He knew he shouldn't give in to this but the whole catastrophe of the day had shattered him. She was Dana. She was Woman. She was Fantasy. A liberation from the black well of grief. He wanted her even if she detested him.

But Dana, too, was in the relentless grip of passion.

She had always known this man could break her heart. Hadn't their relationship always been fraught with intensities? She knew she would bitterly regret this. But for now…for now… In his way he was an irresistible force. Her body was responding to him like it responded to nobody else and never would. She realised in a moment of terrible truth she loved him. That all the emotional ambiguities had nothing to do with her deepest driven secret. She wanted him as badly as he wanted her, both of them wholly dependant on the other to reaffirm Life.

His mouth and the questing urgency of his hands left her breathless, half crazed. For all they had tried, what was about to happen could not be averted. It was even a release to get it out into the open, the dream after midnight become reality.

She was lying on the sand, feeling its coolness against her heated skin. She saw Logan bending over her, his dynamic dark face all taut planes and angles, his blue eyes blazing like the jewels in some primitive mask. Hadn't she known in her heart of hearts this was going to happen? She had hidden from the danger, now she was mad to embrace it.

But it was all *wordless*. Only the air thrummed with the electricity their bodies generated and the soft sound of the moans that bordered on anguish. As a lover he was extraordinary, more extraordinary than in all the little fantasies she had kept to herself.

When his mouth found her nipple it set off an avalanche of pleasure. She had to gasp aloud. Excitement was building so rapidly she could hardly remember to breathe. This was the perfect way of blotting out pain and grief. But at such a risk! Her stubborn resistance to him and the power he projected had been her perfect camouflage. Now this headlong surrender. The *enormity* of it. The intense fear and the rapture. Sensation was obscuring everything. Any need for caution. All she was aware of was her overpowering hunger for him. With a few sweeping motions he removed the rest of her clothing. His blue eyes burned at the sight of her body so perfectly designed for a man's loving. They moved over her so intensely he might have been memorising every inch of her, the fine pores of her skin.

Then he was making love to her with such passion yet a curious underlying tenderness that left her dazed with wonder. Both of them had dropped all form of pretence; the masks they had kept in place for so long.

While the rain continued to drum down on the parched earth and the cave was filled with white-hot flashes of intermittent light, the fire that was inside of them burst into a conflagration that finally gave expression to the bewildering pain/pleasure that had plagued them for so long.

This was ecstasy even if they had lost all sense of the morrow.

Another secret.

It was Dana's first waking thought. Around her was silence and the grey pearly light of pre-dawn. As the light brightened the birds would begin to sing in their trillions but for now the silence rang like a hammer on her heart.

Impossible to describe her night. It had been full of fragmentary-coherent dreams and heart-stopping moments when she awoke with a convulsive gasp thinking Logan's hands were caressing her. Her face flushed with colour at the memory and she turned sideways burying her head in the mound of pillows that smelled so beautifully of the native boronia that perfumed the linen press.

Yesterday had been the most traumatic day of her life. It had started so grimly with Jimmy's funeral yet ended in a dazzling ecstasy that redefined life. Two separate momentous experiences. She wasn't a virgin. She and Gerard had shared a warm, caring relationship which she gradually came to understand was not the passionate overwhelming love she really craved. It was she who had broken off the engagement knowing in her heart the right person was out there for both of them. And so it had turned out. Gerard had found his Lucy, but the man who held her under his spell was already in her life. A man who until yesterday had been armoured in discipline, authority, control.

And after the bubble burst and they came back to cold reality?

Neither of them seemed ready to handle what had happened, accepting no amount of mind power could ever wipe it out. For as long as their lovemaking had lasted, both of them had lost all thought of anything but one another. They had breached the iron rule. To keep their physical and psychological distance.

What now?

So deeply was Dana immersed in her thoughts it took a little time for her to register a small voice was calling her name.

Alice.

Dana sprang up from the bed, pulling on her robe as she went.

"Why, darling girl, whatever's the matter?"

Alice stood just outside the door dressed in one of the pretty pin-tucked batiste nighties Dana had bought for her as a balance to the "sensible" apparel Melinda favoured. Her dear plain little face was streaked with tears and her light brown hair free of its plait stuck out in a tangled nimbus around her head. She went straight into Dana's arms, hugging her.

"I went into Mummy's room but she told me to go away. It isn't time to get up. She said she's sick of me and my silly fears. She's not going to look after me anymore."

Shockingly, it was something Melinda said often. Neither Dana nor Jimmy had been able to stop her.

"Mummy doesn't mean it, darling," Dana soothed. "I expect she's still very tired and sad. This is a bad time for all of us."

"It's worse for Daddy." Alice's voice broke on a sob. "Why did he have to die? I'll never forgive him."

Gently Dana drew the child through the door and shut it after her, feeling the grief and frustration that was in the child's small frame.

"It was a terrible accident, Ally. Daddy had no control over what happened to him." Which sadly wasn't strictly true. "He would never have left you. He loved you."

"Then why didn't he stay? Now I'll be more different than ever. I won't have a Daddy."

Dana couldn't answer that. Although she hadn't the slightest doubt Melinda would remarry soon. Melinda had never felt secure on her own. "Hop in with me," Dana invited. "I'll give you a cuddle."

Alice expelled a soft shuddery sigh. "That will be lovely. There was a beastie in my room."

Assorted beasties and bogeymen had long plagued Alice during the hours of darkness. She was a sensitive, imaginative child and, it had to be faced, emotionally disturbed.

"Wasn't your night-light on?" Dana asked, pulling up the covers and settling the little girl against the pillows.

"Mummy doesn't like me to have the night-light, Dana. You know that. She always scolds me. She said it was all your fault filling my head with silly stories."

Dana stroked the fringe from Alice's eyes. "Don't worry, darling, I'll speak to Mummy about it. She doesn't quite realise how much imagination you've got. Lots of children don't like the dark. It's always been part of childhood. A lot of adults don't like it, either. It's nothing to be worried about."

"I like the light on," Alice insisted, already snuggling down. "Dana, do you think I could come to live with you instead of just for a visit?"

Dana tried to cover up her sadness. This was a terrible state of affairs.

"Darling, how could I deprive Mummy of her little girl?"

Alice gave her a very grave adult stare. "She wouldn't miss me. She said she might put me in a boarding school while she travels the world."

This was entirely new to Dana. "When did she say this?"

She got into bed beside Alice while Alice moved into the crook of her shoulder. "Yesterday. She said I was part of the problem with her marriage."

"Oh, rubbish!" Dana couldn't help herself. It just burst out. Melinda depended on her for many things. She would have to flex what little muscle she had for Alice's sake.

"You're really funny when you get mad," Alice giggled. "Daddy said to me once, if I'm not around, find Dana."

"Well, I am your godmother," Dana answered finally.

"And you love me." Alice gave a great sigh of belonging. "Sometimes I really am scared of Mummy. Even the kids at school think she's awful."

Dana pondered on that. "Awful when she's so young and pretty?"

Alice squirmed. "Miss Eldred said, 'It's just awful what she's doing to that child.'"

It was amazing how she caught the teacher's tones. "Surely she wasn't talking about Mummy?"

Alice shot her another look. "Some days when Mummy picks me up she's in a really bad mood."

"Why on earth didn't you tell me?" Dana was appalled.

"You might be so angry at Mummy you might never come to see her and she wouldn't let me see you," Alice answered in her extraordinary way.

"Alice, I would never desert your mother. Or you," Dana said fervently. "You must believe that. Your mother and I have been together since we were little girls. She's almost my sister."

"Then why does she tell you so many lies?"

The skin on Dana's head actually prickled. "Whatever do you mean?"

Alice looked back in genuine puzzlement. "Daddy said she did. Didn't he tell you?"

Dana took her time replying. "Listen, cherub, I hate to say this but too many people have been doing too much talking in front of you. Why don't you curl up now and close your eyes. It's going to be a long, tiring day, I'm afraid. You'll need your sleep."

"Can't I stay awake and listen to the birds? They're so beautiful."

Dana felt a great rush of affection. "The birds will sing for you another day, sweetheart. Get your rest now. We have a lot of travelling to do."

Alice obediently composed herself, giving an exhausted little yawn. "I hope I'll be as beautiful as you are, Dana, when I grow up."

Dana gave the little girl a hug. "Darling, you're going to be a lovely person to be with."

"I want to have a light about me, like you," Alice breathed, her lashes coming down to rest on her cheeks. "Like the picture of an angel."

"That's lovely, darling." Dana was touched.

"Daddy said about the light, but I know exactly what he meant." Alice suddenly opened her eyes and turned her head along the pillow. "Take care of me, Dana?"

"I'll take care of you as long as I live," Dana said staunchly.

"Swear you'll live a long, long time." There was a sudden rush of tears into Alice's big brown eyes.

"You don't have to worry about that." Dana fought to keep her voice steady. "I'm going to live until I'm a hundred and I get a telegram from the Queen."

"Does she really send a telegram?" Alice giggled.

"Yes, she does," Dana said very softly into the little girl's ear.

"Thank you, Dana," Alice answered simply, and almost immediately fell asleep.

Alice was still sleeping when Dana went down to find herself a cup of coffee. The house was quiet, but Mrs. Buchan, the housekeeper, was in the kitchen making preparations for the day.

"So, can I get you a cup of tea, Dana?" she asked as Dana came quietly through the door.

"A cup of coffee would be lovely. Here, let me get

it.'' Dana put a gentle hand on the older woman's shoulder, hearing the uncontrollable tremor of grief in the housekeeper's voice. Mrs. Buchan, in her mid-fifties, had been in the family's employ since she was a girl. Her husband, Manny, Logan's overseer, had started his working life on the station as a young jack-eroo. Both of them had watched Tyler grow up.

''Toast, dear?'' Mrs. Buchan breathed deeply to calm herself.

''No, I think I'll go for a little walk.''

''How about Alice?''

''Don't worry. She'll sleep for a while yet. She woke up early and came into me.''

''You tell me where that little girl would be without you.'' Mrs. Buchan shook her head sadly.

Outside in the brilliant early morning sunshine, Dana walked down the drive, feeling the crunch of gravel beneath her shoes. There wasn't a single cloud in the sky. It was a deep vivid blue. A sense of foreboding hung over her, the feeling that life was rushing out of her control. She had an acute sense, too, of her own sensuality. Not so long ago she thought she had discovered love with Gerard, but compared to what she had experienced in that explosive storm it now appeared very quiet and safe. Logan had taught her more about her own body than she had learned in a lifetime. She had discovered herself as he had discovered her, unlocking all her closely held secrets. For that time in the cave there hadn't been one tiny part of her that hadn't responded to his touch. Passion at that level was stupendous. It was also perilous. How, for instance, was she going to live without it?

CHAPTER FOUR

RESTLESSLY, Dana veered off towards the lake. She could see the exquisite black swans sailing across its glassy green surface with a flotilla of ducks and other waterfowl in attendance. The dense green perimeter of reeds was illuminated by large stands of day lilies, strap-leafed iris and the water-loving arum lilies with their handsome velvety white spathes. It all looked so peaceful, so beautiful, *eternal,* when Jimmy was gone. He had paid a terrible penalty.

She couldn't fathom why he had told his family of a depth of feeling for her, which he had never shown. Of necessity because of their common bond of love and protectiveness for Alice, they had been drawn closely together. Both had tried very hard to shield Alice from a mother who was cold to her.

Trying to find some defence for Melinda, Dana had come to the conclusion Melinda had been emotionally crippled by the early loss of her parents. Dana had once heard her own mother say Melinda was incapable of showing affection. But she was bonded to Dana. Their kinship made Dana unique and Dana had always made allowances for her cousin. They all had. Perhaps in retrospect it had been a mistake. A little toughening up might have made Melinda a more complete person.

Jimmy's death had precipitated a crisis. Alice had lost the loving, caring parent. It was a bruising reality Melinda could and would not show Alice the affection every child needed. Such coldness and Alice's obvious unhappiness troubled every sensitive person who came into their orbit. Dana herself couldn't count the number of times she had felt its chilling effect. Melinda was such a very difficult person. It was because of this Dana had felt compelled to build up a supportive relationship not only for Alice but for Jimmy, who had suffered in his own way. Perhaps her best efforts had complicated things terribly. Without Jimmy to explain his precise emotional attachment, the family might always believe she had deliberately allowed his feelings for her to develop. Truly it looked a hopeless dilemma.

She didn't hear Logan's approach until he was almost up to her, then she turned, her velvety brown eyes almost black with intensity. It came to her with anguish that she wanted him to gather her into his arms, but from the expression on his face, yesterday might never have happened.

"Have you decided what you're going to do?" he asked tautly.

Even the set of his body had a daunting authority. She looked away across the lake, her heart beating painfully. "If I could stay, Logan, I would."

"So what's so damned important to take you off?"

They were caught in the old minefield of antagonism. "I have a career. A successful career, but I don't have a fortune behind me. Not like you."

"I'll take care of that," he said curtly.

"I know you would, but nothing could persuade me to take money from you, Logan."

"Dana, please." He took hold of her shoulders, turned her to him. "Ainslie is desperately in need of comfort. Sandra, too. You can help."

"I know that." Dana's eyes filled with tears. "And I'm so terribly sad. Please don't be angry with me,

Logan. I'm so upset myself, I feel I want someone to take care of *me*.''

"I'll take care of you until the cows come home," he clipped off. "God, Dana, if I let you, you'd have me eating out of your hands."

Incredulously she heard his words, assimilating them through every cell of her body. "But you can't handle that?" she questioned. What was power without love?

His brilliant gaze was the distillation of his passionate nature. "You're running, too, Dana," he told her bluntly. "Hell, you can't wait to get away. But neither of us is going to forget what happened."

"Knowing you, Logan, you'll give it your best shot." She couldn't prevent the upsurge of bitterness.

He let out a sigh that seemed filled with terrible doubts. "It's going to be a long time before I can part you in my mind from Tyler."

"You've just got to be Number One," she said in a low, weary tone.

"So what are you telling me?" he challenged her fiercely.

"I'm telling you *nothing*. You've already decided what you want to believe."

Her eyes were so dark, so beautiful, they could hide many secrets. He wanted desperately to know them all.

She half turned as her voice broke, hair and skin gleaming in the vivid shimmering light. She could taste the pain it was so intense.

"Dana." He came after her immediately, catching hold of her bare arm. "I'm sorry. God, I'm sorry. I don't even know what I'm saying. We're all hurting. I'm only asking you to use your gift."

"Gift, what gift?" She wasn't comforted by his

touch. She was on fire. Both of them were still on the thin edge of control.

"People want to talk to you, Dana," he said, his eyes searching her face. "They want to confide in you. I suppose it's called healing."

"But it's Alice who's most in need of me now."

"And how are any of us going to find a way around Melinda? No court will take a child off its mother unless the charges are very serious. Melinda may be damned awful to Alice, but it's emotional abuse and it's mostly hidden. How the hell did you have such a ghastly cousin anyway?"

Dana didn't allow herself to consider she had asked herself the same question. "You've always been rough on her," she accused him.

"I agree." His tone was unapologetic. "I don't seem capable of hiding my dislike. Melinda wrecked my brother's life. She tried to wreck this family. She's turning my little niece into a real mess. Frankly, I find that very hard to stomach. What's more, I'm sick to death of listening to you defend her."

"And I'm sick of listening to you." Dana stopped abruptly, afraid she was about to crumble.

"Then isn't it hell for us to want one another so badly?" he retaliated. "I couldn't bear the thought of you out of my life, yet I don't know how to reach you. You're very valuable to us, Dana. We just can't do without you."

"Valuable? I don't deserve that." His words stirred her so much, her heart pounded in her chest. He was alternatively sharp then seductive. No wonder she was in such a state of constant emotional flux. "I know I'm the intermediary between Melinda and the family."

His expression softened. "Alice is in trouble, Dana. You know that, don't you?"

"Of course I do." She bit her lip.

"I can't walk softly around Melinda. Alice is my brother's child, my niece, a Dangerfield. I'm going to make sure she has a good life."

"And I'm going to help you, Logan," Dana responded with fervour. "I promise you I'll have a serious talk with Melinda."

He groaned, his eyes fierce. "I've heard all about your serious talks. I know how much you love Alice, how much she loves you, but in the end all the talk turns out to be a monologue. When has Melinda ever *listened?*"

It was true. "So *you* talk to her." Dana's voice rose. "You're all powerful."

"I intend to," he said decisively. "Melinda will be financially secure for the rest of her life, but she's not getting what she may have counted on. I've seen to that."

"How?" Dana was completely thrown off stride.

"I had a damned good talk to Tyler last time he was home," Logan told her tersely. "As a family we haven't been wasting our time all these years. We've worked hard to hold on to all we've got. The bulk of the money will be held in trust for Alice. I administer that trust, as you know."

"So there's a new will?"

"There is, my lady. I don't mind your knowing. If Melinda is smart, she'll accept it. It will advantage her nothing going out on the attack. I should tell you, too, so you won't get too emotional. Tyler left a legacy to you."

The shock of it almost sent her reeling. *"No."*

"You didn't know about it?" He smiled tightly, like a tiger.

Her face flamed and she was sorely tempted to hit him. "God, Logan, I hate you."

His handsome mouth twitched in bleak humour. "Sometimes that's the way I feel about you. It's rather a lot of money," he added.

"I don't want it." Her turbulent emotions matched his exactly.

"Maybe you could even quit work," he suggested.

"Go on. Have your hateful fun," she cried.

"It would be the only fun I could have at a time like this," he pointed out grimly. "I don't think Melinda is going to like it."

"Melinda can think what she damned well likes." Dana was so angry she fairly trembled. "She does anyway. I don't want to say this, but she lies."

"No kidding."

"Why are we fighting, Logan?" she asked bleakly.

"It seemed like the best solution up until now." It sounded unbearably cynical but at that moment he wanted her so badly he clenched his fists until his knuckles whitened. His brother's death was a terrible tragedy and Dana was his good and beautiful friend.

At the look in his eyes, the half-expected rejection, something seemed to die in her. "I'm going back to the house, Logan," she said.

"That's just what I'm doing," he said.

"Then why don't you take another route?" Her voice was cold and dismissive.

He reached for her, holding her still without any physical effort. "Are you telling me what I can do on my own land?"

She tried to pull away. "I sure am. You're like one of those feudal barons, aren't you?"

"Not that I'm aware," he said coolly, but his blue eyes burned.

"Oh, yes, the whole persona fits you perfectly, just like a second skin."

"Then surely I can demand anything of any beautiful woman who passes my way?" he suggested with the powerful urge to fold her in his arms.

"It's part of it, yes," she hit back.

"Like yesterday?" He was so angry, for a moment his grip tightened painfully.

"I suppose now you think you can have me anytime you want." She was shocked at herself but determined to say it.

"Leave it there, Dana," he warned, his eyes fixed on her.

"It may be years before I have another opportunity," she retorted in bitter irony.

"All right, then." Like yesterday, his strong will fled him, leaving only the desperate hunger he believed nothing else could fill. He swept her into his arms, silencing her lovely mouth with a kiss that was without a skerrick of tenderness, holding the kiss powerfully until her furious resistance yielded in sheer surrender and her own needs were utterly betrayed. When he released her, her face was flaming and her dark eyes sheened with tears.

"You brute!" When she had let herself fall fathoms into that kiss.

"Tell me something I don't know," he said with a kind of self-contempt. "I've always wanted to make love to you, Dana. Didn't you know? Stretching right back to the day when you simply burst into my life like some exotic flower.''

Want? What was want when she needed so much more from him? ''Nevertheless you made sure you kept me at a great distance.''

''I know I *attempted* to.'' His voice was suddenly wry.

''And succeeded rather well. You even got yourself engaged to Phillipa.''

''And I'm very fond of her, but it wasn't the classic love at first sight. Maybe it even had something to do with the fact you were marrying your...Jeremy, wasn't it?''

''Gerard, as you very well know.'' A sudden wind tore at her hair skeined out around her face, causing her to turn away.

''So both of us made a mistake.''

''I like that, Logan. You making a mistake,'' she said in response.

''I don't mean to make another.''

She had begun walking, now she turned on her heel. ''Does that hold some message for me?'' she asked, her face lit by pride.

''You're welcome to see one in it if you like.''

She made a sound of distress and shook her head. ''We can never be together five minutes without this happening.''

It was perfectly true, and under the truth a very good reason. He closed the short space between them. ''And I apologise. Most of it is my fault. But it's just as I told you, I have warring feelings about you, Dana.''

''It's damned hard to live with,'' she said bitterly.

''For you and for me.'' He caught her hand, raised

it to his mouth in one of his totally disconcerting gestures. "I didn't want to upset you. I want you to stay."

"As Alice's comforter, or your mistress?" she asked, unable to resist it, but dazed at the thought.

"Well…both."

Some note in his voice made her look up at him sharply, only to find him smiling at her, that rare, charm-the-birds-out-of-the-trees smile that so illuminated his dark face.

"You're insufferable." She was losing the battle to fight his strong aura.

"I know." He tipped up her chin, kissed her briefly but with a haunting sympathy that stayed with her for the rest of the day.

The will reading went badly. Melinda sat white-faced with bitter resentment as Logan read through the four page document, mute until the moment when Logan announced in dispassionate tones Dana's legacy. Then hell broke loose. Melinda rose so swiftly from her chair that if it hadn't been for its substantial weight she would have sent it flying. As it was, her leather armchair rolled back on its casters, scraping the parquet around the Persian rug.

"I don't believe this." For the first time Melinda showed the anger and hostility she usually kept so carefully under wraps.

"All of us are aware Tyler thought very highly of Dana," Logan said, his handsome face without expression.

"Felt highly of her! Is that what it was?" Melinda was totally unable to accept she was not the main beneficiary let alone Dana had been left a considerable sum of money.

"Please sit down, Melinda," Dana begged. "I won't, of course, be accepting it."

"Of course you *will*," Logan cast her a brief glance. "Tyler counted on you for a great deal."

"He was in love with her!" Inexplicably Melinda laughed as if at a joke. "He revelled in her company, the warmth he wouldn't let me give him. I never counted on my own cousin ruining my marriage."

While Dana drew a sharp breath preparatory to answering, Ainslie burst in. "I think you took care of that yourself, Melinda."

"I did not!" Melinda was too far gone to care. "She was always around us. I can still hear their laughter in my ears. Do you think I'd speak like this if it weren't true?"

"Yes," Dana answered without hesitation. "I've always supported you, Melinda, but I'm not prepared to let you destroy my good name. Stop this unforgivable offence right now. I want to be cleared fully. Jimmy—" She corrected herself immediately. "*Tyler* and I were friends. Our common bond was Alice."

"Before God it's true," Melinda announced ringingly. "I even caught you one time."

A deep unstoppable anger took hold of Dana. She felt she could protest her innocence forever and never be believed. She shot out of her chair like an avenging angel, grasping her cousin's upper arms tightly. "You'll never drag me down, Melly," she promised. "I'll never understand why you want to."

"If you hadn't been around he would have come back to me," Melinda exclaimed with a high moral tone.

"Well, you had to make sure we all knew," Logan said in a harsh voice. "Now that you've got that off your chest, would you mind resuming your seat, Melinda? There's more to get through. Despite your disappointment I'm sure you're going to be very comfortable with five million. Tyler's main concern was for Alice.''

''I can't see why she needs all that money when she has you to look after her,'' Melinda retorted, her pale blue eyes almost colourless with anger. ''I know I can fight this.''

''I would advise you not to,'' Logan looked at her for a space of time. ''I want it on record we'll continue to exercise our rights as Alice's family. We'll want to see her and have a say in her education.''

''Please, Melinda,'' Ainslie implored as Melinda's expression slid into one of regained bargaining power. ''We must all co-operate for Alice's sake. My little granddaughter is all that is left to me of Tyler. I did love him so.''

''He wasn't the husband I imagined he was going to be,'' Melinda continued in the flat ugly tone she had always kept from the family. ''As for your rights with Alice? Well, we'll see. I'm not dependent on you Dangerfields anymore. You never wanted me from day one when you were always so affable to Dana. You should have thrown her out.''

''For having a heart, Melinda?'' Logan challenged, and his voice reverberated around the room. ''Her loving manner with Alice alone would have endeared her to us. You're so anxious to belittle your cousin when she has always been so loyal to you. Why *is* that?''

''She betrayed me.'' Melinda's voice cracked with emotion. ''She took everything I ever wanted.''

''No, Melly.'' Dana let out a long, terrible sigh, at that moment she could have killed Melinda for the lie.

"It was always the other way about. Everything was given to *you*. We all did it. It was a way of compensating for what you'd suffered."

"Well, you don't have to worry about me now," Melinda said in a strange singsong voice. "I've got enough money to live my own life. I bet you're happy with your little sum. You must have planned it all along."

There was total silence in the room, then Logan rose from behind the massive mahogany desk with detached disgust. "Our business is concluded here. Your plane is due in just over thirty minutes, Melinda. I'll drive you down to the airstrip. I'd like to say goodbye to Alice there. May I wish you a safe journey. This has been a terrible time for all of us. I know none of us wants to compound the grief with disharmony in the family. We want the very best for Alice."

Outside in the hallway, Melinda stalked up the central staircase the very picture of outrage, while Ainslie, looking paper white and suddenly frail, clutched at Dana's arm.

"Surely you can't go back with her now, dear?"

Dana was almost at the point of abandoning her commitments but she couldn't. "I must, Ainslie," she said regretfully. "I know Melinda. She says many things she doesn't mean. She really needs me. Alice, too."

Ainslie's expression went wry. "It's wonderful you can feel for your cousin like you do. Today she was absolutely ghastly."

"I apologise for her," Dana said. "I think you should be in your bed. You're in shock. When is Sandra due home?"

"Shortly. Jack is bringing her." Ainslie sighed heavily. "If we hadn't lost Tyler I think they were coming around to announcing their engagement. They've always been very happy in one another's company."

"Yes," Dana murmured. "Here, let me take you upstairs." She slipped an arm around Ainslie's waist, leading the older woman towards the stairs. "I have a number of commitments I must honour, but can't you come to me for a little while. A change of scene. I don't have a mansion but I do have a very comfortable guest room. We could talk and I could bring Alice to see you. Melinda won't mind. Sandra could come, too, if she liked. We could manage."

For the first time Ainslie smiled. "You're very kind, Dana. One can see it in those great dark eyes. I'm tottering today but I just might take you up on your offer. I need solace a million more times now."

Upstairs Dana knocked on Melinda's door then opened it without waiting for an answer. Melinda was standing in the centre of the room vigorously brushing her short blond hair away from her face.

"God, Melly, you must want to hurt me badly to have said all that. What gets into you?"

"Nobody puts any value on me," Melinda explained in a shaking voice. "Sometimes I find the way everyone loves you utterly insupportable. If I had to be born again it would be as *you*. Even my own daughter doesn't love me like she loves you." Melinda threw down the brush and collapsed into a chair. "I'm going to find someone who really cares about me."

"I understand how you feel, Melly," Dana said, wishing her cousin had just a little more iron in her soul. "But you have to learn how to *give*."

Suddenly Melinda's face changed. "Be mad at me, Dana," she said. "You have a right."

Dana sighed. "Be mad at me" had always been her

cousin's way of showing shame or remorse. "I'll go and get Alice ready. I'm all packed. Put your luggage at the door. One of the men will take care of it."

At the airstrip with the charter plane waiting to take them to the nearest domestic terminal, Alice, high in Logan's arms, threw her arms around his neck, burrowing into it, crying with the pain of departure.

"Please, Uncle Logan, don't forget me."

"Miss Dangerfield," he said in a mock-stern voice, "would you mind repeating that?" He lifted her chin so that Alice staring into his eyes saw only love and a devotion that would last a lifetime. Her uncle Logan represented safety and comfort. He was so tall and strong and though he didn't look like Daddy, his voice it suddenly occurred to her was like Daddy's only darker or deeper and more definite somehow. "You could have me back for the holidays," she ventured.

"We could indeed." Logan kissed her cheek lightly then set her down, resting his hand on the top of her head. Alice was wearing a yellow dress that gave off a bright glow, but her smile was small and sad. "Be a good girl, sweetheart. Grandma might be coming to Sydney to stay with Dana for a while so you have that to look forward to, then the Christmas holidays. We'll fix something up with Mummy."

Instantly Alice's cheeks took on a little bloom.

"Goodbye, then, Logan," Melinda said stiffly. "I don't imagine I would be included in the invitation. I've had no refuge here."

"That was one of your choices, Melinda," Logan answered in quiet somewhat weary tones.

Melinda grabbed for Alice's hand and began to walk towards the waiting Cessna, leaving Dana to say her goodbyes.

"It doesn't exactly sound good," Logan murmured ruefully.

"I'll speak to her, Logan," Dana promised. "Things will work out."

"Is that the prognosis for us?" His eyes were jewels; his words so disturbing she put a hand that suddenly trembled to her breast. "*Is* there an us?" She felt the fire run through her, the tremendous swell of desire. Just to stand near was like being trapped in a magnetic field.

"You're very bright, Dana. Very intelligent. There always was an us and always some reason for hiding it. When Ainslie wants to come to you, I'll fly her in. You might find some time for me. In the meantime so you won't find it quite so easy to block me from your mind…"

As his voice trailed off he took her by the shoulders. The next moment she felt his mouth close over hers, its sensuous contours warm, alive, her soft face revelling in the slight rasp of his shaved skin. He kissed her, not gently but matching perfectly the emotion of the moment so her lips yielded beneath his, every inch of her body sensitized and sheened with excitement. Griefs ebbed away as the kiss lengthened, searing her in golden heat.

Logan's brand, she thought. She would never be free of it. At the same time it gave her great energy and the strength to go on.

CHAPTER FIVE

THE next couple of weeks were a mixed bag so far as Dana was concerned. On the one hand she was thrilled and delighted to win a prestigious award for excellence in Children's Portrait Photography, further enhancing her career; on the other, trying to be there for Melinda and Alice proved harrowing.

The loss of one's husband is an enormous crisis in a woman's life and although the marriage had not been a happy one with neither partner making the right moves to improve it, Melinda had fallen into a depression that involved either venting her feelings very forcibly or bouts of sobbing that bordered on hysteria.

Alice, suffering in her own way, had gone back to school, but it was Dana in the main who collected her after school or when Alice's own tantrums became too overwhelming for her teacher and fellow pupils to cope with. The fact Alice's behaviour had been tolerated so long was due to her attendance at a small private school where the teachers had the necessary time to try and establish a good relationship with her and help her over an extremely difficult period in her young life. A school psychologist had even been called in to observe Alice but when Alice had refused in no uncertain terms to have her near, the young woman had thrown up her hands in defeat. Alice's main temper tantrums occurred when the teachers tried to get her to do something she didn't want, as in group activities or when it was time to go home, unless Dana was to collect her. Finally when everyone had done their best and the other parents were beginning to voice their complaints, the headmistress requested an interview with Melinda.

"I'm not going," Melinda told Dana flatly.

"Melly, you'll have to." Dana sat with her arm around Alice's shivering frame. Almost a half hour had gone by since Dana had arrived home with Alice in tow. Alice had pushed another little girl so hard the child had fallen back against a desk and sustained a bruise to the temple. Not only that, the child's grandmother was on the board of trustees. Melinda hadn't answered her phone, so the school had rung Dana who at this stage was well known to them.

"I don't have to do anything," Melinda said, oblivious to Dana's ongoing hassles. "There's something wrong with Alice. It has to be in the Dangerfield's history. There's absolutely nothing wrong with me. When did I ever give trouble at school?"

"Quite often as I recall," Dana pointed out dryly. Melinda right through primary and secondary school had been a controversial little person with a habit of fabricating stories. A kind of payback to classmates out of favour.

"I hardly expect you to stick up for me," Melinda said bitterly. "Everyone seems to think so highly of you, *you* front up to Mrs. Forster. I'm in no condition to sit through interviews."

Mrs. Forster, a handsome woman in her early fifties, received Dana very graciously, listening quietly while Dana explained why Melinda was unable to attend the interview.

"I understand completely." Mrs. Forster's shrewd grey eyes were fixed sympathetically on Dana's face.

"We were all shocked by the tragedy. It explains so much of Alice's behaviour. On the other hand..."

For the next twenty minutes Dana sat patiently through a stream of constant concerns. Alice was highly intelligent but did her level best to hide it. On her good days she was very endearing. She was good with little Samantha Richards, for instance. Samantha had a mild form of cerebral palsy. Alice's gentle kindness at least was judged admirable. But with the others... Here Mrs. Forster threw up her hands. Alice's behaviour was very uneven. She was either aggressive or withdrawn. She wanted to sit in a corner and read books all day, telling everyone to keep away, including her teacher.

Finally it was suggested it might be better for Alice to take time off school while she tried to cope with her obvious unhappiness.

Against Melinda's strenuous protest the school was shirking its responsibilities, Alice had her enforced holiday with Dana, taking her goddaughter at the weekend. To "give me a break," Melinda's own words. It curtailed Dana's social life but she wasn't concerned. Alice was very important to her and in great need of emotional support. How it was all going to end, however, she didn't know.

Ainslie's visit considerably eased the burden. In her grief Ainslie found great comfort in the very nearness of her little granddaughter. Because it suited her, Melinda had offered no objection beyond the mandatory bitter comments to Alice's staying over, and Alice, for her part, sensitive, intelligent little girl that she was, realised her being there was very important to her grandmother. Alice, the school rebel with a history of causing trouble, was markedly different when it came to "hurt people." Just as she took special care with her little friend, Samantha, at school, Alice showed the ut-most concern for her grandmother's well-being.

To Dana's mind they moved closer every day, taking walks in the park together, sharing an ice cream, vis-iting the beach and going for drives. In this way Dana was free to keep up with most of her commitments although she curtailed her hours so she could be home for Ainslie and Alice. Despite Ainslie's obvious delight in her granddaughter, Dana realised it was tiring for Ainslie to keep going when she was physically and mentally laid low. Still, by the time the fortnight was over Ainslie was showing a heartening recovery.

"I feel exactly the same as you, Granny," Alice told her gently, putting a comforting arm around her grand-mother. "We're sad for Daddy, but us two can stick together."

"Yes, darling, we can," Ainslie replied, smiling through her tears. "*Us two*. That is as it should be. Us two from now on."

Logan couldn't accompany Ainslie to Sydney for her stay. Pressure of business had allowed him only enough time to fly her to the nearest domestic airport. Mara was going in for organic beef in a big way and there were many meetings and discussions about this, but Logan had rung to say his schedule was fine for picking Ainslie up for the return flight. Ainslie even suggested she might be able to take Alice back with her, but here Melinda put her foot down.

"I can't begin to contemplate it," she told Dana. "Too far away. And Ainslie knows it. No, Dana, don't bother trying to win me over," she warned, catching sight of Dana's expression. "Alice stays. I have you to help me and I don't want to lose control to the Dangerfields. To hell with them all!''

Dana felt a mounting excitement not unmixed with trepidation as the morning of Logan's arrival approached. Much as some elements in their relationship disturbed her, by the Friday afternoon she felt like a bonfire blazing away merrily.

"You won't find it so easy to block me from your mind," Logan had said. Easy? It had proved impossible. She still heard his voice in her head, still trembled at his remembered touch. She thought she had had a good idea of what it was like to be in love. She had been a little bit in love with all her boyfriends since she had started dating. She thought she had loved Gerard, had become engaged to him, but nothing had prepared her for the enormous heart-stopping pleasure she took in Logan. It was infinitely greater than any pleasure she had ever known. Pleasure, a certain apprehension, the melting heat of excitement. She couldn't wait for him to arrive. The anticipatory glow almost made up for the grinding disappointment she had experienced when he had been unable to accompany Ainslie on her arrival.

She arrived home a little later than she had hoped Friday afternoon, apologising to Ainslie who met her at the front door.

"Darling girl, come in and relax," Ainslie said, drawing her in. "You're much too pressured. I feel a lot of it is due to me."

"Not at all. I love having you here." Dana deposited her things on a chair. "Where's Alice?" she asked.

"She's changing her shoes for joggers." Ainslie laughed, her cheeks pink. "We're going for a walk in the park. She just loves the fountain, the way the sun makes those little rainbows in the spray.''

"Excellent! I can have my shower.'' Dana slipped out of her linen jacket. ''It's been one long hot day. A shower will feel fantastic. What say we have a nice family dinner at Ecco.'' She referred to one of the small superb restaurants in the area, specialising in Italian food as the name would imply. Alice adored ''Italian.''

"Lovely.'' Ainslie stretched out a hand to pat Dana's soft cheek. ''Logan will be here tomorrow, but I want to tell you now how much I've appreciated being here this fortnight, Dana. I've loved having your company, enjoying little Alice. It's not a feeling of visiting. It's a feeling of being *home*.''

Standing outside the door of Dana's apartment, Logan hesitated for a moment thinking up an excuse for why he hadn't let them know he was arriving a day early. Alice enjoyed surprises? Ainslie would greet him as she always did with arms out-thrown. But Dana? He had to confront the fact he had arrived early because he felt maddened to see her. It all came of making love to her. The unbearable involuntary longing. This from a man who had prided himself on his self-sufficiency, his content with his own company. No more. The longing came as a severe jolt. Every day it seemed to get worse. He could hear music coming from inside. A violin. Not classical. Something modern, elegant, distinctive. Probably Nigel Kennedy, he guessed. He pressed the buzzer, gave it a few moments, suddenly aware of a charge of adrenaline. What exactly would happen if Dana came to the door? Would he suddenly grab her? Draw her into an impassioned embrace? Hell, he felt wild enough.

But no one came. The music played on.

Exploratively he put his hand on the doorknob expecting to encounter resistance from the lock, only the knob turned. That was decidedly odd.

He stepped inside, feeling a surge of anxiety. The apartment looked wonderful. Like Dana. The combination of colours of fabrics, of ornamentation, the beautiful flowers.

"Dana?" he called, his tone urgent. "Anyone at home?" Surely in this day and age when security was paramount, she would think to lock her front door.

Beyond the seductively haunting sound of the violin another sound reached his ears. Running water. Someone was home. Maybe Ainslie. Dana and Alice could be out. It was getting on for late afternoon even if the sun was full of blazing sparkle.

"Hello?" He moved farther into the apartment, experiencing a tightening anxiety until someone appeared. He moved past the empty guest bedroom, the sliding-glass door open to the balcony incandescent with massed pink and white daisies in blue-glazed pots.

He found her in the master bedroom, or rather in the shower of the ensuite, eyes closed, head tilted back as the water ran in rivers over her exquisite woman's body. He knew he had to, but he couldn't. He could not look away. His very breath caught in his throat. She was creamy pale to her toes. Swan's throat, delicate shoulders, a tilt to her breasts with their pointed rose nipples, the long curve of her back, the small perfectly shaped buttocks, the slender straight legs. He wished he could draw. He wished he was a gifted painter who could seize the moment, capture it on canvas, so he could look at it forever. But then she reached forward, making an effort with her eyes closed to turn off the faucets. Only a few moments, yet it had been timeless delight. But not for the world would he embarrass her. He moved back soundlessly, deciding the best thing he could do was start all over again.

The doorbell. Dana heard it just as she reached for a towel. Surely they weren't back already? These little walks usually spun out to an hour. Perhaps it was too hot. Hastily she put on her robe, careless of the fact her wet body was leaving sprinkles of damp all over the short pink satin gown. Walking back through the hallway, she shook her long hair free of its coil, feeling its bulk and softness against her nape.

The door wasn't locked, causing her a frisson of anxiety. She hadn't thought to check it after Ainslie and Alice had left, which was a mistake. Usually Ainslie snibbed the lock and pulled the door after her. Better to say nothing however.

"You're early..." she cried, sweeping the door open to confront them. Instead of Ainslie and Alice, Logan was staring down at her with open fascination, his gaze so deep she thought she could drown in that radiant blueness.

"You're right. By a day. And you look so... delectable." In fact she held him utterly. He could smell the perfume of whatever she had used in the shower. Gardenia? The sweet freshness of her skin. Beads of moisture like dewdrops ran from the base of her throat down the shadowed valley between the lapels of her robe. For a moment he thought he would bend his head and tongue up those drops. He badly wanted to. He even stepped forward, his features tautening.

"Welcome," Dana breathed. Her blood was racing as the sensuality that was in him communicated itself

powerfully to her. This complex intimacy. She had
never known anything like it.

"No kiss for me?" he mocked, desperate now for
the taste of her mouth.

"Maybe a gentle one." She stood on tiptoe, shut her
eyes and presented her mouth, every pulse throbbing,
every nerve tingling and alive.

Just to touch her was to realise the depth of his hunger. He gathered her close to him with one arm, amused
yet on fire with the way she had jokingly made her full
rounded mouth even more pouty. Her body against his.
Her beautiful naked body beneath the soft satin robe.
A gentle one? Hell, he wasn't a boy. He was a man
racked with hunger.

The kiss lasted a long time as their defences unfurled
and fell away.

"God, I've missed you," he groaned, his hands
cruising with controlled yearning over her body. This
wasn't the time to act on his feelings. He was already
living dangerously. He'd totally flipped his cool over
this one, velvet-eyed woman.

"I've missed you, too," she murmured, seduced at
every level.

"You can't invite me into your bedroom, I suppose?" To kiss her was to want it all.

"No," she said regretfully, her body alight.

"Damn!" He tried to joke, even gave a little laugh,
when he was thoroughly aroused. "You're obviously
not as reckless as I am." And what a glorious risk! He
bent his head, kissed her again, feeling with a hard jolt
of pleasure the tip of her tongue mating with his.

"Ainslie and Alice will be home soon," she warned
him shakily, trying to fight down her own tempestuous
sensations. "They've only gone for a walk."

"Hell, when I want you so very very much."
Another kiss. This time a little rough. He let his hand
skim her back, feeling the slick satin warmth from her
body. He urged her closer, closer so he could feel her
breasts crushed against him, the thud of her heart.

"Logan!" There was a little flutter of panic in her
soft cry. Panic and acknowledged desire to surrender.

"You're right to be scared," he rasped, moving her
hair away from her ear so he could nibble the succulent
lobe. "I could kiss you until hell freezes over."

"And it's fabulous." She had to swallow hard on all
the emotion that was in her. "But I should get
dressed." Any moment Ainslie and Alice could return.

His eyes were electric. "I think *no* clothes work better," he drawled. "Oh, all right." He relented, dropping his hands before he arrived at a point neither of
them could handle. "Go, then. Put on something pretty,
though you look great in anything. I've a mind to take
us all to dinner."

Melinda chose the following morning to pay a courtesy
call. A gesture so phony, Dana was disgusted.

"Just so they don't decide to whisk Alice away,"
she mouthed at Dana the moment she stepped in the
front door.

As soon as Alice saw her mother, her voice quavered
and she looked like she was about to cry. "Hello,
Mummy," she said anxiously.

"Hello, Alice." Melinda barely looked at her daughter. She walked to the hall mirror and fluffed up her
hair. "Logan arrived yet? A lot of traffic from the
Hilton." She continued to study her makeup intently.

The seemingly offhand remark had the crack of a
whip. "How did you know he was staying at the

Hilton?'' Dana stared at the cousin she knew so well. And didn't know at all.

"I'm not dumb.'' Melinda glanced away from her reflection. "He usually stays there, doesn't he?''

"But he wasn't supposed to arrive until this morning. I told you that on the phone.''

"I know.'' Melinda shrugged carelessly. "But it just so happens a friend saw you all dining out last night and passed it on. Silly to think I might have been invited. Anyway, I gave Logan a call just before I popped over.''

Dismay caused Dana to react forcibly. "Whatever for?'' Once Melinda started talking to Logan everything went wrong.

Patches of red stood out on Melinda's cheekbones, the only indication she was flurried. "Don't be difficult, Dee. Just keeping in touch. I would like you to remember I'm the Dangerfield around here.''

"That's funny. I thought you'd forgotten it entirely,'' Dana retaliated, sickness stirring.

"How you love to have your little digs,'' Melinda responded with venom. "You don't have what it takes to land a Dangerfield. No way. Logan has a dark side to him.''

"You and he both,'' Dana burst out feelingly. "You didn't make any trouble for me, did you?''

Melinda's blue eyes were wide and guileless. "Good heavens, no. All I did was say hello. I wish you all the good things in life a million times over.'' She smiled at Dana as she said it, but Dana was unhappily aware of the jaggedness that was in her. Melinda, she had come to realise, revelled in sowing the seeds of discord. It was almost a sport to her. She had also developed a

compulsion to destroy the blossoming relationship between Dana and Logan.

Dana was sure of it the minute Logan arrived. One
glance at his hard handsome face revealed the difference. One exchanged greeting. The formality was back
in place. The ease and warmth of the previous evening
had just as suddenly been reversed. They were back to
their familiar *distance*. Only Ainslie's gentle presence
as Dana drove them to the light aircraft terminal saved
the situation. The constraints were on. Dana was positive now it had something to do with Melinda.

Melinda, of course, denied it. "Would I do anything
to upset you when I desperately need your help?" She
had rounded on Dana as she and Alice left to go home.

"I'm sure you would," Dana had replied, feeling
defeated and betrayed. Melinda shifted moods so often
she might have suffered from multiple personalities.

With Ainslie and Logan safely back on Mara, things
continued as before. Alice came to Dana at the weekend, unchallenged because Dana simply couldn't bear
to let the little girl languish. Something had to bring it
to a head, but not in a way Dana had ever contemplated. One Sunday evening when Dana returned Alice
to her mother's care they found the house was empty
and a letter addressed to Dana in Melinda's handwriting
propped up on the mantelpiece. Childlike, Alice was
intrigued more than worried. She ran through the house,
room after room, checking her mother wasn't simply
hiding. Her mother's behaviour was often strange.
Meanwhile Dana read through the letter thinking she
would never forget the contents.

Melinda had gone away to find herself. She had in
fact taken a Qantas flight to London that very day. She

made it sound like a harmless joy flight. Obviously she had been planning the whole operation for some time, Dana thought dazedly. Melinda intended to travel the world. She was going to stay in the best hotels, treat herself to some really beautiful clothes. Furthermore she intended to marry just as soon as she found the right man. A man who would cherish her and appreciate all she had to offer. She stressed she needed her freedom. She could not be "shackled with a child." Alice was in good hands. As an heiress she had a secure future.

And to hell with the emotional well-being! Dana leaned back in her chair momentarily staring sightlessly at the ceiling.

"I'm going to get out from under your shadow, Dana," Melinda concluded. "And about time, too. Life has been so damned disappointing. Never what I hoped for. Maybe things would have been different if my mother and father had lived. Anyway now I've got sole control of the money, I'm going to make my dreams come true. Bright and beautiful as you are, you'll never land that lord of all creation, Logan. He'll never forgive or forget the role you played in Jimmy's life. Logan's woman would have to be *perfect*. And he has already decided you're not."

With your help, Melly, Dana thought bleakly, afraid now to contact him.

But despite the pressure of her work, the difficulties of adjustment, despite *everything,* Dana was able to manage. What held her and Alice together was the love they had for each other. On some occasions Dana was able to take Alice along on location, other times she was forced to employ an agency nanny. That was the worst part. Dana ran herself ragged but whenever she arrived home it was to Alice begging her never to leave her again. Much as the kind and competent nanny tried to soothe and please, Alice remained intractable. Eventually Dana had to face the truth. She couldn't cope on her own. Someone had to be on hand full-time to combat Alice's profound sense of loss and abandonment. Alice needed her family around her. She had taken overlong to work up the courage to contact Logan and Ainslie. The reason being her sensed estrangement from Logan the day they had parted. Now the moment had arrived. She could put it off no longer.

"How do you feel about going to visit Grandma and Uncle Logan?" Dana asked one evening, watching Alice put a quite difficult jigsaw puzzle Dana had just bought her together.

Alice who had been hunched over her project sat up straight, a beaming smile on her face. "Oh, that would be lovely! I adore it on Mara. You'll have to come, too."

Dana confronted the issue head-on. "I'll have to stay here, Alice, while I get an important project under way. I have a solo showing early December."

"But after that?" Alice began to look less happy.

"If it's all right with Uncle Logan I'll come later," Dana said, anxious not to disappoint her.

That settled it for Alice. "Uncle Logan will be all for it." She grinned. "Let's go to Mara. It'll be fun."

Dana should have acted there and then but decided to wait until the next day when Alice wasn't around to put through a call. It would be agonising to have to explain Melinda's defection and not in front of the child.

Morning, like most mornings, proved hectic. She was out of the studio for most of the time on a fashion shoot checking in with Becky her seventeen-year-old assistant and apprentice who fielded all her calls. Dana had first seen Becky on a T.V. programme about youth unemployment and felt constrained to offer a job to the tough, valiant little Becky who wanted "to make something of herself." A snap decision that had worked very happily.

"You've had a visitor," Becky told her on the last call-in. "Best-lookin' guy I've ever seen. Tall, dark and handsome with brilliant blue eyes. High flyer. *Very.* Moves in all the best circles, I'd say."

"He didn't leave a name?" As if he *had* to with that excellent description of Logan.

"And he gave me such a smile," Becky crowed. "Said he'd be back. I told him you'd be free for lunch. You're such a terrific compassionate person you're not gettin' to enjoy yourself."

Nerves on edge, Dana took a taxi, thankful she was wearing a favourite sand-coloured Armani suit, an expensive badge of confidence. On a lot of assignments she opted for casual clothes but this had been a high-fashion shoot, something of an occasion. The clothes had been wonderful, especially a red lace evening dress she took quite a fancy to. Christmas was coming up. Lots of parties she realised she wouldn't be attending. Alice was her first priority.

When she arrived back at the studio it was to find Logan looking the picture of cool, hard elegance, wearing a beautiful city suit, his enviable hair gleaming blue-black, shorter, the deep wave controlled with excellent barbering.

"Haven't you led me a merry dance?" he drawled, lifting himself out of one of the leather armchairs and rising to his impressive six-three.

"For once in my life I was hoping you wouldn't hurry up." Becky grinned cheekily. "Logan has been telling me the most marvellous stories about life in the Outback." Too young to hide her enthrallment, Becky's pert, animated little face glowed.

"I'm pleased." Dana inclined her cheek as Logan barely brushed it with his lips. "This is such a surprise, Logan," she said in a poised voice when the familiar charge of electricity was kicking in. "Are you in town on business?"

"One all-important appointment late afternoon," he told her. "It's been set up for some time, otherwise I'm free. Perhaps we could have lunch. Becky has already shown me your appointment book."

"That would be lovely," Dana murmured carefully. "Just give me a few minutes to freshen up. It's been quite a morning."

"Which you handled beautifully I'm sure." Mocking, angry, loving. It was the most seductive voice she had ever heard.

"Dana can cope with anything," Becky piped up loyally. "Even little kids."

It was absolutely *crucial* Becky said no more. Dana shot her a swift quelling look, which Becky, needle-sharp, caught.

"How is Alice?" Logan asked. "I've brought her a present. I'd like to give it to her in person."

"I'm sure you will." Dana felt another wave of guilt and anxiety. Why hadn't she contacted him last night? She was angry at herself. She deserved what was coming. Logan hated being kept in the dark.

They lunched in a riverside restaurant on baby lobster with a piquant lime sauce followed by coral trout.

It was delicious but Dana was so nervous she left most of hers.

"What's the matter?" Logan asked with raised brows. He let his eyes move over her, feeling the pull of attraction, too deep, too threatening. Still he had called on her, never managing to keep his emotions under control. He loved the sleek simplicity of her pale suit, the beautiful silk blouse beneath. He had always admired her dress sense. He had never seen her look anything less than stylish in whatever clothes she wore. But it wasn't simply her beauty that gripped him, it was the slender grace of her body, the way she sat and stood, the colours she wore, the meticulous grooming. She radiated a quiet confidence. Today she looked the successful professional woman she was, but a weight loss was apparent and her lustrous skin had a transparent look, as though she was working herself too hard.

"I'm not all that hungry, I'm sorry," she apologised.

"Are you sure all this dedication to your career is worth it?" he asked dryly.

He would have to know sometime. "It's not exactly my career, Logan." Dana raised her eyes to his, met them fully. "There's been a whole chapter of disasters lately."

"Meaning what?" His answer came swift and clipped, just as she expected.

"I'll tell you, but please don't lose your temper."

Narrow-eyed, he sat back. "It's something to do with Melinda, of course. Has she been giving you and Alice a hard time?"

Now her sense of being in the wrong swelled to huge proportions. "There's no easy way to put it, I'm afraid. Melinda's gone."

"Gone?" His tone bit.

"As in, took off," Dana explained with grim humour.

"Don't tell me with Alice?" Logan asked through clenched teeth.

A waiter approached them, took note of their expressions and immediately backed off.

Dana reached for her wineglass, took a long, calming sip. "No. Melinda left for London all by herself."

"I think you'd better tell me the whole story," Logan suggested in a tone that made her wince, "and don't leave anything out. I knew from the look of you something has been weighing pretty heavily on your shoulders."

"I don't think we should discuss it in the restaurant." Dana's eyes made a quick circuit of the luxuriously appointed room. Several women were staring at Logan with undisguised interest.

"So where would you suggest?" He lifted an arm, signalled the hovering waiter for the bill.

"I want your promise you won't get angry."

"That may be tricky."

"Logan, you look dangerous!" she said, and meant it.

"I might be if you don't get around to telling me," he warned. "Where is Alice? At school?"

Dana could see what was in store for her. "She's staying with a friend of mine. A lovely person. Alice is in good hands."

"Let's get out of here," he said with exasperation.

They went to her apartment to have their long overdue discussion.

"Would you like some coffee?" Dana stalled as they entered the living room.

He whirled her around, compelled her to face him.

"Don't act as though you're frightened of me. That's not you, Dana."

His closeness totally rattled her. He was a passionate man. The tight self-control was more a necessity. "I'm ashamed to say I'm in awe of you, Logan. I always have been."

He made a sound of disgust. "Let's talk. We can have coffee later."

So the whole story came out. Logan listened in silence, making a visible effort not to intervene, though anger showed in his eyes.

"Aren't you feeling a little ashamed of yourself?" he asked finally.

She nodded. "I wanted to ring a dozen times but something always got in the way. We didn't exactly part the best of friends. I'm not such a fool I didn't know that. I've been thoroughly occupied trying to keep up with my commitments and looking after Alice." She couldn't mask her hurt.

His handsome mouth twisted and he stood up, pacing to the doorway that gave onto the balcony. "Whatever is between us shouldn't have stopped you. You only had to make one call and we'd have given you all the help you needed. Taken Alice off your hands. If she needs some counselling it can be arranged. There are no obstacles that can't be overcome."

"No, but there's a whole lot of disarray while you set about tackling the problem. Please sit down again, Logan. You remind me of a prowling tiger."

"Good," he said shortly. "Now you just might walk more carefully around me."

"Surely I've always done that?"

"That's interesting." He turned on her. "Tread carefully yet lure me on at the same time?"

"Is that how it looks to you?" Dana spread her hands, looked down at her ringless fingers.

His eyes gleamed. "Damn right! Only I'm not good at playing games."

"Really?" Their fragile truce was splitting wide open. "You don't hesitate to step over the edge."

"Only with you, Dana," he said very quietly. Too quietly. He moved with coiled energy to where she sat, coming behind her as she sat on the sofa, letting his lean strong hands encircle her slender throat. "I want so badly to believe in you," he said with a curious mixture of sadness and hostility.

"Haven't you ever heard of an act of faith?" She shuddered convulsively as his hands slid down over her shoulders to her silk-covered breasts.

"Maybe I'm too suspicious a man." There was pain now in wanting her. Real pain. The force of it shocked him.

"You would rather allow your doubts to warp you rather than follow your instincts?"

"If I followed my instincts right now, you know what would happen." His voice registered a hot sensuality.

"Oh, I do," she said bitterly, and sprang up, her skin flushed, her eyes deep and dark. "Whatever you want you get."

"You played your part, as well," he charged her, his voice hard now. He wanted to pull her to him, fold her in his arms. He wanted to connect with her at the deepest level, but he heard Melinda's voice in his head, too. Even despising her she had only said what his own family believed. The spectre of Tyler would always be there to haunt them.

Watching him, Dana smiled grimly, suddenly feeling

humiliated. "I can't bear much more of this," she confessed. "Perhaps we shouldn't see one another at all."

"Did you switch on for Tyler, Dana?" he flared.

She threw up her hands. "That's it. The big question! Nothing I could say would convince you otherwise. If you'd like a cup of coffee I'll make it. God forbid, I should keep you from your appointment."

In the kitchen Dana moved quickly, even though her hands were trembling with emotion. To be alone with Logan in this mood was enough to drive her frantic. She was pouring near boiling water over the fresh coffee grounds when Logan moved into the kitchen, instantly charging the atmosphere. It was like all the overhead lights had been switched on.

"Black?" she said stormily when she knew perfectly well. Black. Two sugars.

"I'm sure you know the answer to that." He curled his fingers into his palm, exercising the tight control he had long used around her.

Her lashes were low, sweeping her cheeks. Her hands, like his, weren't quite steady. Next thing he knew the glass coffeepot was skidding along the counter and Dana was crying out.

"Ouch!" Hot coffee had splashed over her hand, causing an instant red stain. Quickly he grabbed her, propelling her towards the sink where he turned on the cold water.

"That must have hurt."

His concern, the sudden tenderness in his voice, quite undid her. "It's all my fault. So stupid." She was trembling all over.

"No, damn it, it's mine. I've upset you. God, I'm a brute." He continued to hold her hand under the cold running water. "Most of it has gone over the bench. It could have been a lot worse. Poor baby."

Why these lightning transformations from accuser to lover? They were nearly destroying her.

"Dana." He put his mouth to the sensitive skin behind her ear, moving her back closer so they were body to body. "Want me to kiss you?"

Desire. The warm oblivion of it. "No." Her denial was pathetic, little more than a whisper.

"Liar." He lowered his dark head, his mouth trailing gently down her cheek.

She lost herself in sensation. Her head fell back against his shoulder and though she kept her arm extended as though on automatic, she lost all sense of injury and the running water.

"I can't help but want you," he murmured, desire and a kind of despair deep in his voice. Maybe some things in life were best left alone. Past relationships. His arms wrapped her completely now, his mouth moving over hers with incredible hunger, capturing it, claiming it for him alone.

She was so physically vulnerable to him. Sheer ecstasy shot through her. Rapture to glory in. She hadn't thought it possible to need a man so much; hadn't thought it possible the depth and abandonment of her own response. Her will was so fragile, melting under the force of his. How had he ever learned so much about her? How had he arrived at such a level of intimacy as though he knew her body as well as his own?

Her head was beginning to swim as passion drove deep. Only a kiss, and her sensuous nature was released. The longer his mouth held that kiss, the more her body yearned. She wanted his hands and his mouth all over her. She wanted that matchless passion even as she realised she might never have his love. These moments for him were a form of imposed blindness.

His long lean fingers were laced into her hair, his body almost supporting hers as she leaned into him, helpless to deny conquest.

"What do you do to me?" he muttered against her throat. "I'm crazy about you. Want it or not."

That element of male hostility had her struggling away from him. "Chemistry I think it's called." Even to her own ears she spoke raggedly.

"And an awful lot of it. Maybe too much for a man to handle. I don't just want to *kiss* you, Dana. I can tell you that." He leant forward, turned off the tap. "Here, show me your hand. I hate to see those red marks on your beautiful skin."

"Don't fuss," she almost shouted, no longer able to act normally.

There was a faint pallor beneath his dark copper skin. "All right. Take it easy." He spoke soothingly, as though women were as fractious as horses. "I don't want you hurt, Dana," he said, his dark timbered voice deep and serious. "I don't want to be hurt, either."

CHAPTER SIX

IN THE following weeks Dana was overtaken by a recurring sense of emptiness and loss. It was almost like a darkness had fallen on her. The urgency of her work propelled her along, nevertheless she was terribly aware something altogether vital was missing from her life. She and the Dangerfields were bound together. She missed Alice greatly. She had become very used to having her little goddaughter under her wing, but through all her thoughts, flamelike, ran Logan. The tragedy was she had allowed that flame to burn her. She had even begun to fantasize about having him for a husband. Logan to share her days. Logan to share her bed.

For the first time in her life she was having trouble sleeping, and even when she did, it was only to have that impossible, unattainable man stalk her dreams. Why had she ever allowed him to make love to her? It had so profoundly changed everything. Logan's lovemaking was all she seemed to think about. Even when she closed her eyes his image moved like pictures behind her closed lids. To lose him now would cut her to the heart. Jimmy and Melinda between the two of them had cost her Logan's trust. Logan thought a great deal of trust. He would demand it totally of the woman he loved. She truly knew what it was to be the innocent victim and it made her ache.

Ainslie rang weekly to keep in touch, always allowing Alice to speak, Alice's words tumbling over each other with her excitement. No reproaches from Ainslie.

Dana had brought her granddaughter closer.
Nevertheless Ainslie told her privately Alice had reverted to a few difficult moods and the occasional tan-
trum which rather shattered the overall harmony. Only
when Logan was at home could the household be assured of no discord. Alice's emotions were not yet in
balance. She seesawed between sunny periods and days
of wilful behaviour that required a lot of love and pa-
tience. She was missing Dana dreadfully, Ainslie said.
Dana was a pivotal part of Alice's life.

"We're all looking forward to having your company,
Dana," Ainslie told her warmly. "I'd love it if you
could see your way to coming to us *before* Christmas.
Some days I desperately need your support. Sandra
spends so much of her time with Jack. My disciplining
skills have blunted over the years, I'm afraid. My heart
aches so for Alice, I should be a little firmer. Logan,
of course, charms her. She's a little angel with him."

Dana could believe that perfectly. Though Sandra often took over the phone for a chat, Dana had no contact
with Logan. It was Sandra who gave her the news
Phillipa had taken to dropping in at Mara. She was
piloting her own plane now, a single-engine Cessna, a
magnificent birthday present from her wealthy pastoralist father.

"I think she's dying to start up with Logan again,"
Sandra confided. "There's no other man in her life and
there's been no other serious relationship for Logan. I
don't know how he feels about Phillipa now but I can
tell you for a fact she's still in love with him."

Just hearing it made Dana's blood run cold. It was
never clear to her why Logan and Phillipa had split up
in the first place. Any man would be happy to marry
Phillipa, she thought. Everything about her was calm,

confident, controlled. She was good-looking in a
healthy, athletic way, not glamorous like most of
Logan's ex-girlfriends, but well turned out, attractive,
a fine companion for the owner of a grand station. She
could just bring it off, Dana thought. Phillipa was far
closer to what Logan really wanted than she could ever
be. Phillipa could never be accused of having had an
affair with the tragic Tyler, either.

In the end Dana didn't send Logan an invitation to
her solo showing. In one way she desperately wanted
him to see her work, admire her artistry and profes-
sionalism, in the other she was unwilling to put herself
through the torture. So emotionally buffeted she had
taken shelter in the calm waters of isolation. Encounter
could only bring ecstasy and anguish. The sense of loss
would go on forever. How to survive without Logan
was going to prove one huge ongoing problem she had
brought on herself.

On the evening of her showing, which took up a
whole floor of the prestigious Stanford Gallery, Dana
dressed to the nines. This was going to be a very social
evening. One couldn't do without the "glitz crowd,"
not that they ever bought anything, but their very presence added glamour and excitement to the occasion.
The serious people from her own world would be there
and art collectors looking to wider fields. Colin
Stanford, the gallery owner, had rung her earlier in the
day to tell her two representatives from overseas galleries had flown in especially after the gratifying reception of her work at the Venice Biennale. Both representatives were from commercial galleries like the
Stanford, one in Berlin, the other in New York. It
would pay her to impress not only with her artistry but

her personal presentation. As one of her colleagues put it laughingly, "the whole package."

Tonight she wore a short slip dress of dark chocolate taffeta covered with exquisite black lace. She always looked good in black. It went well with her hair and skin and the gleam of the taffeta gave the whole outfit an additional lustre. Because the dress called attention to her legs she had invested in a pair of beautiful Italian evening shoes worn with the sheerest of black stockings; gold and jet drop earrings, an antique shop find, her hair a long ash-blond slide. Always light-handed with her makeup she set to a little extra colouring and sculpting so in the end she thought she looked rather exotic. Certainly glamorous enough to fit in with the ultra-chic crowd.

When she arrived the gallery was already so crowded Dana thought anyone who was seriously interested in her work would have to come back the next day when the gallery would be near empty. Colin Stanford rushed forward to greet her, delighted she was looking so absolutely "smashing," something he couldn't take for granted with a lot of his artists. Taking Dana by the arm, he introduced her around, beaming fondly while she was offered a whole lot of compliments. The men were delighted to meet her, blondes always were the centre of attention; the women, either envious or impressed, seemed more interested in what she had on than the wide range of photographs expertly placed around the walls. The showing had a name: "Journey of Life." It featured images from the moment of birth, through childhood, adolescence, the courting years, marriage, midlife, old age, on one's own or in nursing homes, the inevitable images of dying and death. It was a serious body of work. Dana had put her heart and soul into it.

While the champagne and finger food were being circulated and the hum of conversation had reached such a high level the air itself was turned to noise, she was approached in turn by the two overseas representatives who seemed genuinely excited by her work.

"So young to know so much about the human condition," the gentleman from Berlin murmured, seizing her arm to discuss a booking.

The American in the next ten minutes, not to be beaten, offered to "buy up the whole showing." "Australia's too small my dear," he told her. "You have to exhibit in the States."

It sounded as though she was quite a success.

Long-time friends swelled the ranks, people she had known since college days when she had studied film-making and had even made a couple of documentaries and a short film that had received quite a bit of attention. Gerard and Lucy arrived, delighted at the brilliant showing, hugging and kissing her.

"I always knew you'd make the big time," Gerard told her with pride and pleasure. Though he loved his Lucy dearly, Dana would always have a place in his heart. Everyone knows about first love. One never entirely gets over it.

Logan, who had waited for an invitation and deemed it perhaps unwise to accept, found himself reacting badly when one didn't arrive. This was throwing down the gauntlet indeed. And how it stung him! The past month he had found himself toiling through his days with a lack of enthusiasm that was entirely new to him. He had managed his life so much better before he had allowed a woman to slip into his bloodstream exposing his all-too-apparent vulnerability. His life up to a point had been rife with good-looking girls. He had even become engaged to Phillipa whom he had known all his life.

Phillipa was bright and attractive, suitable in every way. She understood thoroughly his way of life and enjoyed it, but he had learned the hard way Phillipa could be as disloyal as the next one. While he had been away on a trade mission to South-East Asia, Phillipa had spent the weekend with an old boyfriend who was still crazy for her. She had claimed later, weeping copiously, it had been just "one of those things." They'd been to a rock concert. She'd had too much to drink. But loyalty shaped his life. He didn't want a woman who could fall into bed so easily. He also became uncomfortably aware he had never loved Phillipa in the first place. Maybe it was all his fault. Phillipa had become aware of his true feelings and sought comfort where she could. In any event, they agreed to break off the engagement. A mutual decision. He didn't want to be taken over by love. He had far too many responsibilities.

His strong feelings for Dana Barry had always disconcerted him. Not only was she extraordinarily beautiful, she was extraordinarily gifted with a warm, giving nature. She aroused such sensations in him, strange hungers that gnawed at him long after she left and Mara was his own again. The relationship seesawed constantly before the sharp winds of doubt. A kind of self-sabotage and mostly on his part. Never a man to waiver, he wasn't doing too well now. The trouble was, he could never reconcile himself to a reality of Dana with Tyler. He has always thought her, for all their complex dealings, absolutely straight. He hated himself for even suspecting her, but he couldn't unload the burden of evidence.

Except for that time in the cave. There all the barriers had been swept aside as their bodies reached a sublime harmony. She had been perfect to make love to, filling him with such pleasure, such a sense of wholeness, he felt the Bible was right. She was his Eve, his missing rib. Was this intense passion something to be seized on rather than cause alarm? It was the end of peace. He knew that. The end of his peace of mind. When there was important, even dangerous work to be done, the image of Dana got between him and the project. In a way it was like leaving one's borders undefended. Maybe this was the way Tyler had felt. Captive and confused. Dana Barry was a crisis in both their lives.

No one challenged him when he arrived at the gallery. He wasn't asked to show his invitation. He simply walked through the door, not stopping to think his whole aura assured him of automatic entry. Why would a man who looked like that ever have to gatecrash anything? One or two even stopped him, trying to gather him into their circle, but he smiled and said he was anxious to view the collection. A futile pursuit, he thought, when the crowd was so huge. Were any of these people genuine buyers or were they simply being seen before going on to the theatre or dinner.

In the end he stood back, as much away from the crowd as possible, seeking out Dana. He knew she was successful, of course. He knew she was very good. Over the years he had seen quite a lot of her work, which was becoming far more meaningful as she matured. His interest was genuine.

"Super stuff!" a distinguished man said as he walked past. American, from the accent.

A small section of the crowd moved suddenly, heading en masse towards the photographs which were beautifully lit and displayed. It was then he saw Dana and something like elation rose in him on a wild wave. Their coming together the way they had, had opened up the floodgates so his whole world looked different and he found himself moving in a strange new landscape. He continued to stare at her, spellbound.

She was the most wonderful-looking creature he had ever seen, beautiful as were others, but so full of life, of sparkle. The laughing, chattering crowd moved around him but he felt compelled to stand and stare at her. She was looking highly polished and sophisticated in a way he had never seen her. Tall on her high heels, beautiful black-sheened legs. The dress was exquisite. Suddenly melancholy, he remembered how well black suited her. The black suit she had worn the day of the funeral. She was laughing at something an attractive young woman said as she hugged her, obviously a friend, adjusting her gilded waterfall of hair before a young man captured her, kissing her cheek soundly then holding her by the shoulders, looking down smilingly into her face.

Hell, the guy was in love with her. Their whole body language was far from casual. They knew one another well. For an instant he felt an unprecedented surge of pure jealousy, which only abated as he saw Dana move back, her expression full of an affection which embraced the young woman, as well.

So he was wrong after all. Just as he could be very wrong about Dana and Tyler. The seeds of doubt once sown spread tenacious tentacles.

A moment later he felt a touch on his arm, dissolving a moment of anguished struggle.

"Good Lord, Logan, what are you doing here? I thought you'd be back on Mara, pulling your weight for the country."

"Good evening, Sir William." Logan turned, smiling to acknowledge the handsome, elderly man at his side. "Actually I know Dana Barry very well. Have known her for some years. Her cousin Melinda was married to my late brother."

"Terrible business." High Court Judge, Sir William Hardy, shook his pure white head. "I'm so sorry, Logan. It must have been a great blow to the family."

The two men stood in conversation for a few more minutes before a colleague sought the judge out. Much as he liked and admired Sir William, Logan had kept his eyes trained on Dana all the while as she spoke to the changing crowd clustered around her. She was obviously very popular with the kind of vibrancy that drew men and women to her. She was very gifted, as well. Now he could see the photographs more clearly as some of the crowd left to go on with their evening. Another twenty minutes or so and he would be free to study the collection in detail.

And then she saw him, her colour deepening with a rush of astonishment, excitement, whatever. It didn't take her long to reach him. "Logan!" she said quickly, almost breathlessly, presenting her perfect cheek for his kiss that wasn't social at all. "Why do you always confound me?"

"It's nothing really," he drawled, blue eyes blazing. He wanted to pick her up in his arms there and then. Carry her away to the quiet opulence of his hotel suite.

Make love to her until she lay rosy and satiated in his arms.

"I'm absolutely delighted you've come!"

He heard the warmth and excitement in her voice, revelled in the transparent joy in her face.

"How could I refuse your personally worded invitation?" He smiled with that part of him that mocked.

"I did *want* to but I was afraid of... Oh, I don't know—" She broke off. "Anyway, you're here and I'm absolutely thrilled."

How could he doubt it when her beautiful eyes, tender and velvety as a doe's, sparkled with pleasure?

She took his hand, her tumultuous feelings for him gathering force, introducing him around with great pride. Everything about him made her heart beat faster, made her feel more alive such was the power and vibrancy he generated. Others felt it, as well. She saw it clearly stamped on their faces.

"You must come and meet two very dear friends of mine," she invited him, brushing her long gleaming hair out away from her creamy neck. It was a trick that tantalised him, making him want to put his mouth to her satiny skin.

Lucy and Gerard Brosnan.

Gerard. The name cut through him. The ex-fiancé. Now he had it. His instincts were never far out. The young woman, his wife, was pretty, with short dark hair, vibrant green eyes, and a pair of engaging dimples in her cheeks. An attractive creature but no Dana.

"They all love you, don't they?" he murmured as eventually they moved off.

"I'm a very lovable person," she joked, a little thrown by his tone. She knew, none better, Logan was a man of strong passions, but she had never seen him exhibit the faintest trace of jealousy.

"One wonders what you saw in Gerard as pleasant as he undoubtedly is." He bent to her ear.

"Perhaps it had something to do with the fact he's not in the least like you. Phillipa, too, has moved on." She felt a strong desire to add, "It appears now she's back," but that would be giving Sandra away. Better by far to keep that inside information to herself.

"Will you let me stay with you tonight?" he asked abruptly in an extremely taut tone.

She had to remind herself forcibly she was on full view of the crowd. Even then her whole body trembled as though she was on the verge of a high fever.

"We both know, Logan, that would be a mistake."

"I want to touch you. I want to make you shiver with ecstasy. I can't seem to get the last time out of my head."

His voice was so sensuous, so rich and deep, it was almost like being made love to. She could feel her whole body quickening, the shooting, piercing little thrills, the startling tightening of her nipples.

"Logan, stop," she whispered.

He took her hand, brushing her with delight. "Don't close me out."

It was the nearest Logan Dangerfield would ever come to begging. She was so excited. On top of the world yet full of confusion that flowed around her like floodwater. She knew the sting of his mocking tongue. She knew the whole range of emotions she incited in him. The underlying hostilities. The deeply implanted doubts.

"Please come and look at the collection," she said,

and gave a little involuntary shiver. "I don't know that I can cope with any more than that."

He laughed deep in his throat, so vividly, vividly alive. There was never any doubt for either of them about what would happen.

The day before she was due to fly to Mara, a long letter arrived from Melinda. Dana sat in her living room for a long while turning it over before opening it. Something about it made her feel physically and emotionally drained. She had done far too much trying to fit all her commitments in before taking off. Now this. Finally she sighed and, using a small silver letter opener, slit the envelope neatly.

A whole store of memories of Melinda came back to her. None of them pleasant. When Melinda had abandoned her child, Dana felt her days of covering up for her cousin were over. There were few surprises. Melinda wrote endlessly of herself. How these days she was looking so good she was turning heads. She had met a lot of very nice people who had "taken her over," showing her a good time. She was wearing her hair differently now. Several lines to describe this. She was wavering about cosmetic surgery. No matter her weight loss she still had a trace of a teeny double chin. In fact she had had one since childhood. A negligible thing. Not even unattractive. She had met someone very interesting only that week. A lot older but someone rich and cultivated. Someone high up in the city, a stockbroker.

Just as Dana was beginning to wonder if Melinda would ever mention her daughter, Melinda advised she had sent early Christmas messages off to the family. A letter each for Logan and Ainslie. A very expensive

card for Sandra, "Never did like her, looking down her
long nose at me." A magnificent life-size doll for Alice
when Alice wasn't a doll child at all. Surely Melinda
knew that. "Max and I picked it together." Melinda
was just beginning to find herself, fighting out of the
trauma of her disastrous first marriage. Obviously this
meant she contemplated a second. "A door has closed
behind me, Dana," she wrote. "I'm starting a whole
new chapter in my life. Maybe I can find time for Alice
later. I do love her, you know, but there's so much of
the Dangerfields in her."

Thank God, Dana thought.

She didn't want to read any more but felt she had
to. "I hope you've forgotten about Logan," Melinda
added a warning. "He's the type to find second-hand
goods distasteful."

Dana flinched. *Second-hand goods?* Did anyone say
things like that anymore? Truth and lies. Melinda didn't
know the difference.

Dana rose with a passion, tearing her cousin's letter
into shreds. Why had it taken her so long to realise
Melinda had never wanted her to find happiness?
Perhaps it was a kind of madness? Melinda had coveted
everything she ever had. She remembered that now. For
the first time in her life Dana began to seriously contemplate a child might be better off without a certain
kind of mother. A mother utterly insensitive to her
child's needs.

CHAPTER SEVEN

THE charter pilot was brisk, businesslike, directing her to one of the rear seats of the Cherokee Six. There were four other passengers, twin boys of around fourteen, old hands at air flights, on their way home for the long Christmas vacation, a very tense elderly man with a clipped moustache who was visiting his sons, and a middle-aged woman with an attractive friendly face returning to Teparri Station where her husband was head stockman. This was after a two-week visit to her sister in the Big Smoke which was still the Outback name for beautiful, bustling, cosmopolitan Sydney. They all began talking to each other in easy Outback fashion except for the elderly gentleman Dana had privately labelled "The Major." The pilot made another quick round of external checks then shut the baggage doors hard. A moment more and he climbed into his seat, glancing over the flight plan.

"Wow, aren't you lucky!" the boys said when they found out she was en route to Mara. "Dad took us there once to watch a polo match. Mr. Dangerfield's team won, of course. He's a great player," Chris, the elder boy by ten minutes, told her, "the homestead is out of this world. Compared to Mara, Dad said our place is a tin shed."

"I bet you love it all the same," Dana smiled.

"It's home." Chris sighed in a happy holiday-time voice. "Can't wait to get there."

Mara was the last stop, the most remote. On Teparri

the Cherokee taxied along the strip towards the hangar, braking to a stop just before a boundary fence. Mrs. Harrison disembarked and waved. Now Dana was on her own. It had been an uneventful trip, clear blue skies, no rogue air currents to lift the aircraft up and down like a yo-yo, which sometimes happened, but tiring. Logan was to have come for her, picking her up at the domestic terminal but at the last minute had to change plans to make an urgent visit to one of Mara's outstations.

Dana was dozing lightly when the pilot's voice reached her, calm but very decisive. "Listen, I want to put down. There's no need to be alarmed. It's just a precautionary check."

Dana jerked forward so suddenly her seat belt cut into her. "There's nothing wrong, is there?" As used as she was to light aircraft, indeed enjoyed flying, she was perfectly aware there was always an element of trouble and danger.

"Just something I don't think I should ignore. Call it instinct. I can't actually see anything wrong. All the needles are pointing the right way. It's just a feeling. I'm very sorry, Miss Barry, but it's best to err on the side of caution. The plane's a bit sluggish."

"Well, you're the boss," Dana said doubtfully. "Where are we?"

"Our exact position is twenty-five miles south-west of Teparri Station. I'm sending a message now to Flight Service to announce my intention to land," the pilot said. "If I *have* to, I'll arrange for our engineer to be flown in. If we flew straight on we'd be over Mara in about forty-five minutes. With any luck at all there should only be a shortish delay. One of the wires might have come off the pulleys. Or—" He broke off, by this time almost talking to himself. "It's the oil pressure. The gauge is dropping."

It was on sunset before Logan flew into Mara, asking his overseer, Manny Buchan, who was waiting for him, if Miss Barry had arrived.

"Not as yet, Boss," Manny answered in his usual drawl.

"What?" Logan, who had begun walking to the waiting jeep, turned back on him sharply.

"What time was she supposed to be here?" Manny asked, surprised by the boss's reaction. He looked shocked and then anxious.

"I would have thought four o'clock. Run me up to the house, Manny. There may be a message."

"Hop in." Manny took the wheel with alacrity. He'd been caught up most of the day supervising a muster so although he knew Miss Barry was due to arrive that afternoon, he hadn't heard when.

At the homestead, Ainslie came out to greet him, her expression matching his own. "Dana hasn't arrived as yet. I'm starting to get worried."

"Did you get onto State Aviation?" Logan referred to the charter service.

"I was just about to when I heard the jeep. You do it, dear." Ainslie's voice sounded strangled in her throat. In truth she was seized by a panic that had never left her. She had lost her husband, Logan's father, to a fatal plane crash over which she was still agonising. Flying was a way of life in the vast Outback but it was never without its fatalities nor would it be.

Logan more than anyone knew the dangers. His father had been a very experienced pilot, as he was himself, but that hadn't helped with mechanical failure. In

his study he got through to the charter service who at
that point didn't know the plane was overdue. It took
ten minutes before they were notified by Flight Service
in Brisbane the pilot had advised them of his intention
to land but there had been no subsequent confirmation
the aircraft had landed safely. A search flight would
have to be organised.

It wasn't enough for Logan. Fierce anxiety rushed
through him. Never a man to panic, he realised his heart
was thudding. His strong features drew together, giving
him a very daunting demeanour. The fellow at the other
end kept talking, explaining the situation, but he found
himself chopping him off, telling him as an experienced
pilot he intended to start the search himself. The only
remaining passenger on the Cherokee was a member of
the Dangerfield family which was to say close to God
in that part of the world. The thought of Dana out there
in the desert was tearing at his insides. It was too soon
to think of anything else.

At that point Alice, who had broken away from
Ainslie, ran into the study causing him to almost jump
at her high-pitched yell.

"Where's Dana? Where's Dana? Is she going to be
killed?"

Logan slammed down the phone, caught the child
and lifted her in his arms. "Alice you'll have to quit
that racket. Where did you get that idea?"

"I heard Retta tell one of the girls the plane was
long overdue," Alice choked.

"Well, you can stop worrying right now," he told
her firmly. "The pilot had to put down. Just a precau-
tion. That means he was being very careful. He radioed
his position, south-west of Teparri Station. You know

Teparri Station. It's not all that far from here. I'm going out to find them now.''

"Really? Aren't you wonderful. Can I come?''

"No, you have to stay with Grandma and I don't want any fuss,'' Logan said. "I'm going to bring Dana home.''

"I can't help being frightened, Uncle Logan.''

"I know, sweetheart.'' He kissed her cheek. "If you like you can wait up, though it might take a while.''

"Oh, yes, *please*,'' Alice breathed in a fervent little voice. "I couldn't sleep anyway. I can't even remember a time when I didn't love Dana. Do you believe in God, Uncle Logan?'' she asked, her child's gaze very direct.

He nodded, keeping control over his own apprehension. "I believe in a Divine Being, yes.''

"He wouldn't let Dana get lost,'' Alice said.

He was airborne just after dusk, flying into a night sky already peppered with stars. Mercifully he knew this part of the world, vast as it was, like the back of his hand. He had the charter flight's last recorded position. The pilot had notified Flight Services he would let them know when he had landed safely. No further transmission had come through but that didn't necessarily mean a crash. He had to hold on to that. There was another scenario. The pilot couldn't contact Flight Services on his VHF on the ground. He would be out of range and he mightn't have checked his high frequency radio before take off. He prayed to the God Alice so staunchly believed in that was the case.

Dana. She was never off his mind. Why hadn't he gone for her? It had been the plan. Now he wished with all his heart he had put the outstation's problems on hold. In a blaze of new knowledge he realised he loved her. Had loved her for some time even when he was crippled by doubt. An image of her slipped into his mind. The image when she was last in his arms. Her beautiful eyes full of magic, her mouth curving, her long gleaming hair spread out over the pillow, her body so warm, so sweet, so silken, desire tightened in him even then. Dana had transformed his life, now the thought of her mortality cut through him like a knife. On odd occasions in the past he had thought himself a man of stone so controlled were his emotions. It was a measure, in a way, of how he had been brought up. Responsibilities, a big heritage, the untimely death of his father, the disaster of Tyler's marriage, then the terrible news that had brought a hard lump into his throat. Men didn't cry. They were trained not to. It was only underneath they took the full brunt of their losses.

Losses?

God, what if…?

When he saw the lights of the charter flight he cried aloud with relief. Shouted at the top of his voice. No crash. His entire body relaxed and his formidable strength flowed back. How strange and extraordinary to find these feelings in himself. The crazy thought that without her he would most likely die? Him? Whose whole life was duties and commitments? No wonder the immense power of these feelings made him fearful.

He landed the Beech Baron on a track baked so hard it was almost as good as a landing strip.

Dana swooped to him, arms wide open like wings. "Oh, Logan!"

He gathered her to him, held her painfully fiercely close, struggling not to kiss her senseless. "What the hell do you think you've been up to, frightening the life out of me?" he demanded, feigning exasperation.

"All I can say is you've found me." She lay her silky head along his chest, feeling the texture of his khaki bush shirt against her skin, her ear attuned to the strong beat of his heart. "Not hurt, either."

"Thank God." His voice was deep and quiet. "Hello, there. Dangerfield," he introduced himself to the pilot who approached hand outstretched.

"I remember your dad well." They shook hands. "Never had the pleasure of meeting you. It's damned good of you to come." The pilot taciturn, but always polite, began to open up to another man. "Trouble with low oil pressure," he said. "Tried to get a message out when we landed. No problem with that, but my H.F. isn't working. My fault, I'm afraid."

While the two men walked back to the Cherokee still in conversation, Dana walked over to Logan's Beech Baron which was resting like some giant wide-winged bird on the desert track. She had known, of course, they would be rescued but she hadn't fancied a night under the stars with a complete stranger, correct as he was. Now Logan had come for her. He really was a knight in shining armour. In *some* ways, she smiled to herself, when he wasn't the impatient, impossible oh-so-arrogant autocrat laying down the law. Just the sight of him made her radiant. Logan Dangerfield in action was a glorious sight.

Dana lifted her head to look up at the stars, marvelling at their infinite numbers, their unique brilliance. The desert air was so pure nothing got between her and them. A series of images like snapshots flashed across her brain. She had camped out under the stars only once. That was when Jimmy was alive and as a special treat he and Logan had allowed Alice, with Dana for company, to experience how wonderful it was to spend a night around the camp fire; sleeping out in the wild bush, along the bend of a billabong. She still remembered the moment when Logan had bent over to check on her sleeping bag, asking her if the ground wasn't too hard. Just an ordinary thing yet as his hand briefly touched her, her heart had leapt like a fish to the lure. She had never managed to keep her calm around Logan but at least her imprisoned heart had kept its secret.

Almost immediately, Logan got a fire going, brewed up coffee he had on the plane to make them feel better. He hadn't stopped to pick up food, but he had a few bars of chocolate and some fruit, which he offered to the pilot. He'd already offered to fly him back to Mara but the pilot made the decision to stay with his plane, apologising again his high frequency radio hadn't been in order. Logan had already transmitted the message the Cherokee had been found with all on board safe. He advised further he would be flying Miss Barry on to Mara Station, her original destination. "How do you feel about a night in the desert?" he asked the pilot, who only grinned.

"The desert is my kind of place. I'm a bit of a loner. Anyway another plane will be here in the morning."

"Just stay put," Logan advised.

On the flight back to Mara, Logan said surprisingly little, wanting to keep the force of his emotions tamed. He expected he'd go crazy but he had promised her once there he would keep his needs under iron control. One hell of a promise when he wanted to claim her this very night. Even the thought of it made him groan aloud.

"What's the matter?" She turned her head, seeking the reason for that sort of pain.

"What do *you* think?" His brilliant eyes flashed.

"Logan, I don't know." She touched his arm.

"I'm thinking of laying you out on my bed. I'm thinking of unbuttoning that silk blouse. No hurry. Nice and slow. Then the jeans. I'm thinking of feeling your satiny woman's flesh under my hand, only it's business as usual. Wasn't that the deal?"

She laughed at the brisk change of tone. "I'm almost sorry we made it."

"*Almost?* Even in this light I can see the blush."

"I have to look to my position," she said. "Your position."

"True. You're Alice's godmother. I'm her uncle. Both positions are sacred."

"Have you ever thought of marrying me?" she asked as she meant to, satirically.

He laughed deep in his throat. "I've thought of it dozens of times."

"And?"

"I'm damned if I know how it would turn out," he drawled. That wasn't fair. "We live in different worlds. Your last exhibition really opened my eyes to your artistry. You're still young. You could have the art world beating a path to your door. How could you turn your back on all that?"

"If you're making excuses, Logan, they're working," she replied dryly.

"I mean how could we make the transition from *family* to husband and wife?"

"I never understood how we made the transition to lovers," she retorted sharply, lying through her teeth.

"I'm going to die of wanting you," he said.

Their arrival back at the homestead turned into a celebration, with station staff coming to the door to check all was well. The word had gone out and everyone was anxious. Mara had had enough tragedies. Though long past her bedtime, Alice ran around ecstatic with joy. Finally she sank with sheer exhaustion to the floor, her feet perched on a footstool, her head on a cushion. "Next time I'm going with you, Uncle Logan."

"Next time?" Logan threw back the last of his single malt Scotch, and set the glass on a side table.

"Next time you have to rescue Dana."

"I don't know that I like the idea of *next* time," Logan said feelingly. "Once is enough."

"But wasn't it romantic?" Alice queried happily. "Did you kiss her?"

"Heck, Alice, I didn't have a chance to." He smiled, his beautiful white teeth in stunning contrast to his dark tan. "I hugged her. That's a start."

Ainslie, who was sitting on a sofa, caught Dana's eyes. "Dear girl, could you pour me just a little more champagne? I really want to unwind. I'm no good with worry anymore."

Logan moved first, on his feet as smooth as a big cat. "I'll do it, Dana. And you're for bed, young lady," he told the excited, yawning Alice, large eyes overbright.

"No thanks. I can't get up. I might sleep here."

"No way."

"Carry me," Alice cajoled. "Some nights it seems like half a mile to my room."

"You will live in a mansion, darling," Dana smiled.

"You have to come, too, Dana." Alice rose, a little wobbly on her feet, going to her grandmother, kissing her soundly. "One of these days, Grandma, I'm going to have a little sip of champagne."

"Happy times ahead," Logan joked, swooping his

niece up. "Are you turning in, Ainslie?" he asked, his eyes on his stepmother's pale face. To his sorrow Ainslie seemed to have aged dramatically since Tyler's death.

"Yes, dear," she murmured, followed by a tired little laugh. "Dana, give me a hand up. I don't think I've ever been so pleased to see anyone in my life."

After Dana had seen Ainslie to her room, she walked along the wide corridor hung with paintings, to Alice's room. Logan was there, tucking her in.

"Uncle Logan and I are good buddies," Alice informed her. "I like that. Good buddies. And he believes in God, Dana. He told me."

"You were having a very serious conversation, were you?" Dana moved to the opposite side of the bed, smiling down at the little girl.

"I was terribly frightened when you didn't arrive." Remembering, Alice's eyes filled with tears.

"Oh, darling, that's awful." Dana's heart smote her. She bent down and hugged her. There had been too many traumas for Alice.

"Uncle Logan kept my hopes up. He told me I could stay up and wait for you."

"I'm safe. I'm home. And your eyes are drooping," Dana said soothingly. "You get your sleep and tomorrow we can talk all you want. I've got books and games for you and a little camera. I'm going to show you how to use it."

"What about now?" Instantly Alice sat upright.

"Not a chance," Logan said in a firm tone. "I hate the idea of you girls going without your beauty sleep."

That made Alice laugh. She snuggled down obediently, and fell asleep wondering what her first picture would be. Maybe one day she would be as famous as Dana and have her own exhibition.

Out in the corridor once more, Logan caught her hand, determination in his fire-blue eyes. "Let's go for a walk," he suggested. "I want to clear my head."

Excitement soared, looped like a bird. Still she said from behind her perpetual shield, "But what's the time?"

He laughed, a sound so attractive it made her senses swim. "What an idiotic question. Whatever the time, it doesn't matter."

As they walked through the moonlit garden their feet crunching on the fallen leaves, they were serenaded by a solitary bird.

"He's singing his heart out for us," Dana murmured. "Sweet and silvery and sad."

"Then it just has to be a song of love," Logan responded, lifting an overhanging branch out of her way. "Love's an agony after all."

"You really think that?"

A gentle breeze was blowing full of the scent of flowers and the wild bush. "I've had a taste of its power," he returned very dryly.

"Is it something you're going to share with me?"

"I think you're perfectly capable of working it out yourself."

"Well I'm not," she said honestly, breaking off a gardenia and twirling it under her nose.

His voice was crisp and very slightly edged. "I think it's transparently clear I'm in love with you."

The thrill of hearing him say it swept through her like a fire. "But you don't trust me?" she said, a great sadness in her eyes.

"In some ways I'd trust you with my life," he admitted.

"But you can't stop thinking about me with Jimmy?"

"I thought you were going to try to say Tyler?" he responded in the same slightly edged voice.

"Jimmy is how I remember him, Logan. I hope that doesn't upset you too much."

"You know it does. I can't exactly say why. I don't blame Tyler for loving you, Dana. You're awfully easy to love."

"We *are* at war, aren't we?" she said quietly, glad of the fragrant blackness to hide the sorrow of her expression.

"It's like something we can't help. But I'm never going to let you get away."

She took a few moments to speak. "Are you going to allow me to marry or are you going to lay down another one of Logan's laws?"

"Why, do you have anyone in mind?" He sounded utterly certain she didn't.

"I'm twenty-six, you know. I want what every woman wants. I want a husband who loves me as much as I love him, children we can both adore, a home to share. I want a purpose in life. I want to push the boundaries of my self-development as a woman, a human being."

He bent his head, kissed her briefly, a mocking gesture. "I think you're doing very nicely. I've said it before, but you have a considerable gift with your photographic images. You're a true artist."

"I hope to be," she answered gravely. "I have other needs, as well."

"You think I don't?"

"Beyond your basic instincts?"

"That's a low blow. Do you seriously believe what I feel for you is *lust?*"

She shrugged, realising it wasn't. "I know some part of you finds me taboo."

He made a sound of frustration. "Surely it doesn't require much understanding to know I have difficulty dissociating you from Tyler in my mind."

"When all you have to go on is Melinda's lies?" She stopped short and turned to him, raising her face.

"Melinda?" He gave a bitter laugh. "We'll come to her later. I had a letter from her. So did Ainslie."

Dana felt her heart sink. "She wrote me about it. What did she have to say?"

"A whole lot of garbage," he answered bluntly. "I really enjoyed hearing about how she's enjoying herself in London, how she's met a new man. I'd be beside myself only Alice is taking her defection unnervingly well. I thought the disappearance of one's mother, even a bad mother, would cause a lot of trauma."

"Children get on with life," Dana said a little awkwardly. "I had thought she'd be more upset myself."

"But she's confounded us all. Her grief is for her father and she was fretting about you."

"Her father was able to demonstrate his love."

"Melinda's your enemy, you know," he said with deep conviction.

"That's an odd word for a cousin."

"I know it hurts." He brushed her words aside. "For some reason Melinda is flawed. She sent me another warning about you. Of course that's what the letter was all about."

"All you have to do is ignore it."

"I did tear it up," he said shortly. "Ainslie made a

little bonfire of hers. Ainslie has just lost her son and Melinda can't wait to tell her about her new man. She really needs help.''

"I'm sorry, Logan. There's nothing more I can do about Melinda. Having one's parents is central to development. Melinda lost hers early. Obviously all we tried to do for her was unappreciated and unwanted.''

"One would have to feel sorry for—what's his name?''

"Max. Maybe she's a different person without her stresses.''

"Without her child, you mean,'' he said incredulously. "In the last analysis, Dana, she wants to hurt you.''

"That's becoming increasingly clear,'' Dana said bleakly. "I'm a little tired, Logan. Can we go back?''

"Why don't we just move into the summerhouse?'' His voice was both intense and ironic. "I want to make love to you.''

"When I don't have your respect?'' she challenged.

"Dana, I never said *that*.''

"And I believe I said I'd never be your mistress.''

She went to turn away from him, suddenly deeply emotional, but he gathered her to him. "Lust corrupts, Dana. What I feel for you is entirely different.''

"Then why do you have to punish me for it?'' She was truly bewildered.

"Because you make me so damned *miserable* when you're away from me,'' he protested, his expression for a moment touched with male outrage. "You get between me and my work. What kind of a thing is *that*? I'm supposed to be entirely focused and all I can see is your beautiful face. It's clear to me that's obsession.''

"Well, it must be a real change for you," she said tartly. "You never did tell me what happened between you and Phillipa. Was she giving you a bad time, too?"

"I didn't worry about Phillipa when I wasn't with her," he said.

"Have a care, Logan. I think you're admitting you got engaged to someone you didn't really want."

He laughed shortly. "You aren't going to tell me you didn't? Anyway that's all in the past."

"Are you quite sure?" She was afraid now of losing control.

"What's that supposed to mean?"

"I think Phillipa's heart is still in your hands," she retorted fiercely.

"Dana, our relationship is over. Why on earth are you mentioning it?"

"Maybe Phillipa doesn't believe it. Something about you puts women in a frenzy." She stopped abruptly, starting to crumble. Her emotions were more fragile than she thought and she'd had a glass too many of champagne.

"Don't you dare cry." He looked down at her intensely.

"Who said anything about crying?" She heard the rising note in her voice.

"Because if you do... if you do, my God, you'll be lost to me."

"We can't do this," she pleaded, but her voice was no more than a whisper on the wind.

"There's nothing in the world I want more."

"Wanting isn't the same as getting." Even when she was trembling in his arms she employed her defence weapons.

"Is it not?" He turned up her chin, allowing the

moon to shine down on her face and reveal the liquid glitter of her eyes. There was such a vulnerable innocence about her. Despite the dreadful letter that had made his heart twist inside him, he wanted to believe in her. So *badly*. "I'm not going to let you go without a kiss."

Though she yearned for him, she resisted. But only for a moment. In the end she could deny him nothing. He knew it. She knew it. So when he released her her heart was hammering and her body was profoundly aroused.

"I guess you're lucky I'm a man of my word," he said, anguish in his harsh tone.

To be together now on Mara. On his own land. And so many barriers still left between them.

CHAPTER EIGHT

IT TOOK Phillipa less than a day to find out Dana Barry was in residence at Mara. The following day she obeyed the compulsion to fly in, the very picture of friendliness. As far as Phillipa was concerned, her love story wasn't over. She wasn't such a fool she didn't know Logan had never been *mad* about her, but she was in love with him, had always been in love with him and he had been very fond of her.

Logan was the most dynamic man she had ever known, the sexiest, the best-looking, the smartest, the richest, a star of the first magnitude. The same hero he had always been in her mind. That little episode with Steve, nothing really, and she was not promiscuous, had cost her dearly. She had lost Logan's respect though there was nothing cheap or shabby about Steve. Steve did love her and he had asked her many times to marry him. In one way she had always known it was wiser to look to Steve as a life's companion. Steve wasn't complex like Logan, neither was he terribly exciting. Logan was incredibly so and very glamorous however much he would deride the term.

Now Dana Barry with her beautiful face and well-documented talents had moved in. Phillipa had always found her very pleasant, well-informed and interesting to talk to, but she was increasingly disturbed by the thought Dana could present a problem just when she and Logan had made up their quarrel and she was once more in his good books. Of course Logan had never told anyone of her little "slip." She didn't expect he ever would, which was her great good fortune.

Once or twice in the past Phillipa had thought she had discerned a very curious tension between Logan and "the cousin," which was how most of them knew Dana. Nothing very obvious or important. Logan and Dana were both very correct with each other, but a certain atmosphere prevailed so that on hearing the news Phillipa and her mother decided immediately Phillipa had best get over to Mara and size up the situation. Phillipa's mother had been planning their marriage since childhood. The breaking off of the engagement had upset her dreadfully. "How could you have lost him?" There was no doubt in Phillipa's mother's mind Phillipa had done all the losing but Logan was still unattached, lending weight to her theory Phillipa and Logan were destined for each other.

Logan was out on the job when Phillipa flew in, but the women greeted her with a genuine warmth. They all sat out on the veranda enjoying morning tea, with Alice sitting close by reading one of the beautifully illustrated children's books Dana had brought her.

"I thought it was high time we got to know each other better," Phillipa said amiably, leaning back in her comfortably upholstered wicker armchair, watching a couple of groundsmen move around the many-acred garden, bringing down yellowing fronds on the tall palms. It always gave her enormous pleasure to visit Mara, one of the great historic homesteads and such a wonderful showcase. The Dangerfields were vast land-owners but Mara was the flagship. It was a compelling enough reason to marry Logan even if he hadn't been every woman's dream.

Mistress of Mara!

Phillipa very nearly cried aloud at her loss. Instead she asked, "How long do you plan on staying, Dana? Long enough to come visit us, I hope?" Phillipa's family, the Wrightsmans, owned Arrolla Station some two hundred miles to the north-east.

"I'd like that, Phillipa," Dana responded lightly. "I'm here until around mid-January."

"No you're not," Alice said, briefly lifting her head. "You're going to stay with me forever."

"But surely, dear, you'll be going back to school?" Phillipa laughed uncertainly, looking towards Ainslie whose expression looked vaguely embarrassed. "And how is Melinda? I expect she'll be joining you for Christmas."

Dana remained silent, waiting for Ainslie to deal with it, but Alice as was her wont, burst in, "Mummy took off. She's over in London now. That's the capital of England where the Queen lives. She's not my mother now. She doesn't want me."

"Alice, darling, would you mind popping into the kitchen and asking Mrs. Buchan for fresh tea?" Ainslie asked.

"Sure, Grandma." Alice put down her book at once. "I expect you want to tell Phillipa all about it."

Ainslie's mouth pulled down. "Thank you, darling."

A brief look of shock passed across Phillipa's cool good-looking face. "Is there a problem?"

"No problem," came Dana's reply, intercepting Ainslie's agonised look. "As I'm sure you'll understand, Melinda is going through a bad time." Dana made it sound convincing. "She wants some quiet time to herself. Somewhere far away."

"Yes, of course," Phillipa murmured, her agreement tentative. Whoever heard of a mother leaving without her child? Of course the marriage had been a disaster. Everyone knew that. "So does this mean Alice will be living here for a while?"

"She's looking on it as a great adventure," Dana said. "And she desperately needs her family."

"You, too, by the sounds of it." Phillipa's gaze shifted constantly from Ainslie to Dana as though looking for some break in a united front.

"Well, we're family, too. Alice is my goddaughter as well as my second cousin. I've been looking after her for a long time."

"She's a dear little thing," Phillipa murmured when she didn't think so at all. She had seen Alice in one of her tantrums with no one in the house outside Logan able to handle her. Ainslie, always a robust woman, was looking almost frail, obviously grieving for Tyler. She wasn't up to looking after a difficult small child, Phillipa thought. Sandra was spending more and more time with the Cordells. In-laws one day. "I haven't seen any of your photographs, Dana, but I read in one of the papers your recent showing was a great success."

"Yes, it was." Dana smiled at the memory. "I'm really thrilled at the public response."

"And she's had wonderful offers from overseas galleries," Ainslie said proudly. "Logan was telling me all about it. He was immensely impressed."

"Logan?" Phillipa showed a glimpse of shock.

"He went to see it, of course," Ainslie said.

"When was this?" Phillipa's lightly tanned skin took on a rosy hue.

Here we go again, Dana thought. "He came to the gala opening," Dana informed her.

"Really? Well, he kept that a secret."

"Was he supposed to have told you?" Dana smiled slightly.

"It probably slipped out of his mind," Phillipa said, shrugging a straight shoulder. "I'm envious, of course. I never can take a decent photograph. Don't have the time really."

"I intend to take hundreds while I'm here," Dana said, excited at the prospect. "I want to make my own contribution to recording this unique environment." She didn't mention some of her best photographs had been used in a conservation battle.

"But surely—" Phillipa gave a little smile "—with all due respect, Dana, there are scores of books on the Australian wilderness? Mumma has dozens. All the coffee table variety."

"But I have my own way of looking at things, Phillipa. That's the point. The photographer's individuality. Great photographers are great artists. I want to make my way."

"I'm sure you will," Phillipa hurried to say. "I know Serena wants someone really good for her wedding but I expect she would be fixed up by now."

"Thanks, Retta," Ainslie said in a rather tired, sweet voice as an aboriginal girl, as graceful and small-boned as a bird, moved out onto the veranda bearing a tray.

"I'd love to do a series of pictures on our aboriginal women," Dana said, making room for the tray, and greatly taken by the beauty of Retta's hands.

"I can help you there, Miss Dana," Retta said.

"I'm counting on that, Retta." Dana smiled.

In the end Phillipa stayed all day and was invited to spend the night just as she expected. It was the routine. Dinner would furnish her with the opportunity of observing Logan and Dana together. Dana appeared to be genuinely devoted to the child, spending the afternoon entertaining her with lessons on how to use a camera, while Phillipa herself went in search of Logan, finding him rounding up clean skins at Cudgee Creek. This was Phillipa's world. She had been born and raised on a large station that ran both sheep and cattle and she was very knowledgeable about all aspects of station life. A prerequisite she had always thought for becoming mistress of Mara. Logan might have a great eye for beauty but he was very hard-headed when it came to making the big decisions. And marriage was the biggest. Dana Barry with her extraordinary silver-gilt hair and contrasting velvety brown eyes was essentially a creature of the big cities. Maybe she might even make the move to the United States if she was that interested in furthering her career.

As it happened, Sandra returned home early, before lunch, with Jack Cordell in tow, throwing her arms around Dana and hugging her. Something that Phillipa found a mite disturbing. Although she and Sandra, who was several years younger, always got on, they had always stopped short of demonstrations of affection.

They had finished a highly enjoyable shooting session with Alice's brand new Olympus MJU, a compact and robust little camera, basically point and click but with excellent results. Now they were resting under a beautiful old ghost gum on a hilltop that looked down on a panorama of flower-strewn slopes and flats, the results of one of the late afternoon storms that worked up with great thunderclouds and little passing rain just a short week before. The flower displays that after good rains could turn into blinding displays of pink and white paper daisies were a vision that could never be forgotten, but the Spring rains had been unpredictable with only isolated falls. Songs and prayer chants had already begun for the longed-for rainy season linked to the northern monsoon when the desert wilderness turned into the greatest garden on earth. Still Alice was happy to photograph the bush that she loved, a goanna resting on a log too lazy to move, three brolgas standing in deep conversation beside the silver bend of a billabong, an obliging aboriginal stockman leaning against a gate holding his horse by the rein, and a desolate pile of rubbish and mortar that long-ago sheltered stockmen touched some artistic nerve in her.

"Thank you, Dana," Alice said, softly touching her godmother's cheek. "I love my camera."

"I'm so glad, darling." Dana was indeed pleased with Alice's vision, enthusiasm and quickness of mind. "I'm hoping this might be the start of a lifetime interest. I started very young." She leaned back and opened the picnic basket they had brought with them. "Fancy a sandwich?"

"Yes, please." Alice accepted one gratefully. "I'll have my drink now, as well."

"This is marvellous, isn't it?" Dana sighed with contentment, leaning back on a cushion. "A glorious place if you have an eye for the wild, vast, open spaces under a perpetual cobalt sky."

"It's our home," Alice said. "Mine and yours."

"And Uncle Logan's." Dana laughed. "He's the boss, so we can't forget him."

"It was Uncle Logan who said it." Alice sipped her home-made lemonade through a pink and white straw. "I think that was lovely of him."

"I agree." Dana's heart melted. "I didn't think he would include me."

"Well, he did. He likes you a whole lot better than you think," Alice pronounced owlishly. "Phillipa doesn't have to come here anymore, does she?"

Dana broke off part of a cookie and put it in her mouth. "Why's that, darling? The family have known her since she was a little girl, just like you."

"Is that why she and Uncle Logan got engaged?" Alice leaned over and plucked an iridescent little beetle from Dana's collar, admiring it then placing it gently on a leaf.

"He may have loved her perchance," Dana tried to joke.

"I don't think so." Sometimes Alice was given to enunciating very clearly, just like her grandmother.

"And what would you know, young lady?"

Alice rolled her eyes. "Give me a break. If you love someone so much, why do you have to hide it?"

"Meaning?" Dana turned to her, startled.

"Kissing and stuff. Hugging. When Uncle Logan speaks to her, he just sounds kind. I thought he might be in love with you."

"Oh, man," Dana sighed. "How did you figure that out?"

"Simple." Alice put out her hand for another sandwich. "His eyes light up. They go all blue and sparkly like Grandma's big sapphire. And he *sounds* different."

"You're really smart."

"Yes," Alice agreed complacently. "Kids are a lot smarter than grown-up people think. I don't think Phillipa likes me."

"I'm sure she does," Dana responded instantly. She didn't like Alice to be hurt. "Some people are better with children than others, that's all."

"No, she doesn't like me, Dana," Alice repeated.

"It's all right. I don't akshly like her. I heard her asking Mrs. Buchan once if I was the naughtiest girl in the world?"

"And what did Mrs. Buchan say?" Dana looked into the big, gold-flecked hazel eyes.

"You bet!"

At that they both broke up.

Because the afternoon was so hot they drove to one of the many beautiful lagoons that formed a network all over the station, leaving the open jeep on the plain and walking down the narrow, winding slope to the moon-shaped pool. Here the calm cabochon waters glinted with a million sequins, with islands of deep pink lotus lilies glowing like sculptures on the sea of green floating pads. Hundreds of golden bottlebrushes and wild gardenias grew close by, spreading their delicious scent over the entire area and filling their lungs. Anticipating just such a swim, both of them had worn their swimsuits beneath their clothes losing no time peeling them off and folding them in a neat pile on the back seat of the vehicle.

Just as they were about to enter the water, Alice caught at Dana's fingers. "Don't go into the deep, Dana," she said, a little catch in her voice.

"Of course I won't." Dana, busy plaiting her hair, stopped to reassure her. "I would never do anything to upset you. You know that."

Alice nodded, brushing her fringe off her face. "Mummy thinks its terrible I can't swim properly. After all, I'm nearly seven."

"Darling, you'll be able to swim a whole lot better by the end of the holiday," Dana promised. "Mummy was expecting a little too much of you."

"She's terribly good, isn't she? Almost as good as you."

"We had our own pool at home, Alice, and my father coached us a lot. I'll give you some lessons in Mara's swimming pool. Now we're going to have fun."

They sported without incident for the best part of an hour, revelling in the open air and pure cold water on their heated skin. This was a timeless place, an oasis of quiet calm, sustaining a wide spectrum of birdlife. Above them a black falcon soared majestically, wings outstretched forever in the search for prey and, undisturbed by their presence, a pair of brolgas began to wade out to the succulent waterlilies on their lofty, stick-like legs.

Afterwards they spread their towels on the honey-coloured sand, their bodies protected for the most part by overhanging green boughs.

"Do you miss Mummy, darling?" Dana asked, concerned despite all that had happened Alice didn't appear to be missing her mother at all or perhaps was bottling up her grief.

"I do sometimes," Alice confided, turning to look steadily into Dana's eyes. "She's Mummy even when I know she doesn't want me."

So small and so brave. So much the victim of Melinda's lack of love and understanding. Sometimes Alice broke her heart. Dana tried to find the right words. "We have to remember, like you, Mummy was frightened and lonely after Daddy died. She needs time to find herself, to adjust to a new life."

Alice sighed deeply. "But she told Daddy she hated him. They had a big fight. It was *terrible*."

Almost moaning in her grief, Dana reached over and

took the little girl's hand. "I'm so very sorry you had to hear that, Alice. But I'd like you to think of this. Sometimes when they're upset and angry, people say things they don't mean. I know you will understand that!"

"You mean, my tantrums?" Alice said immediately in her intelligent way.

"I mean when you're upset and confused. When we sob and rage, it's a protest about something. It means you're not satisfied. Probably Daddy had done something Mummy didn't like. Telling him she hated him was just a reaction, like you tell people you hate them and want them to go away."

Alice frowned, remembering. "I've never said that to *you*, Dana."

"Oh, yes, you have, my girl. Lots of times." Dana tickled her.

"I never ever meant it. You're always lovely to me, Dana. So different from Mummy."

Dana's feeling of regret was enormous. "We'll have a long talk about it, darling, when Mummy returns."

If she *ever* returns, she thought dismally. It was a good thing most women weren't so woefully deficient when it came to loving kindness.

"So this is how some people spend their day?" a familiar voice, pitched loud enough to reach them, called.

Alice stared back, then jumped up excitedly.

"Uncle Logan, Uncle Logan."

"Hi, sweetheart." He flashed her a white smile.

Now another figure emerged. Phillipa, looking a little bit hot and bothered. Logan reached back a hand to her and in another few moments they were down on the sand.

"Are you going to have a swim, too?" Alice asked, so put out by Phillipa's unexpected appearance her voice held a trace of wrath.

Phillipa laughed sharply. "Not today, I think. I don't have a swimsuit."

Her cheeks began to burn. Oh, this was upsetting indeed! And it had only taken one look. One look to turn a pleasant acquaintance into rivalry. When had Logan ever looked at her like that, his blue eyes blazing? It was like a blow to the stomach. Not that she could ever look as good as that in a purple bikini. Not given to envy, Phillipa felt a great wave of it.

Dana, not unaware, came to her feet, her long ash-blond hair sliding out of its loose plait and cascading over one shoulder. Emotions were palpitating in the air like actual heartbeats. "That's a pity," she managed lightly. "It's absolutely beautiful in. The water's surprisingly cold." She, too, had caught Logan's look, the blue-fire eyes, the slight flaring of his finely cut nostrils. She realised, too, Phillipa was disturbed, and no wonder! Logan wasn't supposed to look at her like that, but for once his reaction had been unguarded or maybe he didn't care.

Alice came to their rescue, grasping her uncle's hand. "I'll have all these great photos to show you, Uncle Logan."

He smiled down at her, pleased she was looking so much better than when she had arrived pale and pinched. "So Dana's started you off already?" he asked

"Aren't you glad she did?"

"I sure am. Anything that makes you happy makes me happy. It was very nice of Dana to buy you a camera. I wish I'd thought of it."

"But surely she's too small to use one properly?" For an instant, cool, confident Phillipa couldn't contain a sudden flair of hostility. Something that really shocked her.

"Not at all," Dana answered smilingly. "The one I bought her is excellent for a beginner. Alice is very intelligent and she has a very good 'eye.' I'm very pleased with her. What have you two been doing?" Dana only glanced at Logan, wishing she had at least brought her pink cotton shirt down with her. Never a self-conscious person she now felt extraordinarily aware of her own body and the amount of cleavage her bikini top was showing.

"Doing the rounds, the usual old thing," Logan offered casually, blue gaze flowing over her. "Pip always shows a great interest in Mara."

"It's my favourite place," Phillipa gushed, pleased Logan had reverted to her old nickname.

"Don't you like your own place better?" Alice asked in a vaguely belligerent voice.

"Of course I love it!" Phillipa glanced down at this horrid little girl. "But bless me, it's not Mara. I don't know anything to equal Mara."

"Someone should take you to Kinjarra, or Main Royal, or Bahl Bahla," Logan mocked.

"The devil's in you, Logan," Phillipa said.

"Thanks a lot."

"It only makes you more attractive."

Dana privately agreed. "So, will we go on home, Alice?" she asked. "Sandra will want to see you."

"Nah, not with Jack around," Alice said, startling them all. "They're sort of mad about each other, aren't they?"

"One is supposed to be when one intends to get

married," Phillipa began rather piously only to then blush a bright red.

"One day you'll meet one special guy," Logan told Alice lightly, taking her hand.

"Will I really?" Alice looked thrilled.

"Count on it. I'd say you're going to make one heck of a woman"

"Like Dana." Alice smiled.

Phillipa moved off, striding it out. Half an hour ago she'd been happy. Now she was down in the doldrums, wishing Dana would go back to where she came from.

Dana tried to keep up, but she wasn't wearing shoes and her city feet were very tender. Logan and Alice were a little distance behind her, Alice straggling to protect her bare feet, as well. The track was harder to negotiate going up than down, the sandy earth covered with leaves and twigs and seed pods, abundant little scurrying insects and isolated masses of delicate yellow wildflowers.

"Why don't I carry you?" Logan suggested to Alice.

"Not unless you want to break your back," Alice chortled. "No, I'm okay, Uncle Logan."

"How's it going, Dana?" Logan called, wanting to trap her in his arms. The light was dancing over her beautiful skin. She moved like she was dancing. She had a dancer's lovely strong but delicate legs. That neat little butt just made for a bikini. He could see the slight swing of her small perfect breasts as she bent suddenly, putting her hand down as if to steady herself.

"Ouch!"

They all heard the little sound of pain.

"Dana?" He left Alice's side, moving swiftly, efficiently, up the slope. "What is it?" He grasped her around her bare, narrow waist, bringing her upright.

"Damn. After such a delightful day I think something has stung me."

"Hang on one minute. Just one minute." He moved back to Alice, swinging her into his arms and carrying her to the top of the slope.

"It's probably nothing, Logan." Phillipa frowned, for a moment considering. "A bull ant." When had he ever acted so concerned about her?

"Dana doesn't normally react like that," he answered a little shortly.

"I don't think it's a bull ant, either," Alice said.

"Okay. So what is it? She'd know if it had been a snake."

"It can't be a snake," Alice said with great intensity.

"Next time you'll remember to wear your shoes," Phillipa responded with faint censure.

Alice glared at her but had the sense to keep silent.

Logan reached Dana in half the time it took him to ascent. "Here, hold on to me while I take a look. Where is it, your foot?"

"Yes, the soft part underneath." She was speaking calmly but her foot had started stinging badly.

"You really should have worn shoes. It's always best to take precautions."

"I know, I'm sorry." She laughed a little shakily, reacting to the closeness of his body, his warmth and his strength. "It could have been Alice."

"That must be painful." He held her slender foot in his hand. "A bee sting probably. All the bottlebrushes are in flower. The bees love the nectar. You trod on one or a couple by the look of the swelling. Only other thing is a spider. It's certainly not snakebite."

"I'm pleased about that." Dana's tone was dry.

"There's not a damn thing I can do about it until we get you back to the house."

"I'll survive." She fought down the instinct to reach out to him. Instead she tried to put her foot down.

"What the hell!" Logan stared at her for a long moment then lifted her as easily as he had Alice, into his arms. "You're one lovely creature, Dana Barry. I could carry you for miles."

"The trouble is, I need my clothes."

"Not by me." He gave a provoking little laugh. "That's what comes of being a hot-blooded male."

"Oh, yes?"

"Shall I prove it?"

"Not with *Pip* around."

"Why don't I just kiss you and be done with it?" His gaze touched her, sizzled.

"That seems monstrously cruel."

"Maybe," he agreed.

"Are you alright, Dana?" Alice called anxiously.

"Of course she's alright." Phillipa was dismayed by her own grumpy voice. "Don't worry, dear, Uncle Logan to the rescue."

"He practically loves Dana," Alice said.

For an instant Phillipa felt close to screaming. A remarkable thing for her.

"That is a shame," she clucked sympathetically when Dana showed them the fiercely red, swollen area. "As I've just said to Alice, it's wise to wear shoes, but then, you haven't spent a great deal of time in the Outback have you, Dana?"

"Nonsense, she's been coming out here for years," Logan clipped off. "Listen we'll all go back in the one jeep. I'll send someone back for the other. Dana needs some tea tree oil on that sting and a painkiller."

"Oh, my, what's the fuss!" Phillipa laughed lightly, watching Dana shoulder into a pink shirt, buttoning it modestly over the creamy swell of her breasts. "I rode in a cross-country race once with a broken collarbone."

Dinner made Phillipa even more uneasy. Because there were only six of them, they used the informal dining room which flowed on from the breakfast room adjoining the kitchen. Not that there was anything too informal about it, Phillipa had always thought; a large dark-panelled room illuminated by day with tall leaded windows, a Venetian glass chandelier by night, a huge tapestry on one wall, a matching pair of consoles with mirrors above them on the other, a long refectory-style English oak table with two magnificent oak carvers at either end and eight chairs. Because there were guests there were a series of silver candlesticks with tall lighted tapers down the centre of the table, with a low crystal bowl of yellow roses in the middle.

The Dangerfields were used to living grandly so much so it was bizarre to think just outside the main compound was a great wilderness, as savage as it was splendid and beyond that the Simpson Desert spreading its vast intimidating presence over an area of 15000 square kilometres. Sandra, though she was still grieving deeply over the loss of her brother, had picked up, Phillipa thought, and with Jack to stay, joined in the conversation that ranged over a wide area: local news, the political situation, various hotly debated issues and Dana's highly successful show.

"It must be so exciting for you, Dana, to be invited to New York?" Sandra smiled across the table, looking for a moment so much like Jimmy, Dana had to look down quickly so as not to show her feelings. "You'll go?"

"Of course she will!" Phillipa interjected, wanting nothing more. "It would be so exciting, no artistic person would think of giving up the chance."

"And all the showing sold." Sandra showed her genuine delight. "Now I can boast about you to all my friends. Fancy having an international audience for your work."

Think about that, Logan cautioned himself, his eyes on Dana in her exquisitely soft green dress. Was there no colour she couldn't wear? He knew, first-hand, dealers had been vying to get hold of her work. She had sold every last photograph that evening, in the end to the American dealer because he intended to keep the entire show together.

"After all, you can only go so far here," Phillipa was saying. Almost like a prompt.

Dana twisted the stem of her wineglass, knowing what Phillipa was about. In a way, feeling sorry for her. "My work is really about being an Australian, Phillipa. It's *my* country and *my* way of looking at things."

Phillipa had to force a smile. "I think you'll change your mind once you get to New York."

New York, Logan thought. A world away. Almost another planet. What did an Outback cattleman have in common with a photographic artist on her upward climb to the top? Her talent would get her there. Her beauty, like a lily in bloom, would assure her of a public image. The whole world admired beauty and talent.

Jack Cordell, who had a secret desire to beat Logan at billiards at least once, dragged him off for a game. Logan had tried to cry off but in the end gave in good-naturedly. He had plenty of paperwork to get through and a proposal from a pastoralist colleague to consider a partnership venture, but he always tried to get in some relaxation and he liked Jack. He had known the Cordells all his life and he approved of Jack as a husband for Sandra. Jack was a fine young man from a well-respected family and he was always on hand to give Sandra the kind of comfort and support she needed.

Once the men departed, the women retired to Ainslie's large sitting room. It was a beautiful "blue" room with an entrancing painting of a tree in a green field against a densely blue sky above the mantelpiece. The painting alone was so real it transported the viewer to the green meadow. Dana loved it and the combination of sofas, armchairs, fabrics, a few wonderful antiques and the tall bronze lamps. It was a room as distinguished and restful as Ainslie herself.

They chatted for some time, listened to Ainslie's classical CD's, then Dana excused herself saying there were a number of things involving her studio she still had to attend to. Although she had worked intensive hours to clear her commitments she still had letters on hold which she would now send by fax.

"You'll look in on Alice, would you, dear?" Ainslie said. "It took her such a long time to go off."

"Excitement." Dana smiled. "Don't worry, Ainslie, I'll attend to it."

"I've been no help." Sandra apologised for her absence. "I've needed to be with Jack but I'm going to get closer to my little niece now she's here. I must say she seems a lot happier than I supposed under the circumstances."

"When did you last have word of Melinda?" Phillipa came a little too near to demanding.

It was Ainslie who answered, slowly, reluctantly, acutely aware of Phillipa's disapproval. "Just recently. You must remember, Phillipa, Melinda is a woman in shock."

"She's the most selfish woman in the world, you mean," Sandra burst out, then, catching Dana's eye, apologised. "Sorry, Dana. I know Melinda is your cousin, but she makes me furious. I can't understand how she can do this to Alice."

"Please let's drop it, dear," Ainslie begged, unwilling to discuss family matters in front of Phillipa. Though she had always liked Phillipa, liked the way she was so active in community matters, she had never found her particularly tolerant of failings in others, and her mother, though a bright energetic woman, was a great gossip. Time had to go by before any of them would know exactly what Melinda's plans were for the future.

In her room, Dana drafted a few letters, took her shower, put on her nightclothes then padded down the corridor to Alice's room. Alice was lying quietly, two hands locked beneath pink cheeks, her breathing easy. She looked fine, lightly tanned and healthy. Dana moved the night-light a little further away from the bed. The light was very soft but it was falling across Alice's eyes. She resisted the impulse to kiss the little girl's cheek in case she woke her up, going to the French doors that led onto the upper balcony and catching the gently swaying curtain back into its silk rope.

The night sky was blazing with stars, the sky itself tinted a marvellous dark purple. She ventured out onto the veranda exulting in the warm darkness, the wonderful scents of the bush that rose over and above the more familiar perfumes of the garden. Mara was an incredible place. It had been her first experience of a great Outback station and one that would never leave her. All this was Logan's. Had been his from birth. In a way it was like being born a prince. And tragic Jimmy! To have died so young and so far from home. Now he would never leave.

Dana was just about to turn away from the door when a woman's voice, low-pitched but urgent, reached her from the terrace below.

"How much punishment must I take?" It was Phillipa, and she sounded deeply upset. "I told you it meant nothing. A mad moment. I'm sick with shame."

It was no surprise when Logan responded, "Why are you bringing all this up, Phillipa? It's over."

It was time to move yet Dana was rooted to the spot, her better judgement way off.

"I can't accept that. How can I?" Phillipa, so cool and contained, responded passionately. "It seems to me with a little forgiveness on your part we could get back to what we had before."

"*Were* we so happily engaged?" Logan asked, and his voice sounded dismayingly cool.

"You know we were," Phillipa protested. "We were meant for each other from the outset."

Logan's laugh was brief and cynical. "So as soon as I turned my back you fell into Steven's bed?"

At this point Dana moved back, in the process stubbing her bare toes against a sandstone pot containing a lush golden cane. Shock acted as an anaesthetic. She couldn't believe the impeccable Phillipa with her ho-lier-than-thou manner, had taken such a wrong turn. It would have been funny only the consequences had been disastrous, dashing Phillipa's hopes and dreams.

"You've heard this a hundred times before," Phillipa pleaded. "It was a mistake. We both had too much to

drink. God, Logan haven't you ever made a mistake?" she cried.

"Plenty of them." His tone was hard. "But I'm a great believer in fidelity. Anyway, it doesn't matter anymore."

"But you haven't found anyone else." Renewed hope sounded in Phillipa's voice. "Tell me, Logan, I have to know."

Logan was silent for a few fraught seconds as though measuring her claim. "I don't see it that way at all."

"It's not Dana, is it?" Jealousy distorted Phillipa's normally attractive tones.

"Why would you say that?"

On the veranda above, Dana's face flamed.

"She's very beautiful," Phillipa said wretchedly. "I know how much you prize beautiful things."

"Surely you don't think that's all there is to Dana?" he asked. "Beauty?"

"All right, she's interesting." Phillipa considered shortly. "I've always liked her, unlike that ferocious little pussy cat of a cousin. But Dana Barry isn't the right woman to have by your side," Phillipa said with strong conviction. "On her own admission she's a career woman. She belongs in a different world, not out here."

Logan sounded so taut it was nothing short of hostile. "I appreciate that, Phillipa."

I can't bear this, Dana thought, her frozen limbs unlocking. She began to back slowly, stealthily, towards the French doors, not wanting her movements to be heard nor to wake Alice up.

"It would be awful if you allowed her to disrupt your life." But Phillipa was so upset she was forgetting to keep her voice down. Almost at the door, Dana stood stock-still, desperate to hear Logan's reply.

"I hope I can handle that myself, Pip, with no help from you," he said curtly.

"But I love you. I loved you long before she came into our lives." Phillipa's voice was less audible. "Doesn't that mean anything anymore?"

"This is insane, Pip." Logan's tone was final. "Insane, and I wish you'd stop."

If only Phillipa had, but she was clutching at anything. Things she wouldn't normally have said. Taboo things. "How can I when I feel so *betrayed*," she cried. "I'm not the first woman to lose her man to Dana Barry."

The air started to shimmer before Dana's eyes. She felt dizzy, disoriented. It was all her own fault. In listening had she really believed she would resolve her own dilemmas? What was coming would be worse by far. She knew it in her bones.

"What about her relationship with Tyler?" Phillipa challenged in a burning rush.

"I beg your pardon?" Most people would have shrunk from Logan's tone but Phillipa gave a distraught laugh.

"We all knew the marriage wasn't perfect. How could it be with someone like Dana in the background? Why she showed her cousin up at every turn."

"So?" Logan's rasp cut her off.

"A blind person could see Tyler was in love with

her.'' Phillipa's voice was unnaturally clear. ''I was a guest here at different times.''

What is happening to me? Dana thought.

''You're not so different from your mother, are you?'' Logan accused cruelly. ''Endlessly in search of gossip.''

''I'm clearer eyed than you,'' Phillipa burst out just as fiercely, her nerves frayed. ''My only interest is *you*.''

Dana felt a desire to cry out her innocence, but who would listen? She moved back into the bedroom, standing shaken beside Alice's bed. It was just as well children slept so soundly, so clearly had the voices floated upwards. She was nearly weeping herself with pain and frustration, causing her to put a hand against her mouth, swallowing down hard against the tears. All the hoping and praying in the world weren't going to change the fact they all believed in a terrible triangular relationship between her, Melinda and Jimmy. Jimmy could have put things right, but Jimmy hideously was dead. Melinda *knew* the truth, but Melinda these days was filled with a terrible desire to hurt people. For any young woman to marry Logan Dangerfield would be considered a triumph, a splendid match. Melinda was going to make certain that didn't happen to Dana.

It all went back to sibling rivalry on a scale Dana had never dreamt of.

In a flash of recall Dana remembered her cousin as a child, pretty as a porcelain doll with her apple blossom skin, blond curls and big blue eyes. She remembered clearly, keenly, how her heart had gone out to that little cousin so tragically bereft. It seemed to her now she had fallen over backwards all her life trying to make excuses for Melinda, yet she remembered the times they had cried together locked in one another's arms, their tears mingling. Some subterranean part of Melinda did love her. It had showed itself from time to time. So how could she have ever imagined Melinda could turn on her with such venom?

When she finally moved out into the corridor Dana had to stop abruptly, heart hammering, as she saw a lean, powerful figure silhouetted against the pool of light from an open doorway.

"Dana?"

She wrapped her arms around herself in a futile attempt to protect herself from the overwhelming magnetism that never failed to grab her.

"I was just checking on Alice." She flushed, attempting a matter-of-fact tone and failing dismally.

"So what are you shivering for? It's a hot night," he challenged.

Strongly, purposefully, like a panther on the prowl, he began walking towards her. "How much did you hear?"

No mercy from Logan. "I don't know what you're talking about." Absurdly she lied.

"The hell you don't. You were on the veranda weren't you?" He looked down at her, a hard excitement spiralling up in him at the sight of her. How huge were her beautiful eyes, glittering as if on the verge of tears. How pale that lovely face. Desire jabbed at him so painfully it was like a knife point at the heart.

She scented the wildness in him. "Please, Logan. It's late. I want to go to bed."

"No, Dana. I'd rather you talked to me." He pulled her back against the wall. "I knew you had to be there. I could *feel* you. I could even pick up your scent."

"I'm sorry." There was nothing more she could say.

"I was looking in on Alice. I had no idea anyone was on the terrace."

"But once you heard us you stayed?"

"I made that mistake, yes." Her chin came up. He had never seemed so formidable or so tall. "I didn't want to, but I couldn't move."

"And I bet you're sorry?" His laugh was low and harsh.

"Don't you think it best if I went to bed?"

"And which bed do you belong in?" he asked.

She didn't think. She didn't repress her blind anger. She was swamped by it. Logan's sardonic tongue laced with honey or gall. She struck out at him, breathing hard and furious, her fists clenched, the force of her emotions staggering in their intensity. So this is what it was like to love? To hate? Their mutual sexual hostility was never far beneath the surface.

"You want to hit me. Go on. Don't bottle it up." He taunted her, letting her flail at him, the blows landing with a satisfying thud on his wide shoulders or the hard wall of his chest. "I could use some kind of fight. Only you're hardly a match, are you?" Then his arms were pining her, his hands moving restlessly, ruthlessly, over her lightly clad body. "How do you think I can hold tight to promises when I feel like this?" he rasped.

"I don't know," she answered bitterly. "Since when did you have time for fallen angels anyway?" She tried desperately to keep her traitorous body under control but it was too avid for his.

"Twenty four hours a day, Dana," he gritted. "That's a helluva lot."

She continued to struggle, fighting down her own weakness.

"What? Didn't Phillipa convince you?" she shot at

him, ramming her fists against his chest, trying to put distance between them only she might as well have tried to push back a brick wall.

"What made you do it? I mean…God, Dana." Stifling a violent oath, he grasped a fistful of her silky hair, dragging her head back so his mouth could plunge over hers. Whatever she had done the sheer power of his passion undermined his will, sending it spinning away into space. This wasn't the magic they had known in the cave, or that night they had spent at her apartment. This was treacherous, overwhelming, threatening desire. He could stand no more, his jagged emotions sweeping over him like a flash flood.

She was trembling so badly she thought her knees would buckle. She was shrinking from him yet wild for his touch. She was two people. The woman who loved him, and the woman who couldn't bear his disbelief in her. A disbelief impossible to fight. Only as he took her mouth with such all-conquering passion, the woman in love found supremacy, the other Dana, the victim, moaning with the pain of it all.

He placed his hands on both her breasts, cupping them in his palms, then he bent, lowered his body so he was kneeling, drawing her to him so he could kiss her through the layers of filmy fabric, plunging his face against her, breathing in her body scents.

The excitement of it was so tremendous, her body felt incandescent. Finally she could no longer stand. She pitched forward overcome by ungovernable sensation, her blood in a ferment, her nerves frenetic.

He rose to his feet, lifting her so she slumped over his shoulder, like a rag doll he was holding.

"Logan…Logan…" was all she could say, her voice in an agonised whisper of sorrow, of protest, of an answering compulsive desire. She had to stop him. This one time at least.

Only Logan came to his senses. "I'm going to beat this," he said, and his strong voice shook. For once she was entirely in his power, but it gave him no satisfaction. Holding her captive like some pirate of old, he carried her to her room, throwing her down on the bed so tempestuously her body and mind whirred with reaction and her hair flew wildly around her head in a silver-gilt cloud.

"I won't hurt you if I can help it," he gritted from behind clenched teeth.

She grabbed for his hand and struggled to keep hold of it. "Then start believing in me," she begged, a pulse pounding away in her throat.

"I'm not the damn fool you think I am," he said angrily, pulling his hand away, his eyes in the lamplight blazing like sapphires.

"Okay," she said miserably, feeling utterly defeated. "I'm leaving. I mean that."

His dynamic face hardened to granite. "If I don't want you to leave, Dana, you *don't.*"

"You think you can keep me a prisoner?" she said bitterly, trying to sit up.

"You know I can."

And so he could. "I've always been afraid of you, Logan," she said, feeling the cold steel of him.

"I guess I've always been afraid of you, too. With good reason." He bent, kissed her again, so hard it pushed her head right back to the mattress. "Anyway, Alice needs you. Don't you remember? Her beautiful angelic Dana. Not the Dana who inflames men." With a violent movement he pulled away from her, away from the sight of her, her skin flushed, her eyes so dark and disturbed, her light robe that seemed to have lost its sash thrown back from her body, covered in a mere wisp of some creamy silk material. She looked so delicate, so mesmerizing, her nipples erect against the feather lightness of her nightgown, the long skirt of which had wrapped itself around her, pulling taut across her body, exposing her beautiful slender legs the sun had flushed with gold.

He was hideously humiliatingly aware of his own driving hunger. It bordered on agony but he forced himself to control it, tightly coiling his fingers into the calloused palms of his hands. He had never felt so smothered by desire. So smothered by a woman. And the worst part of all. The worst part…

With one galvanic movement Logan moved back from the canopied bed a fine beading of sweat breaking out on his dark copper skin. He could master it. He could master it. He was his own man.

"I can't stand the thought of another day with you," Dana cried, sick with love of him.

"Ditto, my lady." He had recovered sufficiently to manage a hard sardonic drawl. "This just isn't the right time to do anything about it, though, is it? Christmas is coming, remember? The season of peace on earth and good will to men. Everyone is enjoying having you here with the possible exception of yours truly, but then you're not making things exactly easy. Tomorrow I thought we might put up the Christmas tree. For Alice, of course. At least we both love *her*."

CHAPTER NINE

THE next morning Dana, unwilling to face the day, tried to sink back into sleep but it was too late. She was awake. Early morning sun washed across the room in a wave of bright golden light and bird calls were ringing again and again, carolling across the many species of beautiful native eucalypts that grew in the garden. She lay still on her back feeling the emotions of the night before pressing down on her. How could she carry off the rest of this holiday with Logan feeling the way he did? And all because she had tried to be there for Jimmy when Alice was the real object of her love and attention. She had done everything she could to deny it but there seemed no way to counter the damage. She might even have difficulty trying to explain the situation to an outsider. Where there was smoke there was fire, they would probably say. It was a classic example of mud-sticking.

Dana threw back the bedclothes, moving through the small dressing room to the pretty adjacent bathroom with its Wedgwood blue and white tiles. She was still shocked by Phillipa's admission she had slept with another man when engaged to Logan. Phillipa had claimed alcohol as an excuse and there was no doubt when under its influence the little devils got to work but the excuse hadn't worked. Had she really thought it would with Logan? Probably Phillipa had thought he would never know, when Logan had tabs on everyone even when he was out of the country.

Poor Phillipa! She shouldn't really be feeling sorry
for her but she did. Phillipa was a woman who would
use every weapon when under threat. Phillipa's words
came back to her. "A blind person could see Tyler was
in love with her." What had made her say that?
Jealousy, of course. But had she *really* believed it or
was it a wild charge born of desperation? But where
had she got the idea? Sandra? Sandra had been so
shocked and lost at Jimmy's funeral, her usual sense of
discretion hadn't been working. Had Sandra said something for Phillipa to catch on to? I don't really need
another person to condemn me, Dana thought.

When she walked out into the hallway, dressed in
yellow cotton jeans and a white tank top, her long hair
pulled back into a cool knot, Phillipa chose exactly that
time to emerge from her room.

Dana felt like bolting, making a return rush for her
room but Phillipa had already seen her. She, too, was
dressed in jeans and a pink shirt, dragging on a packed
bag and leaving it just outside her door.

"I always said there was a great deal more to you
than met the eye." Phillipa lost no time addressing
Dana directly.

"Good morning, Phillipa," Dana responded. Keep
calm. Keep cool. Phillipa is leaving. "Is there a problem?"

"I'm not sure it matters anymore," Phillipa answered in a bitter tone. "I never realised it before, but
you and your cousin are two of a kind." She strode up
to where Dana was standing, her eyes pink and puffy
as though she'd been weeping.

"Are you going to explain that?" Dana asked quietly, thinking this time she'd have to put Phillipa
straight.

"I'd be happy to." Phillipa gave a discordant little laugh. "Both of you went after the Dangerfield men. Your cousin caught Tyler by getting herself pregnant. It shouldn't take you long to achieve the same objective."

There was a sudden chill in Dana's voice. "You're getting very personal, aren't you, Phillipa? Offensive, too. I can see you're very upset but I'm not prepared to listen to this kind of thing. Your engagement to Logan is long over, so you're getting into something that isn't even your business."

"Of course!" Phillipa seemed to be trying to hold herself together but failing. "You don't cheat on Logan Dangerfield. No, sir. If you do you end up in Outer Mongolia."

"I'm sorry, Phillipa," Dana said, dipping her head, trying to balance pity and anger.

"*You're* sorry?" Now it was Phillipa's turn to stare. There was obvious sincerity in Dana's voice.

"I know what the pain of rejection is like." After all, she had been rejected last night.

"Well, well," Phillipa mocked. "I appreciate your concern, but only for *you* Logan might have come back to me. Then you had to arrive with your sparkly hair and your big brown eyes. You're as dangerous to my happiness as you ever were to your cousin's."

It was a monument to Dana's control she didn't cry aloud. "You're talking *scandal*, Phillipa," she warned. "You're talking character assassination. Mine as well as Jimmy's."

Phillipa's gaze went cold and triumphant. "I never said anything about Tyler. *You* did."

"I didn't intend to overhear you and Logan talking last night, either," Dana flashed back.

"An eavesdropper. Was it worth your while?" Phillipa asked contemptuously.

"I didn't know about Steve. That would be Steven Mitchell? One of the elite circle." Dana thought she deserved it.

Phillipa flushed violently. "I'm hoping you won't pass that on," she said stiffly, totally ignoring the fact she herself was into trading insults.

"No, I won't. I don't have any time for people who pass on hurtful gossip. I can only tell you this, Phillipa, and I want you to believe it, Jimmy and I *did not* have an affair. The thought never crossed my mind. Not ever. He was married to my cousin. End of story."

"But there's what Tyler said himself." Phillipa shook her head, brooding seriously.

"He never said anything about an *affair*. My God, Jimmy wasn't a liar. A destroyer. Maybe he had deep feelings for me and told his family, but when I think about it, why not? In so many ways he was a lost soul. He was doomed right from the start to walk in Logan's shadow. He never had a proper sense of himself, his own worth. He squandered his gifts and his money. But he was really only looking for love and fulfilment. I grieve to say Melinda didn't offer it to him."

Phillipa frowned severely. "We all knew about Melinda. But are you sure you didn't offer comfort?"

"Look at me, Phillipa," Dana urged. "Look right at me. Do you really think I did?"

Instead of looking at her, Phillipa looked off. "I'm not usually like this, you know," she said bleakly.

"There's a lot of pain in you."

Phillipa gave a wry laugh. "I guess." She reached out spontaneously and touched Dana's shoulder. "You can have Logan if you want, Dana. Have a great life."

"Except Logan doesn't want me," Dana was driven to say. "You see, Phillipa, I don't have the necessary qualifications. Like most women, I can't live up to perfection."

Midmorning hours, after Phillipa had flown out, three of the station hands brought the Christmas tree into the house. It was a specially grown-for-the-occasion casuarina, an annual thing, with the tree to be planted out after. Care had been taken to train the tree as it grew, now the slender grey-green pendulous branches, which naturally mimicked a conifer, showed a pyramid form. A huge sandstone pot had been placed to the right of the staircase in the entrance hall, now the men lofted the earth-balled tree into position.

"Up, up and away!" Alice cried excitedly. She stood within the circle of Dana's arms, her gold-flecked hazel eyes filled with joy. "Doesn't it look marvellous!"

"Wait until we decorate it." Dana hugged her. "Grandma has the most wonderful ornaments. They've been in the family for generations."

"This suit you, Miss," one of the men, the ginger-haired Bluey, called, willing to put it wherever Dana wanted. The top of the stairs if need be.

"That's fine, Bluey. Thank you. It's been beautifully grown. So much a part of this desert environment."

"No spruce's here, Miss." Bluey laughed. "Smells great, too. Want me to bring the stepladder in?"

"If you wouldn't mind, Bluey," Dana said. "We're going to start decorating it right away."

When Logan returned to the house he found the women happily engaged in setting up the tree. Already its slender branches were hung with a glittering array of silver, gold, scarlet and green orbs, baubles and or-

naments of all kinds, things Ainslie had collected over
the years. It came to him he had great affection for the
woman his father had married when he was only four.
Ainslie had never tried to mother him. Something in
him must have held out against it. God knows why.
Maybe his soul dwelt with his own mother. The beautiful creature who had died giving him birth. Said to be
the image of his father, his father had always told him
from the near-empty well of pain, "You have your
mother's eyes. Her beautiful, beautiful sapphire eyes.
Otherwise, you're a Dangerfield."

Ainslie had come to her marriage knowing she was
a kind of rebound, a marriage of convenience, fearing
her husband would never truly love her and her stepson
would never accept her. Neither had happened. Ainslie
was a woman who gave with all her heart, creating her
own special place in the Dangerfield family. A position
cemented when the children came. Tyler, then
Alexandra. Logan remembered he had been ecstatic
when his father told him there was going to be an addition to the family. An addition who turned out to be
Tyler. He had loved Tyler from the beginning, proud
of being big brother, longing for the day when the baby
would be old enough for them both to go adventuring
in the bush.

Only he and Tyler had been opposites.

And they had both fallen in love with the same
woman.

There she was, beautiful, intelligent, gifted Dana, for
all of that unassuming, no conceit in any form, full of
the social graces. Both Ainslie and Sandra had almost
from the start treated her like family. Tyler should have
married someone like Dana, he thought grimly. Dana
would have understood him, been firm enough, de-

manding enough to insist Tyler live up to his potential. Tyler had always been capable of so much better. It was their own father who had never understood him, forever holding up Logan as some impossible role model. It was a wonder they had remained as close as they had, Logan thought with deep regret.

Alice, turning, saw him, cried out, "Uncle Logan, come and see the tree. We've only got a few things more to put on. Grandma's little angels. They're all playing instruments."

"And we must be careful how we handle them, darling." Ainslie smiled. "They're quite precious."

"I know." Alice took a bisque porcelain angel very carefully into her hands. "Look at this one. He's playing the violin. I think I'd like to learn a musical instrument."

"That can be arranged." Logan trod across the parqueted floor, covered with a beautiful antique Persian rug, in his riding boots. "How are you, Dana?" he asked suavely. He'd been out since dawn so this was the first time they'd met up. "Sleep well?"

"Like a top," Dana responded just as pleasantly. "You're just in time to place the Star of Bethlehem at the top. None of us can match you for height."

Alice squealed with merriment. "Ladies don't grow *that* tall."

"You should see Bert Bonner's mother," Logan joked. "I practically have to look up to her."

"Really?" Alice asked, wide-eyed.

"Bert says he has to get up on a box to talk to her. Right, Dana, you can pass me the star." Logan put out his hand, catching her fingers briefly as she tried to hand it to him without actually touching him.

Her fingers tingled with electricity.

"Oh, this is so beautiful!" Alice breathed when the glistening silver Star of Bethlehem was in place. "Can we turn on the lights?"

"Go right ahead." Logan stepped down from the ladder, looking up at the tree that almost lofted to the upstairs gallery. Even in daylight the multicoloured lights were a bright illumination, reflecting each sparkling ornament, throwing a kaleidoscope of colour outward in a halo.

"Perhaps a little more tinsel," Dana mused. "That's if we've got any left."

"Plenty of everything in the attic, dear." Ainslie smiled, then inevitably grew sad. "Year after year we've had a tree since the children were babies, but this is the first time we've had it in the hall. I'm glad you came up with that idea, Dana. It makes a lovely change."

Feeling her grief, Logan bent and kissed the side of his stepmother's cheek. "You're the centre of this house, Ainslie. You've been since the day you came into it."

Ainslie caught her breath. Logan had always had the capacity to surprise her with the perfectly beautiful things he said. For a moment she let her head rest against his shoulder. "It's time to tell you, too, my dear, you've been a wonderful stepson to me. A wonderful brother to my children."

It was an emotional moment that could have turned to tears, but Logan saved it, bowing from the waist, an exaggeratedly formal gesture he managed to pull off with considerable natural grace. "Thank you, Mamma."

Alice came to hold his hand, staring up into his face. "I'm glad I'm here, Uncle Logan. I feel safe."

She, too, seemed on the point of tears. "Your darn right you are!" He picked her up, whirling her around. "I tell you what that tree really needs."

"What?" Alice stared adoringly at him.

"Lots and lots of wonderful presents all around it."

As the countdown to Christmas began, Mara was host to an influx of visitors, younger members of the extended Dangerfield family with their children, friends from all over the Outback popping in and out on private flights, business people from the Outback towns, all wanting to convey their best wishes and enjoy Mara's legendary hospitality at the same time.

The Christmas tree in the entrance hall was now surrounded by a great pile of beautifully wrapped and beribboned presents chosen with care, the papers luxurious, most in the festive colours of Christmas: gleaming silver with ruby, rich gold and emerald, Santa Claus and mistletoe and berries, reindeers, winged angels in flight, all casting their own special glow. The children who came to call found the sight irresistible and Alice for once was in her element playing the small hostess and leader.

Christmas is such a wonderful time of the year it softens everyone's heart and Alice had discovered peace and sunshine in her life. Her "bad moments" when she couldn't cope with the pressures were becoming far less frequent now. There was more understanding in her life, more happy experiences, more encouragement to learn things and build up her own feelings of confidence and inner strength.

Reared in an increasingly unhappy household with her father too little there and her mother not bothering to mask her own unhappiness and frustrations, Alice had not been allowed to grow and blossom. In her new environment she was developing overnight, secure in the love and stability of her family around her. Not that there wasn't the occasional storm, but when it wasn't getting much attention it quickly passed. The thing that most impressed the family was the way Alice was now relating to her own age group, the previous big problem.

"It's not the same as school," she told Dana. "These kids all like me."

Dana took her by the shoulders so she could get Alice's full attention. "So help me they'll *all* like you at school if you're the friendly little person you are here. I'll even go beyond that, Alice, you have the capacity for leadership. It's all up to you, darling, isn't it? You can be anything you want to be. You're clever. You're full of ideas. You're a sensitive little soul. You can afford to take pride in yourself."

"That's right," Alice confirmed with a big smile on her face.

Little trips were organised to entertain, picnics beside the billabongs, where the children looped ropes around the tree and swung out into the water. Even Alice, once a little fearful, tried it, full of life and joy. Her swimming lessons had been progressing and in any case the younger children weren't allowed into the deep.

"You're such a good example to Alice," Sandra told Dana one day as they lazed against cushions watching Alice and the visiting cousins swoop shrieking across the glittering water.

"It's a wonder for her to be within the magic circle." Dana smiled. "Not like school with the other children poking fun at her. Alice loves these children and more wonderfully they love her. Just look at her now.''

''Dana, Sandy, watch me, I'm going to let go,'' she yelled, and fell without a moment's hesitation or fright into the sparkling water where the other children were sporting like small dolphins.

''I do admire the way you handle her.'' Sandra sighed. ''She's changed so much she's almost a different child.''

''Well, she had a tough time of it, don't forget. It was a very bad experience for her seeing her parents fighting. She's escaped all that. She feels loved and secure.''

''Until the day her mother wants her back,'' Sandra warned, waving at little Katy. ''It's all up to Melinda really. She's the mother, right or wrong.''

There was no need to tell Dana. She never stopped worrying about it.

Around this time she also began regular photographic sessions, her mind constantly turning over ideas and possibilities, which, as she moved freely around Mara, seemed to be endless. She had worked a number of times with a well-known travel author and journalist mostly in tropical North Queensland's sugar lands, glorious country, and the wonder of the Great Barrier Reef, which had to be paradise on earth, but nowhere she found so compelling so challenging as the vast Timeless Land. One of the world's harshest environments, it was frighteningly lonely, savage in drought, yet capable of turning on heart-stopping displays of beauty.

When the time was right, she had seen and photographed Mara literally covered in flower. Miles and

miles of fragrant flowering annuals that spread in all
directions as far as the eye could see. The wildflowers
were remarkable but so was the prolific bird life, the
vast spinifex plains, the great flat-topped mesas, the
crystal-clear spring-fed pools, the gibber plains that
glittered like a giant mosaic and the magnificent albeit
terrifying sight of the Simpson Desert, the Wild Heart.

More and more she was filled with the invigorating
ambition to capture on camera the very essence of this
mirage-stalked country, to bring it to people who might
never have a chance to see it for themselves. She was
in a unique position to do that with her ties to Mara. It
seemed to her, too, she would like to do her own writing, convey her own feelings and reactions as she ex-
plored this remote part of the world. Perhaps she could
inspire her readers as she was inspired herself. It gave
her lots to think about. She was grateful, too, for her
technical expertise, though it hadn't come overnight. It
was the result of years of highly specialised training.

Returning one afternoon from one of her treks she
came on a mustering party driving a herd of cleanskins,
cattle as yet unbranded, into one of the holding yards.
Red dust rose in a whirlwind so she parked some little
distance off enjoying the spectacle framed in the dancing gold-shot blue light. Vivid green butterfly trees
grew in clumps all round the area still heavy in white
and mauve blossom, the earth a bright red ocre, the sky
a vivid cloudless blue. It really was a scene for the
cinema screen, she thought. There were even sound effects. Cattle lowing, stockmen riding in among them,
whips cracking harmlessly in the air, urging the beasts
into the yard. Every few minutes one would try to make
a break with no success until a young red bull decided

it was high time to leave the mob and head back for
the hills.

Through the wall of men came a rider, darting his
horse in and out, nosing the errant animal back into the
enclosure. Both man and horse were lightning quick in
their movements, a pleasure to watch. Dana took up a
position with her Hasselblad, aiming it at the tall lean
cowboy, pearl grey akubra rakishly angled on his dark
head, sitting his bright chestnut horse with easy mas-
tery.

She shot off a half a dozen frames before she became
aware of him riding towards her and holding up his
hand.

"What are you up to?"

She lay the camera down. "Does it require an explanation? I'm taking pictures of you."

"Whatever for?" He seemed genuinely puzzled.

"Because your so damned colourful. You look like
the guy in the old Marlboro commercials, only better,"
she said.

"At least I have the sense not to smoke."

"Pretty well everyone has these days. Why don't
you let me take a few more for my girlfriends," she
taunted him. "Most of them fell in love with you on
the strength of that one photo on my bookcase. You're
every woman's idea of an Outback hero."

"That's me." He smiled with lazy satire. "God, it's
hot!" He took off his hat and ran a hand through his
thick hair. His hands were beautifully shaped. She remembered the feel of them on her body. How she found
their faint callousing and strength so exciting.

"If it's not too personal a question," she asked, "are
we likely to see Phillipa again before Christmas?"

He bent the full force of his brilliant gaze on her. "Phillipa is past caring about me."

"So that's a no?" With Phillipa, anything was possible. She might have got her second wind.

"More or less." This with a slight edge. "Her parents might turn up. They won't want to cut themselves off from us in any way."

"I guess not," she agreed laconically.

"Where's Alice?" Deliberately, he changed the subject. "The two of you are always together."

"She's having fun with the children. The last time I saw them they were dressing up in the attic. Someone is going to have to put all the stuff they've pulled out of the old trunks away."

"Don't *you* bother about it," he told her. "Now that you're here, why don't we go for a ride?"

For a moment she couldn't think of anything at all to say. They had been well and truly keeping their distance for just on a week now.

"Is there something wrong?" he challenged with the old tantalising mockery.

"Friendly today, are we?"

He gave a brief laugh. "Dana, you're my pain and my delight. Besides, even my iron control doesn't work all the time."

"Then I'd love to." Just for a second she smiled at him. "You'll have to come with me. I haven't got a horse."

"Mine will take both of us."

"You're joking?" Her eyes widened.

"Dana, I mean everything I say. You're a featherweight, that's okay. Or are you frightened of coming up before me?"

His amusement restored her cool. "It works for Alice. I don't know about me."

"So let's try it."

"What about the jeep, my equipment?" She looked around. "It's valuable."

"Don't fret. Who's here to steal it? Cover it with something. Zack can run the jeep back to the house."

She was fiercely tempted even when her wounded feelings were barely healed over.

"Make up your mind," he said, directing a challenging look into her eyes.

"I can't believe I'm doing this." Dana moved to take care of her camera and equipment, covering it with a light rug. Meanwhile Logan rode back a little distance having a short conversation with Zack, his leading hand. She had one last chance to cry off and drive home, only she was too damned excited. This was the sort of man Logan was. All electricity and excitement, and just to prove it while her mind was in arrears, he reached down for her like a stuntman doing tricks and lofted her into the saddle before him. His enveloping arm was an inch from her breasts, his breath fanning her cheek. She scarcely heard the men's applause. She didn't even remember riding out of the camp. They were heading for the crossing fording it at the shallowest point then galloping up the incline to the sheltered valley beyond.

It was a madly heady feeling galloping across the desert flats, the wild bush around them, the wind tearing at her hair, a great flight of budgerigar, the phenomenon of the Outback joyfully joining in the chase, winging in an emerald green and gold V-shaped formation, as though spurring them on. Logan's face was hunkered down over hers, his left arm locked around her upper body, the tips of his fingers pressing into the swelling flesh at the side of her breast. Just to have physical contact was to feel enormously energised. She thought she could have cheerfully ridden to the ends of the earth with him so infinitely spell-binding was his influence over her. Almost unknown to her, her own hands were caressing the length of his bare arm, moving up and down, stroking the light tracery of hair, holding his arm even closer to her so he had to feel her quickening pulses, the primitive throb of her heart. It was almost as though someone had started up a small drum. Over the flats they went until finally they reached the point where their bodies were burning. Not from the heat that rose in waves from the red sun-baked earth, but the heat within. The great all-pervading flames neither of them could put out. This was part of the sorcery of love, the recklessness, the anguish, the ferocious need for physical fulfilment.

Finally, Logan rode down on a spring-fed pool, clear cool water oozing up from the sandy bed, the pool lined by long reeds the area totally surrounded by stands of desert oaks. He dismounted swiftly, seized Dana, pulled her from the saddle and into his waiting arms. He was mad for her, even dangerous, he thought. In truth he was trying to get a hold on himself, hating the sense of going out of control, but he wanted this woman too much. He could never have foreseen how terribly he would want her.

Forgetful of his strength, he almost lifted her off her feet to kiss her, pushing her head back into his shoulder, covering her mouth passionately as if kissing her was as necessary to him as the air he breathed or the precious water without which a man would die. He kissed her over and over as if this was his one and only chance, his hand moving, moving, deeply massaging her spine, moulding her body ever closer. Her mouth tasted of apricots, her skin smelled like wildflowers after rain. He knew she was breathless, panting in his arms, but she wasn't struggling away. The more he wanted, the more her body gave. He plunged his hand into the open neck of her soft shirt, breaking a button, but anything to get to her exquisite naked breast. Now he understood fully how that one woman could change a man's life. He didn't want an affair. An affair would be wrong. He wanted this woman to love all the days of his life. He wanted to be free of the torment. He wasn't good at giving up the things he wanted.

She hadn't been wearing her hair loose but the wind had whipped it free of its ribbon. Now he grasped a handful of this beautiful long hair he loved, turning her head to the side so he could kiss her lovely neck. She was quivering in his arms. Burying her face against his shoulder, moaning a little as though her heart was breaking.

He drew a breath so sharp it hurt his ribs. "Let me love you," he urged. "I would never force you. But let me love you."

Her eyes were so dark yet at the centre was a leaping flame. She began to laugh, a soft wild little sound, no mirth in it but a kind of acknowledged abandonment. "We said we wouldn't."

"I know." His face was full of urgent hungers, a desire that raged. "You want it though, Dana, don't you?"

Want? She was ravenous. She let her head fall back, stretching her throat. "Ah...*yes!*" She wasn't a woman who had ever expected to be totally dominated by a man yet nonetheless she was. Logan consumed her. It was that simple.

CHAPTER TEN

THREE days before Christmas the peace of the household was shattered when Melinda flew in unannounced and alone. Logan, who saw the four-seater Cessna fly in, doubled back to the landing strip in the four-wheel drive, his eyes focused on the charter flight that was just coming in to land. He felt absolutely no warning. Visitors had been flying in and out for most of December. Usually, though, they always rang ahead to say they were coming. He was familiar with the charter plane. It was one of Westaway's. Ray Westaway was a good friend. It was probably Ray come to say hello and pay his respects to Ainslie. By the time he drove the vehicle to the strip, the plane had landed and the pilot was on the strip, handing down a young woman.

Melinda.

Dismay welled up in him, a fierce sense of protectiveness for his family, Alice in particular. Whatever Melinda was doing here it could only spell trouble. A harsh judgement to some but he knew her too well.

The pilot came towards him, smiling like he was among friends, carrying his passenger's two pieces of luggage. "Hi, there, Mr. Dangerfield. One passenger delivered safely." He turned to include the very pretty blonde who was showing for the first time an unexpected uneasiness? Wariness? Whatever. Dangerfield wasn't smiling. To the pilot's mind he looked positively formidable. This was his reputation anyway. A powerful man who had stepped very neatly into his father's shoes. And he was angry. Quite angry. He had never seen such a blaze in a man's eyes before.

A few minutes later the pilot flew off, feeling mollified Dangerfield had greeted him pleasantly, giving him a message to convey to his boss. He remembered now they were good friends.

On the ground, Logan settled Melinda in the front passenger seat then went around to the other side, opening up the door and climbing behind the wheel. "You're full of surprises, Melinda," he said, trying to view the arrival calmly. "I understood you were enjoying yourself in London?"

Melinda touch a hand to her short, pretty hair. She was doing it a new way and she looked older and more sophisticated than he had ever seen her. "Max hates the cold. He has great friends in Sydney. We're staying with them."

"So it's serious, then, with Max?" What exactly had Tyler meant in his wife's life? he thought with a heavy heart, asking, "What's Max's other name?"

"He's the man I'm probably going to marry," Melinda evaded. "It doesn't matter his name."

"I'm afraid it does, Melinda, as you're Alice's mother."

"I've learned to keep a few things to myself," she said, "for the time being anyway."

"You could have let us know you were coming."

"Don't be awkward, Logan. It was a spur-of-the-moment thing. I wanted to give you all a big surprise."

"Then I have to say I find your idea of a big surprise pretty bizarre. You can't expect us to feel overjoyed about it."

"Well, it was never your way, was it?" Melinda gave him her kittenish triangular smile.

They were even more shocked at the house. The moment Melinda set foot in the entrance hall exclaiming at the Christmas tree, the pervading tranquillity seemed to fly out the door.

"Melinda!" Ainslie tried her level best for courtesy and calm. "This is indeed a surprise. We didn't expect you back so soon."

"Only a flying visit. A week or two to miss the Winter. "Dana!" Melinda held out her arms as Dana for a few moments transfixed started down the stairs. "My very *favourite* cousin."

"Good God, Melinda," Dana responded in a heartfelt groan. "Couldn't you have let us know you were coming?"

"Why, Dee. Don't you like surprising people? I'm here with Max, actually. We're staying with friends of his, right on the Harbour. An absolute mansion. The Goddards. You must have heard of them." She named a well-known racing family then stopped abruptly as though she had given away too much. "I slipped away for a time. I hope you don't mind, but I have a few things to straighten out."

"Of course," Ainslie answered, still shocked. "You're staying overnight surely?"

"I'd like that." Melinda smiled. "I can't be away from Max's side for any longer than that. And Alice, where is she?"

Logan couldn't help the cynical laugh that broke from him. "I was wondering when you were going to mention your daughter." He gestured towards the formal drawing room. "Let's go in and sit down, shall we?" He turned his head briefly to speak to Dana. "Would you mind finding Alice, please, Dana. You could prepare her by telling her her mother is here."

Dana sprang into action almost running through the house. What did Melinda's sudden appearance mean? Was it possible Melinda was becoming more human? Did she intend to resume her God-given role and take Alice back with her? If so, they would miss Alice dreadfully. And what of Alice's feelings? And who was this Max? How serious was the relationship? Was he the sort of man who would be prepared to love another man's child? And *Jimmy!* Had he really meant so little to Melinda she had already put him out of her life?

She came bursting out of the house, finding Alice sitting beside Retta on the grass. They were spreading out drawings, things Alice had completed with Retta acting as teacher. Retta was a very talented artist, both in the traditional aboriginal way and the Western culture. She had already shown Alice an easy way to draw animals.

"There you are!" Dana breathed.

They both turned at the tight, constricted sound in Dana's normally warm melodious tones.

"I've got a good little pupil here." Retta smiled, then with her enviable sensitivity picked up on Dana's agitated feelings. "Everything okay, Miss Dana?"

Pray God it was. "Yes, fine, Retta." Dana tried for a smile that didn't quite come off. "Thank you so much for looking after Alice, but she has to come into the house now."

"Ah, Dana, I'm having a nice time," Alice complained.

"Yes, I know you are, darling, but something has happened. I want to tell you all about it."

"You're not upset about it, are you?" Alice rose immediately to her feet, staring into Dana's face.

"No, dear." Dana turned to address Retta who was

standing quietly nearby. "Perhaps you could collect the drawings, Retta. I'd love to see them later."

"No trouble. Go along now, Alice. We can take a walk together later."

Inside the house, Dana drew Alice into the kitchen storeroom. "Listen, darling, a very big surprise. Mummy is here. She wants to see you."

For answer, Alice reached out, picked up a small can of baked beans and threw it violently against the wall. "If this means I have to go back with her I'm not coming."

"Alice," Dana came close to wailing, taking the child into her arms. "This is *Mummy*. She's been missing you."

"Well, I haven't been missing her." Alice frowned ferociously, twisting away. "I don't want her anymore, Dana. I like things the way they are."

"But will you always, Alice," she pleaded. "Your mother has hurt you, but give her a chance. She's come all this way out here to make amends."

"You take care of me, Dana," Alice said, her light brown head dropping. "Mummy is mean to me. She doesn't like me. She doesn't want me around."

"Alice, please, why don't you let her tell you how sorry she is? Please give her another chance. Mummy was hurt, too."

Alice looked up into Dana's eyes. "You really want this, Dana. You're not punishing me?"

Dana almost reeled back in shock. "Punishing you. Lord, sweetheart, would I ever do that? Would I ever do anything to make you unhappy?"

"Daddy said you didn't know about Mummy."

"Daddy had his own problems. Mummy and I grew up together. We've been together all our lives."

"And what does Uncle Logan and Grandma say?" Alice looked her straight in the eye.

"We're all trying to understand our feelings, darling. Maybe we all can't be together nice and friendly like your cousins and the children, but we have to learn how to cope with what's going on in our lives. You're growing up now, Alice. You're a serious little person. I only want you to greet your mother and listen to what she has to say. Parents must be treated with dignity and respect."

"Kids have to be treated with respect, too," Alice burst out, giving vent to all her pent-up feelings of hurt and rejection.

"You should be happy Mummy's here," Dana said sorrowfully.

"Well, I'm not." Alice reached out and grasped Dana's hand. "This is important to you, Dana, isn't it?"

"Important to you, too, darling." Dana squeezed her small hand, praying and praying Melinda would come into her own and express loving maternal feelings. She had changed a good deal in appearance. Indeed she was looking stunning. With the grace of God she would make up for the hurt she had inflicted on her child.

When they went into the drawing room, Melinda, sitting alone on a Victorian settee, jumped up, a radiant smile on her face. "Alice, sweetie, don't you look well. The prettiest I've ever seen you. Come to Mummy and give me a great big hug."

Alice hesitated a moment, turned and looked at Dana, then walked towards her mother.

"Hello, Mummy," she said composedly. "Didn't you like London?"

"I loved it! I can't wait to go back." Melinda bent

over Alice and kissed the cheek her daughter presented. "This is what is called a flying visit."

"Why?" Alice asked.

"Why what?"

"Why did you come?" Alice asked. "It's a long trip just to see me."

"That's right, and I am a little tired. Aren't you pleased to see me?" Melinda's blue eyes looked hurt.

"You look very pretty," Alice commented.

Melinda brightened. "Well, I know I can never be a genuine beauty like Dee but I can turn a few heads. Why don't you come up to my room while I have a little rest? We can talk. Is that all right, Ainslie?" Melinda turned her blond head.

"Of course, Melinda," Ainslie answered quietly. "I'm hoping when you're feeling refreshed you can tell us your plans."

"Oh, I will." Melinda took hold of Alice's hand. "I've lots to catch up on with my daughter."

"Come with us, Dana," Alice begged.

"Not now, Alice." Melinda gave a little smile. "I know you love Dana, but I'm hoping you can spare a little time for your mother."

"Dear God!" Logan said slowly and deliberately after they had gone. "What does all this mean?"

"I couldn't bear to lose Alice now," Ainslie said piteously. "To take her away to another country! Don't grandparents lose out."

"Who said anything about her wanting to take Alice away?" Logan asked, a vertical frown between his black brows. "It's a good thing Sandy isn't here or we could have a fight on our hands."

"Give her a chance, Logan," Dana implored.

"You *want* her to take Alice?"

"No, no." Dana slumped dejectedly into an armchair. "But she is Alice's mother."

"Of course she is," Ainslie agreed wretchedly. "If only she was a real mother. A real person. I don't think she's changed."

Dinner was a quiet meal with a kind of unbearable tension beneath the superficial conversation. Alice had been allowed to stay up, now she sat beside her mother, wrapped in a blanket of silence.

"Everything all right, my little love?" Ainslie asked, her pale face showing her anxiety. "You're not eating."

"I have a headache, Grandma," Alice said quietly.

"Naturally she's wanting me to stay on," Melinda said.

"I imagine she might, as you're her mother," Logan clipped off. It was driving him wild Melinda just sitting there saying nothing. He had the dismal feeling she was toying with them, playing some preconceived game.

Alice spoke again. "I don't care if Mummy goes." From the expression on her face there could be no doubt she meant it.

"That's not very nice, sweetie," Melinda said.

"It's what I want," Alice exclaimed.

Melinda reached for her wineglass and picked it up. "I can see you've all been doing your best to turn my child against me," she said acidly.

Dana looked directly at her cousin with angry eyes, then she pushed back her chair and stood up. "If you have a headache, Alice, why don't I take you up to your room?"

"I want her to stay," Melinda said.

"I think not." Logan gestured to Dana to go. "This conversation is obviously for the grown-ups."

In her bedroom Alice slumped down dejectedly on the bed. "I belong to Mummy. Is that right, Dana?"

"Pretty well, darling, until you're older."

"So she can take me at any time?"

Yes, Dana thought. "If you want that, darling."

"Well, I don't." There was rebellion in Alice's voice. "I want to stay here. I don't want to go away. I would miss you terribly. I would miss Grandma and Uncle Logan and Sandy. I would miss all the kids when they come to visit. I'd miss Mrs. Buchan. Retta, too. She's so sweet to me. Mara is a wonderful happy place."

This was a dilemma and it was tearing at Dana's heartstrings. "Don't you think you could be happy with Mummy?"

"Not the way I want to be," Alice said slowly.

"Did Mummy say she was going to take you?" Dana didn't like to question Alice too closely but they had to know.

"She was talking mostly about you," Alice surprised her by saying.

"Me?"

"You and Uncle Logan." Alice nodded her head. "She asked how you were getting on."

"And what did you say?"

"I said Uncle Logan loves you and you love him. I can feel it deep inside." Alice clasped her small hands together and pressed them to her heart. "I've been praying you'd get married then I could be your child."

"Oh, Alice." Dana sat down on the bed and caught the little girl to her. "Oh, Alice," she moaned, "this is so very very hard for all of us. I'm your godmother.

I'll always be your godmother. I'll always be there for you.''

"I'm afraid," Alice said.

It took Dana close on half an hour to settle the child for bed, so when she returned downstairs she found the family had adjourned to the library.

"Alice is asleep at last," she said as she walked into the room, acutely aware of the tension that clouded the atmosphere.

"You've quite taken her over, haven't you, Dee?" Melinda said, not troubling to hide her disdain.

"You didn't seem too concerned about doing the job," Logan reminded her very abruptly. "You've obviously come to tell us of your intentions, so we'd appreciate it if you would. Alice has had a very disruptive life. She's only now settling down."

"Why this endless talk of Alice?" Melinda fumed. "She's had a pretty good life. Anyone would think she was suffering some abuse."

Logan stared at her from his position behind the massive mahogany desk. Behind him, above the mantelpiece hung a portrait of his grandfather, a sternly handsome man with a look of power and achievement. It was obvious they were cut from the same cloth. "Ever heard of emotional deprivation," he said.

"It seems to me I know more about it than you do," Melinda retorted. "I'm the original deprived child."

"That's right, the never-ending story," Dana burst out. "Deprived of your parents certainly, Melinda, but not of plenty of love and attention. You've never been gracious enough to acknowledge that. Anyway I would have thought your own emotional deprivation would have made you more understanding. More determined to see Alice would have a good life."

"It's a great relief then, isn't it, she's an heiress," Melinda countered. "Which brings me to my proposition," she went on calmly. "I'm willing to sign papers relating to *your* guardianship of Alice, Logan, if that's what you all want. You don't seem to be able to hide it. There is, however, a price."

"Really?" Logan's voice was marvellously ironical. "How did I know that was coming."

Melinda flushed and stood up abruptly, beginning to pace the far end of the spacious room. A pretty, petite figure in a short, gold-embroidered navy dress. "Max is a wealthy man, but I have no intention of being dependent on him like I was on Jimmy."

"You have a not considerable inheritance from my son," Ainslie pointed out bleakly, glad Sandra wasn't there to hear this.

"I want more," Melinda said flatly. "A lot more. You've got it."

"What sort of money are we talking about here?" Logan demanded, his handsome mouth thinning.

"Another five million," Melinda said as though that was more than fair. "It doesn't seem much for a child and you Dangerfields always figure in the Rich List."

She didn't have long to wait for Logan's answer. "I'm terribly sorry, Melinda," he said very quietly, "but it's not on."

"Logan!" Ainslie stared at her stepson as if to measure the wisdom of his words. What was money compared to the happiness and well-being of her granddaughter?

"See, Ainslie agrees!" Melinda turned on him in triumph. "What about you, Dana? You know how important your opinion is to Logan," she said, with sly meaning.

"I'm not believing this," Dana said, a slight betraying tremor in her voice. "Are you saying you're prepared to *sell* your child?"

Melinda shrugged. "Well, I'd certainly like to see her from time to time. Don't look so damned righteous. You've always told me I'm a poor mother."

"Even so, I'm not handing over another penny," Logan cut across them, rising to his daunting six-three. "So what are the other options, Melinda?" he asked, watching her pretty kitten face suddenly look pinched.

"I'll collect her after Christmas. You won't have her, I'll see to that."

"And Max is in agreement with all this?" Logan looked suave.

"Anything I do is fine with Max," Melinda said shortly. "He's madly in love with me."

"Poor devil! He's happy to take on a ready-made child, is he?" Logan continued.

"He certainly is!" Melinda huffed.

"Then why not take her now before Christmas?" Logan suggested, quite reasonably. "I see no reason to wait. You're Alice's mother. No one can deny that. You want her. Well and good. You can't expect us to keep looking after her. I say take her tomorrow. We have all her clothes ready."

For the first time Melinda appeared aghast and she wasn't the only one. Ainslie covered her face with her hands and Dana sprang up, velvety brown eyes flashing fire. "You can't mean this, Logan. You can't," she cried, knowing Logan had a ruthless streak.

"Indeed I do," he said harshly. "I won't be blackmailed."

"It's Alice's whole life that's at stake." She went closer to him, caught hold of his arm.

"I thought you were the one who was telling us all to give Melinda a chance." He looked down at her. "Something miraculous was to happen and she'd turn over a new leaf."

"Please, Logan," she begged. "Won't you consider it? She can have what money Jimmy left me. I haven't touched it."

"You're not seeing this clearly, Dana," he told her, his blue eyes cold. "I'm the head of this household and I say, *no*. Melinda has received more than enough and I have no intention of getting into a legal battle. If she's going to marry this Max and he is quite happy about assuming the responsibilities of a stepfather, I say Melinda should cut all the anguish short and take Alice now."

"Excuse me, dear. I'm going to bed," Ainslie said, rising a little unsteadily to her feet. "You must do as you think best."

"Let me take you up." Logan moved swiftly to support his stepmother. "I'm sure you and Dana have things to say to each other, Melinda," he threw over his shoulder. "I won't be long."

Both young women were silent until long after the sounds of footsteps had died away, then Melinda launched into a plea, a well-remembered febrile look in her light blue eyes. "Talk to him. Convince him this is the best way to do it."

"What makes you think I could possibly sway Logan," Dana demanded. "He's a law unto himself."

"Come on, Dee." Melinda flashed her a look. "You two have something going, haven't you? You've always been in love with him only you were too stupid to see it."

Dana ignored that. "I'm telling you, once Logan has

made up his mind, no one on earth could change it for him."

"But you must *try*," Melinda insisted with extreme intensity. "Invite him into your bed, that's if you haven't done it already. I bet he's one hell of a lover, too. All that fire! But underneath, he's cruel. He professed to love Alice yet he's prepared to let her go."

Dana, too, was unprepared for his reaction. "What did you expect him to do?" she said wretchedly. "Pay up just like that. Who could ever trust you anyway?"

"You can trust me *easily*," Melinda maintained.

"How's that? You've been a liar all your life. You've lied about me."

"And enjoyed it," Melinda clipped off, crisply decisive.

"Why would you want to hurt me, Melinda? Hurt Jimmy's memory?" Dana asked very seriously.

"I've buried Jimmy," Melinda flashed back. "He was unfaithful to me God knows how many times. If you weren't one of his women it was only because his feeling for you was all tenderness. Dear sweet Dana, the embodiment of all that is good."

"So why did you write to Logan telling him Jimmy and I had an affair?" Dana asked heavily.

"Oh, jealousy I suppose," Melinda cried in exasperation. "What kind of an idiot are you? I've always been jealous of you. Even your friends told you that. Why should you have a man crazy about you? I never had."

"What about this Max?" Dana rushed in, frowning. "What's the big secret about his last name? Does he even *exist*?"

"It's Max De Winter, if you must know," Melinda joked. Then, "No, it's Max Ferguson. No need to tell

Logan, I don't want him checking up on me. Max is a lot older than I am, as I told you, but he's an impressive-looking man and he can give me the life I've always wanted.''

''And he wants a child?'' Dana was starting to wonder.

''Exactly. A ready-made one. He won't want me to fall pregnant. We'll be doing a lot of travelling together. Entertaining. He has a lot of business interests across the Atlantic and here. I could see Alice when we're in the country.''

''Gee, that's big of you.'' Dana shook her head sadly. ''I just don't understand you, Melly.''

''When did you ever?'' Melinda retaliated, sweeping out of the room and up the staircase to her bedroom, where she locked it.

Dam all the Dangerfields to hell! Especially Logan.

Dana waited quite a while for Logan to return. She stood by the window looking sightlessly out over the moonlit garden, desperately trying to keep herself together. Could Logan really bring himself to pass Alice over at this time? At Christmas, when Alice was the happiest she had ever been?

She could understand his anger at Melinda's demands for money. A great fortune to most people but not people like the Dangerfields, the establishment since pioneering days. She'd had to face, much as she regretted it, Melinda would never become the person she had hoped. Melinda was a bitter disappointment, with little capacity for parenthood. So why then, if she didn't get the money, was she going to take Alice? Because the current pivotal person in her life, Max, wanted it? Would a middle-aged businessman who travelled extensively want a small child? Was Alice to be shunted to a boarding school? Why didn't Logan just pay the money? Let her have it. Could he see the loss of her grandchild would shatter Ainslie's life? Let alone hers. Hadn't she sworn to Alice she would never abandon her?

By the time Logan did return, Dana, for all her efforts, had worked herself into an emotional state. It showed in the line of her body, her flushed skin and the glitter in her dark eyes.

"We won't stop here," Logan said in his commanding way, taking her arm and ushering her out onto the colonnaded terrace. "Let's get away from the house. I take it Melinda has gone up to bed?"

"Yes." Her response was brittle but it was the best she could do. "She's beside herself her little scheme mightn't work."

He tried to restrain the abrasiveness that was in him but failed. "So you've finally got your eyes open?"

That stung her. "I'm not like you, Logan, I'm sorry," she answered in a jagged voice. "You have a rare talent for being able to categorise people on sight. I like to give them a chance."

"Well, you must be feeling you've made one hell of a mistake tonight." He tossed her a tight smile. "Your cousin is what's known as a gold digger."

"It certainly looks like it. But she's dealing with the wrong person, isn't she? The toughest negotiator for miles."

"I wouldn't last long if I weren't and I've had a lot more exposure than you to the underside of human nature. Let's walk."

"Anything you say, Logan." She meant to mock him, instead it echoed the pain in her heart. She let him lead her down the short flight of steps onto the circular drive with the lights from the house playing over the three-tier fountain. "Is Ainslie all right?" she asked, looking up into his face. A handsome face. A proud face. "It worries me to see her so upset."

"You surprise me, Dana." He used the sleek tone she knew so well. "Don't you think I can look after my stepmother?"

"I'm certain you *mean* to."

"You can't expect me to adopt your sweet girlish ways. Ainslie's willing to let me handle this situation. Unlike *you.*"

She tried unsuccessfully to hold on to her temper. "That's really weird. Ainslie must know all about your ruthless streak."

"Oddly she regards me as the perfect stepson. What's so ruthless about what I'm doing, anyway?" he countered.

They had begun walking, now she stopped in the semi-darkness of the trees and faced him. "You're prepared to let Alice go?"

"You mean I'm not doing what Melinda is asking," he corrected, his voice hard.

"I can't bear to think about it." Dana began to move on, agitation racing through her blood. How could she love Logan when he tied her in knots?

He caught her up easily, whirling her around. "It might pay you to use your mind and not your emotions. You're tearing yourself to pieces. That's not a man's way."

"Hell no!" She reacted with unconcealed hostility, pushing against his strong hands but he only tightened his grip on her. "Why would the all powerful cattle baron accept blackmail?"

"It's not going to come to that."

"Why? What are you going to do to stop it?" Even when they were arguing her pulses were all aglitter, her heartbeats racing.

"I'm going to call Melinda's bluff. Pulling stunts doesn't sit well with me and that's what's she's doing. It would be great if it could come off. An extra five million to get on with her life." He stared down into her face, shifting her a little so she was caught in the full moon's copper radiance. "You don't really think she wants Alice, do you, or are you still wallowing in all those cousinly marshmallow feelings?"

"You hate women, don't you?" she accused him.

He seemed amused. "Only one of you can drive me nuts and I'm looking at her."

She tried desperately to interpret every nuance in his voice. "I'm scared of what she'll do, Logan. Can't you understand that?"

"Of course I can." He released one hand to cup her nape. "You've had too much trouble dealing with your cousin. Now you have to leave her to me. Are you prepared to do that?"

"I don't have much choice." She moved her head against his hand, unable to resist the basic sensual pleasure.

"No, you don't," he agreed. "But you could have some faith. While you've been thinking of ways to kill me, I've been calling in a few favours."

That would explain his time away. "Good heavens!" Dana stared up at him in surprise. "You should be running the country."

"No thanks, but we now have the lowdown on Max. Max Ferguson is his name. Melinda let slip she was staying with the Goddards. I don't know them personally, but I have plenty of connections who do. One's Eve Goddard's brother.''

Frantically she considered the ramifications. ''Could this damage Melinda?''

He tilted her chin. ''Do you care?''

''I can't help caring, Logan. It's the way I am.''

''Sure.'' His voice softened. ''Anyway, Max is over fifty. He already has a grown up family.''

Dana's eyes widened. ''You can't mean he's married?'' She felt shocked.

''Not exactly. He's divorced.''

''Good grief!'' She had to steady herself against him and he drew her right into his arms. ''The word is out and it's all very confidential, Max would be highly unlikely to want to start another family. He has one and he's a very busy man. The whisper is Melinda is part of a package. She's young, she's blond. Max has always preferred blondes, and she has a nice little nest egg of her own.''

''Most people would call it a lot. Does your friend know if he means to marry her?'' Dana asked, wondering if Melinda had made yet another mistake.

''Apparently she's just what Max needs in his life.''

''And Mrs. Goddard won't say a word?''

Logan shook his head. ''She swears she won't mention the phone call to another soul. I don't know that I can see her doing that in the fullness of time but by then Melinda and Max should be out of the country.''

''Without Alice?''

''That's what we're counting on,'' Logan said a little grimly.

''I know you keep a perfect picture of motherhood in your head, but you'll have to accept all Melinda thinks about is herself.''

"So she was lying?"

"Isn't it something she does all the time?" He took a skein of her hair and twisted it around his arm.

"One of her lies was pretty effective with you."

"Especially when everyone else was saying the same thing."

Her eyes were sad. "You're going to break my heart, Logan, if you don't believe me."

She looked so perfect, a moon maiden, with her lustrous skin and long gilded hair. Her skin was warm to the touch, almost feverish like below the surface there were sparks in her blood. It drove him to straining her to him, the slender, almost fragile body he couldn't get enough of.

"Could I?" he asked.

"You know the answer to that."

"I thought it was my heart on the line?" His voice was deep, caressing, heavy with desire. As his dark head came down, Dana lowered her eyes, feeling the exquisite crush of his mouth over hers, the fierce strength of his arms that excited her so intensely. She knew he was in love with her, perhaps in his heart of hearts *loved* her, but she had gotten to the point where she believed there could be no future for them if she couldn't have Logan's trust.

Dana was never to forget the early part of the next morning. Despite Logan's assurances, his insistence that calling Melinda's bluff would save the day, Melinda was full of qualms. Melinda was a parent who didn't hesitate to project her own conflicts on her child. She had even done her best to cause Dana harm. At some deep psychological level Melinda was a person full of resentments and frustrations. The family was trying desperately to recover from Jimmy's death yet Melinda seemed hell-bent on causing them more pain with her actions. It all added up to the fact Melinda was a loose cannon.

When Dana very quietly entered Alice's room to check that the little girl was all right, instead of a sleeping child she encountered an empty bed. Already suffused with anxieties she checked the bathroom, the veranda outside Alice's room. No sign of her. Next she hurried down to Melinda's room, tapped on it briefly, then finding the door unlocked pushed it open and went in. It was still early. Not quite seven o'clock. She remembered now Melinda hated being woken out of a sleep but her concerns about Alice were making her jumpy.

Melinda had her narrow back to her, curled up in sleep, but there was no Alice beside her.

"Melinda?" Dana didn't hesitate to call urgently. "Wake up."

"What?" Melinda stirred, muttering very crossly. She turned on her back, her blond curls a halo around her small face, one strap of her luxurious nightgown falling off her white shoulder. "What the heck is going on, Dee? Are you throwing me out or what?"

"I can't find Alice," Dana answered, holding her hands together tightly.

"Great!" Melinda groaned. "She'll be around some place."

"She should be in her bed," Dana said worriedly.

"Kids get up early. You know that. What's the matter with you? You're like some poor old mother hen."

"What did you say to her, Melly?" Dana advanced on the bed, such a fire in her eyes Melinda sat up straight.

"Nothing!" Melinda snapped.

"You didn't tell her you wanted to take her back to Sydney with you?"

"It's Logan who decided she has to go," Melinda reminded her angrily. "Always set himself up as the wonderful uncle, too. Now he can't wait to get rid of her."

Dana decided to strike while the iron was hot. "Then you've accepted he won't pay up?"

"You're sure of it, too?" Melinda searched her cousin's face. Dana would never lie to her.

"You know Logan, Melly," Dana said, as if that were sufficient explanation. "He's as hard as nails."

Melinda nodded, biting her lip. "Like that Getty? Remember when he wouldn't pay up for his grandson?"

"That's right, so you might as well forget your little scheme. We'll have Alice ready for you by the time you leave."

"Oh, God." Melinda closed her eyes tightly then she stripped back the bedclothes and stood up, a pocket venus in her peach satin nightdress. She had lost quite a bit of weight and she looked little more than the young girl Dana remembered. "You have to wonder about some people," she said, reaching for her matching robe and putting it on. "I thought you loved Alice?"

"I do." Dana nodded, in one way not wanting to do this but she had no choice. "But you're Alice's mother. We must all focus on that."

"But damn it all, I don't want her!" Frustration distorted Melinda's voice. "I *can't* want her. Max knows I have a daughter who lives with her grandmother. I explained Alice is quite difficult and needs special attention. He understands that, but he doesn't want or need a small child to disrupt his world."

Dana forced her voice to remain even. "Let me get this straight. You've come out here trying to extort money? Is that it?"

"Bunkum. It's justice, Dee. Haven't you ever heard of justice? Alice is the heiress not me."

"And Max is prepared to marry you only if Alice remains with her family?"

"Can you blame him," Melinda retorted, as if Dana was stating the obvious.

"I expect he has a family of his own tucked away some place?" Dana said grimly. "Are you sure he's not married?"

Melinda stood stock-still, suddenly uneasy. "He's *divorced*."

"I guess Logan could talk to him," Dana suggested. "Establish you're not without family."

Evidently that was the last thing Melinda wanted. "Leave Logan out of this," she cried. "I don't want him interfering in my affairs."

"Then I suggest you come clean with your intentions, Melly," Dana said shortly. "Get it over. He'll be as mad as hell but it probably won't go any further. Alice has to have stability in her life. Make Logan her legal guardian. You need have no fears. He'll look after her and he won't deny you access to your own child."

Melinda began to drum her fingers on a small marquetry table. "You're absolutely sure I couldn't break him down?" She glanced at Dana, who shrugged.

"*Convinced*. Logan means what he says. I should have known but it shocked me nevertheless." Hurriedly she turned to the door. "I'll get back to you, Melly.

I'm going downstairs. With any luck Alice might be with Mrs. Buchan eating breakfast.''

Mrs. Buchan was surprised. "I haven't laid eyes on her, Dana. She doesn't come downstairs until around eight o'clock, as you know." She stepped closer, speaking in a confidential murmur. "You don't think she could be hiding? She's done it before. In the old days when life got too much for her."

"Hiding?" Given that Alice was very upset it was more than likely. But where? There were a million wild acres out there. Even the house was huge. "Where's Mr. Dangerfield?" she asked, feeling she needed Logan beside her.

Mrs. Buchan considered. "I fed him breakfast at six. He wanted to be at the Four Mile when the men came in. Other than that I can't say."

"We'll have to search the house from top to bottom," Dana said. "Someone has to go for Logan. Alice could have headed out into the bush."

The search began in earnest and a short time after Logan strode through the front door. "Why didn't I consider this is what she might do?" he said, his eyes flashing. "Alice has always been full of action."

"You don't think she's in danger?" Dana's pale face was showing her anxiety.

"I'll bet my riding boots she's just hiding out." Logan went to her, pulled her into his arms, let her head rest against him as her support.

"My, isn't that a touching scene!" Melinda called, coming daintily down the stairs. "I always knew you two would get together at some point."

"So that made you tell all your lies," Logan confronted bluntly.

"Well, you did get hooked for a time." Melinda

looked completely undisturbed. "Jimmy may have hankered after Dee but even for him she was the princess in the tower. You know, *inaccessible.*"

"But you decided to hang it on him all the same." Logan shook his head, feeling a vast shame and anger. In doubting Dana he deserved to lose her.

"Jimmy ripped my heart out with his infidelities," Melinda retorted. "I owe him nothing. Dana and I have been together since childhood. I love her, I guess. I don't really mind hurting her, either, from time to time. And while you're all knocking yourselves out searching for Alice as though no one else matters, I should tell you she's given to this sort of behaviour. Just her way of looking for attention. I'd advise you to get on with what you're doing and the little devil will come home. She'll be hiding out until she figures it's safe."

"Safe?" Dana asked the question, sounding appalled.

"Until I'm gone," Melinda explained. "The moment she hears the plane take off she'll come out of her hiding place."

"Very likely," Logan agreed, his voice quiet. "But surely you feel some anxiety?"

"Do you?" Melinda countered. "That child's a Dangerfield. I've said it all along."

Melinda flew out at ten o'clock sharp, convinced there was no remote cause for worry and that's exactly how it turned out, though the search continued unabated, spreading out into the bush. It was Dana who found her, given a clue by one of the drawings Alice had made with Retta the day before. It was a picture of the Dangerfield stone chapel, an excellent drawing for a child, showing its Gothic features and the tall spire.

Even an attempt had been made at drawing the intricate design on the beautiful wrought-iron gates that enclosed the grounds. A church. A chapel. Historically, a safe haven.

Alice was nowhere to be seen inside but when Dana called her name, trying to communicate all the love and protectiveness that was in her, Alice suddenly emerged from behind the altar, rising a little stiffly from her cramped position.

"It's all right, I'm here. Were you worried?" She stared at Dana with big over-bright eyes.

"Oh, darling, you mustn't do that again," Dana said when they were through hugging one another. "We're only looking to do what's best for you."

"Not if you mean to send me back with Mummy," Alice maintained stubbornly. "If you hadn't found me I'd probably have stayed here until I heard the plane."

"But you understand, don't you, Grandma has suffered enough grief? She's not young anymore. We mustn't worry her."

"I'm sorry." Alice hung her head, shrinking from the vision of her grandmother's sad face. "I love Grandma, I love you all. I even love Mummy if she'll only leave me alone."

"We must go back to the house," Dana said decisively, holding out her hand.

"I'm not," Alice cried passionately, backing away. "Mummy does what she likes. She doesn't care how anyone feels."

"She's not taking you back to Sydney, Alice, I promise."

"Are you sure?" Alice watched Dana closely.

"I'm certain. I probably shouldn't be discussing this with you now but it might put your mind to rest.

Mummy has decided Uncle Logan can be your legal
guardian. You'll be able to see Mummy anytime you
like but you'll be living here.'' Where you belong,
Dana thought.

Alice held out her hand, obviously imitating her
Uncle Logan. "Will we shake on that."

"I'm pleased to." They shook hands. "Can we go
up to the house now?" Dana asked. "I want everyone
to know you're safe."

"I bet Uncle Logan wasn't worried." Alice grinned.

"He knows all about your bolting."

"What did Mummy say?" Alice gave her an intense
stare.

"Mummy is worried, like the rest of us. Even Uncle
Logan is under some strain. You could have wandered
off into the wild."

"No way!" Alice snapped off. "I could have got
lost."

Dana went to take the little girl's hand, anxious to
return to the house, but Alice escaped, entering a pew
and ramming her small frame into the corner. "As soon
as I hear the plane." Her voice was still wary. "You
can go and whisper to Grandma I'm all right, if you
like."

Dana sighed, lifted her wrist and stared down at her
watch. There wasn't much longer to go before
Melinda's flight. She moved into the pew, reached for
Alice, who fell sideways into her lap.

On Christmas another contingent of Dangerfield relatives arrived to spend Christmas Day and Boxing Day
on the station. It was a yearly ritual with different members of the extended family taking turns. This year because Alice was in residence, younger members had

been invited to bring their small children to join in all
the fun.

Another Dangerfield ritual was the Christmas Eve
party. Not only for the family, but for everyone on the
station. It was set in the Great Hall, built almost twenty
years before to accommodate large gatherings. Now the
whole family, children, as well, had worked to decorate
it and make it beautiful for the party. When Dana
looked in, Jack Cordell and Sandra were perched on
stepladders busy hanging Christmas swags with glossy
green foliage and dozens of gold and scarlet baubles.
Even the dais where the band would be playing was
decorated with a semicircle of ''snow''-tipped
Christmas trees in pots flashing tiny white lights. Like
so many stars. Everything that could be tied with a big
gold-trimmed ribbon was tied. The children loved it;
all the Christmas songs were played constantly, they
hugged one another exuberantly, thrilled they would be
allowed to stay up until nine-thirty. No later. They had
to be in bed and fast asleep before Santa Claus began
patrolling the station.

Dana chose a beautiful gold dress to wear to the
party. Actually it was her bridesmaids dress from a
friend's wedding. She had brought it with her thinking
it was suitable for the Christmas ritual. The bodice was
gold lace, the calf-length full skirt lustrous taffeta. She
even had a small jewelled headpiece to catch up her
hair at the crown. She had debated arranging her hair
in a coil then decided to leave it out. She couldn't fail
to be aware Logan found her long hair exciting. Searing
relief still washed over her at the memory of Melinda's
''confession.'' Maybe it was Melinda's peculiar way of
letting her know she loved her. And it vindicated
Jimmy who could have lived such a different life.

Dana was almost ready to go downstairs and join the others when someone came to her door. Almost certainly Ainslie. Alice, she knew was with the children, every last one of them radiant with happiness and excitement.

"Logan!" She stared up at him, her limbs melting, almost literally because she had to hold on to the doorjamb. "You look wonderful." It wasn't as much a compliment as a plain statement of fact. He was wearing a white dinner jacket with his black dress trousers, a white pin-tucked shirt adorned by a blue silk tie.

He smiled at her, his handsome face a little taut. "Thank you. A man does his best, but no one will be able to match you. You look breathtaking." His blue eyes moved over her with an almost unbearable pleasure. "May I come in for a moment?"

"Of course." She took a deep breath, held it, convinced from the underlying seriousness of his demeanour matters between them would come to a head. She heard herself asking, almost shakily, "Everything's all right, isn't it?"

"Fine." He seemed to come out of a slight reverie. He was standing in the centre of the room, now he turned to face her directly. "I have something to give you before we go down. I hope you'll honour me and wear it tonight. But first I wanted to thank you from the bottom of my heart for everything you've done for my family."

Dana pressed her hands together, fighting an irresistible impulse to weep. "Oh, Logan, you don't have to say this," she implored.

"I do." His reply was harsh, self-judgemental. "I want to thank you for your great loving kindness to Alice. For the way you have supported Ainslie and

Sandra. The way you tried to help Tyler through the difficult times. I even admire your loyalty to Melinda even when we both know she doesn't deserve it. You've been strong through the tragedy that has engulfed us all.''

''Please, Logan,'' Dana begged. ''You needn't say any more. Alice and I are blood kin. I've had all my efforts rewarded. I have love and I have enduring friendships.''

''You must let me finish, Dana,'' he said inexorably. ''I want you to forgive me. I want you to forgive me for ever having doubted you. No matter what I've *said,* I knew you wouldn't fly in the face of honour. I knew you would never betray anyone. Even before Melinda's conscience attack, I *knew.*'' He paused, admitting, ''I do have a hard streak at times. Put it down to the fact I'm not a man who finds it easy to hand over his heart. And yet I have. I love you.'' His blue eyes blazed. ''I love you body and soul.'' He reached out and very tenderly stroked her cheek. ''You fill me with the most beautiful feelings I've ever known. You bring me sweetness and character, dazzling joy. Even when you wring my emotions dry, you're my shining hope. I just can't go on like this. I need a resolution.''

''Oh, so do I!'' Dana responded. It came out like a vow. ''You're everything to me, Logan. I don't *have* a life unless we're together.''

''But your career?'' He cupped her face between his hands, held it still. ''I can't let you go off and leave me. I couldn't bear it.''

''Not even for a short time?'' she asked in a profoundly happy voice.

His mouth twisted into a wry smile. ''How much time are we talking exactly?''

Dana smiled, linked her slender arms behind his neck. "What's wrong with coming with me sometimes? We would manage. I have a lifetime's work out here. A thousand ideas. Anyway, you have some explaining to do. You haven't actually asked me to marry you."

"Okay." He moved her in very close. "Marry me, Dana Barry." He bent to drop multiple kisses on her lips, feather-light so as not to disturb her make-up, the tip of his tongue just entering her mouth. "You know you've always loved me."

All of a sudden she *was* crying, though her heart was filled with boundless joy. This was one of the great moments of life.

"Darling, please don't." His voice was a mixture of amusement, dismay and indulgence. "You simply have no idea what it does to me. And we have to go downstairs."

"I just *need* to…" Dana made a valiant effort to blink back teardrops.

"Here." He removed a beautiful monogrammed handkerchief from his pocket and dabbed very gently at her cheeks. "I can't tell you how much *I* need to give you everything you want." His vibrant voice rang with a passionate seductiveness. "Dana, darling," he warned, "if you don't stop we might have to forget the party altogether."

"No… No… " She lifted her head, paused, inhaled a long deep breath. "Do I look all right?" She stared up so sweetly into his face. Glorious, radiant, she brought a lump to his throat.

"Perfect."

A great sense of peace was moving over him. An intensely felt joy. This was Christmas Eve. He had asked the woman he loved to marry him. Now he reached into his breast pocket and produced a diamond ring so exquisite Dana gasped.

"This is for you, my love," he murmured, gently, so gently, taking her hand. "It belonged to my mother. It was her engagement ring and it's one of my greatest treasures. My father gave me all my mother's jewellery when I was only a boy. 'This is for *your* wife, Logan,' he said to me, and there were tears in my proud father's eyes. 'This is bonding us all together. Past and future. This is keeping our heritage alive.' I've never offered this ring to anyone but you, Dana. I believe now that was the forces of destiny at work. If you would like something else, something of your own choice, you have only to say."

The light in his eyes brought back the tears. She felt for a moment there were other presences in the room. Loving presences who gave them their blessing. "Put it on my finger, Logan," she invited with absolute reverence. "Put it where it belongs."

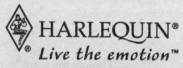

COOPER'S CORNER

Welcome to Cooper's Corner...
a small town with very big surprises!

Coming in April 2003...
JUST ONE LOOK
by Joanna Wayne

Check-in: After a lifetime of teasing, Cooper's Corner
postmistress Alison Fairchild finally had the cutest nose
ever—thanks to recent plastic surgery! At her friend's wedding,
all eyes were on her, except those of the gorgeous stranger
in the dark glasses—then she realized he was blind.

Checkout: Ethan Granger wasn't the sightless teacher
everyone thought, but an undercover FBI agent. When he
met Alison, he was thankful for those dark glasses. If she
could see into his eyes, she'd know he was in love....

HARLEQUIN®
Makes any time special ®

CC-CNM9